What People Are Saying

Wow! What a great book. I feel like I am walking down Garrison Avenue with my ancestors. Having grown up in Fort Smith, this book brought back memories of my childhood. It also mentions things about Fort Smith that we might like to forget, but that are very important in the history of my home town.

George Simmons, Great Nephew of John B. Williams

* * *

While working for the Sebastian County Circuit Clerk's office, I found the court records of the lynching on Garrison Avenue my mother and grandmother talked about. I am intrigued to see its story come out of hiding for others to read. I would encourage others to visit the Records department and research those historical records.

Reginald Moore, Historian, Researcher, and Reenactor

* * *

Joyce Faulkner describes a city facing a new era, becoming what had always been brewing under the surface—a southern town. Her characters are full of life—including Sanford Lewis, a quiet, gentle man who loses his life. Faulkner's story affects not only Sanford, but his family, the black community, the townspeople, and city government. Sadly, it is story of people—good people—facing life when a force larger than all of them swept the soul of this quiet town down Garrison Avenue.

Angela Walton-Raji, Historian and Genealogist

* * *

A one, two punch! An enjoyable novel with characters that draw you in, and an important accounting of one of Fort Smith's most tragic and reprehensible events.

Tom Wing, Assistant Professor of History, Director–Drennen-Scott Historic Site, University of Arkansas-Fort Smith

Garrison Avenue is historical fiction plucked from newspaper articles, archives, and court records of the time. Joyce Faulkner and Micki Voelkel have expertly crafted a heart-wrenching and engaging tale of a young woman's struggle to find her niche in the early 1900s, and her attempts to reconcile a senseless and cruel act against her friend, Sanford (Sandy) Lewis.

Sandra Miller Linhart, award-winning author of *Monica, Lost* and coauthor of *Frozen Tears: The Fort Wood MP Murders*

* * *

A good read where legend, fact and people come together in a narrative of racism, murder, greed and universal human nature. Everything is here and it really happened. There *was* a black man named Sanford Lewis and a white policeman named Andy Carr. They came together in an incident that left them both dead and a community stained for over a hundred years. Joyce Faulkner and Micki Voelkel have made them live again and speak to us today.

Judge Jim Spears, author of *JUSTICE DIVIDED: A Judicial History of Sebastian County*

* * *

Garrison Avenue

Joyce Faulkner
and
Dr. Micki Voelkel

Red Engine Press
Pittsburgh, PA

Cover by Russ Jester

Edited by Pat McGrath Avery

Researchers: Karen Daggs, Mary Kaye Smith

Library of Congress Control Number: 2019938885

ISBN: 978-1-943267-65-1 Paperback

ISBN: 978-1-943267-66-8 ebook

Printed in the United States.

Red Engine Press

For Sanford

&

Andy

Garrison Avenue is historical fiction about the only lynching in Fort Smith, Arkansas, during the Jim Crow era. This was an event that reflected the religious and social mores of the time—plus ongoing racial anxieties. The town had been a Union Fort in a Confederate state. By 1912, it had become a modern city with almost a hundred years of immigration, politics, and business history.

The story is told through the eyes of a young woman who is new to Fort Smith. The townspeople speak for themselves through dialogue—and as such, the reader will encounter language and attitudes that reflect their ambitions, fears, biases, and cultural perspectives. Some of the characters are fictional. Their conversations and behavior reveal their own personalities, ideas that channel those of the various factions in the city—and their attitudes about real historical events in Fort Smith at that time. Many other characters are our interpretations of real people who lived through this event. Some of their words are taken from newspaper interviews and court documents. Since many of the folks who inhabit these pages are the ancestors of people we know, we've tried to present them as accurately and respectfully as possible.

Like all novelists, we hope you will enjoy the story. We also hope it will make you think about things that bind us together as well as stuff that tears us apart. And in the end, we hope we will feel good about where we have been, who we are now—and who we might become.

Joyce Faulkner
Micki Voelkel

The way to right wrongs is to turn the light of truth upon them.

— Ida B. Wells-Barnett

Who's Who

Historic Characters and families are identified with a asterisk.

The McGraths

- Mamie—writer, Julian's wife, Sarge's niece
- Julian—reporter, Mamie's husband, Caroline's son
- Caroline—Julian's mother, widow

*

The Talbots

- Abigail—Caroline's Friend, Garland's wife
- Garland—Abigail's husband, businessman, son of a Confederate soldier

*

The Williams*

- John B—well-known, well-liked owner of the Pony Express and the Horse and Mule Barn on 9th and A Street, friends with the Carrs, McGraths, Talbots
- Jennie Williams—wife of John B, great grandniece of George Maledon—Judge Isaac Parker's hangman, mother of Ray and Marjory, friend of Caroline, Mamie, and Abigail.

*

The Carrs*

- Patrick (Andy) Andrew Carr—Deputy City Detective, well-known and well-beloved police officer, husband of Della Meek Carr, considered to be a straight arrow, heroic police man
- Della Meek Carr—wife of Andy Carr, mother of Pansy, Patrick, Della, and James Carr, sister to James Meek, aunt of Jim Meek.
- Pansy Carr—oldest daughter of Andy and Della Carr

*

The Lewises*

- Sanford (Sandy) Lewis—grandson of slaves, young day worker, son of a preacher, works as yardman for the McGrath family
- Webster Lewis—son of slaves, share cropper in Oklahoma, preacher, father of Sanford Lewis
- Loula Castleberry Lewis—daughter of slaves, wife of Webster Lewis, mother of Sanford

*

The Espositos

- Dino—Italian immigrant, husband of Martina Esposito, father of Roberto (Bobby) Esposito, owner of Esposito's Italian Restaurant on Garrison Avenue, friend of the McGraths
- Martina—wife of Dino, mother of Bobbie, friend of Mamie
- Bobby—son of Dino and Martina, born to be President of the United States

*

Sisters of Mercy

- Sister Clarence
- Sister Alberta—sister of Anna Marie Cavanaugh

*

Ladies of the Night

- Miss Laura*—owner of Miss Laura's 1903 -1911
- Miss Bertha*— owner of Miss Laura's 1912-1940
- Miss Angelica/Anna Marie Cavanaugh—prostitute and sister of Sister Alberta Cavanaugh

*

Fort Smith Policemen

- Bryant Barry*—Chief of Police
- Cathey Pitcock*—City Detective
- Sam Booth*—young officer
- Ed Pennewell*—officer
- R. O. Lacey*—officer
- John Jarnigan*
- William Phillips*
- Philip Ross*

*

The Mathews*

- Reverend William M. Mathews—preacher (great grandfather of the authors)
- Rachel Matthews—wife of William M. Mathews (great grandmother of authors)
- Frankie Mathews—daughter of William and Rachel (grandmother of authors)

*

The McClouds* and Sicards*

- Sam McCloud—father of Ella McCloud Sicard, President of First National Bank
- A. N. (Alfred Napoleon, aka Fred) Sicard—businessman, husband of Ella McCloud Sicard, son-in-law of Sam McCloud
- Ella McCloud Sicard—daughter of Sam McCloud, wife of Fred Sicard

*

Fort Smith Citizens

- Sergeant (Sarge) Elias Eacret—wounded Union Veteran of Civil War, Mamie McGrath's uncle
- Patsy Lincoln—Caroline's childhood friend, teacher at Lincoln high school, editor of the *Fort Smith Bell* newspaper for the black community
- Genevieve Day—housekeeper for McGraths, Talbots, and writer for the *Fort Smith Bell*
- Bebe—housekeeper for the Carrs and friends with Genevieve Day and Patsy Lincoln
- Miss Peach—Sarge's nurse
- Emanuel (Manny) McKnight*—poor teenage boy making his living on Garrison
- Burley Clay Johnston I*—friend of Julian and Mamie McGrath, businessman and entrepreneur, singer, young widower
- Marie DuVal*—daughter of Confederate veteran Colonel Benjamin DuVal, musician, love interest of Burley Clay Johnston
- Theo Lamb—fortune teller, sales lady at Boston Store
- Father Horan*—pastor at Immaculate Conception Parish
- Florence Pahotsky*—Emanuel McKnight's* teacher and protector
- Medora Sparks*—daughter of George Sparks, Mamie's friend
- Fagan Bourland*—Mayor
- Judge Daniel Hon*—Sebastian County Circuit Judge
- Judge Jessie A. Harp*—Sebastian County Judge
- Vincent Miles*—businessman, Head of Police Inquiry
- Artie Berry*—businessman
- Paul Little*—prosecuting attorney
- Chauncey Lick*—businessman, manager of the New Theater
- Dr. A. E. Stevenson*—physician
- Pocahontas Ross*—friend of Sanford Lewis

- Professor W.O. Wiley*—piano teacher from Van Buren
- Till Shaw*—saloon owner and past jailer
- Grover Bourland*—nephew/step brother of Mayor Bourland
- Con Sullivan*—bank robber and son of respected parents
- Howard H. Redner*—Photographer
- Ollie and Sarah Fields*—local farmer and wife (ancestors of authors)
- Colonel J. Bart Parker*—newspaperman with *The Fort Smith Times, Southwest American, The Elevator*, and *The Fort Smith Daily Herald*. Owner of Publishing Company, J. B. Parker and Sons.
- Judge Isaac Parker*—historic nineteenth century figure.

The Séance

Mysterious! Amusing! Instructive!
Consult the Ouija Talking Board for Occult Phenomena
and Astonishing Results!
1909 Advertisement in the Southwest American

January 29, 1909

WHEN I OPENED THE DOOR that night, Abigail scowled. "I saw Mayor Johnston on Garrison and he didn't acknowledge me!"

Behind her, Garland Talbot rolled his eyes. "He was probably preoccupied with city business, sugar." He hustled his wife into the foyer. "You've been jabbering on about it for the last twenty minutes. Let it go."

"I've never been so insulted. What is Fort Smith coming to when a servant of the people can't take time for his constituents?"

"Good evening, Abigail," I said.

"I liked that nice little Mayor Bourland much better. He always tipped his hat and asked how I was doing. That kind of thing matters in politics, you know."

"Yes, I do know, dear." I turned to Garland. "There's refreshments on the side board in the dining room, and the other gentlemen are already in the back parlor with their cigars."

He rubbed his palms together and blew on them. "Did Caroline make those tasty little cinnamon cookies?"

"There's a plate full if Andy and John B haven't seen them yet."

"I better hurry then." He headed off down the hall.

I smiled at Abigail. "Would you like me to take your hat?"

"Good heavens, no. I haven't made my grand entrance yet."

I smothered my amusement and took her arm. "There are six of us tonight."

"Six? Who's the extra lady, if I might ask?"

"Miss Theodosia Lamb, a lovely young woman who just arrived from New Orleans. I met her at the Boston Store the other day."

"Does she shop there often?"

"I am sure she does. I understand the shop girls get first shot at the new merchandise and a nice discount to boot."

"A shop girl?" Abigail's eyebrows rose. "Mamie, I commend your generosity, but a shop girl?"

"Theo promised us an interesting parlor game tonight. I'm sure you'll like her."

"That remains to be seen."

I pushed open the pocket doors to the front parlor. "Here she is, everyone."

Abigail's frown melted into a wide smile as the women set down their teacups and turned to greet her. She grew taller, grander, and more sophisticated as she swooped into the room, the long teal feathers on her enormous hat bouncing as though energized by her personality.

"It's about time, Abigail. I was beginning to think you got waylaid on Garrison again." My mother-in-law, Caroline McGrath, rose to receive Abigail's air kiss.

"I'm always struck by the loveliness of your home, Caroline." Abigail ran her gloved fingers over the mantel above the fireplace and then checked them to make sure they were still dust free.

Jennie Williams and Della Carr smiled up at Abigail.

"Good to see you again, Mrs. Talbot," Jennie said. "We missed you at Caroline's picnic this summer."

Caroline's cheeks reddened.

Oh no, I thought. *Here we go again.* However, although Abigail's jaw hardened and she avoided Caroline's eyes, she focused on our other guests. "I'm sorry too, Jennie. Garland and I would have loved to see you and John B again. Were you and Andy here too, Della?"

"We were. Caroline puts on quite a grand party."

"She does at that. Garland had business in St. Louis and I thought I'd go along for the ride. Great shopping there. Bought this adorable little hat. It's called the Merry Widow." Abigail turned her face to one side and then the other so that Jennie and Della could get a good look at it. "Perhaps Caroline will get her invitations out a bit earlier, next time."

Caroline coughed into her fist. "Um, yes, I certainly will."

I touched Abigail's shoulder and turned her to face a woman standing behind a small round table. "This is Theo. She's going to do our fortunes this evening."

"Our fortunes?" Abigail raised an eyebrow.

"Yes, ma'am," Theo responded. "If you're interested."

"I suppose we shall have to pay you for this window into the future?"

"Oh no, Caroline and Mamie thought it might be fun for you ladies. That's all."

"Fun?"

"You never know what might happen."

Lightning flashed outside the window followed by ominous rumbling. "How does it work?" Nothing could break Abigail's focus once something captured her attention.

I knew Abigail would love Theo's parlor games. In fact, I'd counted on it. "Let's get you some hot tea or maybe some of Caroline's sherry and Theo will show us," I said.

"She's not going to call down the devil on us?"

I hung Abigail's coat on a rack in the corner with Della and Jennie's. "I don't think the devil comes running when a woman at a party crooks her finger."

"I'm not personally in touch with the devil," Theo said. "I deal with everyday ghosts."

"What kind of ghosts?" Della Carr sipped her tea.

"Ones with something to say."

"Ghostly gossips?" Abigail sank into an upholstered chair beside Jennie, her hand pressed to her ruffled bosom in mock horror. "What will Father Horan say?"

"You don't have to stay if it makes you uncomfortable."

"Don't be impertinent, Mamie. Of course, I'm going to stay. A whole team of John B's mules couldn't pull me away."

"Let me hang up your hat and we can get started."

"No, no. Leave it alone. I like it as it is."

"Some sherry then?"

"For heavens sake, Mamie. Let's get on with the main event. I'm quite eager now."

I turned to Theo. "I guess we're ready."

Theo cleared her throat and began. "I want to thank Caroline and Mamie for inviting me." She gazed at each of us in turn. "I was born with a gift, a special sensitivity to people, alive or passed."

The wind made the tree in the front yard shiver and its branches scratched against the window. Jennie sat forward in her seat. I wasn't sure if she was alarmed by the sudden change in weather or intrigued by our guest. "You really do talk with ghosts?"

"More like they talk and I hear them sometimes."

"Tell them about the messages, Theo," Caroline said.

"Yes, I was telling Mamie and Caroline that sometimes ghosts need to tell people something. It might be an undone task or an unsaid sentiment. Sometimes, I can go into a building I've never been in before and they will cluster around, begging me to give their loved ones a final message."

"How extraordinary," Della said. "Surely not every soul is benevolent in death. Aren't you afraid?"

A flash of lightning lit the room.

"Sometimes."

In the silence that followed, we stole nervous glances at each other and then back at Theo.

"So how do they do that?" Abigail's voice made us all jump. "Do they whisper in your ear?" Soft thunder rumbled in the distance.

"Ouija." Theo pointed to a board setting on the table in front of her chair.

"Never heard of it."

"It's a way of asking them questions and allowing them to answer," Theo said. "And of letting other people participate. Relatives and friends or old enemies."

Abigail rubbed her palms together. "So are we going to do this or what?"

For a moment, I thought Abigail's rudeness had gotten under Theo's skin, but she kept her composure and said, "Who wants to go first?"

I figured Abigail would bully her way to the front of the line and she didn't disappoint. "Do we get to ask questions?"

"If we contact someone who wants to talk, you can ask anything you want. No guarantee on the answers though."

"How do we start?"

"I'm going to sit at this little table Caroline provided us and you will sit across from me. The rest of you gather round."

With a flurry of rustling skirts, the ladies rearranged their chairs in a semi-circle around the table.

Seated in front of Theo, Abigail leaned forward."Now what?"

"We are going to put our hands on this planchette." Theo held up a thin, heart-shaped piece of polished wood with felt glued on the back side.

"A what?"

"Planchette."

"What's it for?"

"It's a pointing device spirits use to spell out messages to us."

"Ah." Abigail examined it through her monocle.

"Let me see it too." Della held out her hand.

After everyone got a good look, Theo put the planchette back on the board. "See where it says yes or no?"

Everyone nodded.

"If someone on the other side needs to answer questions with a yes or no, he or she will point to those words."

"How?" Abigail cocked her head sideways.

Theo put the tips of all ten of her fingers on one side of the planchette. "Put your fingers on the other side."

Abigail touched the little piece of wood and it moved. She recoiled and the feathers on her Merry Widow quivered. "What was that?"

Theo's eyes sparkled. "That was someone wanting to speak to you."

"Me? Why me? How do you know?"

"Because it didn't move when it was just me."

Abigail seemed torn between being scared and flattered that someone from the other world wanted to speak with her. Finally, she embraced the exercise and put her fingers back on the wood. "Why isn't it moving now?"

"It needs both of us to speak."

"Show me," Abigail demanded.

Theo touched the planchette. As the wind rose outside, the pointer moved in small circles across the Ouija board. "Feel that? No, don't push it. Let it move by itself."

"Look at that," Jennie murmured as the circles grew larger and more erratic. "Do you think someone is really there?"

"Anyone want to talk to Abigail?" Theo made us all jump.

"I didn't know the spirits were deaf, Theo," Della said and we all chuckled.

"Shush!" A small wrinkle formed on Theo's forehead. "We have to focus."

We stared at the planchette resting under an arc of letters painted on the board.

Raindrops beat on the roof over our heads.

"Anyone you want to talk to, Abigail?"

Abigail stared at the Ouija board. "Who should I ask for?"

"How about your mother?"

"NO!"

"Got a cousin?"

"For heaven's sake. Shouldn't the ghosts want to talk to me?"

The planchette moved an inch and then stopped.

"There it goes," Theo muttered under her breath.

I leaned over her shoulder as the pointer floated first to the M and then to the A. Then it jiggled back and forth between the Y and A.

"What's it saying?" Caroline whispered.

"May," Theo said.

"May?" Abigail's voice went up. "What's that? A month?"

The planchette zoomed up to the word NO.

"A person?"

Ouija pointed to YES.

"My goodness," Jennie gasped. "It's talking."

"Does Abigail know you?"

"YES," Theo confirmed the Ouija's answer and then asked, "What's your last name, May?"

"S - H - I - R -"

"May Shirley?" It was Abigail's turn to gasp. "Maybelle?"

"YES."

We were all struck dumb for a moment. It was Della who found her voice. "Her family called her May."

"Who?"

"Mira Maybelle Shirley was Belle Starr's real name."

"Who is Belle Starr?" I'd moved to Fort Smith from Pittsburgh when I married Julian the year before. I wasn't familiar with all the local personalities yet, living or dead.

"She was quite a character around here until she was murdered a few years back," Caroline said.

"Who killed her?"

"That's just the thing." Caroline pulled her shawl up around her shoulders. "No one knows."

Theo sat quietly as if she were trying to figure out what to say to a local personality made even more notorious by her unfortunate death. Finally, she asked, "Should we call you Belle?"

The planchette shot back to NO.

"Is there something you want to tell Abigail?"

"NO."

"Well, I never—" Abigail stopped when Theo frowned at her.

"Jennie?"

"YES."

Jennie leaned forward. "What?"

"T - E - L -"

"Wait," Jennie said. "I can't keep up. Do you have a pencil and paper, Mamie?"

"Of course." I scurried over to Caroline's writing desk and brought back a page torn from a notebook and a pencil.

Jennie put the paper on the table. "Ask her again, Theo."

"May, what did you want to say to Jennie?"

"T - E - L - J - O -N - B"

Abigail snatched the paper away from Jennie and held it close to her face. "Teljonb? What does that mean? Makes no sense." She handed it on to Della.

"Wait." Della tapped the table with her knuckles. "JONB! It's something about John B."

Abigail snorted. "Old Belle never was much of a speller."

Jennie took the paper back from Della and examined it again. "Tell? Tell John B? Tell John what, May?"

"W - A - C - H - O - U - T - 4 - A - N - D - E - E"

Jennie looked up at Theo. "That's it?"

Before Theo could answer, the planchette swung up to YES and hovered there.

Jennie tapped the paper with the tip of the pencil. "WACHOUT4ANDEE?"

"What's it supposed to mean?" Caroline murmured.

Jennie read the message a second time. "WACHOUT4ANDEE. What's it mean, May?"

The planchette clattered against the board. "T - E - L - J - O - N - T - E - L - J - O - N"

We all looked at each other for a moment before bursting into laughter.

"I hear Belle knew everyone's business back in the day," Della said. "Why would she be any different in the hereafter?"

"I thought the spirit wanted to talk to me, not Jennie." Abigail's mouth turned down at both corners.

"Sometimes the spirits choose someone who's especially sensitive to deliver their messages." Theo soothed her. "Let's try again. Put your fingers back on the planchette."

Flicking off a little teal feather, Abigail obliged and the pointer returned to its aimless circling. "But Maybelle Shirley? I can't imagine why she would choose me."

"Why not?" Della's eyebrows rose.

"I didn't know her well, of course. We were in different social circles. Maybelle had terrible posture, you know. She was older than me too."

The Ouija came alive. N - O - T - R - U - N - O - T - R - U

"No tru, no tru," Jennie read from her paper. "I think she means 'not true,' though."

Abigail sat as tall as her S corset would allow. "Is too, Maybelle Shirley. You were Garland's fall back even before me. And when he met me, you lost him forever."

"N - O - T - R - U - N - O - T - R - U"

"He married me after all," Abigail continued. "You never had a chance."

The window behind Theo shattered and a gust of wind sent Abigail's hat flying across the room. Every one screamed and stood up as rain and leaves blew in.

"What is going on in here," Julian slid open the parlor door and rushed to my side. "Are you okay?"

"I'm fine." But I accepted his hug as Andy and John B thundered in behind him.

7

Garland pushed through them and embraced Abigail who grabbed at the trendy teal feathers floating in the air. "Stop it, Abigail. Stop."

"She was vindictive. A sore loser." Abigail's tinted red hair had come loose from its pins and trailed down her back in long damp curls.

Bits of glass had left tiny dots of blood on Abigail's face and Garland dabbed at them with his handkerchief. "Who, sweetheart? Who?"

"That crazy Maybelle Shirley."

Garland sighed. "Now sugar, you know Belle is dead."

"But she can still torment me, even from the grave."

I caught Garland's eye as Julian went to find a board to keep the rain out of Caroline's parlor. "I'm sorry," I mouthed. I really shouldn't have invited Abigail that night.

Section 1—1910

January 8, 1910
Witnesses Describe Lingerie Parade
The heart of "The Row" was aflame more than twelve hours yesterday, when an oil tank at North First and D Streets exploded. Most of the houses of vice were heavily damaged, but the property owned and operated by Laura Ziegler went largely unscathed. Witnesses described the "Daughters of Joy" escaping the flames in a state of incomplete dress.

Julian McGrath, *Southwest American*

* * *

Church of the Immaculate Conception

April 10, 1910

10 a.m.

Farmer's Mass in B Flat

Soloists and Sopranos

Misses Boyd, Kelly, Breen and Christie

Alto

Misses Danby and Newman

Tenor

Mr. Neville Kelly

Baritone

Mr. Julian McGrath

Bass

Mr. Burley Johnston and Mr. E.E. Edmonds

1

January 31, 1910
The new First National Bank building at 600 Garrison Avenue
opened for business today.

Southwest American

February 13, 1910
The Fort Smith Light and Traction Company added a five-foot-high by four-teen-foot-long electric sign with flashing lights
above the Poe Shoe Company at 710 Garrison Avenue.

Julian McGrath, *Southwest American*

May, 1910

IT WAS HOT. I OPENED both windows in the room I shared with Julian, hoping to catch a breeze. My stomach rolled. Beads of sweat formed on my upper lip. Caroline's egg salad from lunch wasn't settling well. I splashed water on my face, but it didn't help much.

"Are you feeling any better, dear?" Caroline was whipping up a batch of brownies when I rejoined her in the kitchen.

"Still a little dizzy."

She touched my forehead with the back of her hand. "No fever."

"Nothing like that," I agreed. "I'm sure I'll be better as soon as it rains."

Caroline opened the back door and peered out at the steamy-blue sky. "Maybe some cool compresses will help."

"That's a good idea." I opened a drawer in the cupboard where Caroline kept old sheets cut into squares for bandages.

"Cool water, Mamie," she said.

I soaked the squarish piece of cotton fabric.

"Here," Caroline took the damp cloth and wiped my face with it, before folding it loosely and laying it on the back of my neck "Feel better?"

"It does, actually." I felt a wave of affection for my mother-in-law. Since my own mother died when I was twelve, I'd missed that kind of loving attention.

"Sit down and let me fix you a cup of tea." Caroline pointed to the front parlor.

I nodded and sank onto the settee under an open window. While Caroline busied herself in the kitchen, I closed my eyes, enjoying the cool dampness on my neck. I'd almost dozed off when the phone rang.

Caroline stood in the archway between the parlor and the hall to the kitchen. "It's Julian, Mamie. Do you feel up to talking to him?"

I sat up. The butterflies in my stomach had settled and my head was already clearer than it had been five minutes before. "Of course, I want to talk to him."

In the kitchen, Caroline had propped the receiver on top of the big wooden telephone box hanging on the wall.

"Julian?"

"How's my sweetheart?"

"I'm better. It was probably the egg salad."

"I had twice as much as you, darling. Maybe you should give Doc Stevenson a call."

"I feel fine now. Really."

"You're sure?"

I glanced at Caroline who was pouring hot water into a teapot and pretending she wasn't eavesdropping. "Absolutely. What's up?"

"You won't believe the news I have."

"News?"

"New news."

I giggled. "New news is better than old news." It was a silly routine we often went through since Julian had begun working for the *Southwest American*, the city's daily.

"It's about Bud Mars."

"Is he here yet?"

"He's here and so is the aeroplane."

"Did you see it?"

"No but believe it or not, I will."

"Oh, Julian. That's wonderful."

"What?" Caroline mouthed, her eyes wide with curiosity.

"Hold on, Julian. Your mother wants to hear this too."

"Definitely. She'll be excited for me."

I held the telephone so that Caroline could hear.

"I thought the aeroplane would arrive already assembled, but I guess it was too big for the train that way. They unloaded three boxes onto a wagon and are headed out to Electric Park as we speak."

Caroline crossed her hands over her bosom in motherly delight. "So you're going out there to watch them put it together?"

"It's even better than that. I'm going to meet the pilot."

"Oh?"

"Barney was supposed to write about it, but he came down with chicken pox, would you believe. And everyone else already had an assignment. So it's me. Imagine. I'm going to meet Bud Mars."

"That's marvelous, dear. Will you get to see the flying machine up close?"

"I hope so, Mama. Depends on how long it takes to assemble."

"I'd like to see the aeroplane too," I said.

"You will. On Saturday. We'll all go. Today is just a test."

"What if that thing blows up?" Caroline almost shouted.

"Tell Mama it's not going to blow up. Besides, I won't be that close to it."

"So is it just you?"

"No, besides the other newspaper people, some businessmen and friends, I understand."

"Anyone I know?"

"Now you sound like my mother."

Caroline leaned forward, her lips near the mouth piece. "I heard that."

"Seriously, Julian. Who else?"

"I heard Garland Talbot is driving out in his own automobile."

I sighed. "Oh dear, Abigail will make out like he flew the wretched thing himself."

"And Burley's here with me. We'll catch the trolley in a few minutes."

"That's wonderful," Caroline gushed. "The poor dear needs a distraction."

Burley Johnston was a boyhood friend of Julian's. They'd been singing together in a quartet since high school. When Burley's wife and baby son died a few years back, Caroline took him under her wing, whether he wanted the attention or not.

I changed the subject back to more practical matters. "How long will you be?"

"As long as it takes, I guess."

"Should we keep dinner for you?"

"You two go ahead and eat at the normal time. If I can't make it back by then, I'll pick up something at the park."

Caroline took the telephone away from me. "No, we'll wait for you. Tell Burley he's invited too."

"Burley has a mother and she's probably planning dinner for him."

"Tell him I'm making roast chicken and biscuits and gravy. You know how he loves my biscuits and gravy. And Mamie's making chocolate pie with whipped cream on top."

I tried not to laugh. Until that moment, I had no intention of making a chocolate pie.

"I'll ask him."

"I'll even open that good strawberry jam from last year."

"I'll ask him, mama. Just don't surprise him, and embarrass me, by inviting some girl looking for a husband."

"Why, Julian, what makes you think I'd ever do something like that?" She held out the receiver before he could respond.

I took back the phone, laughing. "Have fun, sweetheart."

"Don't worry."

* * *

Caroline's grandfather clock in the hall had just chimed two when someone knocked on the front door. Caroline was in her bedroom and I was finishing the chocolate pie. I wiped my hands and hurried to the front door.

"Mamie." Abigail walked right in as though she didn't need to be asked. "Where is Caroline?"

"She's resting."

"Is she sick?"

"Just a nap. Would you like some cake?"

Abigail stripped off her gloves and handed them to me. "Will I like it?"

"Caroline made it."

"Good." With that, she marched into the front parlor and made herself at home.

I took a deep breath and counted to ten. Although Abigail and Caroline were friends, they were nothing alike. Caroline was warm and generous—and Abigail was—well, Abigail.

"I usually only talk to Caroline," Abigail said as I brought in a tray with the tea and cake.

"Do you want me to wake her?"

"She needs her rest. You'll have to do, if you can stop spreading what I say all over town."

"Perhaps you should wait for Caroline."

"Don't get your back up. I swear, you're the touchiest little thing." She took a bite of cake and closed her eyes. "Mm."

I sat down on the edge of the chair across from her.

She opened her eyes. "Aren't you having any?"

"I had some earlier."

Abigail took another bite, examining me from head to toe while she chewed. "Do you like living out here on Lecta?"

Her question startled me. "Why wouldn't I?"

"All the building that's going on. Noise. Strangers about."

"It's a lovely house. Modern."

"Yes, but not really your taste is it?" She dabbed at her lips with her napkin. "Not what you would've chosen for yourself."

I looked around the room. Caroline and her husband Wilbur had purchased the house only a few months before he'd been killed. Although they picked it together, the decor reflected Caroline's personality. "I would've been happy wherever Julian wanted to be. Home is wherever he is." I blushed at my own romantic notions. "But I was pleased when Caroline asked us to stay with her. Because of who she is, of course, but also because I love this place."

Abigail sipped her tea. "Why do you do that thing with your ring?"

"What?"

"You twist it. Constantly. Miss Fidget."

I put my hands in my lap.

"It's a bad habit. Like biting your nails or slouching."

I sat up straighter. "What was it that you wanted to talk about, Abigail?"

"Yes, well. I guess you're better than nothing."

"What if I'm not?"

"Not what?"

I tried to keep the sarcasm out of my voice. "What if I'm not better than nothing?"

She narrowed her eyes.

I squirmed in my seat.

Seconds ticked by.

I twisted my wedding band and then stopped when I realized what I was doing.

"Garland has nightmares," Abigail said finally.

"Oh?"

"Nightmares about something that happened in Parris, Texas, a long time ago."

"Does he talk about it?"

"Only that he saw a black man burn to death there."

"My God!"

"He says he deserved it."

"How can anyone deserve such an awful fate?"

"He violated and murdered a little girl."

I shuddered.

"Garland still dreams of it. Almost every night." She lowered her voice. "And he cries."

"I would too."

"That darkie didn't deserve a lick of sympathy after what he did."

I tried not to visualize a human form engulfed in flames. "Still, it must have been horrible to watch."

"Garland was old enough to appreciate what had to be done. These people are animals. You have to meet violence with violence or we wouldn't be safe in our beds at night."

"Even so—"

"I'm sure that Negro went straight to hell."

"How did Garland come to see such a thing?"

"His uncle saw a handbill about it and the two of them went down there to bear witness. He said it was the biggest crowd he'd ever seen, close to ten thousand people. Young and old. Families with little children. People from all walks of life. Surely with that many Christians in attendance, it was God's will." Abigail avoided my eyes.

I wanted to comfort her, but I didn't have any insights on what God wanted. "What does Garland think?"

"He doesn't say."

"If he dreams about it, it must bother him."

"Does that make him weak?"

"Why do you say that?"

"The righteous shall rejoice when he seeth the vengeance: he shall wash his feet in the blood of the wicked." She ran her finger around the rim of her empty teacup. "That's from Psalms."

"Seems pretty cold blooded to me."

"Lot's of cold-blooded passages in the Bible. The right thing demands violence sometimes, Mamie."

"But what you describe was so awful. I can understand having nightmares about it."

"I expect more from Garland."

"Why?"

"He's a man."

"Watching someone die like that shouldn't bother him?"

"I need someone to protect me. Someone who can bear the unbearable."

"Things like that come at a price."

"And that is?"

"Perhaps you won't like that kind of man."

"Or maybe that's precisely the kind of man I'd like." She stood up. "It's a crazy world, Mamie. Having someone to figure it all out and act when necessary is what marriage is about."

"Is it?"

"You'll learn."

I wasn't sure that was a lesson I wanted to learn. "I suppose so," I said as I followed her to the door.

"Remind Caroline about the Women's Christian Temperance Union meeting on Friday."

"Yes, ma'am."

"Why don't you come too? The WCTU needs young women like you."

"I hear the Fort Smith group is pretty large. You don't need me."

"Nonsense. We need every one to destroy this scourge. It's dangerous for young women like you to show your faces on Garrison Avenue after dark, what with the bars and saloons and all." She opened the door and we stepped out onto the porch. "Those hyenas get liquored up and can't control themselves when they see proper white women, especially a child like you."

A soft breeze cooled the sweat on my face. "Surely, it's not as bad as all that."

"It is—and worse." She gave me an air kiss. "The meeting is this Thursday. I'll come by and pick you and Caroline up at five thirty."

It was the last thing I wanted to do in this weather, but I nodded and tried to smile.

"And stop twisting that ring." She climbed into her carriage, clicked to her horses and headed toward Rogers Avenue.

* * *

**We move pianos and houseware goods cheap.
Jno B Williams. Call 111.**

*

I set the table with Caroline's good china and put a bowl of Hydrangea blossoms on the sideboard. I was polishing the good silverware when the phone rang again. Thinking it might be Julian eager to tell me about the aeroplane, I picked it up and pressed the receiver to my ear. "Caroline McGrath's number, this is Mamie."

"Mamie? Julian McGrath's wife?" It was a woman's voice.

"Yes?"

"I need your help, Miz McGrath."

"Do you know Julian?"

"Oh no. Someone told me about you. Someone said you could be trusted."

That captured my attention. "I'm listening."

"My name is Anna Marie Cavanaugh. My sister is Alberta Cavanaugh. She's a nurse at Saint Edwards Infirmary. You know, behind Immaculate Conception Church?"

"Oh, Anna Marie. I know Sister Alberta well. I see her at mass often."

"I need to ask a favor."

"What can I do for you?"

"I want you to take a note to my sister."

"Why?"

"It's a long story. I'll tell you when we meet."

"You are here? In Fort Smith?"

"Yes."

"I'm happy to help, but why can't you visit your sister yourself?"

"I don't dare."

My mind raced. "Why not?"

"Because I work at Miss Laura's."

I swallowed—and then swallowed again. "On the row?"

"Yes, ma'am."

"Does Sister Alberta know?"

"Not yet. I'm hoping you'll tell her for me."

I was torn between fascination and embarrassment. "You can't telephone her?"

"No." The voice had dropped to a whisper. "I'll send you a letter when I'm ready. I need you to take it, unopened, to Bertie at the convent. Before you give it to her, I want you to tell her where I am."

"This is awfully complicated, Anna Marie."

"I've thought this through. It's the only way it'll work."

"But—"

"Please do this for me."

"This is a busy week. When will you be ready?"

"I don't know yet."

It was a lot for a stranger to ask, but I was as intrigued. "What's this all about, Anna Marie?"

"I'll tell you everything when we meet."

I thought for a moment. "Okay."

"Thank you, Miz McGrath. Watch for my letter." She hung up.

"Of all things," I muttered to myself.

"Who was that?" Caroline called from her bedroom.

"Julian." The lie slipped out as smoothly as if I'd planned it.

"Is he and Burley on their way?"

"Soon."

"I'll finish dinner in a few minutes. Will you shell some peas and get them to cooking?

* * *

Julian burst through the door. "Mamie!" He grabbed me and spun me around. "We saw it fly. We saw it."

I held on until he decided to set me on my feet. "I thought they were just putting it together today."

"I thought so too. But Mr. Mars wanted to test it once it was assembled."

A handsome young man stood in the hallway behind Julian. "Hello, Burley." I took his hat. "Looks like the two of you had a great day."

"I would've never gone out there or gotten to see it, if not for Julian."

"And to think chicken pox got us in at all." Julian elbowed Burley playfully.

"I can't wait to hear about it. You two go wash up and dinner will be on the table by the time you get back down here." I gave Julian a quick kiss and shooed them both upstairs.

"Sounds like they had fun," Caroline said as we carried food to the dinner table. "Julian always did love anything with a motor."

"First time I saw him, he was putting an engine on a bicycle. I thought he was terribly modern and terribly attractive."

"Don't know where that came from. His father and I were happy with the old ways. We'd still be candle-lit and get around with a horse and buggy if it were up to me. Julian talked me into that telephone too. Always in a hurry to try new things."

"Me too. It was exciting when he came courting in the Boehmer. My grandma didn't want to let me go with him, but he convinced her it was safe and ended up taking her for a ride before me."

"I remember the day he bought that thing," Burley said as he joined us in the dining room. "It had just rained and Garrison was a soggy mess. He drove past, splattering me with mud."

"Oh no," Caroline said. "I hope he apologized."

Burley laughed. "No apology, but he coaxed me into that automobile and we drove up and down the avenue for an hour. Then we went back to Mr. Boehmer's and he put down his money. In fact, he was sixteen dollars short and I covered it after Julian promised me free rides wherever I wanted to go for a year."

"You boys made tips running errands for everyone on Sixth Street."

"Yes, ma'am," Burley said. "From picking up packages at the Frisco train station to driving old Mrs. Stumpf to mass every morning."

"Did I ever tell you about the time I was turning up the avenue from Texas corner—" Julian said from the door, "—and Andy Carr was standing in my lane, waving for me to pull over?"

"That's a new one to me," Caroline said as she sat down at the table.

"Me, too." Burley pulled out my chair before he sat down himself.

After a quick blessing, Julian picked up the platter of chicken and offered it to Burley. "Andy needed a ride back to the court house where he was to testify before Judge Freer and he was late. As we headed up Garrison, he spied Will Manus on the sidewalk in front of the Silver Dollar Saloon. Guess Andy had a warrant on him or something. So he screamed at Will to stop, which about scared me to death, it being so unexpected and all. Will looked over his shoulder and his eyes got real big and he took off running. Andy told me to go faster and get closer to the side of the road. I pushed that Boehmer as fast as I dared, dodging holes and garbage and people. Will could have slipped inside one of the buildings but I guess he wasn't thinking too clear. I figure he'd had a drink or two at the Silver Dollar.

"As we came up alongside Will, Andy never even told me to stop, he just jumped out, and tackled him. They rolled around in the dirt until Andy got the upper hand. Then we took Will to jail and Andy got to court without a minute to spare. I watched him dust himself off as he went into the building like nothing ever happened. Me, I was shaking like a leaf."

We all laughed.

"That's Andy all right," Burley said as he passed me the chicken. "Got more nerve than sense sometimes. After that deal with the bale of cotton, which would've gotten an ordinary man killed, he got hit by a trolley. Everyone thought that was the end of his career, but no, he was back on the streets in a few months."

"What bale of cotton?" I spooned mashed potatoes onto my plate.

"Well the rumor was that back in the day Andy was hot on the trail of some outlaws who pulled off a robbery here in town and then forded the river and hid in a cave up on a rocky hill somewhere in Oklahoma. Andy wasn't having any of that, so he followed them with a couple other lawmen. They found the bad guys pretty easy, but arresting them was another matter. They couldn't climb up without getting shot and those ruffians weren't about to come down. So Andy found himself a bale of cotton somewhere—don't remember how—but they say it was at least two hundred pounds. On the theory that if he padded himself up enough, bullets couldn't get through, he wrapped himself in that whole bale."

"He probably thought those bandits would take him for a ghost." Caroline slathered strawberry jam on her biscuit. "Figured they'd take one look and run away."

"Maybe so, Miz McGrath. And maybe being not quite sure what was coming up that hill after them made those crooks about the worst shots in creation." Burley bit into his drumstick.

"So Andy went after these guys wrapped up in two hundred pounds of cotton and—" I let my voice trail off questioningly.

"They shot at him but he didn't have a nick," Julian said.

I was astounded. "Nothing?"

"Ask Andy one of these days. That story's been going around for years now."

I shook my head. "He's invincible."

"So it seems," Caroline said. "But I still worry. Remember when Theo Lamb did Ouija for Abigail last year?"

"Yeah?" I paused with a spoon of peas an inch from my lips.

"Ouija?" Burley looked surprised.

"We aren't pagans, Burley," Julian laughed. "Was a parlor game that no one but Abigail took seriously."

"What's it got to do with Andy?" I laid down my spoon, trying not to be alarmed.

Caroline lowered her eyes. "Remember that Maybelle was a bad speller?"

Burley, Julian, and I stared at her.

"Who is Maybelle?"

"It's silly, really." I smiled at Burley. "A silly game."

"Abigail believes she's talking to the ghost of Belle Starr," Caroline said. "You know her middle name was Maybelle."

Burley seemed upset. "A ghost?"

"And she talks to Abigail through the Ouija board." Julian mimicked pushing a planchette on Caroline's linen tablecloth.

"Anyway," Caroline continued after we all stopped laughing. "Supposedly Maybelle was talking to Jennie Williams and was telling her to tell John B something."

"And it came out garbled." My heart beat faster. "We never could figure what it was supposed to mean."

"Remember that Jennie wrote it down? The next day, I was staring at that piece of paper stuck between the pages of my notebook and it came to me." She got up and went into the front parlor.

Julian looked at me. "What's going on?"

I shrugged.

We heard the drawer on Caroline's desk squeak. In a moment, she returned to the dining room with the notebook. With one hand, she moved the dishes of food out of the way and spread the page Jennie had written on that stormy night last fall in the middle of the table.

Burley, Julian, and I leaned forward. Caroline had drawn a slanted line between some of the letters and scribbled additional words here and there. "At first, it was just a puzzle. A mental challenge. And then I saw it."

Julian pulled it closer.

"T - E - L - J - O -N - B" now said in Caroline's hand, "TELL JOHN B." and "W - A - C - H - O - U- T - 4 - A - N - D - E - E" now said "WATCH OUT FOR ANDEE." Then, at the bottom of the note, in bold print, "TELL JOHN B TO WATCH OUT FOR ANDY!"

Julian looked up. "What does that mean, do you think?"

"Andy's in danger and only John B can save him?" It was the first thing that came to my mind. "After all, the ghost was talking to Jennie."

"If there was a ghost." Burley clearly didn't think so.

"Theo was putting on a good show for Abigail," Julian said.

"But why would she say something like this?"

"To get your hearts pumping faster." Julian picked up the paper, examined it more closely, and handed it to me.

I read it several times, not believing that what Caroline had discovered was a real message from the hereafter, but intrigued just the same. "Should we tell Jennie and John B what you figured out?"

"It's nothing," Burley said. "Gobbledygook from a scam artist."

"Why scare people, Mamie? Like as not, this is exactly what Burley said. A gypsy trick."

Julian was right of course. I glanced at Caroline. Her eyes were troubled but she nodded.

Burley took a bite of his dinner and chewed slowly. "Besides, maybe what makes Andy invincible is his fearlessness. Something like that, if you let it, can undermine a man's confidence and get him killed."

"I hadn't thought of that." Caroline took the note from me. "I'll keep it where it's been and let's promise each other never to mention it to the Williamses or the Carrs."

We each nodded and, eventually, Julian and Burley began talking about their afternoon and Bud Marr and the aeroplane out in Electric Park.

*

Last week an employee scared off some bad guys who broke into the Brasch Shoe Company. They must have needed shoes something awful.

Patsy Lincoln, *The Fort Smith Bell*

2

May 17, 1910
Aunt Sarah Lewis' house on 923 North Ninth caught fire. The firemen were
afraid Aunt Sarah might be lying inside all burned up, but thank the good
Lord, she was off visiting her daughter. They don't know what caused that
fire but Aunt Sarah was a pack rat so that could be it. Aunt Sarah lost about
$200, but thank you, Jesus, the good woman herself still be with us.

Genevieve Day, *The Fort Smith Bell*

May 21, 1910

ELECTRIC PARK GLISTENED AS WE got off the trolley and purchased our tickets. Once we were through the front gate, we wandered around, enjoying the flowers and deciding what to do first.

"Oh look," Caroline pointed. "There's Theo."

I turned to see a woman sitting in a booth. "Oh, my goodness. I'd never have recognized her."

Julian patted my hand that was curled around his arm. "What kind of outfit is that supposed to be?"

"Some kind of fortune-teller costume, I guess." I thought about saying hello, but there were several people waiting in line to see her. "Does she charge?"

"I would think so," Julian said. "It would get tiresome telling people the same old stories over and over."

"Is that what she does?"

He squinted his eyes and pretended he was gazing into a crystal ball. "You'll meet a handsome young man who will sweep you off your feet and take you to see an aeroplane someday."

I laughed. "Theo tells every woman the same thing?"

"Only on days when there's an aeroplane here. I have it on good authority that last week, the main attraction was a hot air balloon."

"You couldn't pay me enough to sit out here for hours making up stories like that," Caroline said. "There are too many things to see and do."

I glanced up at the cloudless sky. "It's going to be a scorcher today."

"Nothing like spending a pretty day with my pretty bride." Julian guided us toward the merry-go-round. "Would you like a ride?"

I felt cranky and out of sorts, but I squeezed his arm. "Of course."

"Mama?"

"I'll sit on that bench there and watch the two of you."

Julian and I had only gone around once, when I saw Abigail and Garland Talbot approaching Caroline's bench. The next time around, they were chatting with her. By the third circuit, Abigail was waving her hands and stamping her feet.

"What do you suppose is going on there?" I dabbed sweat off my upper lip with my handkerchief.

Julian shook his head. "Something's got her going."

We finished our ride and got off. Julian cleared his throat as we approached them. "Look who's here. Hello, Garland. Abigail, my dear, you look like a ripe tomato that's been squeezed too hard."

"Julian, someone just has to do something about that mean old man." Abigail pointed to a one-legged figure, leaning heavily on a wooden crutch as he made his way up the path toward us. "My own husband refuses to engage in fisticuffs with that...that...Sarge, no matter how much I beg him."

"What?" I smiled at Garland. "You won't smite a crippled man for Abigail? What kind of husband are you?"

He shrugged. "One who will be able to sleep in my own bed beside my sweet wife tonight instead of in a smelly jail cell accused of assaulting one of our venerable war veterans."

"Sounds like a better option to me too." Julian nudged Garland in the ribs. "Abigail is far more charming than the array of misfits, drunks, and ne'er-do-wells who populate our jail house on Saturday nights."

I turned back to Abigail who was glaring at the old fellow. "Why are you mad at Sarge?"

"He had the nerve to insult Colonel DuVal just now."

"Is the colonel here?" I pretended to look for him.

Abigail scowled. "Don't be ridiculous, Mamie. The old gentleman died in aught and five."

"Ah!" I threw up my hands in mock surprise.

"Calm down, sugar." Garland patted Abigail's hand. "Mamie's just trying to find out why you're having a hissy fit this fine day."

"Sarge had the nerve to say that the war was won at Gettysburg. You know how the colonel hated talk like that."

"Abigail!"

"Well, he implied it."

"He said it was over for him."

"Same thing."

"Well, butter my butt and call me a biscuit. Is that little Mamie Eacret?" The old soldier called as he approached us.

"It's McGrath now, Sarge. Didn't you hear I got married last year? It was in the paper, you know." I gave him a peck on the cheek.

"Not much news in the bottom of a whiskey bottle," Abigail hissed.

Sarge ignored her. "I ain't been readin' much these days. Eyes are blurrin' up on me. Besides, there's not much Fort Smith news in the Michigan papers."

"I am sure there isn't." I took his crutch and put my arm around him. "When did you get here?"

"Tuesday. Travel wears me out these days. Been nappin' ever since."

"I'm glad you decided to come for a visit."

"Didn't have much choice. Dad-gummed Michigan winter about killed me last year. When my old nurse got down in her back, I figured it was time to head for warmer climes."

"Good."

"Your Daddy would have been proud, girl. How long has it been since we lost your mama?"

"Nine years."

"Damn." He shook his head. "She was a fine lady. I'd have grabbed her myself if'n Dalton hadn't seen her first."

"This is my husband, Julian. He's a reporter for the *Southwest American*. Julian, this is Sergeant Elias Eacret, my daddy's brother."

Julian stuck out his hand. "Nice to meet you, Sarge. Mamie's told me all about you."

"She tell you I'm her favorite uncle?" Sarge grabbed Julian's hand and pumped vigorously.

"Of course she did, sir." Julian winced and stepped back out of reach as soon as Sarge loosened his grip.

Sarge laughed and so did I, leaving everyone else looking confused. "I'm her favorite uncle because I'm her *only* uncle."

The heat of the day was starting to get to me, but I continued the introductions. "This is my mother-in-law, Caroline."

"Hello, Sarge," Caroline extended her hand.

"Ain't you a beauty, Miz McGrath?" Sarge kissed her knuckles. "If I was still a young'en, I'd come callin.'"

"I hear that you already met Garland and Abigail." I swept my arm their way.

"We go back a long way, don't we Miss Abigail?" He grinned at her. "Ever time I came down to visit kin, I'd go fishin' with her Uncle Joe. I been tormentin' her since she was no bigger than a minnow in a fishin' pond."

"Sarge served with the Seventh Cavalry," Garland said. "Pop rode with old JEB Stewart. They probably faced each other in battle lots of times."

"Deke Talbot was a good cavalryman. I was sorry to hear he got killed."

"I was eight years old. Only saw him a couple times," Garland said. "Don't remember much about him."

"That old boy had a nose so big he could balance a pickle on it." Sarge held his hands a foot apart. "A great big dill one too."

Everyone but Abigail and Garland laughed.

"Y'all here for lunch or to see that lunatic risk his life over at the League Park?"

"We're killing time waiting for the big event. You want to walk over with us?"

"I ain't walkin' anywhere." The old man cackled. "Just about wore my dang fool self out gettin' up here to beat my gums with you folks."

"Where's your wheel chair?"

"Settin' back where ya get off the trolley. The nurse I pay to push me around went to the facilities and I made my escape."

"What's her name? I'll go get her and the chair," Julian said.

"Rosie? No, Rosalie, maybe? Rosemary? Somethin' about a flower, I think. You can't miss her. Got a face like a catfish."

Julian glanced at me and raised one eyebrow.

I shrugged. "What's she wearing, Sarge?"

"I don't know. Somethin' black."

"There you go, Julian. Look for black," Garland chuckled.

"Easier if you look for a wheelchair, young man. The woman will follow the chair." Sarge wasn't as addled as he let on.

* * *

Sarge's nurse turned out to be a massive Negress named Annabelle Peach—and she was dressed in purple.

"Maybe he was thinking of peach blossoms," Julian whispered into my ear.

Blinded by the sun, I shrugged and turned to Abigail and Garland. "Are you coming with us?"

"I already saw him fly it over at the Fort Smith Country Club the other day," Garland grumbled.

"Well, I didn't." Abigail poked him in the side with her elbow.

"Yes, of course, we're coming," Garland said to me.

People were already heading toward the ball park.

"Looks like everyone in Fort Smith has come out for this." Caroline picked up a basket of goodies she'd prepared for us. "I saw Ike and Hannah Apple go by a few minutes ago and there's Chauncey and Carrie Lick."

"Are Jennie and John B joining us?"

"Jennie said their kids are all excited about the aeroplane so I imagine they are," Caroline responded. "John B isn't coming with them though. It's a workday for him."

Miss Peach took Sarge's crutch away from him and handed it to me. Then, she lifted Sarge from the bench to his chair. She didn't even grunt. It was only then that I realized how fragile the old man was.

"It's too hot for that," he whined when she unfolded a small blanket.

We agreed about something at least.

Miss Peach ignored him and tucked it firmly over his lap. Then she dug into a bag she'd brought and produced a jug of water.

"I don't want that!" He tried to wiggle away from her.

"I'm not taking you to League Park and standing out in the heat just to watch you keel over."

"No!" Sarge locked his jaw and refused to open his mouth.

"Then we'll head on back to town." Miss Peach corked the bottle and put it back into her bag.

"I'm betting on Miss Peach," Julian whispered in my ear.

"Depends on whether he wants to see the exhibition or not," I whispered back.

They were still in a stalemate when Caroline and Abigail got up and headed toward League Park. Garland trailed behind carrying both Abigail's basket and Caroline's.

"Are you coming?" I touched Sarge's shoulder.

He nodded, keeping his mouth clamped shut lest Miss Peach get a drop into him.

"We aren't going anywhere until you fill up with water. It's gonna be hot out there." Miss Peach crossed her arms over her bosom.

"I have lemonade. Will that do?"

"If you can get it down him."

"How about it, Sarge? It's Mama's recipe."

He brightened and nodded.

I fetched the bottle from my basket and poured him a cup. While I stretched and rubbed my back, he drank it down and asked for another. I refilled the cup and within a few minutes we were ready to join the growing crowd eager to see Bud Mars show off his flying machine.

Miss Peach pushed Sarge's chair and Julian and I followed at a distance.

Julian whispered in my ear. "Did he know that lemonade was spiked with vodka?"

"Only reason that old man ever showed up for a family function was when Mama lured him with her lemonade."

* * *

The sun was cruel. My wrists and face were turning red and my stomach was upset again. I would've preferred sitting under a shade tree with the others, but Julian found good spots for the two of us in front of the growing crowd. I wanted to see the flying machine less the longer we waited, but there was no way I'd disappoint my husband.

"It's bigger than I thought it would be," I said.

"What did you imagine?" Julian kept his eyes on the strange contraption sitting on a grassy strip of land a few yards in front of us.

"Only thing I ever saw that carried people up into the air was a balloon. With a little—what do they call it?"

"A gondola?"

"Yes. I thought it would be like a gondola with wings."

"I don't know what I expected."

"Are you hot, Julian?"

"Hot? No, not particularly. There's a breeze."

"I don't feel it." I patted my face and neck with my handkerchief. "What kind of wood is that?"

"Bamboo. I'd never seen anything like it either," Julian said. "When I asked about it, Mars said that Glenn Curtiss picked it because it was both light and strong."

Abigail pushed her way through the crowd to where Julian and I stood. "Who's Glenn Curtiss?"

"He's the man who built this flying machine," I told her. "Where's everyone else?"

"Back where trees can cast shade for Sarge, but I wanted to be down here with you two. It's easier to see it."

"Maybe for take off and landing, but it'll be up in the air after all."

"You say that because you're tall, Julian. We ladies don't have that luxury."

I counted to ten before deciding not to point out that Abigail was every bit as tall as Julian and twice as heavy.

"I thought it would look like a carriage or an automobile," she said. "But it's like a skeleton."

"It needs to be as light as possible."

"But where will Mr. Mars sit, Julian?"

"See that big thing that looks like a fan?"

Abigail squinted. "Yes."

"Look in front of that. There's a seat and steering wheel?"

"I see it."

"That's where Mars will sit and control the aeroplane."

"It's that easy?" I shaded my eyes. "Just like a automobile's steering wheel?"

"I guess," Julian said. "I'm not sure how a flying machine works." He looked down at me. "Are you okay?"

"It's just so hot," I said.

"Do you want to sit down?"

"No, no. I don't want to miss this."

"What's wrong with you?" Abigail's voice was so loud that people around us turned to look.

"Nothing."

"Here, how about this?" She produced a flier about the event and fanned me with it."

The air on my sweaty face made me feel a little better, but it irritated me too. "No, please. Let me do it." I snatched the paper out of her hands and waved it in front of my face.

"There he is," Julian said.

Blinking back dizziness, I turned my attention to the aeroplane. A man came out into the field and did something to the engine.

"Is that him?" Abigail said. "Is that Mr. Mars?"

"That's him," Julian confirmed.

Bud Mars went around behind the seat and spun the propeller. At first, it made a weak coughing sound, but then the engine caught. He went back around the wing and crawled into the seat.

A woman stepped forward, said something I couldn't make out for the noise, and then smashed a bottle against the front of the spindly-looking frame.

Abigail held her arm over her eyes. "Who's that?"

"That's his wife."

"What's she doing?"

"She's dedicating the plane and launching it like you would a ship," Julian explained.

"It's not really a ship, though, is it?" Abigail seemed disappointed. "Just a flimsy little stick box. Hardly worth a good bottle of champagne."

Mars revved the engine. The woman waved and backed away. The plane rolled forward, slowly at first and then faster. As the engine got louder, all three wheels really did come up off the ground.

"Oh my heavens, look at that!" Abigail shook her fists in the air like she was cheering a horse race.

The crowd vacillated between open-mouthed awe and noisy reverie. As Mr. Mars rose higher in the air, the noise in my head faded and my sweaty skin turned ice cold. "Julian—" I reached out for him, but he was staring off into the distance. My knees gave way and grass hit me in the face.

* * *

Water in my nose made me choke. I opened my eyes.

"There she is!"

Something fluttered in my face. A bird? My eyes cleared and I realized it was the teal feathers on Abigail's blasted hat. She was staring at me with a bottle of water in one hand and the ribbon from my ruffled neckline in the other. The people around us were stamping their feet, their voices rising and falling in my ears. And then I was out again.

* * *

I was being carried and Abigail's voice was in the distance. "Move, you fools! Can't you see we have a sick girl here?"

"Julian?"

"Shush, my darling, I have you."

I buried my face in his shoulder until I felt him slowing down.

"Oh my God," Caroline cried. "What happened to her?"

"I don't know!" Julian's voice was gruff and I knew he was trying not to cry. "Sunstroke, maybe. She told me several times she was hot but I was so excited about that damned aeroplane I didn't pay attention." He laid me on Caroline's quilt they'd spread on the ground.

"Oh the poor dear," Caroline murmured. "Look how red her face is."

"Out of the way," a woman's voice that I didn't recognize bellowed.

There was a ripping sound and the clatter of glass. People mumbled in the distance.

"I'll find him," Julian said.

Who? It was so confusing.

"I should have kept on fanning her," Abigail said. "But she didn't want me to. She's never liked me. Never trusted me."

"Nonsense, Abigail. Of course, Mamie likes you." Caroline seemed to be standing above my head.

Abigail's sobs were loud and annoying. I wished she'd be quiet. Just for a little while.

"You did what you could, sugar." Garland's whisper was loud enough to wake the dead too. "You stay here. I'm going to help Julian."

Help Julian with what? "Oh," I cried and opened my eyes as someone put something wet on my face. "What is that?"

A freckled-faced black woman was kneeling over me.

"It's Annabelle Peach, Miz Mamie. Your husband is trying to find Dr. Stevenson. We saw him a few minutes ago. In the meantime, we need to get your body temperature down. Do you understand?"

"My head hurts," I moaned.

"You lay still, missy." She unbuttoned the top of my blouse and laid my damp handkerchief on my throat. She pushed up my sleeves, wrapped my arms from wrist to elbow in something shiny, then she poured water up and down them. "I need your help, Miz Talbot. You too, Miz McGrath."

"Yes, we're here," Caroline said. "What can we do?"

"We've used all of my petticoat. I need the two of you to start tearing your own into strips and squares."

"In front of all these people?" Abigail was aghast. "It's scandalous."

"Don't be ridiculous." It was Caroline. "If you're worried that people will talk about you, then rip up Mamie's. If you don't she could die. Is that what you want?"

Die? "Oh," I whimpered as the heat from my body warmed the wet cotton on my face, neck, and arms. "I feel like throwing up!"

Miss Peach rolled me onto my right side, tucked a corner of the quilt underneath my body, and held my chin while I retched into the grass. "There, there. We got it." She stroked my hair while I sobbed from humiliation and misery. I touched my face. *Funny. There're no tears.*

"He's coming. I can see him now," Miss Peach said.

Someone was pulling on my clothes. *Miss Peach? Abigail?*

"Mamie, I'm here, sweetheart." Julian took my hand. "I brought the doctor."

"My head, Julian!"

"I know."

"I want to go home."

"I'll get you home if I have to carry you the whole way." He stroked my hand. "She's so hot, Doc. They've been putting water on her all this time and she's still hot. And her lips? Why are they so swollen?"

"We need to get some of it down her." Dr. Stevenson opened my blouse and pressed a stethoscope over my heart.

"We need more water. I've used everything I brought for my-self and Sarge," Miss Peach was in the distance. "How about you, ma'am. Do you have any left?"

"I have half a bottle," someone said. "It's all I have left what with the kids and all."

"Thank you, Jennie," Caroline called. "Where's John B?"

"He's at the Pony Express."

"We didn't bring the Boehmer today. We came by trolley."

"There's a telephone back in the Electric Park. I'll call and have him bring the wagon," Jennie said.

"Tell him to bring more water too," the doctor said over his shoulder. "And have those folks inside bring some as well. This girl is burning up."

"I will," Jennie Williams voice sounded like she was already half-way there.

"Doctor, look! Blood!" Abigail was being dramatic again and I hated her for it. However, even in my dazed state, I knew what that meant and I didn't want to know it.

Dr. Stevenson put his mouth next to my ear. "Mamie, are you with child?"

I couldn't get the words out so I nodded.

"Mamie?" Julian sounded shocked.

This wasn't the way I'd dreamed of telling him. "I wasn't sure yet."

"We need to get her somewhere I can examine her more throughly," Dr. Stevenson said. "Somewhere we can put her in a tub would be even better."

"Here's another bottle of water." It was Miss Peach. "A little boy gave me his." She slid one arm under my shoulders and lifted me up. "Slowly, Mamie."

The first sip was wonderful and I begged for more.

"I said slowly." Miss Peach raised her voice.

I ignored her. Grabbing the bottle, I drank in loud gulps, water streaming down my cheeks onto my bodice.

"Mamie!" Julian pulled the bottle out of my hands,

"Oh," I cried and vomited onto the grass again.

*

May 21, 1910–Constable Andy Carr, the most noted officer of Sebastian County, was shot while foiling a burglary. As Carr entered the yard, the burglar fired point blank at his heart. The bullet crashed through Carr's coat, penetrated a pair of gloves and a bankbook in his chest pocket before striking the officer's star pinned to his shirt. Knocked to the ground, Carr recovered and chased the burglar several blocks.

Julian McGrath, *Southwest American*

3

June 25, 1910
Last week Forest Park Cemetery hosted a caravan of Fort Smith ladies to
show new burial facilities. Mrs. Caroline McGrath, widow, said, "When it's
my turn to die, I shall be laid to rest on this property, beyond the prettiest
grove of trees in our city. Her companion Mrs. Garland Talbot disagreed.
"Oak Cemetery is just as nice and all the important people lie there,"
she stated.

Julian McGrath, *Southwest American*

June 26, 1910

I STUCK MY HEAD INTO the front parlor where Caroline was working a quilt with Abigail Talbot and Katherine Mivelaz. "I'm going out this afternoon."

"Where did you say?" Caroline held her hand to her ear.

"Downtown. I'll be back before dinner."

"It's hot out there again today," Abigail said. "Are you sure you feel up to it?"

"It's always hot in Fort Smith." It came out crankier than I intended. "I can't stay in bed and cry forever."

"No, you can't," Caroline said. "You've been cooped up in that bedroom for a month now. Time to get out and get some fresh air and a little exercise."

"My carriage is out front if you want to borrow it."

"I think I'll just take the trolley in, but thank you, Abigail."

"It's a bit of a walk. At least let your yard man drive you to the trolley stop and bring the rig back for me. You could pay him and I'm sure the extra money would make his day."

Remembering how awful I felt the day I lost the baby made me consider Abigail's offer. I glanced at myself in the hallway mirror. Still pale with dark circles under my eyes, I bit my lips and pinched my cheeks. It didn't help.

"These young people don't remember what it was like before we had electricity." Abigail was always louder than anyone else. "You didn't just pop on a bonnet and catch a trolley not six blocks from your front door."

"No you certainly didn't," Caroline agreed. "You had to hitch up the horse to the carriage and then hope the mud didn't swallow you and the poor beast whole. On a good day, the ride to Rogers Avenue took as long as it takes to get to Garrison from here now."

I slipped money into my Dorothy bag. "I can walk. It's not that far."

"Just as well," Abigail said. "Who knows if that Negro can even handle a horse and buggy. It's not like the old days when everyone learned when they were young."

I closed the door behind me and stood on the porch. I was through being sad. Lots of women lose babies and then go on to have big families. That's what Julian had said. Besides, I'd only begun to suspect that there was a baby. It hadn't seemed real yet. It wasn't like Cecilia Walker who lost her baby in the seventh month. Not like the grinding grief Burley Johnston must have gone through, losing first his wife and then several months later that beautiful baby boy. No, what Julian and I had gone through wasn't like that.

I took a deep breath and let it out slowly. There. All done. I hurried down the steps, pausing at the front gate to raise my parasol. I stopped to pet Abigail's old black horse Trekker who was tied up out front. It was only three blocks to Rogers and two blocks over to the trolley stop. By Greenwood Avenue, I was smiling again.

* * *

The trolley was half full when I boarded.

"Morning, Miz McGrath," the motorman said. "It's good to see you up and about again."

"Good morning, Mr. Dyer. It's good to be out again." I sat across the aisle and behind him, as was my custom. Caroline's old friend, Patsy, sat in the back, her arms full of books. I wanted to wave at her, but she hid under the brim of her straw hat and I knew better than to call to her. There were rules about how black and white folks should act in public and neither of us dared challenge them, at least not on trolleys in the middle of the day.

I stared out the window, wondering about Patsy. Caroline had shared a notebook full of her letters with me and I found them enchanting. I wanted to sit next to her and talk about the books she was toting, and about what she and Caroline did when they lived on Caroline's grandfather's farm in Southern Arkansas back when they were girls. I wanted to know why Patsy had never married and why, after graduating from college, she moved back to Fort Smith to teach at Lincoln, the colored high school.

As we neared downtown, the sky darkened. I peered out the window, worried that rain might interfere with my errand. Smoke. I wrinkled my nose. Something was burning in Fort Smith again.

The motorman braked before my stop.

I leaned forward. "What is it, Mr. Dyer?"

"Hard to say. Looks like some kind of ruckus down the way. A fire maybe."

I sighed and stood up. I had an appointment with Anna Marie Cavanaugh at one pm at the Hotel Main. Maybe all the excitement would be over by the time I finished my visit with Sister Alberta. The motorman opened the door and we all climbed out of the trolley.

Mr. Dyer was right. There was definitely a fire somewhere downtown. Patsy's eyes smiled at me over her spectacles. Then she headed toward Garrison Avenue beyond Immaculate Conception Church. I watched her for a bit before walking toward St. Edwards infirmary.

A fire wagon rushed past. Then an automobile honked and swerved to miss a barefoot boy carrying a mess of catfish. City Detective Cathey Pitcock smacked the boy's head with his baton. "Are you stupid, Manny? Stay out of the road. Want to get yourself killed?"

Manny McKnight howled and dropped his catch to cover his head with both arms as the policeman raised his arm to strike again.

"Mr. Pitcock!" My voice was louder than I intended.

Cathey Pitcock turned toward me, scowling. "Who the he—" He paused mid-curse. "Miz McGrath?"

"How dare you hit that child?

"A boy like that has to learn the rules or he'll turn into a pest."

"And beating him will teach him the rules?"

"Yes, ma'am, it sure will."

I turned to Emanuel McKnight. "Go about your business. Shoo."

The boy smirked at the cop before scampering off down the road toward Garrison Avenue.

"Miz McGrath, I'm the law around here." Pitcock tapped his palm with his baton. "I say who can go and who can't."

"Then you should have, Mr. Pitcock." I walked on, in a huff.

Before I went into the infirmary, I allowed myself a quick glance over my shoulder. Pitcock was gone.

I came out twenty minutes later carrying a basket Sister Alberta had given me for Anna Marie. My conversation with the nun had been uncomfortable. Anna Marie's profession was apparently not news to Sister Alberta. She'd already heard about it from her brother in Oklahoma who heard about it from a neighbor who visited Miss

Laura's on a business trip to Fort Smith. He'd recognized Anna Marie even though she called herself Miss Angelica and painted a mole under her left eyebrow when she was on duty at the brothel.

Anna Marie was right to avoid visiting Sister Alberta. A prostitute didn't just wander into a nunnery for afternoon tea. Not in Fort Smith. The local gossips, led by Abigail Talbot, no doubt, would spread the word across two counties within hours. The days of anything goes on Garrison Avenue were over. Businessmen like Sam McCloud, the Eads brothers, Rudolph Ney, Chauncey Lick, and Artie Berry were focused on making the area a reflection of the Twentieth Century—safe, modern, and cultured. And profitable, of course.

I walked down Garrison, avoiding the crowd mulling about, eager to see what was going on. As I approached the Hotel Main on the left side of the street, I saw the new First National Bank just beyond it. Julian's company rented a suite on the third floor. I imagined he was covering the fire.

As I got closer, the smoke burned my eyes. A baby-faced cop encouraged people to leave the area. Most folks retreated, only to return as soon as he moved on. Everyone wanted to see what was happening, including me, but the rancid smoke made it hard to breathe or see much.

Firemen were hooking up hoses to the pumper they'd parked by the curb. Nervous horses shied and forced their riders to go around the area. Automobiles were parked hither and yon, their drivers leaned on their front fenders, watching. I squeezed around and through them to get to the hotel only a few yards away.

Riding a bicycle loaded with packages, Manny McKnight wove through the crowd, alternately on the sidewalk and the street. Just as he passed me, he braked to avoid a hound dog, and landed on his back at my feet.

I'd had enough. "Manny, shouldn't you be in school?" I bent to help him pick up the boxes that had scattered all over the sidewalk.

"Aw, Miz McGrath. Studyin' ain't for me." He stacked them on the rack behind the seat of his bike and secured them with a rope. "I quit for good."

"What did Miss Pahotski say?"

"It don't matter what she says. I'm thirteen."

I doubted he was that old but I put my hands on my hips and scowled. "Thirteen's old enough to get in big trouble."

"I got me a job delivering things to Miss Laura's for Mr. Ney."

"Just delivery, right?"

"Aw, Miz McGrath, don't say stuff like that." He avoided my eyes. "My mama done hit me with an ugly stick and I ain't got me no three dollars. Them women won't take to the likes of me."

"Did you have lunch?"

He hung his head.

"Uh huh. Go get yourself a sandwich." I fished a coin out of my bag and tossed it to him. "Not candy."

"Yes, ma'am." He crawled up on his rusty bicycle and pedaled away, dodging people, wagons, and fire hoses.

"I mean it, Manny!"

He disappeared into the smoke and dust.

I stamped my foot and coughed. "Boys!" Covering my mouth and nose with my handkerchief, I hurried into the Hotel Main.

"Mamie, how are you?" Della Carr was heading toward the door as I came into the lobby.

"My dear Della, what brings you here today?" I looked around, hoping that Anna Marie would avoid approaching me while I was engaged in conversation with the wife of a deputy constable.

"I was supposed to have lunch with Andy, but the Palace Drug Store is on fire and he couldn't stand not being a part of the action."

"So he abandoned you?"

Della's laugh was hearty. "It's not the first time."

"Will he be back?"

"Not likely. He loves a good mystery. He's still trying to figure out what happened to that guy who disappeared when the McKibbon building burned."

"Does he think this fire is connected to that one?"

"It would make his day if it was and I'm sure he'll check it out. If it's a really good lead, the kids and I might not see him at the dinner table tonight."

Out of the corner of my eye, I saw a prim young woman sitting in the lobby. She wore no jewelry and her clothes were plain and unfashionable. Deliberately so.

I returned my attention to Della. "So what're you up to now?

"I'm going to peek in at the Boston Store and then head on home. Andy knows where to find me."

"It's a mess out there. Do you have a handkerchief to keep the soot out of your nose and eyes?"

"Is it that bad?" Della pulled a handkerchief out of her sleeve. "It seems like this town is always burning down."

"It's good to see you, dear." I gave her a hug. "Watch out for those idiots in their automobiles and the trolleys."

"Andy will have their hide if they run me down," Della laughed. "Getting hit by a street car is his claim to fame."

"That's only funny because he survived."

"That man keeps me on pins and needles. Never know what he's going to get into next."

"You be careful and give my love to that daredevil husband of yours." I tried not to think of the ghostly message in Caroline's notebook as Della hurried out the door.

The young woman stood up as I approached. "Mrs. McGrath, I'm Anna Marie."

"I wasn't sure it was you." I took her hand. "But now, I see how you resemble Sister Alberta."

She blushed. "I wish that was more true than it is. She's the beauty in our family."

"You both are lovely." We headed to the dining hall.

"Did Mrs. Carr see me?"

"If she did, she didn't realize I was here to meet you, so no harm done."

A waiter led us to a window table. I set the basket on the carpet beside the table.

"It's so beautiful in here." Anna Marie sat down across from me. "The Goldman is grander, more modern, but I love the older trappings, don't you?"

I looked around. "I don't think that fancy new place up the street will hurt business here."

"The Main feels like home away from home," she said.

"Do you know Della?" I tried to sound blasé.

"I know of her, and everyone knows Andy."

I leaned back in my seat. "She would never guess about you. No one would."

Anna Marie shrugged. "If I'm ever to have another life, I hope not."

The waiter brought tea and finger sandwiches.

"Sister Alberta said to tell you thanks for thinking of her when you needed help." I selected a sandwich from the tray. "And that she misses you."

"Me too." Anna Marie put several spoons of sugar in her tea. "It's kind of you to do this for us, Mrs. McGrath. I couldn't think of anyone else we could trust with our secret."

"Ooo, pimento cheese." I took a bite of my sandwich. "Please, call me Mamie." I swallowed and took a quick sip of tea.

"Mamie."

"You must tell me how this all came about."

"It's a long story."

"My throat is raw from all the smoke. I'm not going back out until it clears and that crowd thins a bit." That was only half true. I was dying to hear a long story.

"Bertie was already a nun when our parents moved the rest of us to Oklahoma," Anna Marie said. "It was hard to accept that we wouldn't see her much anymore. I adored her. She was fun to be around, always joking and making everyone else laugh."

I smiled. "She's still like that."

"One time she sent me a book. I guess no one told her I never learned to read."

"Why?"

"Why?" She wrinkled her forehead. "It wasn't that I didn't try. I went to school. The teacher had lots of other students who weren't as stupid as me."

"Does Sister Alberta know now?"

Anna Marie folded and unfolded her napkin. "I don't think so. She still sends me letters. One of the girls at the house reads them to me. But I can't write her back, you know. Even if I could write, I wouldn't. Unless it was an emergency or something."

"What about the letter you sent me?"

"Miss Laura did that for me."

"You could telephone Sister Alberta."

She ducked her chin. "It's been a long time."

"You didn't talk to her when your parents died?"

"I didn't go to the funeral."

"Why?"

"I was already working in the row. No one back home knew it then. Our brothers still don't know." Anna Marie studied her own hands.

I chose not to be the one to tell her who did or didn't know about her professional life. "I didn't mean to embarrass you."

"I know."

"It's just that she's in the convent at the head of Garrison—"

"And I am in a whore house at the foot?"

I nodded. "Twelve blocks away."

"Not what Mama and Papa wanted for their youngest daughter."

I focused on my teacup, at a loss for what to say to her.

"It's not a bad life, you know. I have a room and clothes and food. A doctor takes care of—you know."

I did know but didn't want to acknowledge it. "And the men?"

"They're usually nice. They're there to have a good time, after all."

I was embarrassed that I'd asked that question. "So why did you pick me for this errand?"

"Theo Lamb comes to the house often. Oh no, she's not—" She lowered her eyes. "—one of us. She brings Tarot cards or a Ouija board to entertain our guests."

"Dear Theo. She's everywhere, it seems. Always working."

"I think she needs the money."

I hadn't thought of that, but Katherine Mivelaz did tell Caroline that Theo entertained at social events all over town. That was good enough for Abigail. She engaged Theo to come to her home twice a month to chat with the shade of Maybelle Shirley.

"So you asked Theo for someone who would act as a bridge between you and your sister."

"It's about a friend. A man named Marky. He showed up at the house after being burned in a fire. He was ill and in pain so Miss Laura let me hide him in the basement and look after him."

"Why did he come to you in his hour of need?"

Anna Marie shrugged. "Mr. Marky was a regular."

I don't know why that hadn't occurred to me. "Oh."

"He thinks someone is trying to kill him."

"Why, do you think?"

This was the first time I'd talked to Anna Marie for very long. Our first two conversations had been quick telephone calls with her explaining what she needed me to do. She seemed like a sweet girl, not at all what I expected of a prostitute.

"I don't know," she said. "I don't know him as well as he seems to think I do."

"Why didn't he go to the police after the fire? They'd protect him."

"Mr. Marky's suspicious of policemen."

"You mean Mr. Marky's a criminal?" I was aghast.

"He's not a ruffian. He's an accountant who found mistakes in the books he was reviewing."

"I see." I was involved in shielding a thief from the law. *What would Julian say?*

"He didn't steal anything if that's what you're thinking."

"Anna Marie, I don't know what to think."

"He was working for a company in Saint Louis. He told the police there about the problem which made the people he worked for angry. They threatened to kill him if he testified at the trial. So he took off and ended up here in Fort Smith last year."

"So he thinks the fire was an attempt to murder him."

Anna Marie nodded. "Miss Laura is spooked and wants Mr. Marky out of the house as soon as possible in case someone finds him and intrudes on business."

"And he won't leave?"

"His burns were serious. They are healing but there will be scars. He hired the room at the McKibbon under a false name but the police have a description of him, you know. And the people trying to kill him know he's alive because no one found a body. He can't walk down the street without someone recognizing him."

"So what's in the basket Sister Alberta gave me?"

"Clothes. A disguise so he can get out of town before the St. Louis gang finds him."

People started streaming into the hotel. Some headed on up to their rooms, others came into the dining hall for a cool drink and a late lunch. Still others went straight to the bar. The relative silence we'd initially enjoyed disappeared.

"I better go now," Anna Marie said.

"You don't have to. Stay and have a custard with me?"

"You never know who might show up in here, Mrs. McGrath. What if someone recognized me here with you?"

"I've enjoyed this delicious little adventure." I dabbed my lips with my napkin. "Of course, it'd be much more fun if I could tell someone about it."

Anna Marie's eyes grew larger. "Oh no, you mustn't. It'd be dangerous for Mr. Marky. And maybe not so good for Bertie or yo—"

"Don't worry, dear, I won't tell a soul, not even my husband."

More men came in, dirty and reeking of smoke.

"I really need to go now. Thank you again. Mr. Marky will be so grateful." Anna Marie picked up the basket from Sister Alberta that I had delivered. "If you see me on the street looking a little different from the way I do now, please don't speak."

"Of course, I'll speak, Anna Marie."

"And don't call me Anna Marie."

"Why?"

"Because that's not the name I use down there."

This game was getting to be quite a lot of fun, but I knew it wouldn't seem that way to her. "Of course."

* * *

The waiter hurried up to my table. "Would you like something else, ma'am?"

"Is it all over out there?"

"The fire's out, although there's some work yet to be done and some cleanup."

"Did Mr. McGee and his employees—are they okay?"

"I imagine they are ma'am. No one said anything about injuries. Not even the firemen."

"The building?"

"Gutted, they say, but I'm sure it'll be repaired soon enough."

As I walked through the lobby, a familiar voice called to me. "Mamie McGrath."

"What are you doing here, Burley?"

"We're performing here tonight. For a bachelor party. Didn't Julian tell you?"

"He did, but I forgot all about it. Forgot it was tonight at least. Aren't you early?"

Burley chuckled. "By several hours. I just thought I'd drop by and get the lay of the land. They set up things differently for every occasion, it seems."

"Well, it was nice to bump into you."

"Tell Julian to get here by seven o'clock. We go on sooner than we thought so I added another song to our repertoire."

"Of course." That meant I had no choice but to tell Julian about my afternoon as soon as he came home to change for the program. I'd have to lie about my mission and that scared me.

As I left the hotel and boarded the trolley for home, I tried out different fibs in my head. I could say that I'd ordered a new pair of gloves at the Boston Store. But then Reverend Mathews got on the Trolley and sat down across from me.

"Good afternoon, Mrs. McGrath." He tipped his hat.

"Reverend Mathews."

"I hear you've been sick. I do hope you're feeling better."

"I'm fine, sir."

"Don't overdo. This weather is hard on strong men. It must be especially uncomfortable for a tiny slip of a thing like you."

My heart pounded. The good Lord had sent a man of the cloth to warn about the perils of lying. Besides, who would guess I'd had tea with a prostitute anyway?

4

September 21, 1910
An Oklahoma man was found dead behind a saloon on Garrison Avenue,
slumped over a beer keg. Officer Carr told me it didn't look like anyone killed
him. Unless you don't count that old demon drink.

Patsy Lincoln, *Fort Smith Bell*

October 9, 1910
We congratulate Miss Louisiana Spencer for taking second place for her
tasty chocolate meringue pie at the Twenty-Third Annual St. Boniface Lawn
Social. Miss Lou cooks for Mrs. Garland Talbot who entered the pie contest.
Of course Mrs. Caroline McGrath won the blue ribbon prize for her famous
buttermilk pie. No one makes pie like Miss Caroline.

Genevieve Day, *Fort Smith Bell*

IT WAS A CLOUDY AUTUMN day. Our yardman, Sandy Lewis, was working in the back and Caroline was still upstairs in her room. I was enjoying the last of my breakfast coffee when I heard someone banging on the back gate.

"Miz Mamie, it's me, Manny McKnight."

I peeked out the kitchen window. Oblivious to the noise Manny was making, Sandy raked leaves into a pile beside the porch inside the fence.

"Miz Mamie?" It was almost a whine.

I opened the window over the table and stuck my head out. "What is it, Manny?"

Everyone felt sorry for the boy. He roamed the streets looking for food and something to do. Julian's boss at the newspaper, Colonel J. B. Parker, paid Manny to tell him any rumors he might pick up on Garrison Avenue. John B let him spend the night in his barn from time to time. Once in a while, some kind housewife gave him patched-up-hand-me-down clothes her own children had outgrown.

"I gotta note from Miss Angelica burning a hole in my pocket."

"Come on into the yard then."

"Cain't. Gate's locked."

"No it's not. We don't even have a lock for it."

He pushed against it. "If it's not locked, it's stuck."

I went to the back window. "Sandy, will you see why that gate won't open?"

Sandy propped his rake against the fence and pulled on the gate. "Looks like them hinges is rusty. Want me to fix'em?"

"Yes, please."

Sandy crossed the yard and rummaged inside the shed while Manny shook the gate and muttered curses under his breath.

"I can hear you, Manny."

"How you gonna hear what I say way off in there, Miz Mamie?"

"I don't know, but I can."

"I'm in a hurry here, ma'am." He gave the gate one more kick. "I gotta give you this letter and be on my way." It was an old wound. Caroline wouldn't allow Manny to come in the front door because he tracked in mud on wet days and dust on dry ones. Abigail claimed that he smelled bad every day and wouldn't let him on their property at all.

"No reason to get ornery about it. We'll get you in soon enough."

Sandy came out of the shed with an oil can and a hammer. "This oughta fix it."

I nodded. "Thank you, Sandy."

He set to work oiling the hinges and manipulating them until the gate finally squeaked partway open.

Manny, impatient and red-faced, slammed the gate back into Sandy's face, cutting his lip and leaving a streak of blood on the white-washed slats.

Sandy froze—his clenched fists pressed against his thighs, his eyes shut.

"Manny, there was no call for that!" I wet a cloth and flew out the door. Guiding Sandy to the porch step, I pointed. "Sit down." I squatted and dabbed the cloth at the corner of his mouth.

He flinched. "No ma'am. That won't do." He took the cloth away from me and held it on his lip.

"I'll get the alcohol." I hurried inside to fetch it.

Manny was leaning against the fence, his arms folded over his chest when I came back out. Something about his expression infuriated me. "Sandy never did you any harm, Manny."

"I didn't do nuthin but open a sticky gate. This nigger was in the way is all. It's not my fault he's dumb as a bag of hammers."

"Stop it!" I stamped my foot. "Don't talk like that."

"Miz Mamie!" Sandy's deep voice boomed.

Shocked, I whirled on him.

He looked into my eyes. "That ain't how it works around here, ma'am."

The social rules we lived by were rigid. Even though I might risk the disapproval of my neighbors if I was too solicitous of Sandy's situation, he would pay a much higher price for my mistake. It wasn't fair, but Sandy was right. That's how it worked in Fort Smith.

"What is it, Mamie?" Caroline called from her room upstairs. "What's going on?"

"Nothing, dear," I said over my shoulder. "Just refreshing Sandy's jug of water."

"Did he finish already?"

"Not yet."

"Tell him not to dawdle." Caroline's voice trailed off into a yawn.

The three of us in the backyard waited for her to say something else. When she didn't, we relaxed.

"I better finish up, like Miz Caroline said." Sandy handed me the bloodstained cloth. "I'll clean that blood off the gate before I go."

Before he could pick up the rake, Manny pushed past him and kicked the neat pile of leaves, scattering them across the yard again.

"Manny!"

"Leave it be, Miz Mamie," Sandy said. "I'll get that too."

I sighed and motioned Manny to come inside the screened-in portion of the back porch. "What is your problem, young man?" I kept my voice low.

"I told you. I got this note from Miss Angelica."

I held out my hand and he dug a folded-over envelope out of his back pocket. "I'm sposed to wait in case you want to answer her."

"You had anything to eat today?"

He shook his head. " 'Ceptin' for candy Miss Angelica gave me."

"Stay right here."

"Aw, ma'am. I got places to go."

"I said sit!"

He made a face but stayed put while I went inside. Rummaging through the ice box, I grumbled, "Why can't anyone control this kid?" I crumbled cornbread into a bowl and warmed up pinto beans and ham to put on top of it. Carrying it out onto the porch, I set it down on the table and handed him a spoon. "Eat slow or you'll have an upset stomach."

Manny dug in while I poured him a glass of milk.

"Slow down. You don't have to rush."

"Hungry," he grunted between bites.

"It's okay. There's plenty."

He gulped down the milk. "How I always eat."

As I poured Manny another glass, I watched Sandy finish up the yard and clean the blood off the white-washed gate. "Wait here." I got up and went outside.

"He's a kid," I said to Sandy as I handed him his money.

"Yes, ma'am."

"He has no manners."

"I have no problem with that boy." Sandy slipped his pay into his pocket.

"I appreciate your patience."

"Ha!"

I cocked my head, not understanding his spontaneous reaction. "What?"

He shook his head. "Sorry, ma'am. My mistake."

"Will you be back next week?"

"If y'all have work, I sure need it."

"When you come, we might as well plan on refreshing the fence and the gate. My husband will leave some paint in the shed."

Sandy nodded and disappeared around the corner of the house.

"Why does he get to come and go the front way?" Manny swallowed the last of the beans and held up his bowl.

"He works for us." It was a lie to spare his feelings. I had no idea where the boy went to clean up, but wherever it was he didn't go there often enough.

"He's a nigger."

"He takes care of our yard."

"Why did you hire him and not me?"

"Have you ever done yard work?"

"No, ma'am."

"Painted anything?"

He spooned a bite of beans and cornbread from the refilled bowl I set in front of him. "How can I learn anything like that if people won't hire me?"

It was a fair question. I poured myself a glass of milk and sat down across the table from him as he ate. "Why did you quit school?"

"Warn't for me. When would I ever need numbers?"

"If you could figure, Mr. Tilles might give you a job in his store."

Manny snorted. "That ain't gonna happen so why bother?"

I knew he was right but I didn't want to accept it. "Manny, you need to keep yourself better. Take more baths, keep your clothes clean. And learn some arithmetic. It would make it easier to get a job."

"You and Miz Pahotski! Always with the dreaming. There ain't no point. Not in Fort Smith. Not for me."

I gritted my teeth. "What's going to happen to you, Manny?"

"Don't pretend you care, ma'am. You won't let me in your house. Hell, you won't let me in your front yard. You might give me a bite once in a while and I thank you kindly for that, but that's all I can hope for from you."

"Oh, Manny, how can you say that?"

He stared at his feet to avoid looking at me. "Pardon my sayin' this, Miz Mamie, but you'd call a lizard an alligator. Fact is, to you, I'm not even as white as that nigger you hired instead of me."

* * *

While Manny finished his lunch, I sat at the kitchen table and opened the envelope he'd brought me. Two fifty-dollar bills folded inside a piece of scented stationary. Puzzled, I read Anna Marie's note.

Mamie,

Mr. Marky said to say thank you for your help. He left town two days ago. He would like for you to give this money to my sister to pay for the clothes.

Anna Marie Cavanaugh

Puzzled, I folded the money and put it back into the envelope. *Why would Mr. Marky send me so much money for Sister Alberta? Why not have Manny give it to her?* I slipped the note into my apron pocket and glanced out the screen door. Manny had finished eating and was waiting for me to come back out with a message for the woman he knew as Miss Angelica. I fetched a quarter from the jar of coins we kept in the pantry and went out on the porch. "You full now, Manny?"

"If I was an inch taller, I'd be round, ma'am."

"Lord, you remind me of my uncle." I smothered a smile. "Tell Miss Angelica I said 'Okay.'"

"Just okay?"

"That's it." I handed him the quarter.

"Miz Mamie, there's no need for you to pay me again. Miss Angelica done broke her piggy bank on this deal."

"I want you to do something for me."

He frowned. "Like what?"

"Sandy's going to be painting that fence out there next week."

"That ain't nothing to me."

"It could be if you show up in time. I'll have Sandy show you how to paint."

"That might get folks around here all riled up."

"Just learn to do it, Manny."

He stared at the coin in my palm. "How much folks pay for fence painting?"

"Enough for a new pair of shoes."

He glanced at his bare toes. "I don't ne—"

"Just do it." I dropped the quarter into his hand and stormed back inside the kitchen, letting the screen door slam behind me.

"Miz Mamie?"

I closed the kitchen door and locked it.

"Ma'am?" He tapped on the wood with the quarter.

I pulled back the curtain over the sink window. "What, Manny, what?"

"What time next week?"

* * *

"Leave it alone, Mamie." Abigail took a bite of Caroline's buttermilk pie. "That boy's a lost cause. Right now you feel sorry for him, but if you don't watch him, he'll steal you blind."

"He's got no one to look after him." Caroline blew on her tea before taking a sip. "He's no worse than any other kid in this town."

Abigail wrinkled her nose. "He's probably crawling with lice."

"He needs to learn a skill. That's all."

"He needs a scrub brush, lye soap, and hot water. Often," Abigail said.

"Maybe we can encourage a bath in the back yard when he comes to paint?"

"Mamie, you need of a child of your own."

Still sore from the ignominious end of my pregnancy, I bit back a tart reply.

"Sandy won't mind teaching him?" Caroline came to my rescue.

"I didn't ask him yet, but why would he? I'll pay him to do it."

Abigail rocked in her seat, disapproval smeared across her face. "Be realistic, dear. He might think you'll give the work he's been doing to Manny."

"I hadn't thought of that."

"Perhaps you can get Manny a job somewhere else," Caroline said.

"Where?"

"Why don't you ask John B? He knows the boy."

"He already lets that ragamuffin come in out of the rain now," Abigail snorted. "He might think he's done more than his share."

"John B and Jennie are good folks. I bet he'll find something for Manny to do." Caroline offered Abigail another piece of pie.

John B was a jolly person. Everyone liked him. He'd stop and talk to anyone on the street, asking after family and sharing the latest joke making the rounds. He just might be the answer for Manny.

* * *

True to his word, Manny showed up the next week eager to learn how to paint. In fact, he got there before Sandy. I let the boy in the back gate and encouraged him to sit at the picnic table in the screened porch. He was eating black-eyed peas and cornbread when Sandy came around the house.

"Afternoon, ma'am.' Sandy nodded. "Sorry I'm late. The first trolley was full today. Kids going out to the Electric Park. I had to wait for the next car."

"Can we talk?"

He glanced at Manny inside the screen porch. His smile faded. "Yes, ma'am."

I walked out to the shed and beckoned Sandy over.

He looked around nervously. "What is it, Miz Mamie?"

"I want to talk to you about Manny."

"I don't know much about that boy, ma'am."

"No one does, but he's a child with no one to learn from, you understand?"

"No, ma'am. I don't know as I do."

"He's not going to be able to take care of himself properly if he doesn't learn some skills."

"That boy is plenty smart, ma'am, and folks would hire him to do odds and ends, but he stinks to high heaven."

"I know. That's where you come in."

Sandy scowled. "There's not enough money in the world to make me scrub up that white boy."

I tried to hide my embarrassment. "I'll pay you to teach him to paint this week. Next week, I'll pay you to teach him to repair the gate hinges. Week after that we can think of something else. But starting today, I'm gonna lay down the law about bathing. Miss Caroline won't let him in beyond the porch, so he's going to have to use the backyard. I was hoping you would show him where that big tin tub is in the shed and where to find the bucket to get water from the well. For the time being, you can have him heat it up using the leaves and twigs to start a small fire." I took a breath. "I put some towels and lye soap out there yesterday. And some of Julian's old clothes. I just need you to show him where everything is."

Sandy bowed his head, and I was afraid I'd insulted him.

"I'm sorry, Sandy. Julian's at work and there's no one else to ask. I'm too small to handle Manny. And of course, there are folks who'd say it's inappropriate for me to be around an undressed boy his age." I blushed.

"It's okay, Miz Mamie. I'll get that boy started."

"I'll tell him he has to be polite."

"Ha," Sandy snorted.

* * *

"I ain't taking a bath!"

"People don't want you around because you're dirty."

"I don't care." Manny folded his arms over his chest.

"How are you going to get a better paying job? Business people expect employees to come to work clean. We aren't doing cowboys and Indians anymore."

"Baths don't matter for lots of jobs."

"Name one."

"Coal mining."

"You plan on working the mines, Manny?"

We stared at each other for a few seconds. "Why not?"

"Then why are you here?"

He stuck out his lower lip.

"Are you listening to me?"

He looked at his feet.

I snapped my fingers. "Manny? Pay attention!"

"I'm so poor I cain't afford to pay attention, ma'am."

I pointed to the old tin bathtub Sandy had fetched from the shed and set up on the back lawn.

Manny's shoulders slumped. "Having to take a bath to paint a fence! Whoever heard such craziness?"

"Sandy will help you heat up the water. From now on, you want to work for us, you take a bath first. Understand?"

"Yes, ma'am."

"There's clean clothes on the back porch. And shoes."

"I hate shoes," he grumbled under his breath.

"Manny!"

He turned around and headed toward the shed.

Sandy was leaning on a rake waiting for Manny to accept my conditions for employment, controlled amusement flickering on his face.

I waved. "Thank you, Sandy."

"Welcome, ma'am."

I turned and went into the house.

Caroline sat at the table sipping her morning tea. "You're a big-hearted girl, Mamie McGrath."

"I learned from the best." I sat down with my back to the window. "Let's pretend we aren't watching the drama that's about to take place in the backyard."

"Think he'll come back next week?"

I shrugged. "I think maybe he doesn't bathe because he doesn't have access to a tub."

"That and maybe he never got into the habit."

"What's happening?"

"Sandy's keeping the fire going while Manny's pouring the first bucket of water into the tub. The funny part is that Manny keeps checking to see if we're watching. He's probably figuring ways to get out of the bath and still collect the money."

"No bath, no painting. No painting, no money."

"Sandy seems to be a nice young man." Caroline leaned back in her chair. "His dad's a preacher. Patsy and I've known him for years, just didn't realize Sandy was one of his kids until the other day."

"Really?"

"Webster works a farm across the river. Sandy helped out growing up, but now that he comes to Fort Smith to get jobs that pay cash, his younger brothers work with their father now."

I peeked over my shoulder. Manny was pouring the first bucket of hot water into the tub while Sandy heated up the second. "They seem to be getting along okay."

"Sandy's used to kids, I bet."

Manny trudged back to the well with the empty bucket.

"Doesn't mean he's used to this one."

* * *

The bath was a long, noisy affair. The voices in our backyard would lower and then a squeal or laugh or angry shout would startle us. Impatient with it all, Caroline went back up to her room before the event played itself out. I watched and waited as Sandy encouraged Manny to scrub his filthy toenails with the stiff brush. The boy tried whining but Sandy refused to budge. Eventually, Manny complied even though he complained that it hurt.

When he was done, I averted my eyes as Manny crawled out of the tub and Sandy handed him a towel. The next time I looked, they were painting the fence.

5

November 1, 1910–Mr. Beale got hurt on Garrison in front of the new First National Bank. The old gentleman was trying to get onto the trolley but just missed it. He was rushing to catch up when he ran into the pole that supports the trolley wire. His wife says he'll be okay soon.

Miss Patsy Lincoln, *The Fort Smith Bell*

November 1, 1910–Beginning today, the Hotel Main will be conducted on the European plan. The dining room service will be a la carte and a special merchants lunch will be served daily from 12 to 2PM for 50 cents.

Southwest American

"WHY, MAMIE MCGRATH. WHAT ARE you doing out here?" Abigail bent to give me an air kiss on each cheek. She and Garland Talbot stood on the sidewalk in front of Immaculate Conception Church. "Where's Caroline and Julian?"

"Caroline's already inside. In her usual spot. You just missed Julian. He's on his way to work."

"And you little love birds were lingering in front of the church for a last minute chat. How sweet!"

I tried not to show my irritation. Having to be here at all was annoying enough.

"You look pale, Mamie. You feeling poorly?"

Garland's eyes were puffy and his cheeks were red.

"What a question!" Abigail smacked Garland's arm with her gloves. "Don't you listen to him, Mamie. You look great considering what you went through last summer."

"I'm fine. It's been months and I'm fine." I tried to slip around them and start up the stairs to the tall wooden doors.

"Can't let a fragile little thing like you climb those steps without an escort." Garland offered me his arm. "It's the least I can do to thank you for coming today."

I glanced at Abigail for help. "Go on,"she urged. "You Yankee women pretend to be tough but Southern gentlemen take care of women folk here."

"I'm fine. I go up and down these steps five times a week."

Garland took my hand and placed it in the crook of his right elbow. "See? Isn't that better? And safer?"

I gave up and let him escort me to the top of the stairs. "Thank you, Garland." He smelled of cigars and whiskey, and now my hand did too.

"Wait here."

I contemplated making an escape, but there was no where to go inside the church and the two of them would surely find me and make a fuss in front of the whole congregation.

Garland was puffing as they approached me.

Abigail reached out to straighten my hat. I flinched and backed away. "There now." She pretended she had actually fixed me in some way. "That's much better."

Garland opened the door and Abigail glided past him, like a grand ship setting out to sea. I followed her into the vestibule and up to the holy water font. She removed her right glove and tucked it under her left arm. A husky Fort Smith policeman came in behind us and then two women. The women waited a moment, but Abigail wouldn't be rushed through her ritual and they went around us. Dipping her bare fingers into holy water, Abigail crossed herself slowly.

The policeman coughed.

"You better take care of that cough, Mr. Pitcock," she whispered. "A little whiskey and honey should do the trick."

Pitcock puffed out his cheeks. "You shouldn't be teasing a man in my condition, Mrs. Talbot. I worked late and now I'm up earlier than I like. I just want to get in there, do a little business and go my merry way." He shuffled several long-stemmed flowers from one arm to the other.

Abigail took her time working her damp hand back into her glove. "This church is not designed for men in a hurry. Ask Father Horan."

"I'm a Baptist, Miz Talbot. The padre and I don't see eye to eye."

"If you're always this ru—"

"Come along, Abigail. You're creating a line." Garland took her arm and escorted her through the inner doors. She tried to jerk away and their noisy whispers caused heads to turn. Reacting to the curious congregants, Abigail put on an imperious smirk and nodded toward one side and then the other as they walked down the middle aisle.

I turned to apologize to Mr. Pitcock but he glared at me too. Not wanting to deal with him in the vestibule, I blessed myself and hurried after the Talbots.

They were maddening to be around on good days—even without a cranky sleep-deprived cop breathing down my neck. And today wasn't so good. We were there to attend Mr. Guckenheimer's funeral and I hated funerals, especially for people I didn't know. The only reason I came was because Caroline accepted the invitation for both of us and I couldn't get out of it.

Abigail walked on ahead of me, but Garland stopped and waited until I passed him. I'd discovered that Garland's manners were a thin veneer when his disdain for my opinions became obvious. At first, I was insulted. But after I lost the baby, I took pleasure in besting him at bridge, in political discussions—even in mathematics. When Julian told him that I played chess, he was shocked. So I challenged him to a game and enjoyed his lies about business commitments and time constraints that prevented him from sitting down across a board from me.

"Come, dear." Abigail turned to me. "I don't want to get caught up in that mess when everyone comes crowding in."

I slowed and pointed toward the Captain Hugh Rogers' stained glass window on the right. "There's Caroline."

Garland stepped on my heel and cursed.

"Garland," Abigail hissed. "We're in the house of God."

"Don't get your knickers in a knot. The good Lord has forgiven a ton of cuss words over the eons," he muttered. "Especially in Fort Smith."

"What will Father Horan say about your vile language?"

"He'll say it's better to cuss a nagging woman than to beat her." He patted her hand. I expected Abigail to make a fuss, but she smiled and the spat was over. Just like that. They chose a seat in the front row. I guessed they wanted to be close to the dearly departed, although I couldn't imagine why since Mr. Guckenheimer had been a low-down, stinking scoundrel, according to Garland.

Eager to get away from them, I slipped into a pew to the right and sidestepped to sit behind Caroline. I put my hand on her shoulder and she acknowledged me with a pat.

Since the deceased didn't know anyone in Fort Smith or have family close, Caroline and I had agreed to host a private visitation the night before. Our front parlor wasn't a big room, but then Mr. Guckenheimer didn't have many friends. Only the Talbots and a shiny-faced fellow with a lumpy, red nose and a Lincolnesque top hat showed up at first.

"Dear, Caroline." Abigail had given my mother-in-law a quick hug, designed to express affection without crushing their old-fashioned crinoline clothes. "Thank you for this. You know how I am about dead people."

I doubted Abigail didn't want Mr. Guckenheimer at her home because she had an aversion to dead bodies. She simply didn't want to pay her cook to stay late and serve hors d'oeuvres to strangers.

"Mamie, Caroline, Julian. This is my associate Orrin Fellows," Garland had said as we welcomed them into our home.

"Nice to meet you, Mr. Fellows." Julian extended his hand. "We've known Garland for years now, but never quite understood his business."

"Oh, it's quite simple." Mr. Fellows shook Julian's hand. "He's a salesman."

"But what exactly do you sell?" I turned to Garland.

"Whatever people are buying." Garland got a kick out of his silly little game. I did not.

"It's lucrative," Fellows said. "And I expect it will be even more so as time goes by."

"What is lucrative?"

"Business."

I was beginning to wonder if Garland was involved in something shady. He would never give me a straight answer about what he did for a living. Julian had never noticed or cared about Garland's evasiveness until I pointed it out. Now, we joked that Talbot's Mercantile sold nonexistent items to phantoms.

Caroline had pushed the coffin so that it was opposite the pocket doors and centered in the room. "Shouldn't we open the lid?"

"Oh no." Mr. Fellows wrinkled his considerable nose twice like a nervous rabbit. "Mr. Guckenheimer has been gone for quite some time now. It could be unpleasant, you know."

"Oh?" Caroline backed away from Mr. Guckenheimer.

Abigail's voice rose. "Exactly when did he die?"

"Four weeks tomorrow."

"Two weeks ago," Garland's voice blended with Fellows.'

"Which is it?" Julian was amused by the old boys' confusion regarding Mr. Guckenheimer's time of death. Caroline and Abigail were less so.

"Two weeks," Garland insisted.

"At least two weeks." Mr. Fellows bobbed his head in agreement.

Caroline took another step back from the coffin. "Did the folks at Putnam prepare him?"

Fellows and Garland looked at each other and then their shoes,

Abigail clapped her hands. "Well?"

"Actually, he died in Fayetteville and was prepared up there." Garland still avoided Abigail's eyes.

The front bell rescued the moment. I opened the door to find a businessman from one of the leading Fort Smith families. "Hello, Mamie." He took my hand and bowed his head. "I understand you're holding a visitation for Mr. Guckenheimer?"

I was surprised to find such an elegant gentleman standing on our porch, but I welcomed him in. "Mr. Talbot is in the parlor."

Garland and Mr. Fellows stood as we came into the room.

"Nice to see you, sir." Garland's handshake seemed overly enthusiastic. "Have you met my associate, Mr. Orrin Fellows?"

"Garland's told me a lot about your business."

"I think you'll be pleased, Mr. Willoughby." Fellows offered his gloved hand.

"It sounds like a good investment."

"Arnold, how are you?" Abigail swooped in like a pigeon eager for the first breadcrumb at a picnic. "I didn't know you knew Mr. Guckenheimer."

Arnold Willoughby bent to kiss the back of Abigail's hand. "You're sense of humor is adorable, my dear."

I glanced at Julian questioningly. He shrugged.

"Arnold and I were childhood sweethearts," Abigail announced to the room.

"In the third grade," Mr. Willoughby clarified. "We wiped down the blackboard at the end of the day. Profoundly romantic stuff."

Abigail batted her eyes first at Arnold Willoughby and then at Garland.

"Would you like some refreshments?" Caroline intervened with a plate full of cookies.

"No, I came to invest in Garland's project, Mrs. McGrath." Mr. Willoughby turned to Garland. "You and Mr. Fellows have come up with a clever way to take advantage of a political opportunity."

Garland blew out a quick puff of air. "You won't regret it, sir."

"I like to be covered, no matter what comes down the pike, Garland." Mr. Willoughby pulled a piece of folded paper out of his breast pocket. "I assume my check is good?"

Garland glanced at the check and handed it to Orrin Fellows who grinned broadly.

"Your check is more than fine. I have the documents here for your signature." Mr. Fellows pointed to Caroline's desk.

With a flourish, Mr. Willoughby wrote his name. "Thank you for thinking of me, Garland."

"Will you at least have a drink to celebrate our deal?" Garland pointed toward a bottle of whiskey setting on the sideboard.

"The missus would have me shot. I've been a teetotaler since our wedding day thirty-five years ago."

Garland and Mr. Fellows glanced at each other.

"What?" Abigail's voice broke the sudden silence.

Keeping his eyes on Mr. Willoughby, Garland threw back a shot of whiskey. He wiped his mouth with the back of his hand

and laughed out loud. Mr. Fellows put the documents into an envelope and handed it to Mr. Willoughby who's grin turned into a wry chuckle and then a guffaw.

Caroline and Julian and I looked at each other.

"What?" I mouthed.

Julian shrugged but soon started laughing just because they were. Caroline and I smiled but we had no idea why. Neither did Abigail apparently.

Mr. Willoughby patted Mr. Guckenheimer's coffin merrily as he headed for the front. I stood on the porch and watched him as he went down the sidewalk, swinging his cane and humming to himself.

I went back inside. Garland and Mr. Fellows were clicking whiskey glasses and chortling.

"What?" Abigail stamped her foot.

Garland kissed her cheek. "What what?"

The doorbell rang and I found another well-heeled Fort Smith resident standing on our porch.

In total, five local businessmen and a partner in a fancy law firm visited us between seven and nine o'clock. All celebrated the signing of some kind of contract with a shot of whiskey, except for Mr. Willoughby, of course.

After everyone left, Garland and Orrin ate heartily from the small spread of sandwiches and cookies Caroline and I'd laid out in the kitchen. They toasted Mr. Guckenheimer's trip to the hereafter with additional shots of whiskey. And that was it. The Talbots and Mr. Fellows left shortly after nine pm.

Several men came for Mr. Guckenheimer the next morning and his ornate coffin was already parked in the middle aisle just in front of the altar at Immaculate Conception when we arrived at ten. I didn't recognize anyone but the two women who came in when we did and a nun in the back row seemed familiar. I tried to figure out who she was as I walked past her, but she was kneeling, elbows on top of the pew in front of her, covering her face with both hands.

We'd no sooner settled in when a loud crash made me jump. The door to the vestibule flew open and three tough-looking fellows hurried down the middle aisle, puffs of dust rising from their boots with each step. The fellow in the lead laid two carnations and three roses on top of Mr. Guckenheimer's coffin.

That's odd. I'd never seen that particular ritual before. It was then that I noticed Detective Pitcock's flowers lying on the lid too. I looked around but the husky police officer must've already left.

The other two men paid their respects the same way—one with a handful of daisies, the other with seven roses. Then they all clumped back down the aisle and out the front door of the church. I was pretty sure that I'd never seen any of them at mass before, although one did cross himself before leaving.

I was still pondering the identities of Mr. Guckenheimer's strange mourners when a preacher from a little church outside Greenwood marched down the aisle to lay a bouquet on the coffin before turning on his heel. After he passed us, I nudged Caroline and she shrugged. I turned around to watch him leave. The nun in the back row was writing something in her prayer book with a thick yellow pencil.

For the next forty minutes, people came and went, all leaving floral mementos for a friendless dead man. In all that time, Father Horan never showed up to perform a service. Around nine forty-five, the nun in the back row collected all the floral offerings and carried them down the aisle and out into the front vestibule. The doors had barely closed behind her when four muscular pallbearers came in the side door and rolled Mr. Guckenheimer out.

Once the coffin was gone, Garland nudged Abigail. She crossed herself and allowed her husband to help her stand. They paused at Caroline's row.

"It was nice of you to come, Caroline," Garland said. "I am sure Mr. Guckenheimer and his family would thank you for your kindness, if they could."

Abigail squeezed Caroline's hand and nodded to me before Garland swept her back up the center aisle and through the front doors.

I waited while Caroline finished her meditation. Then, I slipped out of the pew and knelt in front of a statue of the Virgin Mary holding the Christ child. After a moment of prayer, I lit a candle for my baby that never was, and a second one for the family Julian and I were hoping to have soon. When I turned around, I glimpsed a flash of black and white in the choir loft and then heard heavy foot-falls and the soft closing of a door. *Who was that nun?*

I met Caroline at the end of her pew and we walked out together.

"That was the strangest funeral I've ever seen," she said as we went down the steps. "It was more like a prayer vigil."

"Why no mass, do you suppose?" I took her arm as we crossed Thirteenth Street and passed the new Goldman Hotel.

"I can't imagine."

"So many people paid their respects today. Why didn't they show up last night? And why didn't anyone stay?"

"Perhaps they didn't know him well enough to dedicate a whole evening to him?"

"To be such an unknown bad guy, he got more flowers than the prom queen at St. Anne's. Who *was* he?"

"Garland danced around that question, didn't he?" Caroline said. "All he told Abigail was that the man was an associate from Pennsylvania. I didn't know Garland had ever been to Pennsylvania."

As we approached North Tenth and Garrison, we saw John B. Williams. "Well, aren't you two a sight for sore eyes."

Caroline gave him a quick hug. "And don't you look all trimmed and elegant?"

He chuckled and stroked his chin. "We can thank Bert Stewart for that. What are the two of you up to?"

I adjusted my parasol to keep the sun out of my eyes. "We just sat through the oddest funeral. A friend of Garland Talbot's died. He was down on his luck with no friends and family to send him on his way to the Almighty."

"May I ask the name of the man who died?"

"It was a Mr. Guckenheimer," Caroline said.

"Guckenheimer?" John B threw back his head and laughed.

"Yes. A lonely soul, apparently."

John B wiped his eyes with a knuckle. "Did he have a first name?"

Caroline looked at me and I shrugged.

"Garland never told us Mr. Guckenheimer's given name," Caroline said. "But then we never asked what it was either."

Eyes twinkling, John B tipped his hat. "It's lovely seeing you this fine day, but I have an errand to run."

"Of cour—" Caroline's turned around to watch John B stride up North Tenth toward the Pony Express, still chuckling. "What was John B laughing about?"

I shaded my eyes. "Mr. Guckenheimer's funeral?"

Section 2

January 1, 1911
Building Projects Bring Modern Face to Downtown
Several important projects have come to fruition this past year or will be nearing completion in the coming year. New buildings beautifying our downtown include the brand-new six-story First National Bank at Sixth and Garrison, the Goldman Hotel at Thirteenth and Garrison, the New Theatre on North Tenth Street, and the new Union Station being built on South Seventh. Garrison Avenue merchants offer our citizens shopping, dining, and elegant entertainment facilities. As is painted on the roof at John B Williams' Horse and Mule Barn, "In Fort Smith, life is worth living."

Julian McGrath, *Southwest American*

* * *

February 7, 1911
Immigrant Criminals in Detroit
Seemingly mere school boys, the Detroit Purple Gang has already made a name for itself in bootlegging, robbery and hijacking. Led by the four Bernstein brothers, they attacked the Pavlov family business and stole shipment after shipment of whiskey from Oleg Pavlov and his sons Oral and Konrad. Out of luck, whiskey, and money, the Pavlovs left Michigan permanently.

Detroit Times

6

May 4, 1911
Little Says No Gambling Dens for Fort Smith.
Slot machines must go is the edict that went out today from Prosecutor Paul
Little's office. Owners of slot machines and persons having them in their
places of business must remove them by Thursday or arrests will follow.

Daily Arkansas Gazette

May 21, 1911
Due to the worsening condition of the brick pavement, the Commercial
league proposes repaving Garrison Avenue with wooden blocks.

Julian McGrath, *Southwest American*

May 30, 1911
We remember our dead from the War Between the States with today's Memo-
rial Day celebration downtown at noon. Official Ceremonies kick off with a
parade down Garrison Avenue.

Julian McGrath, *Southwest American*

"ROBERT E. LEE WAS A sick old fool." Sarge drained half a glass of Mama's special-recipe lemonade. "Who in his right mind risks it all when the odds are against you?"

"Robert E. Lee was a saint!" Garland slammed his fist on the table, almost upsetting Caroline's tulip vase. "A saint."

Abigail yawned and stared out the window. I stole a peek too. Sandy and Manny were putting down their paint brushes and wiping their hands on an old towel. Caroline had gone outside to give them milk and a plate of oatmeal cookies.

"He put the Third Arkansas in an impossible position at Gettysburg. They died like flies at Devil's Den," Sarge said.

Julian and I exchanged exasperated glances. Sarge and Garland had been arguing about the war all morning. Caroline's clock showed ten forty. We planned on going into town to watch a parade at noon. Still an hour before we could leave and the two of them were already slurring their words. I crossed my eyes and Julian suppressed a chuckle.

"He had them on the run. He was going for the final thrust." Garland illustrated Lee's thrust with his fist, nearly throwing himself out of his chair.

"How the hell do you know?" Sarge's voice was raspy from years of tobacco and drink. "Were you there?"

Garland held up his glass and I filled it. "Were you?"

Sarge lowered his voice to a raspy whisper. "I was."

Julian set up straighter. "You were at Gettysburg?"

"I fought on East Cavalry Field with Custer."

Sadness flashed across Julian's face, and awe "I didn't know."

Sarge patted Julian's shoulder. "I know ya didn't, son."

Garland threw down his lemonade in one gulp and belched.

"Garland!" Abigail whirled around in her seat and whacked him on the head with the back of her hand. "That's rude!"

His eyes darkened. "You better watch them gloves, sugar."

Something about their exchange made me shiver. I touched Julian's shoulder and when he looked up at me, I mouthed, "Enough."

He turned back to our guests. "What do you two think of old George Sparks' new theater they are building on North Tenth?"

"Fancy enough." Less interested in architecture than the glory of lost causes, Garland's chin drooped towards his chest.

"Too fancy to rob." Sarge finished the rest of his lemonade in one gulp.

Garland caught himself and startled awake. For someone who was the soul of elegance while sober, he was a disgusting drunk. And lately, he seemed to be drunk more often than not.

Irritated, I gathered the glasses, and the half-full pitcher of spiked lemonade, and carried them into the kitchen. I should have lied and pretended we were out of lemons or sugar. However, Garland always had a flask of vodka with him and they would have guzzled that straight even if I'd offered them buttermilk chasers. I poured the last of the pale yellow "elixir," as Sarge called it, down the sink. When I returned with hot coffee, Caroline had come in from the backyard and was telling everyone about how Sandy was teaching Manny to do lawn work.

Garland stared out the window, grinding his teeth as he watched Sandy and Manny chatting while they ate Caroline's cookies. "It's not right how that dirty kid wanders the streets all the time. You just know he's a thief."

"Why Garland," Caroline said as he poured him a cup of coffee. "That boy doesn't need to steal to live. John B gives him a place to sleep when he needs it. Flo Pahotski keeps him in books and pencils."

"Mr. Ney pays him to deliver goods to the row." I offered Garland a pinch of cinnamon for his coffee, but he shook his head. "And we feed him when he works for us and pay him enough to keep him from starving in between his other jobs."

"How do you know that?" Abigail narrowed her eyes.

"Manny told me so," I was tempted to narrow my eyes back at her but I knew Caroline wouldn't approve.

"How do you think that one feels about him?" Garland pointed at Sandy who had finished his milk and cookies and was now opening a fresh can of paint. "He probably takes whatever you pay the boy as soon as you go back in the house."

"Sandy's been with us a long time now and we trust him," Caroline said. "Besides, I'm sure Manny can take care of himself. He's a scrappy little guy."

"If something went missing, I'd be more likely to suspect Manny than Sandy." Julian laughed. "He's been known to pocket a handful of candy if he can't find anyone to give him any."

"I don't imagine Sandy has a problem with Manny. They seem to get along." I stretched and squirmed in my chair. My growing belly made me awkward and no position was really comfortable in the eighth month.

"Get along?"

"Well, they do share a fondness for Jack London," Caroline said as she sat back down. "And Hopalong Cassidy."

"Who doesn't like Hopalong?" Julian chuckled. "There were good bad-men and there were bad bad-men." He put a hand over his breast as he quoted Mulford's latest novel.

"The killer by necessity and the wanton murderer," I joined in with the next line.

Julian and I smiled at each other.

"That's not a book for a proper young woman, Mamie." Abigail wrinkled her nose like the stink of old Hopalong was too much to bear. "Especially one who is about to become a mother."

"What's wrong with a cowboy novel?" Julian was teasing, but Abigail didn't know how to banter back

"It's—it's undignified," she sputtered.

"Reading? Or reading Hopalong?" I was only half-teasing.

Sarge spoke up. "You're just like your mother. Stubborn."

"I can think of worse things to be."

"Mamie's not stubborn. She's determined," Julian said.

"Whatever it is, I admired it in Susanna and I'm glad to see her daughter's inherited it." Sarge winked at me and I relaxed.

Abigail, on the other hand, was still riled, and I was still her target. "You'll tire of her sauciness when the roses on those cheeks start to fade. Then you'll appreciate the things a woman brings to a marriage." Abigail poked Garland who'd dozed off once again. "And I doubt a cowboy novel will measure up to a good apple pie, especially for a man who grew up eating Caroline's cooking."

"Now, Abigail," Sarge interrupted. "You think a pretty girl who enjoys a good Hopalong tale from time to time can't be a good wife?"

"It's about priorities. A woman's job is to see to her family and home. If she's doing that right, there's no time for dime novels."

Julian squeezed my hand. "Mamie's doing just fine. She makes me happy and that's what I want."

"That's because the two of you live in Caroline's house, eat the food Caroline prepares, and use all the things that belong to Caroline. When that's no longer the case, you'll change your tune, no doubt."

I sucked in the insult with my next intake of air. *Was I really such a burden to the household? Had Caroline confided her frustrations with me to Abigail, her closest friend?*

"Abigail!" Caroline's voice was so loud, it made us all jump. "How dare you speak to my dear Mamie like that? Or Julian?"

"I'm sick of seeing them take advantage of you. They live here for free, neither of them lifting a finger to support themselves. Not one dime of Julian's salary finds its way into your pocket. Look at her. She's eating you out of house and home. At this rate, the next time I visit she won't fit through the door. They're leeches, draining everything you and Wilbur worked to build all those years."

Mortified and angry, I stood up and headed toward the hall, but Julian held tight to my hand. "Don't you dare—," he roared.

"You have no idea what you are saying," Caroline interrupted him. "They stay here because I beg them not to leave me every time they talk about building a home of their own. I tell them this is their home now and always."

I stared at Caroline with my mouth open, the tears drying on my cheeks. I'd never seen her angry before and it was glorious.

Abigail shook her finger at Caroline. "There's no fool like a lonely widow."

"Wait a goldurned minute here!" Sarge rolled his chair between Caroline and Abigail. "You two are beginnin' to sound like me and Garland, only you ladies usually have better manners than us old scalawags."

"She lets those two—"

"Stop it. I been teasing you since you was the prettiest girl at the church social and we all let you be bossy cause most of us men treasure beauty more than sense. But there's no need to tear into your best friend like that. No need."

"But—" Abigail's voice quivered.

"No buts about it. Caroline's been as good to you as she has to these young'ens. You ain't got a reason to be jealous."

"Jealous?"

Sarge raised a bushy brow.

"What've I got to be jealous about?"

"Caroline's got a son. One who will take care of her. About to give her grandchild, too."

"It's not fair," Abigail stamped her foot.

Caroline put her arms around Abigail. "I know, I know."

I swallowed the meanness in my heart. Caroline was the saint, not Robert E. Lee. And certainly not me.

"Maybe it's fair after all," Sarge said. "Caroline has a son and daughter-in-law who love her and right now they do her the kindness of lettin' her love them. Later on, she'll see how much they care for her. You have a husband who loves you, Abigail. He's a cankerous, foul-breathed, besotted, rebel-lovin,' old coot. But he's yours, I'll give him that much."

Garland nodded his head toward Sarge. "Thank you, kindly, Elias. I'm glad you see I have some redeeming qualities."

"You're welcome, Garland."

Julian clapped his hands together and we all jumped. "So now that we've picked each other to pieces during our Sunday morning interlude, lets bind up our wounds and head out."

Caroline patted Abigail on the back. "Better now?"

Abigail pushed away from Caroline. "I was always fine, Caroline McGrath." She avoided my eyes—and Julian's. "It was you that had the problem."

* * *

"I'm coming." I hurried down the front steps to where Julian and Caroline waited.

Julian helped me into the back seat of the Boehmer. "Are you okay?"

I straightened my hat. "I'm fine."

"Don't let that old woman get to you. She's meaner than an razorback hog."

"Really, I'm fine. It's over."

Caroline turned around in her seat. "Abigail's jealous of you, Mamie. Just as Sarge said. Life's not been as generous with her as it's been with you."

I touched Caroline's arm. "If I'm not doing my part, you'd tell me?"

"It's the opposite, dear. I love you like you were my own daughter, not my daughter-in-law. You don't have to work for that, it just is. That you do all that you do though, tells me volumes about who you are here." She touched her own heart. "You and Julian are my world."

"Thank you, Mama." Julian patted her cheek.

"Be careful with her," Caroline admonished him. "We don't want another heat stroke."

Julian gazed into my eyes. "We most certainly do not." He kissed my forehead. "That hat's not going to be enough for a sunny day like today. Where's your parasol?"

"Here." I held it up.

"Open it now."

"I don't want to lose it if you go too fast. Jennie Williams told me that John B gets to going so fast that she can't keep her hats on her head and her parasols inside the wagon. Cars go even faster than wagons."

"Then I won't go fast."

"I'll pinch him if he loses control, Mamie." Caroline turned to face the front of the car. "We've wasted enough time arguing about the war to last me a lifetime. Let's go have fun."

"You've got plenty of water, Mamie?"

"I do and I'm fine."

"Don't snap at me, darling. I just don't want you getting sick like you did last year." Julian tapped a basket in the floor. "So I brought extra just in case."

He was adorable.

A loud beep behind us made me jump. "Will you get on the road, for God's sake?" Garland hit the horn on his car twice more.

"Ignore him," Abigail called. "He's still mad about having to pick up Miss Peach to take care of Sarge at the parade."

"We're gonna miss the whole dadgummed thing." Garland was still slurring his words. "Took ten years off my life waiting for that woman." He pulled out around us and accelerated.

"It's not like you never saw a parade before," Abigail was saying to him as they passed with Sarge and Miss Peach in the back seat.

Glad to see them go, I put up my parasol and leaned back in my seat.

* * *

Julian left us off in front of the Hotel Main and drove around the corner to park the Boehmer on Rogers. Caroline and I stood on the curb, careful to keep our faces shaded from the harsh noontime sun.

The marchers were forming in front of the Frisco Station. All around us hawkers sold ice cream and flowers and pretzels and newspapers. Men carrying musical instruments hurried past us to their meeting point.

Caroline shielded her eyes with her forearm. "Who's that nun?" There were hundreds of people lining both sides of Garrison Avenue.

"Where?"

"Look across the street, to your right. Just even with that trolley pole?"

A beautiful Negro woman dressed in blue was engaged in conversation with a nun holding a basket.

It would have been easier to just point the black-habited woman out to me, but it was impolite to point and Caroline was never rude. "Who's that woman talking to her?"

"That's Ruth, dear."

"She is beautiful."

Caroline smiled. "Fort Smith has always drawn the most exotic peoples. Traders, Indians, Negroes, Gypsies. Soldiers. Even the white folks around here are colorful. It's good that we're finally getting some legitimate theaters opening up, but there's always been something to see or do on Garrison."

"Or gossip about," I chuckled.

"As Wilbur used to say, if there isn't something going on, someone will make up a yarn and pass it off as truth just to keep from being bored."

Two colored men came up to Ruth and said something. The nun handed her the basket. Laughing, she staggered backwards two steps and almost dropped it. One of the colored men took it from her and together they headed toward the river a few blocks away. The nun headed back up Garrison, toward the convent behind Immaculate Conception Church, I presumed.

"I've never seen that nun before," I said. "Do you suppose she's been transferred to St. Anne's?"

Caroline examined the woman through her lorgnette. "She's wearing a Sisters of Mercy habit. So maybe."

A well-dressed man met the nun at the corner of Seventh and Garrison.

"Is that Garland?"

Without the benefit of Caroline's lorgnette, it was hard to tell. "Could be. If it is, then where's Abigail?"

"Looks like he knows the good sister well."

Caroline had a point. The figures were two blocks away, but I could tell that they were engaged in an animated conversation.

"What're they talking about?"

A Gypsy woman crossed Garrison Avenue to join them.

"Is that Theo?"

"Theo?"

"The one with the scarf around her head?"

Caroline moved the lorgnette further away from her face then closer.

I squinted. "I think it is."

"That's quite a get-up," Caroline said.

"What're you two doin'?"

Miss Peach wheeled Sarge up to us.

"Just trying to figure out if that Gypsy is someone we know," I said.

"Well, of course, you know Theo. Get that thing away from me." Sarge slapped Miss Peach's hand as she tried to put a hat on him. "She works at Electric Park. Tells fortunes."

"Seems like that woman is all over town these days," Caroline said.

"Looks like Theo knows Ruth. She dances on a little platform across from the Frisco."

"How do you know that?"

"Behave, you old coot," I laughed. "Julian told me about their little business. Ruth dances to draw a crowd, then her brothers come out and sell their medicinal wares."

"Hello, Miz Caroline." A tall middle-aged man approached with a tiny woman and a little girl. "Miz Mamie."

"Reverend Matthews. Mrs. Matthews," Caroline said. "Did you bring Frankie down to see the parade?"

The little girl hid behind her mother's skirt.

"Say hello to Miz Caroline and Miz Mamie, Frankie," the bespectacled woman pulled her skirt out of the child's grasp.

I smiled. "Don't you look pretty with all those curls?"

"Mama did my bow." Frankie bent over so we could see the green bow pinned in her strawberry blonde hair.

"Wow, Frankie. Think your mama will do a bow for me?"

Frankie shook her head. "She only makes them for me!"

We all laughed at her sassy reply.

I decided right then and there that the little treasure under my heart, thumping to get out, must be a girl. "I guess I better practice hair-bow tying then."

"Come on, Frankie, let's find a good place to watch the parade." Rachel Matthews held out her hand to her daughter. "Frankie can always sit on her papa's shoulders, but if we can't get up front, I can't see a thing."

"Me either."

Caroline and I waved as the Matthews family headed down the avenue toward the river. When they disappeared into the crowd, we turned back to face Garrison.

Two horses pulling a wagon full of corn approached. Old Mr. Fields was hurrying to get his rig off Garrison in preparation for the parade. He nodded at us and we waved back at him.

A ball rolled out into the avenue a few inches in front of the horses' front legs. Both of the beasts startled and then one shied. A small boy squeezed between Caroline and me. I reached for him but the tips of my fingers grazed his shirt. Mr. Fields yelled and tugged at the reins. Focused on his toy, the child scooted under the pawing hooves oblivious to the danger.

A woman behind me screamed, "Bobby!"

"Boy, little boy, come to me quick!" I held out my arms.

The child picked up his ball and turned toward us, grinning. The horses reared and screamed, trying to break free of Mr. Fields' control. As he realized the danger, Bobby's joy turned to horror and he froze just as the team surged forward.

I dropped my parasol and ran to fetch him.

"Mamie!" Caroline reached for me, but I was already in front of Mr. Fields' rearing team. I pushed Bobby and he went down, sliding backwards on his bottom. However, before I could get to him to see if he was okay, I tripped on an unevenly-laid brick and fell hard on my stomach. I closed my eyes, expecting the horses to trample me or the wagon to roll over my body. Instinctively, I turned on my side, trying to protect my abdomen.

The horses leapt over me. For a moment, I thought I was safe, but in a heartbeat, the wagon bore down on me. I covered my eyes with both hands. The noise was almost unbearable. I thought I'd already died and the devil's minions were welcoming me to hell. And then, I realized that though the wagon had passed over me, all four wheels missed me.

I rolled onto my back and opened my eyes.

"I'm alive!" I'm sure I said it out loud before I realized that my dress was caught on a hook on the wagon and I was being dragged down the block. I don't know where my hat went but my hair had come undone and covered my eyes and mouth. The heel of my left shoe hit another uneven brick and broke off. I could hear Mr. Fields yelling at the horses. My arms and legs flopped like I was a rag doll bumping down the street. Fortunately, my cotton bodice tore after only a few yards and I was left lying on my back in the middle of Garrison Avenue, stunned.

"Lie still, Miz McGrath." It was a man's voice. "It's Till Shaw."

I had no idea who Till Shaw was but his eyes were kind and his voice soothing.

"Don't let the cars run over me."

He took my left hand. "Don't you worry about that, ma'am. John B's got traffic stopped at Texas corner and the coppers will be here any minute now."

I tried to touch my stomach with my other hand but my arm wouldn't work. "My baby," I sobbed.

"Mr. Lick went to call the doctor. You hang on."

My lips were bleeding. "Julian?"

"Don't you worry, ma'am. I sent my boy to find him."

"Get out of the way, go on." Abigail pushed onlookers aside, poking some with her parasol, elbowing others.

Caroline squeezed under her arm and knelt beside me. "Lay still, Mamie. They say Doc Stevenson is coming as fast as he can."

I reached for her with my right hand, but my arm was bent between my elbow and wrist and I was overcome with pain when I saw it. "Is the baby okay?"

Caroline's forehead crinkled. "We'll pray."

"Mamie!" Julian knelt over me.

I coughed and a piece of broken tooth flew out of my mouth. "I tried to do everything right this time, Julian, but when I saw that boy, I didn't think." I was babbling.

He pushed my hair out of my face.

I couldn't bear seeing his pain so I closed my eyes. I'd failed him again.

"There's the doctor." It was Till Shaw's voice again. "Hold on, Miz McGrath, he'll be here in a minute."

I must have passed out because the next thing I knew, I was being put into a carriage. It rocked as Julian put me in the seat and covered me with a blanket.

"Julian?"

"Rest, my darling."

His face blurred and then I was asleep.

7

June 1, 1911
**After Rescuing Child on Garrison, Heroine Dragged by Wagon,
Badly Injured**

Julian McGrath, *Southwest American*

STRANGE NOISES WOKE ME. SQUEAKING and voices.

"That's a fine bit of steel, Garland. Was it your dad's?" It was Julian.

"Not likely. My dad's older brother used to make them, though. Back in the day, folks called them Arkansas Toothpicks. A sort of specialized Bowie knife. They used them to hunt, to skin bear, gut a deer. Fierce damned weapon, I'll tell you. Lots of hill folk took them to war. Wore them in a sheath slung across their backs if they were infantry, hooked to their saddles if they were calvary. They could whip them out and kill a man before he could draw a pistol from its holster. This here one's for show. See all the engraving?"

"Where did you get it?" That was Andy Carr's voice.

I opened my eyes. I was alone in the bed I usually shared with Julian. The windows were open and a light breeze cooled me.

"Traded a shotgun and a lady's derringer for it. Plus a fifty."

Squeak, squeak.

"Hoo, Garland. That's some fancy dagger. Too dear for my blood though." That was definitely John B Williams.

Was I dreaming?

"So what're you planning to do with it?" It was Julian again.

"It's an investment. I'm gonna put it away for a rainy day."

Squeak.

Andy Carr laughed. "When it rains, you're gonna need cash, Garland. Not some fancy sword—"

"Dagger," John B corrected.

"Arkansas Toothpick," Garland insisted. "It's a piece of history."

"It's just one more thing for people to kill each other with." It was Andy again.

I looked around the room. It was dark. *Where were they?*

Squeak.

I relaxed. They were on the porch under my open window and one of them was sitting in Wilbur's old rocking chair. I closed my eyes and I dozed off, their voices drifting away on the breeze.

* * *

"I think you're going to need some help around here, Julian. This is a big house and Mamie's not going to bounce back in a month like she did with the first one." It was Andy. "That little thing has had a tough couple of years."

"You're hard on your women, Julian," Garland snorted and they all laughed.

Squeak. Squeak

I opened my eyes. Everything hurt. My arm, my leg, my cheek, my teeth, the deep scratches on my back. My belly. My feelings.

"I'd give anything to save her from all the pain. It kills me to see her hurting like this."

Oh, my beloved Julian. My heart beat faster, but I couldn't move or call out to him. *Was I awake or not?*

"I know what you mean," Andy said. "When Della was having our five kids, I felt useless as teats on a boar hog. Here she was going through all kinds of things from swollen feet to what looked and sounded like excruciating pain. And I'd tell her that I loved her enough to do it for her, but she looked at me and said, 'You'd run out that door in the middle of the baby being born if you heard there was a shootout on the Avenue.' And I'd say, "Della, darling, you know me well."

They laughed and laughed.

Squeak.

* * *

The front gate clicked and people on the front porch below me stood up.

"Colonel Parker, sir. Can I help you?"

"I just came to see how that amazing young woman you married is doing, Julian." I didn't recognize the voice. Maybe I *was* dreaming?

"She's pretty beat up, sir."

"After what she did, I'm surprised she's alive. Is there anything I can do for her? For you?"

"I can't think of anything, sir."

"Maybe when she is up to it, you can write an article about what happened to her? We'd run it front page. Maybe with a picture of her with that boy?"

"I would be glad to write it," Julian said. "But Mamie is in no shape to talk or pose for photos right now."

"I understand. "How about you talk with the family of the boy she saved and get his picture now?"

"I can definitely do that." Julian sounded excited.

"Maybe when Mrs. McGrath has recovered, you can help her write her account."

"I'll be glad to help her write up something, but she is perfectly capable of writing it on her own, Colonel Parker." Julian sounded amused.

"She sounds pretty special, young man."

"She is, sir."

"I'll see you at the office."

"Thank you. See you soon."

A moment passed and the front gate clanged again.

"Is Colonel Parker your boss?" It was Burley.

"He is."

"Imagine him coming to see Mamie like that."

"I'm sure he's a nice man," Julian said. "But he's a newsman too."

"Are you going to tell her he came to visit?"

"When she's up to it."

* * *

"Mamie. Wake up. Come on. Open your beautiful eyes. There ya go." A woman with a red bandanna wrapped around her head, and a wide smile was leaning over me.

"Do I know you?"

"Not yet."

"Why are you here?

"I'm your new best friend."

My lips were swollen and my front teeth hurt. "Jus what I need." I tried to laugh but even that hurt. "What's your name?"

She pulled a sheet up under my chin. "Genevieve."

"Genevieve, can you help me? I need to—you know."

"Sure thang, darlin.'"

After we'd taken care of my private business, I was dizzy, and thirsty. Genevieve gave me water, helped me back into bed, washed me, and covered me with clean linens. It felt wonderful.

"Now let's get some soup into you. I know your mouth is sore, but you need to eat to heal. Miss Peach done showed me how to beef up the broth for you."

I was already exhausted and even though I was hungry, I was afraid food would hurt more. But I leaned forward obediently, eyes on Genevieve's while she spooned beef broth and mashed up noodles into my mouth.

"There now, Miz Mamie. We've had a big morning. Let's close the shades and take a nap. Okay?"

I nodded and closed my eyes.

* * *

"Where's Genevieve?"

"She's home with her own family today," Miss Peach switched on the lamp.

"No," I moaned.

"It's time, Mamie." Sarge sat beside my bed while Miss Peach fussed with the curtains.

I squinted. "It's too bright in here already." I threw my good arm over my eyes. "Close them. I mean it, Miss Peach. Leave the shades down."

Miss Peach ignored my demands and tied the curtains back.

"I'm not ready."

She grunted as she pushed open the sash.

The sound of rain pounding on the roof over the porch below my window was pleasant, but not enough to lighten my mood. "Please. I like it dark and quiet."

"Light's better for you, missy." Miss Peach poured water from a pitcher into a basin. "Let's get you cleaned up."

I frowned. "I'm not in the mood for this."

Miss Peach stuck an arm under my shoulders and forced me into a sitting position.

I screamed, more out of frustration than pain. "Get away from me! I didn't ask either of you to come up here and bully me."

"Settle down. This won't take long." She reached for the bandage that covered the lower half of the left side of my face.

"Stop, stop!" I jerked my head back.

The bandage came away in her hand.

I screamed and then rocked back and forth, sobbing. "Please, it stings."

"Hush now, Miz Mamie." She soaked a cloth in water and dabbed at the wound.

"What are you doing now?"

"Cleaning it."

Actually, it didn't hurt as much as I was afraid it might, but I held my breath, waiting for it to.

"Looks like these stitches are ready to come out."

"No." I flinched, but that didn't really hurt either. Just an unpleasant tugging sensation.

"That's better." Miss Peach put salve on the wound on my cheek.

"Aren't you going to put the bandage back?"

"No. It's closed as much as it's going to. No need to keep it covered. It'll scab over now."

"Wonderful." I preferred to hide the hideous gash from Julian.

"Let's get you some fresh linens."

"Can't you just leave me alone?"

She stuffed one of Caroline's pillows into a clean case and smiled at me. "No ma'am."

"Maybe I just want to lie here and die. Did you ever think of that?"

"Not once."

The woman was infuriating.

"Why should you get to molder away when I got to be up and around?" Sarge cackled. "I been a cripple for forty-eight years. I know ya gottta take time to lick your wounds, but you been doin' that for two weeks now."

"I'm not ready to get up and I'm not ready for visitors—and I'm definitely not ready for you!"

Miss Peach tossed the pillowcase I'd been lying on over her head and replaced it with the fresh one.

I covered my face with my hands.

Sarge leaned forward. "Mamie, unless you're gonna lay there until moss grows on your upper lip, it's time."

"I want to die."

"No, you don't, honey."

"I do, I tell you."

"You're the only kin I got left, girl. Why do you think I came back down here?"

Tears ran down my cheeks. "Don't do this, Sarge."

"Do what?"

"Blackmail me."

"Funny." He lowered his voice. "I thought I was lovin' you."

That did me in and I sobbed. "I'm not tough enough to bear this."

"Sure you are. Besides, that young man downstairs is scared to death you're gonna check out on him. Don't you think you owe him another think?"

"This isn't what Julian signed up for when we got married. He wants a family. What good am I if I can't even do that?"

"You got a lot of young years yet, sugar," Sarge said. "Who knows what will happen? Okay, so not havin' that baby to raise is gonna change your plans. What else do you want to do?"

I sniffed. "What did you do?"

"What do you mean?" The old man's lower lip twitched.

"I mean after you lost your leg. What did you do?"

"I drank myself almost to death." He managed a sour grin. "Don't go by me, Mamie. It's been a complicated life. Didn't have to spend forty years feelin' sorry for myself, hatin' those blasted traitors who not only walked out on us, but tried to destroy us—"

"And took your leg."

He patted his chest looking for either a cigar or his flask. Finding neither, he sighed and I figured this cozy family chat was over. "And took my favorite leg. The bastards."

"The bastards," I murmured. "You must have hated them. Just hated them."

Miss Peach added another pillow behind my head and I felt like I was sitting up for a change. She propped my bad leg up on a third one. "There,"she said through clenched teeth, "There."

I turned my head to look at Sarge. "So what did you do?"

"I got even."

I couldn't hold back my irritation. "Sure you did."

"I did actually."

"How?"

"Those rebels wanted to defeat me. Change the way I see my country. They didn't just back out of a deal or choose to ignore our laws. They attacked us. They tried to inflict a hurt that would last a lifetime."

"So—"

"So I didn't let them. Every time I wake up in the mornin,' it's like pokin' my saber into the corn-fed belly of the Confederacy. Whenever I enjoy a good meal or a fine cigar or salute the stars and stripes, I get back at them."

"It's been half a century, Sarge."

He sighed. "They wasted our national treasure. Destroyed families. Homes. Farms. For what? So they could treat good people like Patsy and Genevieve and Miss Peach and Sandy like cattle? That's why they started that war, you know. I'll never forgive them. Never."

"Not everyone in Fort Smith were Union. A lot of folks around here still think the rebels were right to do what they did. If you still feel that way, why did you come back from Michigan?"

"Because Arkansas is my home too. And because you and I are all that's left of our family."

I felt my anger slipping away. "I'm sorry, Sarge."

He patted my hand. "War sounds good until you're knee deep in it. Then it takes a lifetime to get over. I'm gonna outlast them all." His eyes glittered. "I'm gonna be the last one down. And then I'll hate them in my grave."

Miss Peach gave us each a pill with a buttermilk chaser. "It's time to get you back down those stairs, Mr. Eacret." I'd never heard her speak so kindly to Sarge. Maybe she had a soft spot for cantankerous old fools too.

"Promise me you'll get over this, Mamie," Sarge said as she helped him out the door.

I blinked back tears and nodded, even though I knew I'd still be angry in my grave too. I just didn't know who or what to be mad at.

* * *

"Mamie, darling. Wake up." It was Julian but he seemed so far away. "Mamie!"

I opened my eyes. "What?"

He was standing by the bed, holding my hand. "You were crying, love."

"I was?"

He used his thumbs to caress away the tears lingering on my cheeks. "It's a beautiful day." He helped me sit up.

"Yes?" I covered my mouth with the fingers of my good hand. Since my accident, I lisped words like 'yes' and 'house.' It was embarrassing, especially in front of my husband.

"Dr. Stevenson said we need to start getting you some fresh air."

"Why?"

"You need exercise and a change of scenery. It'll make you feel better." He caressed my right cheek.

"Oh." I jerked back from him.

"Does that hurt?"

I shook my head. "Was afraid that it might though."

"How about breakfast on the screened porch? Some coffee and oatmeal sound good?"

I nodded. "But I'm scared to go down the stairs." I'd avoided trying for days. "What if I fall?"

"I won't let you fall."

I knew he was concerned about my weakened state, but he was even more worried about my continuing sorrow. I only saw our daughter once before they whisked her away, but I knew she was already dead when she was born. She'd stopped moving a few hours after the accident. However, it was over a week before the pains began. Little Julia never took a breath.

It was my fault. A mother's one and only job was to take care of her children, before and after birth. I'd failed at that basic womanly responsibility twice now. And Dr. Stevenson had told us it wasn't likely I'd conceive again anytime soon, if ever. I was devastated. Julian didn't share his grief with me, but I knew he was heartbroken.

"Let's stand up, okay?"

I nodded. "My robe? Can you get it first?"

He collected it and helped me put it on over my nightgown. "How about just slippers? Something to keep your feet warm? I'll carry you downstairs."

I was shy around him since the accident, embarrassed by my injuries and my inability to get past them.

"I'll try not to hurt you," he said as he lifted me.

I didn't know where to put my arm so I held it close to my body as he carried me down the steep wooden staircase. When we reached the main floor, he went straight through the kitchen out onto the screened-in back porch. Caroline had moved a cushioned chair outside and Julian eased me into it, careful to avoid bumping my leg.

"How's that?"

"It's good. Thank you."

He smiled. It was the first time he'd done that since he let Caroline and me off on Garrison the day I tangled with Mr. Fields' wagon.

Caroline tucked a blanket over my lap and draped a crocheted shawl over my shoulders. "I have cream of potato soup for you," she said. "And I cut up boiled spinach real fine."

I picked up a spoon. My mouth was sore and several of my teeth were loose. The broken one ached. I sipped the warm soup and swallowed quickly.

"Okay?" Caroline hovered nearby.

"Yes, thank you." I took another bite—and another.

"Look at you." Julian pulled a wooden chair up to the small folding table he'd assembled for me and sat down. You'll be back in the pink before you know it."

I forced a closed-mouth, half-moon smile.

The front bell rang.

"Who could that be?" Caroline got up. "It's too early for the ice man."

"A few more bites." Julian tapped my tray.

"I'll try."

"Mamie, darling. You have company." Caroline escorted a handsome couple onto the porch. "This is Mr. and Mrs. Esposito."

My old self would have smiled and stood to greet guests. That wasn't possible now though and I didn't know what to do. I needed to cover my mouth but that left me no way to reach out to them.

Julian stood and shook Mr. Esposito's hand. "I'm glad to see you again, sir."

I had no idea who these people were or why they were visiting me. Embarrassed and confused, I laid down my spoon. "Mr. Esposito. Mrs. Esposito," I mumbled behind my hand.

"Call me Martina, please."

"Martina."

"Do you remember me?"

The woman's dark eyes were familiar. I shook my head.

"I am the mother of the little boy you saved."

"Bobby?"

"Roberto, yes."

"Is he okay?" I'd not seen or heard about the boy again after that wagon rolled over me. At first, the enormity of my own situation pushed little Bobby out of my thoughts. Then, since no one had mentioned him in the weeks since the accident, I assumed he'd been killed or mangled by the horses' flying hooves.

"He's fine. A few scrapes and bruises. He's already healed," Martina said. "In fact, he's here. He wants to tell you something."

"Me?"

"Yes. Is it okay?"

"I would like to see him, but don't you think all of this—" I nodded toward the bruises and scabs on my arms and the cast on my leg. "Don't you think this might scare him?"

Caroline touched my shoulder. "Bobby saw what that wagon did to you, Mamie. He needs to see that you are getting better."

"They say you'll be well soon," Mr. Esposito said. "When you are, you must come to our restaurant. For you, it'll always be free."

"Thank you, Mr. Esposito, but—"

"Dino, ma'am."

"What?"

"For you, my name is Dino."

"Dino."

"So you'll come when you are better? To our restaurant on Garrison? Esposito's?"

"Of course." The idea of going anywhere was overwhelming, but I realized there would be a time when having an Italian dinner would be appealing.

"We'll have a party, just for you and your friends," he said.

"That isn't necessary. I'm just glad the boy is okay."

"We owe you so much. Roberto is our first child. He was born in America. That makes him an American. Perhaps some day, he'll be President of the United States."

"Perhaps he will." I was surprised at how comforting that thought was.

"He'll have my vote, sir." Julian squeezed my hand.

"Okay, then?" Martina cocked her head.

I wanted to smile but my broken tooth and the scar on my face made me self conscious. I settled for a nod.

"I wanted to come sooner, but they told me you weren't up to it yet," Dino said while Martina went to fetch Bobby.

"I'm glad you are here." I said it to be polite but once it was out of my mouth, I realized it was true. My grief was no less, but the sense of hopelessness had ebbed.

Martina led her son out onto the porch. I'd only glimpsed him before pushing him out of the path of Mr. Fields' wagon. He was a handsome child with brown eyes and lustrous dark hair like his father.

"Here is the lady who saved you from the horses," Martina said to her son. "You must tell her thank you."

"Thank you." Bobby studied his shoes.

"He's bashful in front of strangers," Martina said.

"Me too." I found myself staring at Bobby. He was perfect except for a scab on his right knee. "Did you get your ball back?"

He stuck out his lower lip. "A kid took it."

"Oh no."

"It rolled into the street and a bigger kid stole it."

"I'm sorry."

"I was scared."

"Of the horses?"

He shook his head. "Of the bigger kids."

I forgot to cover my mouth when I smiled. "I'm sure your Mama and Daddy will get you another ball."

"They're mad."

"Oh, Bobby!" Martina squeezed his shoulder. "Not mad. But you let go of my hand and ran out into the street. You could have been killed. Mrs. McGrath got hurt trying to save you. You must do what Mama and Papa say. Always."

Bobby's sigh was dramatic. "See?"

I laughed in spite of myself. "How old are you, Bobby?"

"Four." He held up three fingers.

His father nudged him with his knee. "One more, Bobby."

"Oh yeah." He giggled. "What's that?" He pointed to my arm.

"Bobby!"

"It's okay," I said and then I realized that it really was okay. "It's where I hurt myself on Mr. Fields' wagon."

His eye widened. "A boo boo?"

I nodded.

"What's that?" He pointed to my cheek.

"Another boo boo."

"Does it hurt?"

"A little."

"Want me to kiss it?"

"Sure." It came out before I thought it through.

Dino picked up his son. "Be gentle, Bobby."

"Okay."

The boy puckered up long before his father got him close enough to kiss me. "That's a boy. Easy."

Bobby's lips grazed the cut on my cheek. "There," he muttered. "All better?"

I ran my fingers over the cut. "Yes. I think so."

"Let's go!" Suddenly shy, he dashed to his mama and wrapped his arms around her legs.

Julian chuckled. "You're gonna be a great doctor, Bobby."

I leaned back in my chair, exhausted.

Dino took his wife's arm. "It's time we should go."

Julian stood up. "It was kind of you to come see us."

"Martina?"

She turned to face me.

"Thank you." It came out a hoarse whisper. "I didn't know it until now, but I needed to see him."

Martina nodded and guided her son out the door.

* * *

June 7, 1911
Guests at the LeFlore Hotel, 316 Garrison Avenue, complained about miss-ing items. While investigating, a guard caught a man carrying clothes in the hallway. A search of his room uncovered a thin steel file and a chloroform outfit, including a hose to inject the drug through keyholes to incapacitate occupants. When they were sleeping soundly, the thief entered their room and took their belongings.

Julian McGrath, *Southwest American*

It was too hot to spend my days upstairs in our bedroom, so Julian carried me downstairs to the front parlor every morning before he left for work. I could have managed on my own, but I didn't. And even though I was able to get around during the day, I chose to sit in a chair, with my legs on a footstool, watching Sandy work in the yard.

My head was empty, thoughts pushed away by intense emotions. There was the loss of our baby girl, of course, but something else bothered me even though I knew it was absurd. I'd never been beautiful, but the scar that split my left cheek from just below my eye to the corner of my mouth was grotesque. I either avoided mirrors or wept in front of them. I did self pity as well or better than Sarge and I'd only been at it six weeks.

One morning, I was alone in the house. Julian was at work, Genevieve wasn't supposed to arrive until noon. I'd insisted that Caroline shouldn't miss another mass because of me. "I'm just going to mope around like I do every day," I told her. "You should go on with your life."

"When your body is ready, you'll be too." She kissed my forehead. "I'll be back in a couple hours. Sandy is out back if you need anything. And you can always telephone for help if something goes wrong."

It felt good when she left. Not that I wanted her to leave, but it felt normal to be on my own again. After a few minutes, I got up and went to the sideboard for a cup of tea. Caroline had left me a note.

Apple cake with walnuts in the kitchen. Whipped cream in the ice box. Your favorite. Love you.

Caroline really was the dearest thing. I limped into the kitchen. She'd already sliced the cake into six wedges. I used the knife to lift a piece out of the pan. It took some doing with one hand, but I managed. It felt like an accomplishment. I was about to sit down at the table when someone knocked on the back door.

Thinking it was Manny looking for work, I got up and opened the door.

"Hello, Mamie. I thought you might like some company." Patsy Lincoln's arms were full of books, magazines, and newspapers. "And I figured you'd need some new reading material by now."

Perhaps it was Patsy's broad grin, but the blues slipped away. "Come on in. I was about to sit down to a bite of Caroline's apple walnut cake. You must have a piece with me."

"Lawd, that girl sure can cook, can't she? I'd love some."

"Come on in then.

"Where do you want me to put all of this?"

"There." I gestured with my good arm. "I'll take a peek at them while we chat."

Patsy stacked the reading material on the table. The second piece out of the pan crumbled a bit, so I took it for myself and slid the plate with the better slice across the table to Patsy. "Tea or milk?"

"Milk, please." Patsy put her straw hat on the chair beside her. "How's that young man doing for you?" She nodded toward the window at Sandy working in the back yard now. "I know his mama and daddy and if he's not doing right by ya'll, I'll get them down on him."

"We love Sandy. We wouldn't be able to keep up with this place without him."

"That's good because he might need the money one of these days. His mama told me at church the other day that Sandy's found a girlfriend."

"Oh?" I pretended to be shocked.

"Yes, ma'am, he sure has. Loula said she's a pretty young thing named Pocahontas."

"Good for Sandy. You think he's serious about her?" I fetched the whipped cream and set it on the table between us.

"He's serious but I don't know about Pocahontas. She's a wild one. Too young to take much of anything serious."

"Does she go to Lincoln?"

"She should—but no, she's not interested in school. Smart but stubborn. Likes to do things her way. About drives her mama and poppa crazy sometimes."

I liked Patsy. I especially liked her stories about the things she and Caroline did when they were children living on a farm in Pope County after the Civil War. Caroline's grandparents had owned Patsy and her mother and brother until 1865 when Mr. Lincoln freed them. You'd think a thing like that would have made it hard for them to be friends, but they'd figured out a way. In front of their neighbors and friends and any grown ups, they pretended Caroline was in charge. When it was just the two of them, Patsy led the way.

"How long have you been teaching at Lincoln?" I handed Patsy a big spoon.

"Long time." She plopped whipped sweetened cream onto her cake. "I've seen lots of fine young people go through those doors. Some went on to college and found good jobs."

"You sound proud."

"I am." The mound of cream almost hid the cake. "Think I have enough?"

"I don't know, Patsy." I giggled. "There might still be a bite uncovered."

"I don't want to leave y'all short." Her eyes sparkled.

"Julian won't be in until late. Besides, Caroline made this cake to cheer me up."

"Feel cheerier?"

"Of all the things that I thought about doing, I don't guess any would've made me any happier than eating sweets with you."

"Good." She took a bite of Caroline's cake and sighed. "Just as I remembered it."

I poured her a glass of milk and because hers looked so good, I poured myself one too. Sitting down at the table, I took a bite and held it in my mouth for a moment, "Oh my, it's heaven."

"It is, isn't it?" Patsy refolded her napkin every time she used it. Caroline did that too.

"So how are you doing?"

"Healing." I didn't share how scared and frustrated I was.

"And what're you up to while you're doing that?" Patsy didn't know how to give up.

"That's just it," I lowered my eyes. "I can't think of what to do with myself. So I sit and stew about this or that."

"Sounds boring."

I sighed. Patsy had a way of getting right to the heart of things. "Abigail made a big stink that morning, the day I got hurt. Julian said it was because I was going to have a baby and she was jealous."

"Maybe." Patsy finished her cake and folded her napkin. "The Abigail you see isn't the real one, you know."

"Lord, I hope not."

"We'll save that story for another day. What the row was about?"

My eyes burned. "She said that Julian and I take advantage of Caroline, living here and not doing our share."

"You were pregnant."

Usually, I appreciated Patsy's bluntness, but on this day, less so. "Caroline does everything so well. She cooks better than anyone. She has a wonderful eye for decor. She loves puttering around with her flowers. I try to help whenever I can, but she only allows me to do so much. She loves her home and enjoys keeping it. What Abigail said stung because it's true. I feel like I'm a burden."

"What does Caroline say?"

"That she loves me. Of course, I've been down twice in eighteen months. She may feel differently now there's no grand baby to look forward to."

Patsy leaned over the table and took my good hand. "Caroline adores you, Mamie. Yes, she wants grandchildren. She and Wilbur wanted a bigger family too, but it didn't happen for them either. So now, she dotes on you and Julian. It makes her happy to have you around."

"She's a saint."

Patsy squeezed my hand. "She is, at that."

I got up and awkwardly wrapped a cloth around the remaining cake. "But even if I forgive myself for not being Caroline, who am I now? Everything changed in the blink of an eye."

"So that's what's getting you down."

I shrugged. "If I'm not going to be a mother, what will I be?"

"How long before that cast comes off your arm?"

"Next week, even if I have to saw it off myself."

"How's your other arm?" Patsy put our dishes in the sink. "Can you type?"

"Do I need to?"

"Let me rephrase that. Can you write?"

"I went to school." I finished the last of my milk and started cleaning up. "And I was pretty good at sketching. Why?"

"Sit down." She pointed to my chair.

I was happy to oblige. "Okay. What?

"I have an idea." She rinsed our dishes and stacked them beside the sink to drain. "You know I have a little newspaper?"

"The *Fort Smith Bell*?"

"Just like Ida B. Wells. Of course it's only a four-page fold-over, but it's important to the Negroes around here to have something about and for them. Why work myself to the bone teaching these folks to read when there's nothing for them to read?"

"Who's Ida B. Wells?"

"She owned her own newspaper in Memphis until a bunch of white men ran her plumb out of town."

"Why?

"Mostly cause they didn't like what she had to say. It scared them, I think."

"What scared them?"

"Her articles complained about all the lynchings."

"Oh." That took the fun out of our conversation. "Wasn't that dangerous for her?"

"Most certainly. But she kept right on writing."

"My Lord, she's brave."

"She is."

"And you write about such things too?"

When Patsy smiled, her nose wrinkled between her eyes. "One of the many things I do."

I changed the subject back to me. "I'm not much of a writer, not like Julian."

"Nonsense. You can read. And if you can read, you can write. And if you can write, you can tell stories people want to hear."

I tried not to sigh. "I used to write quite a lot."

"Why did you stop?"

"Nobody reads the silly things young girls put in their diaries."

"You might be surprised." Patsy picked up one of the magazines she'd brought me and thumbed through it. "People love hearing about other people's experiences." She opened it and pointed to an article about women's fashion.

I realized she was manipulating me, of course, but I reached for it anyway. It was the July 1902 issue of *McCall's* magazine. I ran my fingers over the cover—a drawing of a young woman standing in front of an American flag. "My mother always liked this magazine. We'd go downtown Pittsburgh to have lunch and shop. The last thing we'd do before Daddy came to fetch us was buy a *McCall's* or a *Saturday Evening Post*."

Patsy leaned forward like she was going to share a secret with me. "You should do it, Mamie."

"What are you suggesting?" I knew very well what Patsy was doing, but I wanted to hear her say it.

"You're a smart woman. And you're interested in all kinds of things—fashion, local activities, family stories, history, travel."

"I wouldn't know how to begin."

"Begin by reading these newspapers and magazines." She pointed to the stack she'd set on the table when she came in. "And then you write an article for each one of them. Then you send them to the editors."

"It sounds like a lot of work."

"What else do you have to do?"

I was taken aback by Patsy's blunt challenge. Yet, for the first time since my accident, I was interested in something. I opened the April, 1911 edition of *Woman's World*. "I could, couldn't I?"

Patsy grinned. "Nothing stopping you." She put on her hat. "Your mama would be proud, Mamie. Even that old coot you call an uncle would be."

I doubted it would be that easy, but self pity was a bore. "Thank you, Patsy. I'll think about it." I stood up.

"I know you will." Patsy stepped out on the screened porch and closed the door behind her. I watched her through the back window as she stopped to chat with Sandy before going out the back gate.

I made myself some hot tea and settled down to read *Women's World*.

* * *

"Caroline told me you were better." Abigail appeared at my bedroom door. "And that you have a job."

"A couple actually. Julian's editor is going to let me do a lady's column and I'm submitting a story to *Women's World*."

"Never knew you to say much. You've always been such a shy little thing."

"I'm not shy." I lifted my chin. "Just quiet."

"What're you going to write about?" She sank down in the rocker beside my bed and propped her folded parasol next to her knee.

"I'm going to write about the people of Fort Smith."

Abigail narrowed her eyes. "The black ones too?"

"Maybe." Actually, I hadn't planned on that but Abigail pushed me to the edge of social rebellion.

"How are you gonna do that, Miss Priss? Just go visit them?"

"Why not?"

"You know why." Sunlight streaming through the window onto Abigail's monocle created a glare that made my eyes water.

I blinked. "I'll visit their businesses."

"What will people think?"

"I guess they'll think whatever they want to think." It wasn't much of an answer but I tried to make it sound like it was.

"My you're brave."

I gritted my teeth. Abigail's sarcasm was meant to discourage, but it echoed my own response to Ida B. Wells' determination. "I'll find a way."

We sat in silence. The seconds ticked by. I stared at my hands folded in my lap and then looked out the window.

"Then I'll help you," Abigail said as if it was settled.

"I don't need help."

"Yes, you do. You aren't from here. I know everyone and everything that goes on in Fort Smith. Have Genevieve make us some tea and I'll get you started."

"Give me strength." I shook the little bell Caroline had brought down from the attic.

"Mrs. Julian McGrath. Writer." Abigail was so annoying.

"Yes, ma'am?" Genevieve appeared at the door.

"Mrs. Talbot and I would like some tea and cookies."

"Coming right up, ma'am."

"That one working out for you?" Abigail gestured with her head as Genevieve went down the stairs.

"She takes good care of all of us. Especially me."

"Never cared for her myself. When she worked for us she broke my favorite Limoges pot."

"I like her just fine."

"You wait. Either she'll end up breaking Caroline's treasures or she'll steal you blind. You know how they are."

My smile was sour as Genevieve set the tea on a low table in front of the rocker. "I made snicker doodles this morning." I pointed to the plate.

Abigail picked up one and nibbled on the edge. "No you didn't."

I chuckled. "You're right. They're Caroline's recipe but Genevieve baked them."

"In that case, I'll take two."

I'd have knocked her hat off, but she was out of range. "Take three."

"Wonderful idea, my dear" She put three cookies on the edge of her tea cup. "Now get paper and pencil so you can remember what I'm about to tell you. Remember Alderman Lowrey?"

"The one who accidentally shot himself?"

"Well, I heard from Katherine Mivelaz at our last quilting bee—she's a Maledon by birth you know—who heard it from Marie DuVal who got it straight from Chief Barry's wife that it absolutely wasn't an accident." She took a sip of tea and bobbed her head as though her pronouncement was set in stone.

"Some one murdered him?"

"Well, he was alone in that room but the window was open you see and no one could ever find the spent bullet. So what does that tell you?"

"I have no idea."

"That means the bullet had to go out the window."

"Ah."

"Someone had to be in that room with him and when he or she shot him, the bullet went through his head and out the window." Abigail spoke slowly as if she were explaining to an infant.

"Couldn't the same thing happen if he shot himself?"

Abigail raised one eyebrow. "Surely not."

"Maybe he stood in front of that window at just the right angle so that the bullet would go through his head and out the window. You know, either by accident or to avoid damaging his home."

"Well, if you aren't going to take my word for it—"

"It's not that." I tried to soothe her in spite of my amusement. "It's just that I'm not writing a gossip column."

"If you wait around for proof, someone else will beat you to the story. Besides, gossip sells papers. People are curious about each other."

She did have a point. People loved knowing each other's private business. Especially women. Why else did they gather in an endless assortment of clubs, associations, and private teas to discuss the latest town scandal? And on the rare occasion when a baby born six months after the society wedding of his parents wasn't the topic of conversation, they'd share old tales of murder and mayhem. Fort Smith was almost a hundred years old. The citizens were waist-deep in both ancient and modern rumors—and the ladies loved it. "What kind of stories do you like to read, Abigail?"

A beam of sunshine came through the window and reflected off her monocle. "Why Mamie. I thought you'd never ask."

* * *

It took me a week to write a short mystery using Alderman Lowery's suicide as inspiration. My fingers were stiff, making my script awkward and hard to read. But sitting alone on the back porch while Genevieve hummed as she did our laundry and Caroline took her daily nap, I felt both independent and secure. And that freed me to enjoy the story I was creating.

I finished the piece with a dramatic flourish, wrote a letter to the editor, folded the ten page tale, and stuffed it into an envelope. I was just about to seal it when Genevieve said from the back door, "Don't you wanna make a copy of that? What if that fella you're sending it to tries to steal it? Or it gets lost in the mail bag? You know, delivered to the wrong person?"

Mouth open, I looked up at her. "Oh my, I hadn't thought of that." I took the story titled, "When Murder Came to Town," out of the envelope and smoothed out the fold creases.

Genevieve brought me more paper and a new bottle of ink. "Just in case you need them, ma'am."

"Thank you, Genevieve. You're so thoughtful."

"I think what you're doing is wonderful, Miz Mamie. You might be struggling a bit while your body's healing, but your mind's hard at work. I can't wait to read that."

"Actually, I like composing, but making a copy less so." I opened and closed my hand. Maybe I'll take a nap first. We can send it off to Saint Louis soon enough."

"Want to go upstairs?"

"Those stairs are more than I want to tackle right now. I'll just stretch out on Caroline's settee in the front parlor."

"Here, let me help you up." Genevieve stood behind me, put her arms under mine and lifted me up so that I was balanced on my good leg. "Don't you worry now. I got you."

I leaned against her and hopped on my good leg while Genevieve helped me get my balance. "Without the cast, I'm afraid to put my weight on it," I puffed through my broken teeth.

"Anyone would be. That was a bad break. Let's do this together. I won't let you fall, I promise."

"Okay," I said as I stretched my bad leg forward and gingerly put my weight on it."

"There you go!" She sparkled with delight at my achievement. "Does it hurt?"

"No." I was giddy over my single-step achievement.

"Another?"

I nodded and she let go of me.

"Oh no. I can't do it."

"Ya think?" Genevieve backed away from me.

I balanced on one foot for a moment before taking a step forward on my own, my first without a crutch. Thrilled, I took another. "Okay. Okay. Okay," I chanted as I took three more.

"Look where we are now." Genevieve helped me fall gently onto the settee and then lifted my feet so that I could turn sideways and lay down. "Want some more pillows?" She stuffed Caroline's embroidered throws around and under my head and shoulders.

"No, this is fine. Thank you." I was thrilled with my five-step achievement, and tired.

She opened a window on each side of the room to allow the breeze to blow through.

I'd been awake almost six hours, the longest since my accident. I fell asleep almost as soon as she left the room.

An hour and a half later, I opened my eyes. Genevieve was in the kitchen, singing as she cooked.

I pushed myself to a sitting position. It hurt, but not as bad as I'd expected it to. "Genevieve?"

"Yes, ma'am?"

"I need help—you know, the water closet?"

"Be right there." She appeared in the hall, wiping her hands on her apron. "I was jes talking with Miz Peach. She's more experienced with helping sick people than I am. I told her about you walking that little bit this afternoon. She says it's time you get a cane and start getting some exercise. Building those muscles back up."

"I don't have a cane."

"I'll bring one tomorrow." She helped me up on my good leg and we hobbled to the bathroom. "She say two more weeks and you be good as new."

After we'd taken care of business, Genevieve helped me out on the screened porch again.

"What's this?" I pointed to a new stack of paper on the table. It was covered in much neater handwriting than my own.

"I hope you don't mind, Miz Mamie. I read your story while you was sleeping. Had me both laughing and crying. But your accident's not been good for your penmanship. So, I made you a nice clean copy to send off to that editing man in Saint Louis."

I picked up the stack of paper. "Where did you learn penmanship like this, Genevieve?"

"From Miz Patsy at Lincoln. Or at least I got started there. Had lots of practice since then. Not everybody in my church can write like that, so's I help out from time to time. Work with Miz Patsy on her newspaper from time to time too."

I was stunned. Even in my better days, I'd never been able to write as well as Genevieve. "Will you make me another copy for my files?"

"Sure thang." Her grin deepened her dimples. "You pay me to be here. Whether I wash dishes, help you up and down those stairs, or make copies for you, makes no difference to me."

I felt my excitement grow. "Okay, deal. Would you address the envelope and post it on your way home?"

"Be glad to. This be more fun than some other things white folks want me to do.

8

July 15, 1911
Squire Kate has no use for 'blue laws,' hobble skirts, harem skirts, or Dr.
Mary Walker costumes. "I am against the suffragette idea, and do not desire
to see women voting."

Southwest American

September 28, 1911
George Sparks' Dream To Be Realized with Opening of the New Theater

Mamie McGrath, *Southwest American*

September 29, 1911

"IT'S SO EXCITING." CAROLINE LEANED over my shoulder as I tapped at the shiny new typewriter Julian had bought me. "I've never been to an opening show before. Wilbur was such a homebody."

I was excited too. Julian had pitched the idea of a column designed to appeal to women, written by a woman, meaning me—to Colonel Parker. This piece about the New Theater would be a trial run to see if what I did would interest the ladies of Fort Smith. "Have you decided what you're going to wear?"

"I think the green silk. It's too dressy for every day and inappropriate for mass. I can't let Abigail outdo me, you know." Caroline had changed her mind twice in the last twenty-four hours. "What about you?"

"The burgundy lace. It's fancy and I haven't worn it much because of the baby and then the accident. And it doesn't require a corset which is easier for me."

"Does the arm still hurt, dear?"

I wiggled my fingers. "Not as much. Typing is easier than lacing up a corset, though."

"We'll need to choose our hats carefully. I hear they make you take them off if they're too big. Something about making it easier for the folks behind you to see the stage."

I sat back in my chair, thinking about my carefully-selected head piece with dark netting to soften the visual impact of my scar.

"It'll be fine." Caroline whispered in my ear.

"Do you really think so?"

She brushed my hair back from my cheek. "It's not so bad we can't hide it with a little powder. It makes you look interesting."

"I don't want to scare the horses." Joking about the scar made me feel less ugly.

"It's just during the show," Caroline said. "All eyes will be on the stage."

I slipped paper into the typewriter. "I'll think about it."

Caroline sat down on the couch behind me with a cup of tea and the morning newspaper. I typed, "Fort Smith's Pride - The New Theater."

"What did you say used to be at the site where they built the theater?" I turned around in my seat to face her.

"The Old Red Mill," Caroline said. "Was there as long as I can remember. Patsy and I used to walk past it to go shopping. I heard they used it for a hospital to take care of soldiers during the war. The cyclone got it and they finally tore it down just before you moved here. It wasn't nearly as swell as this theater, though."

"It's sad that Mr. Sparks didn't live to see it. It must be bitter-sweet for his family." I turned back to the typewriter and tapped, Red Mill Inn.

"Della Carr told me that Andy told her that George Sparks got the idea from a theater in New York." Caroline examined an ad in the newspaper. "Thought it would liven up Fort Smith to have one like it. It's supposed to be beautiful on the inside."

"Mr. Sparks must have been quite a fellow. He was young to be a bank president."

"George was a good businessman. He and Annie did a lot for Fort Smith. Abigail knew her well. They were in the Daughters of the Confederacy together."

"Abigail?" I tried not to giggle.

Caroline smiled. "Oh yes, the group raised money for the statue that sits on the courthouse lawn. It was supposed to replace the one in the National Cemetery that the cyclone took, but the Secretary of War at the time wouldn't let them put it there. Something about the inscription they put on it."

"I bet that was a row."

"It was. Abigail was in a tizzy for weeks." Caroline shook her head. "She called Secretary Root everything from a polecat to a rattler's belly. The ladies were so upset that the town wrote a special ordinance allowing them to put it on the courthouse lawn."

"Why they don't let it go, I'll never know. No statue is going to bring back those boys."

"Whoo, girl. I agree with you on that one. Wilbur's folks were Union. Fort Smith was a Union town before all that fussin' got started. But it's still touchy around here, so you ought to keep those opinions to your self. Abigail and her friends will get themselves tied up in a knot and you'll never hear the end of it."

I stared at the blank sheet of paper in the typewriter awaiting my eloquence. "Any interesting stories about Mr. Sparks?"

Caroline lowered her lorgnette. "Hm. Other than being rich as the dickens?"

I nodded.

"Well, after Annie died, George started taking his daughter with him when he traveled. Around about 1907 or so, he and Medora went to California for business. While they were there, they decided to take a short vacation up to Portland, Oregon where they had friends."

I looked up. "Medora Sparks?"

Caroline nodded.

"I know her. We met at a party Julian and I went to with Burley last year."

"I'm not surprised," Caroline said. "She's about your age."

"She's lovely."

"Yes, she is."

"So?"

Caroline looked confused.

"Medora and her father were on vacation?"

"Oh yes. They were on the SS Columbia. It was supposed to be modern, complete with electric light bulbs. It'd had a series of small accidents but whatever those problems were, they were supposed to have been resolved. It was foggy the night it happened. I don't remember if the ship was at fault or the ship's captain. Either way, they were rammed by a freighter. Both George and Medora ended up in the water. George got Medora up on a raft or boat or something, but must have swallowed too much water while doing it. Drowned right in front of that sweet young girl."

"Oh, no. I hadn't heard how he died. Guess I thought he was sick."

"It was a horrible tragedy. Lots of people were killed. Medora was young and strong. Only about fifteen or so at the time. It must have been terrifying. My heart went out to her and her brothers. They lost both parents within four years."

"So what's Mr. Sparks' connection to the New Theater?"

"After he died in 1907, they created a foundation to finish what he started. The theater will support his children."

I leaned on my elbow. Images of Medora and her father fighting the cold, dark water filled my mind. I wondered if the pretty young girl dancing with Burley at that party would be willing to share her story with me. I made a note in my diary to call Medora next week. Maybe I could write an article about the tragedy and tie it into the opening night of the theater her father had envisioned.

* * *

"How did you ever afford it?" I held a large diamond and emerald broach in the palm of my hand.

"Don't you like it?" Julian was a terrible poker player. His left eye twitched when he was anxious.

"I adore it!" I held it against the bodice of my shirtwaist. It was bulky. Not at all like the delicate jewelry my husband usually gave me.

"It belonged to my grandmother Kathleen McGrath. She brought it over from Ireland hidden in a compartment she carved from the pages of her Bible.

I lowered the broach to simulate wearing it as a pendant. "Why did she do that?"

"They were her grandmother's. A gift from a wealthy suitor who died before they could announce the banns. They say that neither of them ever wore it. Perhaps they were afraid to go about with such an expensive piece on display."

I tried not to sigh. "Perhaps."

He dropped his eyes. "I thought that maybe—"

"I love it, Julian—and you." I kissed his cheek. "I'll cherish it."

"You don't have to wear it. My great grandmother was quite stout. I imagine that's why it's so big."

"I'll wear it. I promise."

He put his arms around me and laid his cheek on the top of my head. "I've nearly lost you twice. Maybe it'll be your lucky charm."

I doubted the ugly old thing had ever had any charm, lucky or not. "I got lucky the day we met, Julian."

"No more accidents, then. I can't stand seeing you hurt."

A tear spilled out of my right eye and wet my cheek. "I promise."

* * *

I sat at my dressing table, staring into the mirror. Although completely healed, the scar was an angry red welt. I ran my finger across it. No amount of powder was going to hide it and it was never going to go away.

I'd bought yards of soft black netting to add to my hats. I twisted it loosely around the crown of my largest evening hat, looking for a way to drape it subtly across the left side of my face. Frowning, I turned my head first left and then right.

"You're still beautiful."

I jumped and spun around. "It's not that, Patsy. Really."

"What then?" She sat down in Caroline's rocking chair that Julian had moved into our room during my recovery.

"I'm different now. The scar's the most visible change, but it's more than vanity."

Patsy took off her straw hat and laid it on her lap. "How're you different?"

I turned back to the mirror. "I'm stronger than before. More interested in things like politics and—" I paused, searching for the right words to explain how I felt. "—how people really are."

Patsy didn't laugh like I thought she might. "It's more than that, isn't it?"

Watching the reflection of her eyes in the mirror, I nodded. "Up until now, things happened to me. Julian. Our lost babies. Caroline. Sarge. Even you and Abigail and Garland. I never sought out any of you. You all came into my life like tornadoes, rearranging my world by your very existence."

"And now?" Patsy's voice was soft and reassuring.

"Now I feel like making things happen for myself."

"You might run into a few roadblocks, you know. There are rules about that."

I took a deep breath. "Then I guess I better learn to push harder."

"Where do you start?"

I thought for a moment. "With what I write."

"What will you write about then?"

"Things that matter."

"Good for you." Patsy stood up. "You inspire me."

As the door closed behind her, I whispered to myself, "No, you inspire me, Patsy."

I threw open my chiffarobe. I found the burgundy lace dress I intended to wear to opening night at the New Theater and laid it across the bed. It was simple and modest. Something I'd bought long before my accident, it no longer suited the person I was now. I inspected the two hats that were dressy enough for such an event. Both were black and understated.

"Maybe the first step isn't what I choose to write about after all," I muttered to myself.

* * *

Caroline stood at the bottom of the stairs. "Are you ready?"

"I'm coming."

I dipped my pinkie into the small pot of rouge I'd bought at the Boston Store and rubbed color onto my lips and cheeks. Then I powdered over it to make it seem less obvious. I smiled at myself in the mirror. I looked and felt healthier than I had in a long time. Not wearing a hat for an evening out wasn't unheard of, but the way I'd wrapped the netting into a turban secured with a small bow was unusual. So was the use of Julian's Grandmother's broach to hide the knot. Other than my wedding band, I chose not to wear any other jewelry. The look was formal, unusual, and flattering to my face.

I headed down the stairs, pulling on my elbow-length, black leather gloves.

Abigail frowned. "What have you—"

Garland put a hand on Abigail's arm. "You're beautiful, Mamie."

"Thank you, Garland."

Della Carr smiled up from her glass of wine. "Where did you get that outfit? It's stunning."

"My secret," I said merrily. "Where's Andy?"

"Out chasing bad guys as usual." She wore a simple, deep blue silk that showed off her figure and highlighted her complexion "He'll meet us at the restaurant."

"Jennie, how are you? I haven't seen you in ages."

"I'm fine. Just fine." Jennie Williams leaned forward in her seat. "Chasing kids. Our boy Ray was such an easy baby. Now he's a charmer like his daddy. He helps out around the house. Bringing Bebe drawings and me flowers." She glanced at John B affectionately. "But our little Marjory is a character. Rescuing her from angry roosters and getting her down off the roof wears me out."

The mention of children still caused a pang in my heart, determined as I was to go on with my new life.

John B handed me my own glass of Cabernet. "Julian called and said he will meet us for dinner at the Goldman Hotel. He has a deadline."

"I was afraid of that." I took a sip of the dark red wine. "He took his dinner clothes with him this morning just in case. This is delicious, by the way."

"John B brought it for us." Caroline gave me a quick kiss on the cheek. "You'll have to show me how to do that with my hair, my dear."

It was the first time she'd ever asked me to teach her anything. "Thank you, Caroline. Your opinion matters." Her support felt good.

"Where did you get those jewels, Mamie?" Abigail gestured with her glass. "They are exquisite."

I touched the broach above my forehead. "Julian gave them to me this morning."

Abigail leaned down to examine them. "Those emeralds match your eyes."

"I'm sure that's what he was thinking when he gave them to me."

* * *

Newly-installed electric lights lit up Fort Smith as our caravan of automobiles and carriages approached Immaculate Conception Church.

"This town has certainly changed in the last few years," Garland said over his shoulder as we paused at the intersection of Rogers and Garrison Avenue. "First the Goldman Hotel, then the new First National Bank, now the New Theater. People are starting businesses and hiring employees. I smell money."

"And there's more higher-class activities on the Avenue every day. When we close down those bars and saloons, a lady will be able to walk down Garrison without being accosted by drunks and thieves and ne'er-do-wells." Even though she loved her port, Abigail had just been elected secretary of the local Women's Christian Temperance Union—and she'd become annoyingly passionate about her new mission.

Garland sighed.

I smothered a giggle since Garland loved booze as much as Sarge. They were a strange pair—Abigail and Garland. I made a note to ask Caroline how they ever got together.

Abigail turned around in her seat to further lecture us on the finer qualities of Fort Smith. "We have political groups, ladies' social events, theaters. More and more people with means are moving here. Better neighborhoods, finer civic facilities. We are no longer the rowdy western town we were ten years ago."

"Yes, dear." Caroline gazed out her window. "We are becoming more modern every day."

I sank back into the leather seats of Garland's Buick. *And I'm becoming modern too.*

As we approached the church, I saw Sanford Lewis waiting at the trolley stop a half block away. He was smiling down at a small Negro woman. "If he looks up, I'll wave," the new me thought. But when the trolley arrived, a well-dressed white man sitting on a bench, stood up and elbowed past them to board first. Then a white family with three children hurried to board before them, taking the five last seats.

As the conductor turned Sanford and his friend away, the old me realized that not even the new me could change the world. I stared at my hands. They were still folded in my lap. I was ashamed but I didn't dare wave to a colored person in public. I watched as the two teenagers stepped back onto the sidewalk to wait for the next car.

Garland turned onto North Thirteenth Street and pulled up to the curb in front of the Goldman Hotel. "The Talbot party," he said to the doorman who helped us out of the car. "There are four more in the automobile behind us."

"Yes, sir."

When we'd all arrived, the doorman escorted us into the hotel. "The dining room is to the right, sir."

"Go on," Sarge said. "I need to take care of a few things. I'll join you in the dining room."

"Do you need help?"

"Even if I did, I wouldn't expect it of you." He was sobering up at last. "You go enjoy yourself. Miz Peach will take care of me."

I squeezed his shoulder. "We'll see you in a few minutes."

As we crossed the lobby, an elegant couple approached us with wide smiles. Abigail extended her hand, but the woman brushed past her. "You are the talk of the town, my dear."

It wasn't until the woman touched my arm that I realized she was talking to me.

"The way you saved that child. We've been looking forward to seeing you up and healthy again," her husband said. "You and Julian must join us for dinner one of these days."

I blushed. "We'd love to, Mr. Sicard, Mrs. Sicard."

"It's Fred and Ella,'" Mrs. Sicard said.

"Thank you, Ella."

"I'll send an invitation next week."

The Sicards turned to Caroline, John B and Jennie, and Della.

Ella squeezed Della's hand. "We can't thank Andy enough for his dedication to keeping Fort Smith a safe place to do business. Father often reads about Judge Freer's court cases in the newspaper —and tells us about Andy's antics."

"He lives for his job," Della responded as she often did to Andy's admirers.

"You must worry."

Della's wide smile faded. "I do—but he wouldn't be happy doing anything else."

"We wish you well, dear." Ella turned to me again. "I've come to expect Andy's heroics, Mamie. But you move me to do more myself."

I bit back tears. "Thank you, Mrs. Sicard—Ella."

"We have to rush. Father is waiting. We'll see you soon."

"Soon." My smile was still crooked from the partially-healed gash on my cheek and my desire to hide my broken tooth, but I was thrilled that the daughter of the President of the First National Bank knew who I was. Maybe the worst of my long ordeal was over.

* * *

Abigail glared at me as the Sicards hurried to join Mr. and Mrs. McCloud who were being escorted into dinner.

I pretended not to notice and followed Caroline toward the restaurant.

At the dining room door, the host gestured toward our table. "I believe three of your party have already arrived."

Julian, Burley, and Andy rose as we approached.

"My God, you're lovely." Julian kissed my cheek and led me to a seat beside his.

Likewise, Andy greeted Della affectionately and guided her to a chair between his and mine.

I expected Burley to be alone, but there was an empty place setting next to him. I gestured toward it with my head and raised my eyebrows. He blushed and shrugged. "Just a friend," he mouthed.

"Of course." I wondered which young woman had hooked him for the evening.

"I'm glad to see you back in the pink, Mamie. You look wonderful." Burley's compliment was unexpected. My first impulse was to touch my cheek, but I resisted it and this time I wasn't as worried about my smile.

John B sat between Jennie and Caroline, joking about his good fortune. Women loved John B. He was confident, amusing and handsome. At social events, he made sure every lady had a drink and subjected her to three full minutes of his semi-flirtatious charm. If there was dancing, he made sure every unescorted woman—plain or beautiful, young or old—got a chance to dance. Jennie didn't seem to mind. In fact, she seemed proud of his social generosity. They'd been married several years, but he treated her like she was the prettiest girl in the room. I hoped Julian still sent loving glances my way in ten years.

Abigail and Garland, however, weren't having a good evening. She was in an extraordinarily bad mood. Nothing met her expectations, not even their position at the large round table between Jennie

Williams and me. She wrinkled her nose when Garland ordered whiskey. He ignored her glare and tossed it down in a single gulp. She sent the waiter back twice until he found the fancy tea she wanted, then she made another face at her first taste. "Needs more sugar," she explained when she realized we were all watching her.

"Mamie. Julian." Fagan Bourland was working the crowd, stopping at each table to speak with his constituents.

Julian rose to shake his hand. "Nice to see you, May..."

"Oh Mr. Mayor. It's wonderful to see you." Abigail pushed back her chair and hurried around Julian to grab Mr. Bourland's hand. "Did you get my invitation to speak at the Women's Christian Temperance Union meeting in August?"

At first, the diminutive mayor retrieved his hand from her grasp and said, "No, I didn't." With that, he moved on to the next table.

Abigail flushed. "I'll send another invitation on Monday," she said to no one in particular as she sat back down beside Garland.

"Ever the politician," Burley said behind his hand.

"He loves pressing the flesh," Julian muttered. "But don't expect anything of him. It's all about him."

Mayor Bourland was talking up Ella Sicard a few tables away from us. She was polite and responsive, but something about her posture made me think she found him as tedious as I did. I'd lived in Fort Smith long enough to have heard about his scandalous love triangle that led to a murder. Fagan Bourland had no right to put on such airs.

I glanced at Abigail. As annoying as she was sometimes, I thought how the mayor treated her was unforgivably cruel. I wanted to comfort her, but couldn't think of anything to say that wouldn't make her feel worse.

"I'm planning on attending that meeting," Caroline said a little too loudly.

"Me too." Della Carr wasn't known to care much about politics.

"And me." Jennie Williams folded her hands on the table.

None of these women thought much about whiskey one way or another. They were simply comforting a friend in a way that she would value.

I swallowed the lump in my throat. "And I."

Julian squeezed my hand under the table.

"I'm a veteran," Sarge bellowed. "If I want a nip to chase away the demons, what's wrong with that?"

Heads turned as Miss Peach pushed the old man toward our table.

"Now there's the reason we should all support the Temperance Union." My voice was louder than I intended and everyone at our table and those surrounding us laughed.

Miss Peach must have heard my flippant comment too because she avoided my eyes to keep from laughing. Her reaction was endearing—and after all, she'd taken care of me during both my crises. I suddenly wanted to learn more about her as she pushed Sarge up to the spot at the table the waiter had prepared for him. She locked the wheels in place, stood up and turned to go.

"Won't you stay and eat with us, Miss Peach?"

"Mamie!" Abigail whispered loudly.

Miss Peach looked left and right as if afraid someone had heard my comment. "No ma'am. But thank you kindly. I packed my own dinner."

"You are welcome to join us anytime."

"Oh no, ma'am. Really. No need to cause trouble."

"Trouble?"

The table was quiet as Miss Peach made a quick exit.

"Mamie, you're a damned fool," Sarge growled as he picked up his menu.

"Why?"

Julian tugged at my sleeve. It was only when I saw his concern that I realized Miss Peach—even though she had light-skin and freckles—was a Negress all the same.

I glanced around the table. Everyone was quiet. John B avoided my eyes.

As I contemplated my almost unrecoverable faux pas, the silence at our table drowned out the murmurings of the crowd around us. Then, Jennie Williams turned to John B and asked what he wanted for dinner. As everyone began talking again and the tension drained away, I caught her eye and mouthed, 'Thank you."

Chief of Police Bryant Barry was a welcome distraction. He followed the mayor around the room—shaking hands and smiling at the diners. With his white beard and gracious manners, he reminded me of my father. Unlike the mayor who seemed high strung, the Chief was relaxed and I felt comfortable in his presence. More importantly, he was kind to Abigail—and he distracted those around me from talking about my embarrassing social mistake.

Two other men waited while Mayor Bourland and Chief Barry busied themselves with the art of politics. Cathey Pitcock, the policeman who'd left flowers on Mr. Guckenheimer's coffin in that strange non-funeral funeral, seemed bored. I recognized the other man as Mr. Orrin Fellows who'd attended Mr. Guckenheimer's visitation in our parlor.

The mayor and his cronies had just settled into a table toward the front of the room when the maitre d' guided a beautiful young woman to the seat next to Burley.

"Mamie, this is the amazing Marie DuVal."

"Mamie." Marie nodded to me as she sat down. "I was so sorry to hear of your accident. I'm glad to see you are back on your feet."

I was in awe. Marie DuVal was an accomplished musician. I'd seen her perform at several events around town. "It's wonderful to be back," I murmured.

"I know how that feels. I had an accident a few years back, you know."

The waiter set a glass of sweet tea in front of me. "No, I didn't know. What happened?"

"A gas stove exploded. The back of my dress caught fire. It hurt so bad, I thought I was going to die. It took months to recover. I was in California when it happened, and my father, the colonel, had to bring me back by train. Every bump and rattle set my teeth on edge."

"That's awful."

"I got over it."

"You must be so strong." It was almost a whisper. "I was such a baby about my accident."

Marie's posture was straight, her complexion perfect. "I just decided that I wasn't ready to die—and if I was going to live, I better get on with it."

The waiter laid an open menu on the table in front of me. Some of the options were old favorites. Others were dishes I'd either never tasted or ever heard of. I looked up at Julian first—and then Marie. "I think I just made the same decision."

* * *

**For Good Photos Go to the Redner Photo Co,
16 ½ North Sixth, Phone 2260**

*

The New Theater entrance was on North Tenth Street, three blocks west of the Goldman Hotel and not far from John B's Horse and Mule Barn. After our fancy meal, Julian and I decided to walk. Electric street lights and bill boards lit Garrison Avenue. The town was as busy at night as it was during the day.

A familiar-looking man touched the brim of his Stetson as he passed us. "Julian. Mamie."

I turned to watch as he hurried down the street. "Who is that man?"

"That's Till Shaw. He owns a saloon—maybe two. He's bought some land from the Sisters of Mercy out on Towson Avenue. However, the original owner willed it to the sisters and the children of the lady who died are suing them. It's a mess. All Till wants to do is open a business on that land and the deal has been delayed time and again. It's in the paper all ..."

"No," I interrupted. "I know him from somewhere."

"Where?"

"I think he disentangled me from Mr. Fields' wagon."

Julian turned to watch the retreating figure. "Could be. I was so focused on you, I didn't count noses."

"He was kind and reassuring."

"Then I need to thank old Till one of these days."

"It's wonderful to be out and about." I slid my hand through Julian's crooked arm. "I've missed it."

"There's nothing like strolling down the avenue with my girl."

I gestured to the left with my head. "Such a difference between the atmosphere on that side of the Avenue and this one."

Saloons and bars on Texas Corner, where Towson intersected with Garrison, were alive with activity. As we watched, a large Negro man staggered out to the curb and unfastened his belt.

"Oh my God, what's he doing?"

"Turn your head, Mamie." Julian sounded angry. "He's urinating off the curb."

"In sight of where Fort Smith's fanciest people are gathering to celebrate the realization of George Sparks' dream theater?" The idea was outrageous—and funny.

A Fort Smith policeman yelled and shook a baton at the drunk. The Negro ignored him and continued with his business.

"When you put it that way, it's pretty ironic." Julian's anger melted away as we watched the cop grab the man by his shirt collar and drag him away from the curb, midstream. "Medora's dad was so into architecture and bringing business and class to Fort Smith. He's probably rolling over in his grave."

The cop threw the drunk against the front of the building and began beating him with his baton. The stunned man cringed, ducking and shielding his face with his forearms.

"Why is he beating that man?" I took a step forward.

"Where do you think you're going?" Julian pulled me back, "You're half his size."

I struggled to pull free from Julian's grasp. "He was just peeing in the street, not murdering someone."

"I'll take care of it, but you stay here."

I nodded, but when he released me, I took a step forward.

"Don't even think of it, Mamie. They are both dangerous right now. I said I'll take care of it and I will."

Under Julian's arm, I could see the cop still whaling on the Negro who was covering his face with both hands—and sliding down the wall onto his bottom.

Julian was halfway across the avenue, dodging automobiles and carriages, when two more policemen arrived. They pulled the first cop off the Negro and lifted the big man to his feet. I saw a flash of red and realized his face had been bloodied.

I ran across the street myself, passing Julian and narrowly-avoiding being rundown by Jim Brewer's fancy automobile as he crossed Garrison to short Towson.

"Mamie, you're going to get yourself killed if you don't change your ways."

"Sorry, Jim."

He headed toward his business on North Tenth and B.

"Mamie!" Julian was close behind me now.

The two new cops each took one of the Negro's arms and the original cop began beating him again—this time with his fists.

"Stop it, you're hurting him." I pummeled the burly cop's bicep with my fists.

Strong arms pulled me away.

The man beating the drunk was Cathey Pitcock, the cop I'd seen with the mayor not an hour before. We faced each other, panting.

"Mrs. McGrath. I know you been through a lot, ma'am—but this won't do. It just won't do."

"You're hurting this man."

Pitcock shrugged and handed me over to Julian who slipped one arm around my waist protectively.

"I'll tell them all." I gestured to the crowd gathering in front of the New Theater on North Tenth, just across the street. "I'll tell the mayor."

Pitcock laughed. "Sorry, you feel that way Miz McGrath. I don't know where you come from, but down here we don't put up with fancy ladies sassing the police over a damn nigger."

"Enough!" Julian stepped between us. "Now if you guarantee us that you'll stop beating this man, Mrs. McGrath and I will go about our business. You can either arrest this man or let him go, but if you continue beating him, I'll arrange for a photographer to follow you around. You won't even know he's there. And he'll take a picture at just the right moment, when you are smooching up some woman or punching a drunk in the face. Then, I'll make sure everyone in this town sees what you've been doing."

Pitcock glanced at me and then back at Julian and then back at me. "Mr. Lacey and Mr. Jarnigan will take this man now. They deal with niggers every night." He motioned for them to take the prisoner away.

"He didn't hurt anyone. He's just drunk. No different from most of the fine gentlemen we dined with at the Goldman tonight."

"Ma'am, I know your health is fragile. You think you know what's what, but you don't know a thing about them people. You ain't got any right interfering with police officers trying to do their duty as best they can." He tapped on the window of the bar with his knuckles and for the first time, I saw wide-eyed faces staring at us through the glass. "See them birds? They're just waiting to see what's gonna happen next. If we let this man do what he was adoin,' why the whole lot of em will be out here with their trousers around their ankles." He snarled at the people inside the bar and they backed away. "Yes, ma'am. You do this kinda thing and one of them bulls are gonna think you're an easy target and then someone's gonna get killed."

"Don't hurt him any more."

Pitcock showed his teeth. "Any thing you say, ma'am." He gestured with his head and Officers Lacey and Jarnigan hefted the drunken Negro to his feet and shoved him into the street.

"Come on, Mamie. It's over now." Julian tugged at my arm.

"Where are they taking him?"

"Jail, ma'am. Unless you want him pissin' on them fancy shoes of yours."

"Come on, darling. You've done what you could." Julian guided me across the avenue.

"I don't like that man."

"Me either," Julian said. "He would've killed that guy if you hadn't stopped them."

"Maybe the other two would've stopped him."

"Maybe."

I turned to him. "I'm sorry I spoiled the evening—again."

"I wish I had your courage, sweetheart—but next time, let's find another cop to break up a fight. They held back because you're a pretty white woman of a certain class. If you were a man, they'd have tossed you in the clink too."

* * *

An impressive crowd had gathered around the entrance of the New Theater. Carriages were lined up all the way to A Street waiting to release their elegantly-appointed passengers.

"There's Medora Sparks." I pointed. "Isn't she lovely tonight?"

"This must be a bittersweet moment for her family," Julian said. "Even more exciting than the dedication of the new First National Bank building last year."

"I'm sure it is."

"The Sparks, the Neys, the Apples, the Licks, the Cravens, the Berrys, the McClouds and Sicards, John B Williams and his brother Leon, George Rye, and other businessmen have invested heavily in Fort Smith. They've built neighborhoods that reflect the dream we share about what this community can be."

"That was lovely." I tugged at his arm. "No matter how long I try, I'll never be able to speak or write like you do."

The corners of Julian's mouth twitched. "Thank you, my dear. We write different things for different audiences."

"It's not that. You see things that I miss. I never thought about what money can mean to a city like Fort Smith."

He laughed. "And I would have been oblivious to what Pitcock was doing to that man. I may have vision, Mamie McGrath, but you have heart."

With Julian's words warming me, I pushed the drunken Negro's plight out of my head and focused on the design of the theater and the crowd filing into it.

* * *

As we took our seats in the middle section, in the third row, the atmosphere in the theater quivered with expectation. I looked around. The stage curtain was an elaborate painted scene. The theater itself was fresh and modern. I glanced at my handsome husband. He must have felt my gaze because he took my hand and squeezed it.

We watched as Fort Smith's most successful citizens, dressed in their finest clothes, filled the auditorium. Medora Sparks and her brothers and their families were given the best seats—not too far from the stage but not too close to the orchestra. Artie Berry and his wife Fannie sat in the row in front of us. The McClouds and the Sicards were right behind the Sparks family.

Burley and Marie were across the aisle from us. I hid a delighted smile behind my gloved hand. They were more interested in each other than they were us—or the play for that matter.

"You think that's the one?"

Julian shrugged. "They certainly have a lot in common."

I opened my program. The play was *The Third Degree*. I turned the page, squinting in the muted light.

"There they are!" Abigail's voice startled me. "Right up front."

Julian stood up and I turned around in my seat.

"There. Don't you see them?" She ignored the usher and elbowed her way around George Rye and his wife as they made their way to their seats.

"Oh, dear."

"Be nice." Julian patted my hand. "It's her first night out as an officer of that non-drinking club she's in."

I laughed. "Like anyone but her fellow members would know that."

"Shush." Julian held a finger to his lips. "Madam Secretary has arrived."

"Abigail was afraid we wouldn't be able to sit together, but I told her the seats are numbered." Garland followed the usher to our row with Caroline and Abigail in tow.

"It's a new theater." Abigail's voice rose. "How could you be sure how Mr. Lick set up things?"

"Chauncey's a good businessman," Garland retorted. "No way would he charge ten bucks a pop for unnumbered seats."

"Be quiet," Abigail practically shouted. "You want everyone in town to think you're a cheapskate?"

Red-faced, Caroline scuttled past Julian and then me, sitting in the seat right next to mine, thank goodness.

"Whoever designed this place must have been mad. Green and lavender? A burgundy ceiling? Really?" Abigail stepped on my feet as she squeezed past, the feathers on her Merry Widow blocking out the lights for a moment.

"Where's Andy and Della?"

"They're a few rows back." Caroline patted my hand. "Just in case Andy gets antsy and wants to leave."

"And John B and Jennie?"

"John B wanted to stop by the Pony Express first. Check on something, I guess. They'll be along soon."

I glanced at Julian who smothered a smile. We both knew that was an excuse to get away from the quarreling Talbots.

"It's from *Midsummer Night's Dream*," Caroline said behind her hand.

I cupped my ear with my hand. "What?"

"The painting on the fire curtain. It's from *A Midsummer Night's Dream*. You know, Shakespeare?"

I stared at the painting, mesmerized. It was lovely. "I've never read it, I'm sorry to say. What's it about?"

Caroline thought for a moment. "Transformation."

I inhaled and sat back in my seat. *Yes. Transformation.*

"Are you okay?" Julian's eyes were filled with concern.

I smiled at him. "Yes, my love. I think I'm finally okay."

He lifted my fingers to his lips and kissed my knuckles. "At long last."

* * *

"Wasn't Garland behind you?" Abigail twisted her handkerchief. "I thought you went for the automobiles together."

"No, ma'am." John B held open the door of his carriage so Andy and Della could climb in. "But Jennie and I sat in the last row of the theater. We were the first out."

"There's lots of folks downtown tonight, Abigail. And it's a bit of a walk to where he parked near the Goldman," Jennie said as John B helped her into their vehicle. "John B left our carriage at the Horse and Mule Barn. That's closer."

"If he doesn't show soon, call a hack and get these ladies on home," John B said to Julian behind his hand. "Or go down to the Pony Express and call me to come get you. Manny McKnight is there cleaning up until 10:30."

"We'll be fine. The trolley is still running as well." Julian put his arm around my shoulders.

Andy stuck his head out the window. "It was a great night for Fort Smith. You better say that in your article—for old George Sparks' sake."

"You know I will." Julian tipped his hat.

John B clicked at the horses and they eased into the slow-moving traffic on North Tenth.

"Miz Mamie, I'm taking this old coot home. It's not that far." Miss Peach looked tired herself. She probably had the old man tucked in by eight most nights.

"Did you enjoy the play, Sarge?"

He yawned. "It was long."

"Say good-bye, Mr. Eacret." Miss Peach turned the wheelchair around and headed up the Avenue toward Immaculate Conception Church.

"Bye!" Sarge's wave was limp.

"He doesn't look well." I stared after them.

"He's tired. He'll be out arguing about Massard Prairie tomorrow," Julian said.

"Where do you think Garland is?"

"I really don't know, Mamie." Abigail's frustration with Garland had made her snappish. "He said he'd bring the automobile around right away."

"There's still considerable traffic," Caroline consoled her. "Let's relax and enjoy the night air."

The crowd had begun to thin when Garland stumbled around the corner of Garrison and North Tenth.

Abigail took a step toward him. "Garland?"

Garland's elegant shirt was stained and hanging out of this trousers—and his nose was bleeding. "I'm fine." He tripped and would have fallen except for Abigail catching him and Julian grabbing his arm. "I jes had a lil run-in with a one-armed bandit."

"Is everything okay over there, Mamie?" Medora Sparks called from a carriage.

"We're good, thanks. Garland tripped. That's all."

"Hope y'all had a good time."

"We did. The theater is just beautiful."

"It is, isn it?" Medora leaned back in her seat.

We stood there like everything was fine until Medora's carriage disappeared onto Rogers before we turned back to Garland.

"Are you hurt?" Abigail seemed more angry than concerned. "Did he steal your wallet?"

"Who?"

"The bandit."

"It was a slot machine, woman. Not a real person."

Abigail's face flushed. "You gambled instead of fetching our car?"

Garland swayed back on his heels. "More like I jes opened up my change purse and dumped it in the river."

"How did you get this drunk so fast?" Abigail dusted sawdust off his lapel.

"I worked at it." He belched.

"I thought that lawyer—"

"Little." Julian interrupted me. "Paul Little."

"That's the one." Garland spun on me, bristling with drunken indignation. "No slot machines. No bootlegging. No drinking in Fort Smith at all if he gets his way. Gonna run some good people right outta business. Someone oughta put a bullet in that son of a..."

"Garland!" The electric lights glinted off Abigail's monocle. "Lower your voice."

"I can do and think what I want."

Abigail straightened her shoulders and lifted her chin. "You forget that I am an officer of—"

"Never happen," he growled. "No matter what laws you pass, people love their whiskey."

"Yes, I know." She wrinkled her nose. "You stink of it—"

People peered out of the window of Northum's saloon. And a cop stood in the middle of Garrison, watching us.

Julian waved at him. "Just a little family tussle, Officer Lacey."

The policeman nodded. "Keep it down to a roar. Lots of fancy folks in town tonight."

Julian smiled and said through his teeth. "And some fancy people behaving badly."

Anxious lest Julian's sarcasm further agitate the Talbots, I tugged at his sleeve. "Shush."

Garland covered his mouth and backed away from us.

"What is it?" Abigail's voice went from angry to concerned. "Are you okay?"

Garland heaved twice before he threw up his expensive meal from the Goldman onto the street. Then he staggered backward until he felt the brick wall of the theater and slid down it until he was sitting on the sidewalk.

"Garland, darling." Abigail produced her handkerchief and knelt to wipe his face. "Why didn't you come get us?" When he seemed to be recovering, she straightened his collar. "The show's been over for an hour."

Actually, it was more like thirty minutes, but I chose not to point that out.

Garland put his elbows on his knees and covered his face with his hands. "When I came out of the theater, that pretty lil thing that works at Miss Laura's was waiting for me. You know the one with the mole there?" He nearly poked himself in the eye.

He had to be talking about Anna Marie Cavanaugh. Miss Angelica. After I helped her with the burned man hiding in Miss Laura's basement, she called again a couple months before my accident. She'd decided to learn to read and write and asked me where to start. I sent Manny to deliver a primer from my youth and she called yet again to thank me.

Abigail's eyes widened. "Miss Laura's?"

"She said a friend of hers wanted to talk to me."

"So you just went off with her to who knows where?"

"My mama taught me to be a gentleman." He belched and we all winced, half expecting another torrent of vomit.

Caroline touched Abigail's shoulder—her voice low. "We should go now."

Abigail shrugged off her hand and stared down at Garland. "Where did she take you?"

"To see Orrin Fellows." Garland hung his head. "At Till Shaw's. I owe him some money and he wanted to see me."

"For what this time?"

"Cards."

"So, slot machines, whiskey and now cards?" Abigail stamped her foot. "How much do you owe now?"

"Look," Julian interrupted. "This isn't any of our business. We shouldn't be hearing this."

"Stay." Abigail pointed at us.

"No," Julian insisted. "We have to go home. This is Mamie's first night out, and she's exhausted. Where's the car?"

"Gone." Garland spun around, facing back down Garrison toward the river. He stood there a moment, blinking—before he turned to face us again.

For once, Abigail was speechless.

"Garland, what happened to your car?" Caroline stepped between them. "Where is it?"

Tears filled Garland's eyes. "I don't know."

I gave Julian a gentle push and he stepped forward.

"Did you park it back at the Goldman? Near the church? I'll go get it."

"They took it, Julian."

"Who?"

"Orrin and that little whore from Miss Laura's."

"Why? How?"

"I owed Orrin more than a lil money." He wiped his upper lip with his shirt tail. "A lot more money than that one-armed bandit had in it. More than I could win if I was any good at poker."

"You sure you're not making a mountain out of a mole hill?" Abigail huffed.

"It's complicated, sugar. He thinks I stole Mr. Guckenheimer."

"You stole a body?"

Garland leaned against the building. "It wasn't me. Mr. Guckenheimer didn't arrive in Tulsa intact after the funeral a few months back."

"Someone cut him up?"

Julian coughed into his fist.

"No, of course not. The coffin arrived but—uh, Mr. Guckenheimer didn't. And Orrin is blaming me."

"Why would—"

Julian caught my eye and shook his head.

I bit my lip.

Abigail put a hand on Garland's shoulder. "So they took your car?"

"I'm sorry, sweetheart." A tear rolled down Garland's cheek. "They already had it out front of Till's and when I couldn't produce the money, Orrin gave that—lady—the eye. She stepped outside and gave the driver the signal. It was headed down Towson last I saw it."

All anger drained out of Abigail and she took him into her arms. "There, there."

"I loved that Buick."

"I know you did." She patted his back. "We'll find it."

"You think we can?"

"Of course. And if we don't, we'll survive. We always do."

* * *

Julian and I left Caroline and the Talbots in front of the theater and hurried towards John B's Horse and Mule Barn, less than a block away.

"Why we put up with them is beyond me," Julian growled.

"Abigail is your mother's friend." I struggled to avoid cracks and bumps in the street.

"Ha!"

"Seriously, Julian. Caroline is fond of Abigail." I winced. His grip on my hand hurt and the heel of my left foot had pulled out of my shoe.

"My mother is the kindest human being on earth. The Talbots—both of them—take advantage of that." He quickened his pace and I hobbled along behind him.

"Caroline is a strong woman," I puffed. "No one takes advanta—"

Julian stopped dead still and I would have passed him up but for the fact he held fast to my hand. "So now you're telling me about my mo—" His frown faded. "Oh, Mamie. What am I doing, yelling at you?"

I peeled his fingers off my hand. "Indeed."

"I'm sorry."

I straightened the turban covering my hair and slipped my foot deeper into my shoe.

"This was supposed to be a nice evening, but they ruined it. And now, I've hurt you."

"I'm fine, Julian."

"You're sure?"

I considered my words. We seldom argued and I knew the Talbots were the source of his foul mood. "I'm not quite ready to run like this."

"I know."

"They're so miserable with each other, they make everyone else miserable too."

He waited while I caught my breath. "Are you ready?"

"Either leave me here or go slower."

Behind us, the New Theater lights went out and a second later, John B's Mule and Horse barn lights flickered out too.

"I'm not leaving you here in the dark."

I folded my arms across my chest.

He pulled out his pocket watch and squinted at it. "It can't be ten thirty yet. I guess Manny's not one to stick around without supervision."

"Should we head back to the Goldman? There'll be taxis there."

"Can you make it?"

I sighed. "If you give me a minute to pull myself together."

He checked his watch again.

"Dark is dark." I chuckled.

He shrugged—and put the watch back in his pocket.

A half block in front of us, the Arkansas Garage was still lit up—and of course, a half block behind us the bars and saloons on Garrison Avenue glittered.

"Ready now?"

I took a step toward the Arkansas Garage and its lights went off too. "I guess that fixes that." I turned around to head back to Garrison where Caroline and the Talbots awaited us.

Julian took my elbow, far more gently than he had my hand when we started this fool's errand. "No reason to hurry now."

A sudden roar behind us made me jump. "What's that?" I spun around to see a set of headlights pulling out of the Arkansas Garage and heading our way. I turned back and limped a few steps toward Garrison.

The automobile pulled up beside us. "Is that Julian McGrath skulking out here in the dark?"

"It's me and my best girl, Jim. We're in a bit of a fix. Think you could give an old friend a ride?"

"Hop in." Jim Brewer leaned across the seat and threw open the door. "Think you can make it, Mamie?"

"If it means I don't have to wander around in the dark trying to keep up with my long-legged husband, I'll find a way to get in."

Julian put his hands around my waist and boosted me into the backseat. "What kind of car is this?"

"Any kind you want to make it," Jim said as Julian went around to claim the other front seat. "In my house, we call it a race car."

"It's quite different from the Boehmer." I ran my hand over the nice leather upholstery. "Does it go very fast?"

"Just got it in day before yesterday. They say it can go sixty miles in an hour, but I haven't taken it out to see that for myself yet."

"Sixty, you say?" Julian patted the dash. "That would be some race."

"JW and I are planning a little road trip next spring to check these babies out. Gonna see how fast it'll take to get to Waldron and back." He pulled up to the corner of Tenth and Garrison.

Caroline was standing there alone.

Julian opened the door. "They left you here?"

She held up her arms and Julian lifted her up to the first step. She squeezed into the seat beside me. "Mr. Pitcock came by and Abigail told him all about Orrin Fellows stealing Garland's car. He said he would take care of it for a piece of Mr. Guckenheimer's take. And Garland said that was okay with him as long as he got the Buick back tonight. So they went off with him. Abigail was planning on bashing Mr. Fellows' head in with her parasol. Good thing she didn't bring it with her to the theater." She paused to catch her breath.

"I can't believe he left you alone on Garrison this time of night." Julian fumed.

"It was no problem. Mr. Stewart, the gentleman who owns the barbershop, came by with Sandy Lewis. They said it wasn't proper for them to talk but they'd watch out for me. See?" She gestured with her head.

Sure enough, the men sat on a wagon, talking with each other, while keeping an eye on Caroline at the same time.

"That was nice of them."

"Very." Julian nodded to them as Jim turned left onto Garrison and headed toward Rogers.

Bert Stewart touched the brim of his hat. Sandy clicked to the horses and they headed out to wherever black people lived in Fort Smith.

"And dangerous for them," Jim said as he fussed with the gears.

"It's a shame," I murmured.

"It's the way it's always been. No sense in changing now."

We veered right at Immaculate Conception Church and headed out Rogers toward Lecter Avenue.

"Does this automobile have a name?" I broke the silence.

"This here's a 1911 Hudson 33. The new version is supposed to have a starter button. Even little things like you could manage that."

I leaned forward and gripped the back of the front seats, "Is that so?"

"Jim, you're gonna get me in trouble again." Julian laughed.

"How hard is it to learn to drive?"

"Not hard at all if you're just driving. Keeping everything working smoothly is the thing. That's why I take JW with me usually. That man is a natural-born mechanic."

I leaned back in my seat, imagining myself driving a magnificent automobile like the Hudson 33.

9

October 24, 1911
Miss Nelly Duff and Mr. Neville Kelly were wed at the Immaculate Concep-
tion Church yesterday morning at 9 am. Miss Marie DuVal played Mendels-
sohn's wedding March as the bridal party entered and exited the church.

Mamie McGrath, *Southwest American*

October 28, 1911

I SAT AT THE KITCHEN table with my pen poised over my note-book. The back gate opened. Sandy and a middle-aged man came up the steps of the screened porch and tapped on the door.

"Good afternoon, Miz Mamie." Sandy took off his cap.

"Good afternoon." I smiled at him through the screen door. "It's a beautiful day, don't you think? Maybe a little chilly, but beautiful."

"Yes, ma'am. It surely is." He paused. "This here is my pa."

The man was an older, huskier version of Sandy. "I'm Webster Lewis, ma'am."

I opened the door. "Come on in and I'll make us some hot chocolate."

"Oh no, ma'am. No need." Webster glanced left and right and over his shoulder before facing me again.

"Don't be silly. It's warm and cozy in the kitchen. I was about to make some anyway."

"Thank you, kindly ma'am," Webster said, "But we don't want any trouble."

"It's okay, really. My mother-in-law is here. And so is my husband. He'll even have hot chocolate with us if that makes you feel better."

Webster smiled. "Yes, ma'am. It would."

I waved them in and opened the door to the house proper. They stepped into the kitchen, looking around and it struck me that Sandy had never been in our home before.

"Please sit." I gestured at the table. "I'll fetch Julian and Caroline."

They sat down across from each other, their hats on their laps. I went up the hall to the front parlor where Julian was reading the newspaper and Caroline was embroidering roses on a handkerchief.

"Julian, Sandy and his father are here. They'd like to talk to us."

He laid down the paper and took off his glasses. "Of course."

"I've said I'll make some hot chocolate. Would you like some too, Caroline?"

She finished her stitch. "That sounds delightful. I'll join you in a minute."

Julian and I went down the hall to the kitchen. Sandy introduced his father to Julian while I rummaged in the ice box.

"Go ahead," I said. "I can work while we talk." I took out a bottle of milk and poured it into a pan.

"I hear you're a preacher," Julian said as they all sat down.

I set the pan on the stove and turned the flame down low.

"I told them about you, Pa." Sandy half-smiled at Mr. Lewis.

I spooned cocoa from the box into a bowl and added sugar and a half-teaspoon of cinnamon to it.

"Hope you didn't tell them I'm a fool for cinnamon in my cocoa." Webster grinned and nodded at me.

"That's the way I know to make it," I said. "Only person who does it better is Miss Caroline there, but she keeps her recipe secret."

"Don't listen to her, Webster," Caroline said from the door to the hall. "That young woman can do anything she sets her mind to."

Webster and Sandy half rose to greet her. "Nice to see you again, ma'am."

"It's been a long time," Caroline said. "Patsy tells me you and Loula have quite a family now."

"We got Sanford here—he's my oldest—and there's four more young'uns back at the farm."

"You must give Loula my love. Tell her I use her recipe for cornbread just about every week."

"Yes, ma'am. I sure will."

Caroline squeezed past the table and took down plates from the cupboard. "I baked some good old-fashioned pear cake this morning. It ought to go great with cocoa."

I glanced at Julian and mouthed, "They're old friends?"

He grinned and shrugged.

Caroline could bring anyone—from the King of England to Italian immigrants to a black sharecropper into her kitchen—and make them feel welcome and comfortable. I folded my arms and chuckled. "Caroline, is there anyone in the state of Arkansas that you don't know?"

"Let me see. I think there's a family from Poland just got here. Friends of the Neys, I hear. Haven't met them yet. I understand they make some kind of stuffed noodle thing."

"Stuffed with what?" Webster played along.

"Mashed potatoes."

"I may not be Irish or Polish but I do like me some mashed potatoes." Webster's laugh was hearty, the kind that made everyone else want to laugh too.

"Until Mama hooks up with the Poles, looks like we're going to have to make do with pear cake." Julian joked back.

Sandy sat across from his father. He seemed pleasant enough but a little lost for words.

"Sandy's done a lot for us the last year."

Sandy shot me a grateful look.

"He's always on time, knows what needs to be done and does it."

Webster winked at Sandy. "Any fool can work. Takes brains to do it right the first time."

"Aw, Pa." Sandy held out his mug for me to fill with chocolate.

"Yeah, he's coming along. Not bad for eighteen. His mama and I are awful proud of this boy."

"Almost nineteen, Pa."

Caroline set her cast iron skillet on the table and removed the kitchen towel she'd used to cover it.

"That smell is heavenly, Mama." Julian grazed her cheek with a kiss. "You know, back when I was a little fellow, I didn't like pecans. Which was a shame because we had this row of pecan trees in the back yard. So Mama started baking them in cakes and pies. And that won me over to her way of thinking pretty fast."

"An old mama trick," Webster said. "Turn what we have into what we want."

Caroline put thick slices onto plates. "Nothing to do with pecans this time. Was all those pears coming ripe." She gave the first two plates to Webster and Sandy, before serving Julian and me.

We waited until she sat down. Then, Julian turned toward Webster. "Would you say the prayer, Reverend?"

"Thank you, son. This is like old times."

Julian glanced at me. "Yes, sir. It is."

Shocked into silence, I bowed my head.

"Almighty Lord. Thank you for this time together with old friends. Bless Mr. Julian and his beautiful wife, Miz Mamie. And send your loving care to Miz Caroline. And see to it that my boy, Sanford, who is standing on the edge of manhood—grows in righteousness every day of his life. Amen."

"Amen," we all echoed.

"That's the white version." Webster winked at me. "The colored version goes on for another twenty minutes."

At first I didn't know what to do, but when Julian chortled, I relaxed and laughed too.

Webster took a sip of the hot chocolate. "See, God—He got a sense of humor, Miz Mamie."

"How's that?"

"I think this here ain't Cinnamon in this cocoa."

"I was so worried about using too much, maybe I didn't use enough?" I took a quick taste of mine. "What *is* that?"

"Aren't you gonna ask me why God has a sense of humor?"

I felt my cheeks flush. "Why does God have a sense of humor?"

"What ever it is, I love it." Webster's cackle made us all laugh.

Caroline sipped her cocoa. "It's chili powder—and Webster's right. It's wonderful."

"How could I have made a mistake like that?" I went to the cupboard where Caroline kept spices. "It's clearly marked, Cinnamon." I held up the canister for effect. "Of course, this isn't the one I used." I held up a second one labeled Hot Pepper Powder. "This one is."

"Whatever it is, it's tasty." Julian held up his mug. "More please?"

Webster poked at Caroline's cake. "You sure there are pears in this here pear cake, Miz Caroline? Seems like there's lots of surprises in this kitchen."

"Only when I'm in it, Mr. Lewis." I laughed and sat down to my spicy hot chocolate and pear cake.

After we finished eating, Webster wiped his mouth with a napkin and leaned back in his seat. "Guess y'all's wondering about why Sanford and me showed up at your door this fine fall day."

"I only wonder why your visits are years apart. Patsy is here just about every week—like the old days. Caroline paused. "Guess those times weren't so good for your folks."

"No, ma'am. Not so much."

"Patsy and I were too young to understand all of that."

"I know."

"Funny world."

"Ma'am, it was your grandpa. Not you. And it was my grandpa, not me."

"Patsy said if it wasn't the white farmers it was the Indians."

I glanced at Julian. He avoided my eyes and I knew the explanation would have to come after our guests left.

"That's a mighty sad subject, Miz Caroline."

"Not all of it. Patsy and I had fun."

Silence filled the kitchen except for the little squeaks the kitchen chairs made when we moved.

"Can we talk about why we came a calling?" Sandy's voice was low and cautious.

I set my cup on the table. "Is there a problem?"

"Not a problem. A question."

"Ya, see, Miz Mamie. Sanford here's a hankering for a better job than working for Joe Alexander or you folks."

I turned to Sandy, "Is it money?"

"Not exactly. Well, that's part of it, of course. I want to learn to drive. If I get good at it, maybe I can get a job chauffeuring the town big wigs around or maybe drive a hack. That's steady and pays more than I make now."

"Have you ever driven a car?"

"Down to the end of Mr. John B Williams' short driveway out on Grand Avenue and back to his house. I was trimming his yard a couple weeks back and Mr. Brewer he showed up in one of them fine automobiles he's selling over at the Arkansas Garage. He asked me to tell Mr. Williams he'd like to talk to him."

"Tell em what old John B said about that," Webster urged.

Sandy laughed in spite of himself. "He said, 'Does that old'— pardon me, Miz Caroline and Miz Mamie, but this is what he said, 'Doesn't that old son of a gun know I make my living off of horse-flesh, not his noisy contraptions?'"

I laughed. "John B will come around. He's an adventurous sort."

"Yes, ma'am,"

"He strikes me as more competitive than adventurous," Julian said. "He might not take out on his own, but he'll give you a run for your money if you challenge him."

"One time Mr. John B was workin' with Deputy Andy to take down some big colored fella who stole a pig from Joe Alexander's Farm." Sanford was more animated than I'd ever seen him. "That boy took out running across the cornfield with the porker under one arm. It was late in the season and them plants was chest high. By the time Deputy Andy and Mr. John B got there, that guy was already across the river. But they pulls out their pistols and starts following his trail, stopping once in awhile for Andy to look over a broken cornstalk. They was in there for an hour—maybe two. When they came back, they was eat up with chiggers and ticks—and sweating worse than the pig that ole boy stole from Joe. I brought em each a jar. John B gulped down all of his and asked for more. Andy drank two or three swallows and splashed the rest on his face. I asked him if he wanted more too—and he said, they needed to get back to searching that cornfield. John B was beet red, but he tells me he don't need anymore either. They combed that cornfield till nearly dark."

"John B's proud," Julian said.

Caroline patted his hand. "Or loyal."

"Miz Caroline, you always could see the good side of things," Webster said. "When I was a little bitty feller, you told my ma that when I played hooky from work to go swimmin,' I was jes enjoying the Almighty's gifts."

I envied the easy companionship Caroline had with her friends—and that she always chose observations about them that were kind.

"Anyway, about the automobile, Sandy." Caroline sat down across from him.

"Yes, ma'am. Mr. Brewer wanted Mr. John B to take a look at the fancy new car so after grumbling about it a bit, he goes out and they talk and while they do, I just had to go peek at it."

"That Hudson's beautiful," I said. "Jim gave us a ride home in it a few weeks ago. The seats are as soft as a puppy's ear."

"Yes, ma'am. They sure are. Anyway, Mr. Jim Brewer convince Mr. John B to go for a ride in it and they waved me to go too."

"And I bet John B loved it."

"Miz, Mamie, that man was in hog heaven. We drove all over his land, and up and down Grand Avenue. Mr. John B is a waving his hat at his kids playin' out in the yard and a hooting and laughing like nobody's business. Miz Jennie, she came out on the porch with her arms crossed, grinning and shaking her head when he honked the horn. It was the funnest day I had done in awhile. Jes riding in that automobile with the wind in my face was great, but then as we pulled up to Mr. John B's porch, he turns around and asks me if I wanted to drive it."

"And you said no," Julian teased.

"Mr. Julian, I was so excited I think my tongue froze up on me. All I could so was bob my head up and down."

"So you drove it?"

"Yes, ma'am. Mr. John B gets in the back seat and I climb into the driver's seat and Mr. Brewer, he explained what I needed to do. Cain't say as I remember all the details but it took me some time to figure out the gears. I wasn't as fast as Mr. John B, mind you—but I drove it down to the end of his driveway and then back. And as I got down outta that automobile, Mr. John B and Mr. Brewer said I did good."

"That's wonderful, Sandy," I said. "And I'm jealous. I'm going to work up the courage to do it one of these days."

"Oh no, ma'am. That's what I came to ask about."

"Ask about what?"

"Sanford here, he wants to learn to drive your car so he can drive you around," Webster said. "He wants to get good at it so he can maybe get to cars or maybe even trucks. He just needs practice."

"Why, I think that's a grand idea." Julian clapped his hands together. "We've been mostly taking the trolley into town lately, but I am sure both Mama and Mamie would prefer to be driven around for their functions."

"But Julian—"

He raised his eyebrows and I knew he preferred to have this conversation privately. "You know our Boehmer is pretty old these days."

"Yes sir." Sandy grinned.

"It's not near as fine as Jim Brewer's Hudson."

"I know, but maybe not so fancy is easier?"

"Or maybe it's more trouble than a new one."

"Maybe." Sandy looked like he was about to burst with anticipation.

"How often do you two go gallivanting around town?" Julian looked at Caroline first and then me. "Couple days a week?"

"That sounds about right," Caroline said. "Of course, you'd need different clothes if you are going to be our chauffeur."

Sandy frowned. "What kind of clothes?"

"I'm sure we can set you up with the proper uniform." Caroline pretended to be stern and business like. "What do you think, Mamie?"

I was torn between Sandy's good fortune and my own plans to acquire a Hudson 33 with a push-button starter. "I think Sandy would be handsome dressed in a chauffeur's uniform."

Squinting, Julian calculated in his head. "You can still do the yard once a week if you want, but we'll pay you a dollar a day to drive these fine ladies around Fort Smith."

Sandy's eyes lit up. "Okay, Mr. McGrath. Which two days?"

"How about Mondays and Wednesdays? Is that okay with you, Mama?"

Caroline nodded.

"Mamie?"

"Sounds wonderful." I was already planning the places I wanted to explore.

"When do I start?"

"Whoa, boy." Webster patted Sandy on the shoulder. "You gotta learn to drive first. And then ya gotta get some practice in."

"I'm pretty busy at the newspaper right now, Sandy. How about we plan the next couple Saturday afternoons so I can introduce you to the joys of driving the Boehmer?"

"Yes, sir. Where?"

"You show up here at one o'clock this coming weekend and we'll start the lessons."

"I'll be here." Sandy was overjoyed.

"Thank you, Miz Caroline, Mr. Julian, Miz Mamie." Webster stood up. "I shore appreciate your kindness to my boy."

"Sandy's a good worker, Webster," Caroline said.

"He's my shining star, ma'am. And the center of his mama's life. We got big plans for this one."

* * *

November 13, 1911
Whirling Winds Damage Temple of Justice

Southwest American

November 14, 1911
Mr. Joe Parker says that the whole building shook like crazy during that storm on Saturday.

Genevieve Day, *Fort Smith Bell*

November 29, 1911
Courthouse Foundation Not Sound

Patsy Lincoln, *Fort Smith Bell*

December 24, 1911
Finances Won't Permit Building of New Courthouse

Southwest American

Section 3 – 1912

January 8, 1912
Mr. Joe Parker is not dead after all. Identified as a corpse two weeks ago after being hit by a car, Parker started a drunken row down on Garrison. Judge Freer fined Parker $5 since he was not dead.

Genevieve Day, *Fort Smith Bell*

January 20, 1912
Mr. Rudolph Ney will take his daughter Elizabeth to college in Staunton, Virginia. While away, he will take a short vacation after devoting himself to a heated period of Boston Store business.

Mamie McGrath, *Southwest American*

February 9, 1912
Next week, the Joi Theater will welcome the Haganback-Wallace Animal motion picture. With 4000 feet of film, it will be the greatest program ever shown in Fort Smith.

Julian McGrath, *Southwest American*

1 0

Saturday, March 23, 1912
Mine Surrenders Fifty-Two Dead.
Fort Smith Victims of the McCurtain Mine Explosion Buried Today

Southwest American

Saturday, March 23, 1912 9 a.m.

"YOU MIGHT AS WELL TAKE the rest of the day to spend with your family, Genevieve," I said as I cut into my boiled egg. "We're shopping this morning and then tonight, we're going to have dinner at Esposito's. That's the restaurant little Bobby Esposito's family owns."

"I'll be glad for it, ma'am. I got company coming tonight."

"That'll work out nicely then." Caroline sat down for breakfast. "Morning, everyone."

"Morning, Mama." Julian rattled his newspaper. "Looks to be cool today. Should we just rent a hack? I think it's time to give up on the Boehmer."

"Sandy will be disappointed again." Caroline poured milk into her tea. "Seems like every time we plan for him to practice driving, something happens—wouldn't start, bad weather, no brakes."

"I want to learn to drive too," I said.

Julian lowered the paper. "Really?"

"Why not?"

"I can't think of a single reason except the Boehmer's current mechanical problems."

I laid down my napkin. "Actually, I thought I'd buy a new car."

"Well, I'll be!" Genevieve nearly dropped the plate of hot biscuits she was bringing to the table. "One of your own?"

"I'll give you and Caroline and Julian rides of course." My heart thumped in my ears. "It'll be a way to pay my way in this household. Especially since folks prefer your cooking to mine—yours too, Genevieve. And while I like things clean, my physical limitations the last couple years have limited my contributions in that arena."

"Oh dear, you don't need to do it for that reason." Caroline buttered her biscuit. "Now that we have Genevieve, I'm not doing so much either. Don't know why I ever resisted hiring someone."

"Why do you want a car?" Julian seemed amused.

"Because it'll be practical. I can come and go as I please."

"You can do that now, dear," Caroline said.

"It's not like you need one of your own," Julian said.

"No, I don't need one. I want one. I have more than enough money from what Pa left me. And I can use the money I earn from writing for fuel and repairs."

"And?"

"It would be fun, Julian. Fun!"

He chuckled. "It would definitely be fun."

"I even have one picked out."

"Oh?"

"Remember that night that Garland's car was stolen and Jim Brewer gave us a ride in the Hudson 33?"

"You want a Hudson 33?" He seemed astounded, yet impressed. "You've given this a lot of thought?"

"Months of recuperation gave me opportunity for thought. I was going to say something about it last winter before Webster and Sandy visited, but when they did, I didn't want to, you know—"

"Rain on their parade?"

"Exactly. At the time, I was unsure of how well I'd be. How strong. I was thinking, I could keep Sandy with me to handle the crank. But now that the Boehmer has become a problem and spring is upon us—well, maybe I should buy the new car now and have Jim Brewer teach both of us at the same time."

Caroline smiled behind her teacup. "Sounds like you got it figured."

"I was also waiting until Jim got the new 1912 Hudson 33 in stock."

"Why is that, dear?"

"Because the 1912 model has a push-button starter. He tells me it should be no problem for me to start—even with my weak arm."

"That's one less thing!" Genevieve's laugh was hearty.

I looked into Julian's eyes. "And it comes in red."

"Oh well, red then."

"So you like the idea?"

"I love it."

* * *

10:30 a.m.

Jim Brewer met us at the door of the Arkansas Garage. "Look who's come a calling!"

"The missus made a decision, Jim." Julian shook hands with him.

"I'm glad to hear it. I wasn't sure she was serious."

"She's dead serious." Julian patted my hand that was curled around his left arm.

"The red one." I pointed.

"How soon do you need it?"

"Yesterday." I was giddy with excitement.

"I have things to do, first. That car just came in on the train yesterday. We need to check it out, make sure everything that's supposed to be tight is and everything that's supposed to move does. This is Saturday. It's only me and JW here all day. How about we do all the financial dealings now and you can take delivery on Monday morning?"

"When can you teach me how to drive it?"

Jim frowned. "Teach you?"

"I'll pay of course."

"This is a big automobile."

"So?"

"And complicated."

"We talked about this before, Jim." I tried to hide my irritation. "You even sold me on the push-button starter."

He blushed. "I assumed you would have a driver."

"I'll have either Sanford Lewis or Julian with me most of the time."

"So you won't need to drive it." Jim brightened.

"I won't need to but I want to."

"Could you change a tire?"

"I can learn."

Julian folded his arms across his chest. "What's the problem, Jim. Don't want to make a sale?"

"We've been talking about this for months," I said.

"The Hudson 33's a big heavy machine. I'm trying to be your friend. Yours and Julian's. Especially after all that you went through last year."

"Thank you for the concern, but do you want to sell me an automobile or not?"

He glanced at Julian.

I stamped my foot in frustration. "I'm the customer here."

"You heard the lady, Jim." Julian put his arm around my waist.

"Monday. I'll get all the papers in order and make sure JW checks out the mechanics. Aside from a driving lesson for yourself, do you want us to spend time with the young man who will be your driver?"

"Yes. Include Sanford Lewis in our agreement too."

Jim wrote something in a book on his desk. "Where did you get this idea, Miz Mamie? I don't know of any women driving a motorcar around these parts."

"Harriet Quimby."

"Who?"

"She's a fellow writer in New York. She got her pilot's license last year."

"There you have it, Jim. Harriet Quimby is a pilot. Things are changing," Julian said.

"I surrender." Jim laughingly held up his arms.

"Okay." Julian clapped his hands together. "Is this negotiation over?"

"I'll sell you the car, Miz Mamie." Jim lowered his voice to a penitent whisper. "Sorry to have offended you. I meant no harm."

"I'm sorry to be so touchy."

"There you go. Done deal." Julian chuckled.

* * *

Southern Millinery Company
908 Garrison Avenue

We have a Complete Stock and Artists to create Designs
We Will Be Pleased to Open a Charge Account
With Any Responsible Party

*

Garrison Avenue 3 p.m.

As I was coming out of Maggie Mitchel's dress shop, I paused on the sidewalk to note an idea in my notebook for an article about Maggie's expertise with modern attire.

"Mamie McGrath!"

"Chasing bad guys again, Andy?"

"Looking for a wayward daughter."

"Oh no. Whose?"

"Mine."

"Oh dear, hope she's okay."

"I'm sure she is. She's got her eye on some young man that she shouldn't have."

"How old is Pansy now?"

"Eighteen."

I laughed. "Poor dad."

Andy took off his hat and wiped his face with his forearm. "Let me buy you a cup of coffee. You may be just the person to give me a clue about this kid."

"I'll try."

"Let's head up to Padgett's Cafe. It's close enough that if we hurry, we might miss the rain."

We'd no sooner got in the door than cold raindrops splashed against the front windows.

He pulled out a chair for me. "How's Della?"

"Enjoying having her brother and nephew live with us."

A waitress poured Andy's coffee. "How about you, dear?"

"Coffee's fine," I said to her.

"Think I should make another pot, Andy?"

"Up to you, Sophie."

I took off my gloves and laid them on the table. "So what's going on with Pansy?"

"Growing up too fast. Too pretty for her own good. She knows it too. Got that from her mama."

"I had several cases of puppy love about that age. I wouldn't be too worried."

"I've seen too much," Andy said. "I don't trust any of these young hooligans."

"There's plenty potential sweethearts in Fort Smith that you and Della will like. But in the long run, you'll have to trust Pansy to find the right partner."

He shook his head. "That's my baby. I want her to stay young and pure and safe."

"Isn't that like trying to call back a bullet after you've already pulled the trigger?"

"They're all gonna be grown soon enough. I want them to make good decisions."

"You can guide them."

"Andy Carr!" A man approached our table and stuck out his hand.

"Good to see you, Will. Mamie, this is Will Henry. Had to roust his bony butt a time or two. Will, this is Julian McGrath's wife, Mamie. She's becoming quite a well-known writer."

"Nice to meet you, ma'am. Aren't you the little lady Ollie Fields ran over with his wagon last year?"

"The very same. It was a manful effort on his part, but I survived anyway."

"Good for you." He stood over me for a moment. "Well, you look out for this old boy." He pointed at Andy. "He don't give a body in trouble much wiggle room. When I was a dumb kid looking for folding money to spend on a sweet young thing in Spiro, I stole fifteen head of cattle from a neighboring farm. Turns out, unbeknownst to me, a couple of them steers belonged to my mom. Never did figure out how old Andy here knew it was me."

"Wasn't that hard. The fellow at the city weight scales figured you for a scoundrel and gave me a call. And you showed me and everyone else that you were guilty by running away when you saw me."

"Taught me a lesson."

"I hope so. I take no pleasure in running people in. It's my job though—and I intend on doing it well."

"Yes, sir." Will shifted from foot to foot. "Guess I'll head out now. Nice meetin' you, Miz McGrath."

As Will Henry left, I asked, "Nice young man?"

"Hot head."

I sipped my coffee. "Ah."

"That there's the kind of thing I want to protect my Pansy from."

"Of course."

There was an uncomfortable pause in our conversation.

"I hear you're looking after Manny McKnight."

"Me? Hardly. I had the young man who does our yard teach him a few things. Gave him some of Julian's old clothes—and we feed him on occasion."

"He's gonna get himself in trouble. Been spending time with the mayor's rambunctious nephew Grover. Nothing serious yet. I suspect they've been picking pockets, but no one's pointed him out. Yet."

I sighed. "He makes it so hard to help him."

Andy downed half his cup of coffee. "He does."

More silence between us.

"I've been meaning to tell you."

"Shoot."

I took a deep breath. "It may be nothing, but I'm worried about Garland Talbot."

He straightened in his seat. "You have my attention."

"Garland likes his booze."

Andy rubbed his chin. "I wonder how that works with Abigail."

"Not well, I'm sure—but there's more. A year or so ago, Garland acquired a business associate named Orrin Fellows." I described Anna Marie Cavanaugh's mission to help the burned man hiding out at Miss Laura's, the strange viewing and funeral of Mr.

Guckenheimer, Garland's sudden money problems, and the loss of his automobile on opening night of the New Theater.

"A Mr. Guckenheimer?" Andy choked back a laugh.

"Yes, did you know him?"

"Not personally." Eyes twinkling, he motioned for Sally to refill our mugs. "What does this Orrin Fellows look like?"

"He's short. Thin. Pushing 50. Maybe. Always wears a vest under his jacket and a top hat even during the day. Spectacles. And Andy, there's something wrong with his face."

He frowned. "How so?"

"It's shiny."

"Shiny?"

"I can't explain it any better than that."

Andy leaned back in his seat. "Like that new nun at Saint Anne's?"

"New nun?"

"Got here about a year ago?"

"I didn't know there was a new nun, but—" I put my hand on Andy's wrist, almost causing him to spill his coffee. "—there was a nun at Mr. Guckenheimer's funeral."

"What did she look like?"

"A Sister of Mercy. Didn't see her face."

"Why?"

I closed my eyes, trying to visualize the people at Immaculate Conception Church that morning. "She covered her face with her hands." I opened my eyes. "Like she was praying. And when I walked past her on my way out, she turned her head the other way."

"Who else was there that day?"

I thought for a moment. "Business men. A cop."

"A cop?"

"Rude." I tapped the table with my fingers. "Put a flower—can't remember what kind. Pit—"

"Pitcock?"

"Yes, Pitcock. I mentioned some of this to John B a few weeks ago."

"Hmm. So that's what he was talking about." Andy fished a coin out of his pocket and tossed it on the table. "Excuse me, Mamie. I have work to do."

Surprised by the suddenness of my dismissal, I sat back in my chair.

He put on his hat. "Any idea what was in that basket Sister Alberta gave you for Anna Marie?"

I shrugged. "Clothes."

"Shirts? Pants?"

"I assume. I didn't open it and look."

"What exactly did Anna Marie tell you about this burned man?"

"That he was an accountant and he found out that his boss was a crook."

"What was his name?"

"Mr. Marky."

"Thanks for sharing this, Mamie. I'll check it out."

"Take care of yourself, Andy."

He raised his hand as he headed out the door.

* * *

7:30 p.m.

Julian presented me with a nosegay of three pale pink roses tied with a matching silk ribbon. "Let's make this date unforgettable."

"They're gorgeous!" I held them to my nose. "But why?"

"To celebrate your recovery?"

"How about rejoicing that little Bobby Esposito is alive and well?"

"That too. And that you have become quite the writer."

I laid the flowers back on the paper they'd been wrapped in. "Who knew I'd have such a knack for turning rumor into drama?"

"And comedy. That last piece about Sarge and Garland fighting over whether President Grant was a teetotaler pretending to be a lush or a lush pretending to be a teetotaler had everyone laughing."

"Except Garland," I said as I brushed my hair. "He thought I was making fun of him."

"Don't worry, sweetheart. He'll get over it."

"I'm going to write about the local Women's Christian Temperance Union group next."

"Think that will upset Madam Secretary or tickle her?"

"Hard to predict," I said. "I hope she sees it as a good thing."

Julian combed his mustache and applied a touch of wax to it. "I wonder if her involvement is a bid for popularity or a deeply held ethic?"

"It may be personal. Garland's been drunk the last few times I've seen him. And not charmingly tipsy either."

Julian put on his dinner jacket. "If I was Abigail, that would be enough to send me into the arms of the Fort Smith Temperance enclave."

Tucking the ends of the bow into the folds of the turban I'd created with a scarf, I peered out our bedroom window. "The rain seems to be slowing down."

"It's not wet enough to keep people at home, but I'm afraid it's going to be muddy."

"We'll have umbrellas." I pulled tendrils of hair out from under the turban and curled them around my fingers.

"As long as it doesn't pour and we stay on the sidewalks, we should be comfortable enough," he said.

I pinned Julian's grandmother's brooch on my turban. "I'm excited to see the Espositos again. Their visit with Bobby was the turning point for me."

"Perhaps you can write about them. Immigrants coming to Fort Smith with nothing and opening the most popular Italian restaurant in town. Colonel Parker loves that kind of thing. I'm sure he'd publish it."

"Good idea." I opened my notebook and wrote, "500 words about Esposito's."

"Sounds like Abigail is doing less and less with Garland."

"I think that's Garland's choice, not Abigail's."

"Let's not let that happen to us, okay?" He nuzzled my neck.

"Since I got over the accident and started writing, I'm happier than I've ever been, Julian. We know each other better. We share ideas. I go to bed each night looking forward to the morning."

"And I don't get drunk every night and twice on Sundays."

"Thank goodness. Why do men do that?"

"I don't know about men in general," he said. "But Sarge uses booze to tamp down pain and grief. Garland, on the other hand, tries too hard. It's like he has this giant empty spot and he can't eat enough or drink enough or gamble enough to fill it."

He let go of me and I sat down on the rocker to put on my shoes and button them up. "Why didn't he and Abigail have a family?"

"Ah. Now that's a story. Patsy told me that Abigail had three brothers and a sister. Her sister and the youngest boy had some kind of disease or condition. They were fine when they were born but by the time they were eight or ten they had symptoms—and by the time they were teenagers they couldn't walk at all."

"How awful."

"Abigail had to help her mother take care of them. According to Patsy, the girl was stunning and everyone was drawn to her. When you add the fact that she was also sick, Abigail must have felt overshadowed."

"I'm sure."

"Anyway, both of those kids died in their twenties."

"Oh no!"

"Apparently, there were other kids like that in her mother's line and doctors told Abigail that the condition was passed down through the woman. So she decided not to have children."

"So that's why she's like she is," I murmured.

"Yes, I think so. At least partially."

"And it explains Garland too."

"Some." Julian helped me put on my coat.

"Now I feel bad that I've been mean to her." I picked up my nosegay. "Abigail's petty and foolish, but she also tells a good tale. Her tips are overblown, but there's always a kernel of truth to them."

"She's had to be resourceful. When she was thirteen, her father got tuberculosis and died—and the landowner decided to do something else with the farm."

"What did they do?"

"They moved to Fort Smith. Both the healthy boys got jobs at Eads' Brothers, building furniture. And Abigail," he tried not to smile. "—worked as a shop girl at the Boston Store."

"Oh, I see." I caught Julian's eyes and we both convulsed with laughter.

Someone knocked on the front door.

"That must be the hack driver."

I took his arm. "Let's just have fun."

"Absolutely, Mrs. McGrath."

8 p.m.

"Oh, Julian!" A handsome black carriage, trimmed with brass fittings awaited us. Two beautiful horses stamped their feet and neighed, their foggy breaths highlighted by the moon which was just emerging from the clouds. "It's lovely."

The hack driver helped me into his cab and Julian crawled in behind me.

"I'd almost forgotten how romantic a horse-drawn carriage can be," I said after the uniformed driver closed the door and crawled onto the seat up top.

"It's usually used for weddings or funerals now, but Mr. Weindel was more than glad to let me have it for my girl's special evening."

As the carriage turned onto Rogers, I relaxed into the soft seats, holding Julian's arm with one hand and the nosegay in the other.

"Looks like everyone's going to town tonight," Julian said. "There's Manny McKnight."

"Oh, do pull over and let me tell him something."

Julian put his arm out the window and tapped on the roof of the carriage. "Pull over next to those three boys on the right. Mrs. McGrath wants to talk to one of them."

"Yes sir." Mr. Weindel guided the horses to the side of the road where Manny and his friends were walking.

I leaned out the window, "Manny!"

"My Lord, Miz Mamie. You gave me the heebie-jeebies. I thought you was a hearse coming outta that mist."

"What're you doing tonight?"

"I'm busier than a cat covering crap on a marble floor. What does it look like?"

"Come on, Manny," an older boy said. "That blue-gummed moke might still be following us."

"Manny, please introduce me to your friends?"

"That there's Grover Bourland. His uncle's the mayor. And that's Harold. He's like me. Nobody special. Boys, this here's Miz Mamie McGrath."

"The one that tangled with ole Ollie Fields last year?" Grover squinted up at me. "Glad to meet you, ma'am. They says them horses tore you up."

"Nice to meet you, Grover."

"I hear you're in the paper all the time. Guess that makes you some kinda big wheel in Fort Smith." He leaned on the carriage.

"Back off, son." The driver pointed his whip at Grover.

"I ain't doing nothing."

"You're spooking the horses."

"Them well-bred fillies are high strung, like Miz McGrath here."

Julian leaned forward so that the boys could see him. "Evening, gentlemen."

All three of them stepped back from the hack.

"Manny, come by on Monday. I have work for you. We've got leaves clogging up the gutters."

Manny looked back at Grover and Harold. "Told you I had a job out this part of town."

"Monday. Say ten am?"

"I'll be there."

Julian sat back in his seat and tugged at my hand.

Just as Mr Weindel was about to start up again, I stuck my head back out the window. "So what's a blue-gummed moke?"

"Mamie." Julian muttered under his breath.

"Wait a second," I said over my shoulder.

"What you wanting know, Miz Mamie?" Manny wiped his nose on the back of his hand.

"A blue-gummed moke?"

The three boys looked at each other and laughed.

"Mamie." Julian took my arm.

Grover grinned slowly. "It's a nigger so black that his gums are blue instead of pink. They's first cousins to the boogyman. If'n they see ya, they'll chase you down and try to bite that pretty lil neck of yours, ma'am. One bite and they's gonna put you six feet under."

"Alright, that's enough. Get on along, boys." Julian bellowed.

"C'mon, fellas." Harold elbowed Grover. "They's gonna think we ain't coming and we won't get to see it."

"See what?"

"That pretty black woman that dances under the bridge down by the Frisco. Her brothers sell whiskey in little jiggers like this." Harold held his finger and thumb a couple inches apart.

"Medicine." Manny's whisper was loud enough for me to hear it too.

"Yeah, they sell medicine." Harold stared into my eyes and snickered.

"Mamie." Julian touched my arm again. "They'll be waiting for us."

"Y'all don't get in any trouble."

"We's just gonna try out some free medicine samples is all," Manny said.

"Good night then."

The boys set off toward town and I sat back down on the leather seat beside Julian.

"Let's go." He tapped the roof of the cab.

"Manny would step in a puddle rather than walk around it," I sighed.

"He's a kid, sugar."

"That's one of the reasons he's so dirty all the time."

"He's got family somewhere."

"Wherever they are, they aren't here to watch out for him."

* * *

Minutes later, Mr. Weindel pulled up in front of Esposito's. He hopped down and opened the door of the cab. "Here ya go, ma'am."

"Thank you, Mr. Weindel."

"Pick us up at ten forty-five." Julian slipped a coin into the driver's palm.

Mr. Weindel climbed back onto the rig and clicked to the horses.

The restaurant was busy—and noisy. We went through the dining area and up a single flight of stairs. Julian knocked on the door and Martina Esposito greeted us with warm hugs. "It's good to see you again, Mamie."

"Thank you, Martina." We sat down on a small sofa. "I've been eager to see that beautiful boy of yours."

"Boo." Bobby Esposito sprang out from a door behind us. "I'm a ghost tonight."

"Why're you a ghost?"

"Because you can't see me."

"You're right. I can't see you."

Bobby giggled. "Your booboo's better?"

"Yes. See?" I stretched out my arm toward him and open and closed my hand.

"Mine too." He lifted his pajama pant leg. His knee was smooth. Not a trace of that day remained on his body.

"I go to school now."

"You do? Can you read?"

"Yep."

"Really?"

"I can read." He sounded offended that I doubted him.

"Show me."

"Okay." He dashed off into the other room.

"He's excited about books these days," Martina said.

"Here." Bobby ran back into the room with a book in his hand. "Want me to read it to you?"

"I'd love it."

"I gotta sit in your lap though so you can see the pictures."

I held out my arms and the dear little thing practically leapt on me.

"It's about a lion." He pointed to the cover. "And a little girl named Dorothy. And a shiny man."

I glanced at Julian and mouthed. "Shiny man!"

"And a wizard."

* * *

"I'm afraid Bobby wore you out, Mamie." Martina turned out his bedroom light.

"I loved his antics. He's so smart."

Martina's eyes glowed with maternal pride. "He's our little Mr. America."

A knock at the door distracted us. "It's time," Dino Esposito said through the crack.

"Let's feed you." Martina gestured for us to come with her.

"What about Bobby?" I couldn't help but ask.

"His grandmama shares the room with him. She'll watch over him."

We descended the stairs. Martina pushed open another door and we were overwhelmed with light and voices and the smell of garlic.

"Surprise!"

Four large round tables loaded down with salad and fish and spaghetti and sausages filled the room. Sitting around those tables were the smiling faces of friends and neighbors and family. Dino poured each of us a small glass of Chianti. "To Miz Mamie McGrath who saved Roberto Esposito, the future president of the United States!"

Julian and I held up our glasses in response to the toast. I smiled at Caroline who clearly had been complicit in this little surprise. She mouthed, "I love you," and I choked back a tear.

Sarge was there too—red eyed, but there. I nodded to Abigail and Garland, who seemed to be holding hands even while Garland swayed in his seat.

"I thought Abigail had lost Garland for tonight," Julian whispered in my ear.

I shrugged. "I'm sure there's a story." Somehow, knowing about Abigail's brother and sister—and the reason she and Garland had never had children—made her seem less of a bully.

Burley was at the next table, but Marie DuVal was nowhere in sight. I nodded, grateful for his presence. Medora Sparks and her husband sat beside him. I waved to her and she wiggled her fingers back. Julian's editor, Colonel Parker was on the other side of her. He gave me a thumbs up.

An older couple sat by the front window. I'd never seen her before, but he was familiar. "Who's that?" I said out of the side of my mouth to Julian.

"That's Oliver Fields, Mamie. Ollie and his wife Sarah. The man whose wagon nearly crushed you."

"Oh my goodness. I didn't recognize him all slicked up like that." My eyes drifted to the next table. "Oh, there's Father Horan and Sister Alberta." I waved.

"Neither John B and Jennie nor Andy and Della could make it. Both send you their good wishes," Julian whispered in my ear.

I relaxed into my seat, enjoying it all. How far I'd come since moving to Fort Smith!

* * *

9:30 p.m.

The cool night air, after the damp day, felt good on my cheeks. We stood on the sidewalk outside Esposito's. I was talking a little too loudly, laughing at jokes I usually didn't find funny, pressing my nosegay to my face from time to time. Our friends and family and fellow citizens had showered me with attention—this time for something I did, not because something happened to me. Dino

Esposito's food had been hearty and delicious. And we'd enjoyed several glasses of his homemade Chianti.

Abigail had already lost Garland when she gave me a parting air kiss. "He snuck out for a drink with his buddies over at Till Shaw's," she said. "He thinks I don't know." She looked down at me and sighed. "You've done well here, Mamie."

"People have been kind."

"They are. But it's you too, my dear. Hang onto that sparkle."

I was surprised that her comment mattered to me. "Thank you, Abigail."

A cab pulled up and the driver jumped out to open the doors.

"We'll be home in a few minutes, Mama." Julian helped her and Abigail into the back seat of the automobile.

"Goodnight, Miz Talbot. Miz Caroline." Burley tipped his hat. "It was nice to spend the evening with such lovely ladies."

"Don't give me that, Burley Johnston." Abigail laughed. "We all know who you'd have rather spent your evening with."

We waved as the taxi bearing Caroline and Abigail headed up Garrison Avenue.

"I appreciate that you showed up for my surprise party, Burley."

"It's a night none of us will forget soon." Burley untied the reins of his horse and led it back up Garrison. At Sixth, he crawled into the saddle and turned north, heading for home.

Julian and I waited on the corner of Garrison and Fifth Street for Mr. Weindel. "It's almost bright as day," I said. "The electric lights make it so much easier to be out at night."

"What's that?" Julian stared toward the church at the head of Garrison.

I cupped my ear. "Yes, what is that?"

Passersby also turned toward the church eight blocks east of where we stood. As the sounds grew louder, people came out of the bars and restaurants—and stood on the sidewalks, listening intently and looking around. An elegantly-dressed couple stood on the porch above the Hotel Main's front door. Windows opened in the buildings around us and people stuck out their heads, craning to see what was happening.

Dino Esposito came out onto the curb. "What is it, Julian?"

Julian shook his head. "Some kind of ruckus down around Ninth or Tenth."

"I need my gun." Dino went back inside.

"It's like a hum. Electricity?"

"Voices," Julian said.

Hand in hand, we left our corner and moved toward the noise, a step at a time. Dino locked his restaurant and hurried to catch up with us. He had a pistol with a long barrel tucked in his belt under his apron.

"Look," I pointed.

A small figure ran toward us. I squinted. "Manny?"

Panting and looking around, he stopped in his tracks. "Some damned nigger done killed Andy Carr, ma'am."

"What? Where?"

"Shot him in the head."

The image of a friend—one I'd chatted with only a few hours ago—being shot in the head, literally took my breath away.

Manny turned to run back toward the Hotel Main.

"Where?" It came out a hoarse whisper.

"Where, Manny?" Julian's voice was louder, clearer.

"I done told you, Mr. Julian. In the head."

"No, I mean where is he? Where's Andy?"

"I didn't see him, but they say he's laying in front of the Pony Express. Dead as a doornail." He turned away from us again.

"Where're you going, Manny?"

He ignored me and disappeared down the alley beside the Hotel Main that led from Garrison to Rogers.

Shouts and screams came from further up the street. People poured out onto the streets as the theaters let out or restaurants closed. Voices grew louder as the news that Andy was dead spread.

"What about Della and those kids? What will happen to them?" I let go of Julian's hand to fish through my bag for a handkerchief. When I looked up, I saw a group of people coming our way.

"Dino, will you look after Mamie, please?"

"What? Wait. I don't need a babysitter."

But it was too late, Julian was already running down the middle of Garrison to meet the crowd.

Dino took my arm. "Come with me, Miz Mamie. I'll let you back into my restaurant. You can stay with Martina. I'll lock up after you. You'll be safe."

"No, I have to see about Andy. He's a friend."

He pointed toward the growing crowd. "Can't you see what is happening? This is no place for you to be right now."

"Thank you, sir, but no." I jerked my arm out of his grip and ran after Julian who was already a block ahead of me. My skirt was narrow around my ankles—and I was wearing shoes with heels. I didn't breathe or blink or think of anything but to get to Andy. It felt like I was flying up the Avenue after Julian—and then I saw them.

Officer Lacey was pulling a Negro man by the arm. The prisoner's lips and eyes were cut and blood streamed down his cheeks. Every few steps, he'd stop and struggled to catch his breath. To get him going again, the cop poked him in the side with his night stick. Or in the stomach. The second time he did that, the colored man cried out and fell to the ground. Demanding that he stand up again, Lacey jerked his arm—and his scream set my teeth on edge.

City Detective Pitcock limped a few steps behind them, grimacing.

I stopped, wondering what was wrong with him.

When the black man fell this time, the older cop waddled forward—and bashed the prisoner with his baton, knocking him to one knee.

A growing gang of teenage boys urging the cops to, "Kill that nigger," followed close behind them.

Lacey struggled to pull the Negro to his feet again,

Pitcock, encouraged by the chants, lifted his arm to smash the young man again.

I was in the middle of Garrison Avenue less than five feet in front of them. "Stop it," I demanded.

The cops—intent on kicking their victim, lips curled back from their teeth—elbowed in front of each other to get at him.

"Stop!"

"This is official business, ma'am." Pitcock panted. "Get back." His cheeks were bright red and he was sweating even though it was cold out.

The men and boys cussed me and shook their fists. I sensed movement to my right. Garland Talbot stood on the sidewalk in front of Till Shaw's Saloon a few feet away. He swayed forward onto his toes, then back on his heels.

"Garland, tell them to stop!"

He raised his glass in a drunken salute. "Cheers."

The bloodied young Negro reached out to me. "Miz Mamie."

His nose was flattened and pushed sideways. White bone glowed through his split scalp under the flickering billboard lights. Beneath his swollen lips, I saw that they'd broken his front teeth. "Miz Mamie." His voice was raspy. Unrecognizable.

Horrified, I backed away.

"Help me."

My heels hit the curb and I fell onto my behind.

The young black man lurched toward me, but Pitcock and Lacey grabbed him and pushed him toward the alley across street. Pitcock looked at me over his shoulder. "Get out of here, Miz Mc-Grath. Before you get yourself kilt."

A rush of bodies pushed past me. I was disoriented and confused. I cried out. Dino found me. And then Burley. Together, they helped me to my feet. As we backed away, people lined up on both sides of Garrison Avenue yelled, "Lynch him" or "Let me do it" or "Murderer."

"No, don't hurt him." I shouted after the crowd.

A drunk stopped and stood over me, leering. "You the kind of woman that likes niggers?"

"Get out of here," someone shouted and pushed the young man away.

"Stop them," I grabbed at my rescuer's pant leg. "They're hurting that boy."

"Shush, Mamie. Please." It was Burley.

"I thought you went home."

He squatted down beside me. "I heard the racket and came back to see what was happening."

I rubbed my eyes. "Where's Julian?"

"Where he always is. In the thick of things. Writing it all down."

Dino pushed through the crowd following the cops and their prisoner. "Is she hurt?"

"Not yet, but we need to get her out of here." Burley helped me to my feet.

A man with thick dark eyebrows paused. "Are you crazy? Them niggers are pouring out of the bars down around Texas corner. They have a taste for sweet young things like you. You catch their attention, we'll be hanging more than one of them bastards tonight."

"Get out of here, Joe," Burley said. "We'll take care of Miz McGrath."

The man waved a long-barreled pistol in my face. "Don't think you can change what's happening tonight, ma'am. It's been a long time coming. Long time! Them damn gorillas think they own this town. Think they can murder a white man in front of God and everybody. We cain't let them get away with it, and we won't. We're gonna crush them." He touched the brim of his hat with the barrel of his gun before disappearing into the crowd again.

We froze as another mass of screaming men, curious onlookers and cops enveloped us.

"Back to my restaurant, Miz Mamie," Dino said after they passed us. "Please. I need to check on my family."

"He's right." Burley took my arm and guided me to the sidewalk. "People aren't thinking this though. They're scared and mad. If you get in their way, they'll hurt you. Stomp you to death."

The next thing I knew, I was sitting at a table in Esposito's restaurant.

Dino brought me a shot glass half-filled with a brown liquor. "Drink it."

I wrinkled my nose. "What is it?"

"Drink it."

I touched the top of the liquid with the tip of my tongue.

"Toss it back," Burley encouraged me. "One quick swallow."

I swallowed the sweet drink in one gulp. "Oh my God." I coughed.

Martina, now in her dressing gown, made strong dark coffee and brought it to us. "What in the world is happening?"

"Someone killed a policeman," Dino said. "And a lynch mob is forming."

"A lynch mob?" I looked up—first at Dino and then at Burley.

Burley nodded almost imperceptibly.

"They're going to kill that man?"

"Probably."

"We have to stop them."

"Yes," Martina put an arm around my shoulders. "We must stop them."

Burley and Dino exchanged glances.

Burley squatted down in front of me. "How?"

"Where were they taking him?"

"Probably to the jail on the courthouse lawn."

"We could telephone the mayor," Martina suggested.

"Yes, call the mayor first."

Dino went into the kitchen and clicked the receiver. "Yes, please connect me with Mr. Bourland. No. Not the judge. The mayor. Mayor Bourland. What? Thank you."

We waited in silence. I thought of Andy lying in the street in front of John B's business. I closed my eyes, hoping that John B was with him when he died. Hoping that someone had gone for Della.

"Okay, then. Thank you." Dino hung up the phone and came back into the restaurant where we were sitting. "The operator. She says everyone is calling the mayor but no one answers at his home or in his office."

Someone tapped on the window. We turned and saw Sarge and Miss Peach.

Martina unlocked the door. "What happened to you, Sarge?"

"Never saw so many people in town—night or day," he grumbled as Miss Peach rolled him in.

I stood up and embraced Miss Peach. She froze, arms at her side—eyes wide. "Miz Mamie. Please."

I stepped back. "I'm so sorry this is happening."

"Mmhm, I'm sure you are, ma'am. I'm no fool. It's not you or Mr. Julian or Miz Caroline out there making that racket."

I felt my face reddening. "I know you're not a fool. I just—"
Actually, I didn't know where the impulse to hug her without her
permission came from. "I'm the fool." I lowered my eyes.

"We couldn't get through that crowd to get back to Mr. Eacret's
apartment." Miss Peach changed the subject. "We tried to get in, but
most places had locked their doors."

"Probably afraid someone would rob them during the hubbub."
Burley pulled out a chair so Miss Peach could push Sarge in under
the table beside him.

"Probably," she said. "But we was stuck. Couldn't go home.
Couldn't stay where we was. So we came back here."

"I'm glad." Martina set a coffee pot and a large plate of cannolis
in front of them.

"I'll go in the kitchen, ma'am."

"Oh no. We're locked up in here together. Who's gonna tell
anyone? You?" She pointed at Burley.

Burley shook his head.

"You, Mr. Eacret?"

"Ha!" Sarge chortled. "Not unless I start soberin' up."

Martina's laugh was warm and low. "Then I guess we better
keep the whiskey flowing until this blows over."

Sarge tapped the table. Dino set a glass in front of him and filled
it to the brim. "I'm good at keepin' secrets," he said after the first
sip. "Sit down right here, Miz Peach—and catch me if I fall over."

"How about the police department?" Burley redirected our attention back to the problem at hand.

"No," Dino said. "They'll be busy trying to fight off those ruffians. How about the Chief of Police?"

"Bryant Barry?" I visualized the courtly gentleman I met last fall
in the Goldman Hotel dining room. "Yes. Please try Chief Barry."

Dino bowed his head and went back into the kitchen.

"Maybe Father Horan?"

"He isn't a law enforcement man, Mamie." Burley sat down
across from me. "And besides, not everyone is Catholic here in
Fort Smith."

"What about Mr. Tilles? Or Mr. Ney?"

Burley snorted. "I doubt many of the people out there trying to
break into that jail are Jewish. Or practicing Baptists or Episcopa-
lians or Methodists."

"Who then?" I was beyond frustrated.

"Kids. People in town for business. Train passengers passing
through. Ruffians—as Mr. Esposito calls them—tanked up in one of
our many fine saloons."

"People tryin' to change the results of the Civil War," Sarge bellowed, swaying in his chair. "Deceitful traitors!"

"Shush, Mr. Eacret." Miss Peach patted the back of his hand and he quieted.

"There has to be someone who can stop them."

"Who?" Burley's voice rose.

I pushed back my chair and stood up. "Me."

"Miz Mamie," Miss Peach uncharacteristically broke in. "There are more people out there on Garrison Avenue than I ever saw in one place in my life. A thousand. Maybe more. Ain't none of us is gonna stop what's happening. It's too late for that." Tears ran down her cheeks, but her voice was firm. "No little thing like you is gonna save that black boy now. But I appreciate it, ma'am. I do. His folks will appreciate it. But that boy's already good as dead."

I grasped the back of the chair. I knew she was right, but I couldn't accept it.

Dino appeared at the door between the kitchen and the restaurant. "Chief Barry is already on his way."

I sighed in relief. "Posse is coming."

* * *

When we got to the women's jail with Pocahontas, the biggest part of the crowd was leaving the men's jail. We drawed the conclusion it was just excitement and it was over. So we left her there and went back to work on our beat from Eight Street to Texas Corner.

Officer Ed Pennewell, interview with Mamie McGrath

Chief Bryant Barry ran into the jail yard and up to the door yelling, "Order, gentleman. Order!"

Tol Dean, Police Inquiry Testimony

The boys in the mob were running away from the jail and they said, "That goddamned fool Pitcock will shoot you."

J. B. Parker, Police Inquiry Testimony

When I seen what they were going to do, I said, "My God, this won't do," and I did everything I could to keep them from it.

Officer William Phillips, Police Inquiry Testimony

11:30 p.m.

We sat silently, thinking about what was happening outside the door on Garrison. After the last round of whiskey, I cradled my head in my arms and laid it on the table. My cheeks and chin were wet. I didn't know if I was crying or drooling.

"How are you, Mamie?" Burley said.

"Scared. Drunk. Angry. Ashamed." I sat up, wiping my face on my sleeve. "You?"

"I'm thinking I'm a coward. If I can't stop those men from doing this, I should at least bear witness. I hope the cops have stopped it by now. Maybe they've hidden that man away in a secret cell. Or maybe those people in that mob have come to their senses and gone on home."

I thought about the nameless Negro who'd murdered Andy. Rage rose up in my heart, and confusion. How did that happen? Why? That man—that murderer—should have been arrested and tried. Della and the kids had a right to know how and why it happened. Andy had been a lawman for years. He'd rescued children, protected women, and brought in thieves and murderers. He'd been shot, hit by a trolley, and bruised up in fights. A month or two ago, a bad guy had got the jump on him and locked him in a closet in one of the rooms at the Hotel Main. He was in and out of trouble all the time, but Andy survived. Always.

I looked at Burley. "You're saying you want to watch it?"

He got up and put on his hat. "I'm a citizen of this town, same as anyone else. I'll feel just as guilty watching as I do hiding here."

"Don't be a fool." Sarge swayed in his chair. "The nightmares are the same either way."

"Maybe that man is safe in jail and we can turn our thoughts to Della and the kids."

Sarge grunted. "Fat chance."

I stood up. "I'm going too."

"I ain't lettin' you do that, Mamie." Sarge punctuated his slurred command by hitting the table with his fist. "You're the only kin I got left."

I put on my coat. "I'll still be your kin after tonight."

Without a word, Martina got up and went into the kitchen.

"I'm still armed." Dino said. "I'll go with you."

Martina came back out of the kitchen. "Mamie, I'll worry about you, but if you must do this—you must." She handed me a long-bladed butcher knife. "Don't let them hurt you."

I hugged her. "I'm grateful we're friends, Martina."

Dino opened the door. The three of us went out and he locked it behind us. The rumble in the distance told me the mob was at the jail in the courthouse grounds two streets over—on Parker Street.

An unusually large number of people milled around on the street and sidewalks. The theaters had closed a few minutes before and those audiences had spilled out onto Garrison too. Some had planned late night snacks or a drink after the show, but those who wanted to go home found themselves waiting as taxis, trolleys, and automobiles squeezed through the traffic into and out of Fort Smith.

Judge Harp's raucous political rally had concluded and those people filled the bars and restaurants too. However, as word of Andy Carr's murder circulated, the attendees seemed confused and impatient. A curious few wandered back over to the courthouse to watch or join the assault on the jail.

Till Shaw's Saloon seemed relatively quiet for a Saturday night. I peered in the window. Bartenders were serving whiskey to business men with valises, waiting for the midnight train at the Frisco a couple blocks away. A number of city government employees stood at the bar, drinking beer and plotting political strategies with each other.

"Maybe it's over," I said.

"I doubt it." Dino looked around. "Those hooligans intent on hanging that young man are still at the jail."

"That's probably where Julian is now," Burley said.

A loud roar startled us. Then we heard thuds and cheers.

Burley took a few steps into the alley. "They're trying to break into the jail," he called.

I switched the knife from one hand to the other and wiped the sweat of my palm. "Let's go see what's happening." I said to Dino.

We hurried into the alley after Burley who was following the noise. He was halfway across Rogers when we caught up with him.

"Whoa, no, you don't." Burley grabbed my arm.

I whirled on him, eyes blazing. "Why not?"

"It's dark and dangerous over there on good nights. You don't know what's happening."

The pounding and cheers made clear what was happening.

"Go back, Mamie. You could be terribly hurt if they knock you down. And who knows what kind of evil these men intend tonight?"

"Please, Miz Mamie. Listen to Burley." Dino flinched as another crash and cheer told us that the crowd had finally broken the jail door. "I'll go back with you."

At that moment, a flushed young man raced across the courtyard toward us. "We got that bastard. We got him."

"Will Manus? Is that you?"

"I ain't got time to talk, Dino." He held up his hands and grinned. They were covered with something dark.

I recoiled.

"A little nigger blood too much for you, Miss Priss?" He waved his gory hands in front of my nose.

"Stop that."

Will turned on Burley. "You gonna stop me, singer man?"

"If he doesn't—" Dino pulled that long-barreled pistol out of his belt and pressed it into Manus' stomach. "—I will."

Will backed away, hands in the air, laughing. "If you were gonna shoot that thing, I'd already be dead, Dino."

"Don't try me. Get away from Miz McGrath and go your merry way." Dino threatened.

The crowd noises were getting louder.

Will's eyes glistened in the half light. "Can't hang him back there. Nothing strong enough—but them trolley poles in front of the Hotel Main oughta do fine. Come watch the show."

Burley shuddered. "Get out of here, Will. Now."

Will Manus ran down the alley, laughing.

"We better leave too," Burley said. "They're heading back to Garrison anyway."

I nodded and we retraced our steps. Halfway through the alley, we heard a horse's hooves on the bricks behind us. I pressed myself against the wall as a man on a horse pulled a tottering figure behind him. Unable to keep up, the prisoner fell and was dragged a few yards, screaming as dirt and pebbles tore his flesh.

"Con Sullivan," Burley muttered under his breath.

"Who's he?"

"The wayward son of good people, Mamie."

Con Sullivan jumped down out of the saddle, pulled the Negro to his feet and pummeled him with his fists. In a moment, the rest of the crowd was on him too.

"No," I yelled but my voice was lost in an ocean of grunts, laughter, punches, and screams. I gave up and ran toward the fight, intent on stepping between the black man and his tormentors.

Burley picked me up and threw me over his shoulder. Dino followed as Burley carried me past a half dozen boys, led by Grover Bourland and his friend Harold, beating and kicking the young black man.

"Let me go, Burley. I mean it."

He hauled me out onto Garrison.

"Stop it." I fought him. "You can't throw me around like a piece of baggage."

"Take her." Exasperated, Burley set me down in front of Dino Esposito.

"NO!" I turned to run—and ran into John B.

"Get out of here, Mamie." He grabbed my wrist.

"John B, you have to stop them."

His mouth turned downward and his jaw muscles twitched. "I already tried. I told them that Andy's still alive. At least for now, but they ignored me."

"Andy's not dead?" Dazed by the news, I tried to step back from him, but the crowd had grown so tightly packed that I couldn't.

"He's as good as dead, though." He let go of my wrist.

"Oh, John B," I cried. "It can't be true. Not Andy."

He took off his old stetson and held it across his chest. His jacket was loose and his pants were tucked into his muddy boots. "He's hurt bad though."

"What happened?"

John B's eyes were impossible to read. "I'm not sure. I thought he was behind me. We were trying to arrest that boy. I'm hitting him—hitting him. And there's noise. Jim and JW start screaming and pointing. I run over to see—"

Dino tugged at my arm. "Now, Mamie."

The sounds of blows intermixed with the Negro's screams emerged from the alley.

"You don't want to see this. Go. Get away from here. NOW!" John B turned and headed toward the sounds.

I glimpsed a muscular man dragging the Negro toward the trolley into the middle of Garrison. John B tried to elbow his way through the men surrounding them but was quickly rebuffed. Surprised that the rioters ignored him, I realized that he wasn't armed. He was arguing with someone on the sidewalk under the Hotel Main portico when a cheer distracted me.

I turned to watch the leader of the mob tie a fat rope around the neck of the trembling prisoner just before dozens of onlookers filled the space between where we stood and the pole.

Cars braked. Horses cried out and then quieted. Pedestrians gathered. Heads poked out of the windows of neighboring buildings. The balcony above the entrance to the Hotel Main filled with the well-dressed and curious. We were only a few yards away, but my view was blocked by taller people. Bodies pushed against me from all sides.

Dino let go of my arm.

"What's happening," I whispered.

"They're trying to get a rope through the cross bar." Burley said.

Standing on tiptoes, I could just see the top of the pole. At that moment, a rope hit the cross bar and clattered back out of sight.

A man shimmied up the pole with rope tied around his waist, but he slid down before he could thread the rope over the cross beam and secure it.

"Nice try, Henry!" a deep voice in the crowd encouraged him.

A minute later, the same figure made it back up near the cross beams. "Will Henry," I breathed. "I met him this afternoon when I was with Andy Carr at Padgett's."

Henry slid down again, laughing at his inability to achieve his mission.

"There's Julian," Burley said.

"Where?"

"Up there." He pointed at the portico above the entrance to the Hotel Main. "A bird's eye view."

Julian's glasses glinted off the street lights and electric billboards. I tried to get his attention, but he was absorbed in the spectacle playing out below him.

Finally, a small figure shimmied up the pole and climbed onto the cross beam.

"Manny!" I cried out in the sudden silence.

"Do it Manny." A familiar voice behind me called.

I turned around, shocked to see Ollie Fields and Sarah. Her arms were crossed and she avoided my eyes. Mr. Fields was so enthused over the lynching that he never even noticed me. "Kill him," he yelled.

Manny reached down and reappeared with the rope. He seemed to be receiving instructions from below. He put his hand behind his ear as if he was having trouble hearing and then nodded. Holding onto the pole with one arm, he threaded the line over the crossbeam and handed the end down to a someone below him.

The crowd cheered while Manny looked out over Garrison Avenue and shook his fist in the air triumphantly.

"My God, Manny."

"You know this boy, Miz Mamie?"

"That's Emanuel McKnight. He does odd jobs for us from time to time."

"I'm sorry." Dino bowed his head.

Manny slid down the pole. For a minute, all I could see was the rope tighten and loosen around the cross beam. Then it caught and suddenly, we saw the young Negro being pulled upwards, his hands on the rope around his neck, his feet kicking. His mouth moved as he tried to relieve the pressure, but I couldn't hear what he said.

A woman shrieked as the rope slipped and the figure dipped down out of my sight. She turned and pushed her way between the tightly-packed bodies. "Please," she said as she fought to get away from the sight. "Please stop them." It was Anna Marie Cavanaugh, followed by Orrin Fellows. She grabbed my hands. "Please, Mamie."

I shook my head. "I can't."

Orrin Fellows put his hand on her back, avoiding my eyes.

"I can't. I have to—" She covered her mouth as he pushed her past me and through the crowd.

Immediately, people surged forward to take their places.

"Die, you bastard. Die!" It was Will Henry who'd backed away from the pole and was now, only a few feet from us.

I glared at him.

He must have felt my venom because he caught my eye and his smirk faded.

The crowd parted briefly. I glimpsed the Negro closer to the ground. Con Sullivan pulled the rope around his neck so tight that his victim winced and tried to pull away.

Then another man took hold of the line arching up over the cross beams and pulled, jerking the Negro upwards.

Men in the crowd chanted. "Joe, Joe. Hang 'em, Joe."

"Who's Joe?"

"A local cattle wrangler," Dino said into my ear. "And one of my regular customers."

Andy Carr's murderer kicked and fought the rope. Despite the brutal beatings he'd endured, I marveled at his strength and desire to live.

"Dear God have mercy and take this sinner quickly," a baritone behind me intoned. I turned to see Reverend Mathews, eyes closed, holding a Bible to his chest.

I turned back. I could just see the Negro's head before he dropped below my line of sight again

I clutched Burley's arm. "Do you think they stopped? That it's over?"

"We can only hope," he said out of the corner of his mouth. "That boy has suffered enough."

"No! Look!" Dino pointed.

I stood on tiptoe, straining to see. Another man, older and better dressed than most of the others, climbed the pole.

"Damn," Burley breathed. "John Stowers."

Dino sighed too. "Yes, that's John."

"How do you know him," I murmured.

"He was the contractor I used to create my restaurant."

There was a flash and then another one. "What's that?" I rubbed my eyes.

"Someone's taking photographs."

"Who?" I was horrified and intrigued by the idea.

"Maybe the newspapers?"

I hadn't thought of that. I looked up to the portico, searching for Julian. He was gone.

John Stowers hooked first one arm over the cross bar—and then one leg. With a loud grunt he hefted himself upward until he was sitting on top the pole. The crowd noises softened. Slowly, hand over hand, muscles bulging with the effort, John Stowers pulled the Negro up. The victim fought for air, but he was weakening. I took a sympathetic breath for him, held it while I counted my own heartbeats—and then blew it out.

The hangman let the black man drop. The sound echoed across Garrison Avenue.

"Oh my God," a woman behind me screamed.

After a moment, face grim in the neon lights, Stowers pulled the body up again. The Negro's head was tilted at a sickening angle—and it was clear that the young man was finally dead.

Another voice joined Reverend Mathews in the Lord's prayer. I turned to see Father Horan standing beside Reverend Mathews.

I crossed myself and joined in as did Dino and Burley. As we finished, I saw Cathey Pitcock standing on the sidewalk in front of the Main, calmly smoking a cigarette. He caught my eye, hacked up phlegm and spat it on the sidewalk.

The noise increased and I turned back to the scene in front of me. Stowers hoisted the body almost to the cross beam, put his feet on the Negro's shoulders and swung him around to face the crowd filling Garrison Avenue. The Negro's neck was stretched out three or four times its proper length. His face was a bloody pulp. His hands were torn. And someone had put a bullet in the back of his thigh.

There was a collective gasp. Hundreds of unwitting witnesses around me backed away. An older woman fainted into her husband's arms. Business men groaned and shook canes or umbrellas at the leaders of the mob. Sarah Fields backed away, gagging into her handkerchief. Mr. Fields followed after her, meeting my eyes defiantly.

A high, reedy voice rose over the din. "You're crazy. Crazy. How did that bring Andy back? What kind of fools are you?"

I fought through the diminishing crowd. The voice went on and on.

"Mamie!" Burley called from behind.

I pushed forward, sweat pouring down my face.

People turned to face me. It was only then that I realized that the screeching voice was my own. I stopped. Eyes wide, I covered my mouth. Only then was there silence.

"Mamie, Mamie—darling." It was Julian. He put his arms around me.

"Did you see what they did?"

"Yes," he said into my neck. "I saw."

"How could they?"

"I have no idea."

Dino put his hand on Julian's shoulder. "Who was he?"

"Who was who?"

"Him." Dino pointed to the hanging body.

"He was our yardman."

I swallowed and squinted up at the corpse. "What? Who did you say?"

Julian turned to me and put his hands on my shoulders. "That's Sandy, sweetheart. Sanford Lewis."

11

I seen the chief running by. He said, "How're you boys? I'm in a hurry."

Officer Sam Booth, Police Inquiry

I saw the chief that night and asked him if he needed help. He muttered something and ran off. I figured he didn't need us for anything and we was busy anyway.

Ed Pennewell to Mamie McGrath

I got a telephone message that there was a problem at the jail. I took a trolley to Garrison and then ran to the courthouse. Along the way, I saw Pennewell and told him to come along quick.

Chief Bryant Barry, Police Inquiry

We was waitin' at the Frisco. Several drunk boys and men was staggering around the station, showin' off their bloody hands and tellin' us that was one nigger down and a bunch to go. They boarded the train as our friends got off and we hurried on home as fast as we could. At the time, we didn't know it was the Reverend Lewis's boy, Sanford, who died.

Genevieve Day to Mamie McGrath

March 25, 1912

IT WAS EIGHT O'CLOCK MONDAY morning when I heard voices downstairs. Julian was sleeping. He'd worked through Saturday night into early afternoon Sunday. His first article about the riot on Garrison Avenue appeared in the Sunday morning edition, a few hours after the lynching.

I got dressed and tiptoed down the stairs. Soft sobs echoed in the hallway. Wondering who was visiting so early in the morning, I peeked into the front parlor. Caroline was handing Abigail a handkerchief.

They looked up at me.

"It's Garland. He didn't come home Saturday or last night." Abigail wiped her eyes.

"I'm sure he's okay."

"See," Caroline murmured. "If anything was wrong, we would've heard by now."

"Maybe he had too much to drink Saturday and he's still hung over."

"Maybe." I'd never seen Abigail in such a state. "He's never been gone two nights without telling me ahead of time."

Caroline squeezed her hand. "He needs to be alone to think about things."

Abigail sniffed. "He's sensitive, you know. Extra sensitive about things like that."

"Yes, dear, I do know."

"Would you like some hot chocolate?"

Abigail peered at me through her fingers. "You won't make it will you?"

"I'll have Genevieve make it."

"With mint leaves and whipped cream?"

"With all of that."

"You'll tell her to go easy on the vanilla?"

"I'll make sure she uses Caroline's recipe."

* * *

In the kitchen, Genevieve was crying too.

"Oh Genevieve. What can I do for you?"

She waved me back while she composed herself. "There's not much anyone can do, ma'am. Hearts of mamas and aunties are breakin' all over town."

"Go home. Take care of your family. We can survive without you one day."

"No, ma'am. My family needs me here, makin' a livin.' Seein' Miz Abigail like that tore me up all over again."

I pulled up a chair and sat across from her. "Why, Genevieve? Abigail hasn't been especially nice to you."

"No ma'am, she ain't. But that woman's outsides cover up some mighty unhappy insides. I cain't help but feel sorry for her on a good day. But today, I dunno. She made me think about all this meanness." Her hands knotted up into tight fists in her lap. "Sanford was his mama's pride and joy. Loula once told me that he brought her presents that he drew or carved since he was no bigger than a pissant. One time when he was maybe five or six, he painted a leaf and put some big ole eyes on it and a toothy grin and gave it to her, proud as punch. Was jes a lil thing a kid'll do, but she cherished it."

I sat down beside her. "He was a private person. I didn't know much about him, except that he wanted to learn to drive. To be a chauffeur. He was kind to us and to Manny." I dabbed at my own streaming eyes. "I can't imagine how scared and hurt Sandy was when they were doing that to him."

"Me either, ma'am." She cried again, a single convulse—and then she straightened her shoulders. "What was it you needed, Miz Mamie?"

"Hot chocolate. Caroline's recipe. Abigail was explicit. I'm not to make it."

Genevieve's chuckle was part sob. "Yes, ma'am. You better get out of here then, lest that lady think you been messin' with the chocolate."

"Are you sure you want to stay?"

"Pardon, my sayin' this, ma'am. There's no safe place in this world and not enough work days to waste one, no matter how blue I am."

"If you need to take a minute now and again, please do."

"Ma'am, you look pretty upset too. Maybe you should take a few yourself."

"I thought the worse that could happen had already happened. But Saturday night taught me different."

* * *

Genevieve was pulling out the ingredients for Caroline's hot chocolate when I returned to the front parlor.

"—and that awful Mr. Fellows causing troub—" Abigail stopped speaking when she saw me.

"Genevieve's making our hot chocolate." I said. "I didn't even touch a pot." I held up my hands to show they were empty.

Abigail raised her precisely-drawn eyebrows. "Have I hurt your feelings somehow, Mamie?"

I shook my head and sat down. "Are you feeling better?"

"I'm scared for Garland. You might not know it to look at him, but he has a tender heart. He had a tough upbringing, what with his father dying so young and his mother being left with just a soldier's pension. Enough is not enough for him now."

I suspected enough was not enough for Abigail either, but I held my tongue.

"I'm sure Garland will come home soon," Caroline said. "When you are upset, home is where you want to be."

"That's why I can't understand this. He hates crowds like that. A bad experience as a young man."

I nodded, thinking of Garland's nightmares about the death of the colored man in Texas that Abigail had once told me about.

The phone rang and I got up to answer it.

It was Colonel Parker. "It's this afternoon, Mamie. Tell Julian we need him down here by one."

"What's this afternoon, Mr, Parker?"

"Word is that Judge Hon will send this to a special Grand Jury. Got two witnesses they're going to question late this afternoon. And the city council aldermen are about to rebel against the mayor. Gonna be a big day."

I blew my breath through my broken front teeth and it came out a hiss. "I'll wake him up right away."

The phone went dead.

"Hello?"

Silence.

"Anyone there?" I replaced the receiver, and headed upstairs to wake Julian.

"What did I ever do to her?" Abigail whispered loud enough for me to hear her. I went into the bedroom I shared with my husband and shut the door a little louder than I intended.

"What's going on?" Julian murmured without opening his eyes.

"Your boss called. He wants you downtown. Witnesses are going before a Grand Jury this evening."

He pulled a pillow over his face.

I stood in front of the mirror and stuck my tongue out at myself.

"What's wrong now?"

I spoke to his reflection. "Abigail."

"What else is new?"

"She's upset because Garland hasn't found his way home yet." My eye caught Martina Esposito's long-bladed butcher knife laying on my dresser. I picked it up, wondering what to do with it.

Julian stretched. "I bet he's lying low. He was part of that mob."

"You saw Garland?" I wrapped the knife in a yellow scarf and put it beside my jewelry box.

"I saw him. Him and Stowers. That crook Con Sullivan. Orrin Fellows. Young Jack Hale. Joe Tucker. Sam Smith. Will Henry. Will Manus. A bunch of kids including Grover Bourland. Manny McKnight. Half the drunks in the city. George—"

"Shush." I whirled around. "Don't tell me anymore."

"I saw them, Mamie. I can't name them in the newspaper unless they're arrested. But I saw them. I was as close to them as I am from you now. Closer. I followed them to the jail. Watched our so-called cops melt away into the night. Saw one of them whisper in Stowers' ear. Saw the crowd use a railroad tie to break dow—"

"How do you know what the cop was telling people?"

"Because he whispered in my ear too." He held his head in his hands.

"What?"

"He saw me standing outside the fence around the jail and he came up to me, grinning like a hyena."

I sat down on the edge of the bed. "What did he say, Julian? Specifically."

He looked up into my eyes. "They put the bastard that killed Andy in the nigger holding cell. On the second floor."

"No!"

"That's what he said. Not just to me, either. I saw him tell Tucker too. And Garland."

I stamped my foot. "No way did Sandy kill anyone. Certainly not Andy Carr.

"I'm not saying he did. Just that's what the cop was telling people."

"He's lying, Julian."

"I know. Hell, with a little thought, half of those men out there trying to get into that jail would've realized it too. But they weren't thinking. They were caught up in the moment."

"Didn't anyone stop and say I'm not going to be a part of this?"

"Plenty decent men walked away. They still thought Sandy murdered Andy, but they had no stomach for a lynching."

"They could've rushed the jail. Fought the ringleaders. Protected Sandy." My voice rose.

"They could've, but they didn't."

"Why didn't the police stop them?"

"Chief Barry tried."

"When was that?"

"Before the crowd got the railroad tie. The courtyard around the men's jail was packed with people. I didn't even try to go in. I found a rock pile and climbed up on top. The old man came running from Garrison. He tried to squeeze through the mob several times. But they closed ranks and wouldn't let him through. Finally, he found a way in. Don't know how. I lost sight of him for awhile. But then, there he was blocking the door with his body. A fool could see it was too late for that, but he was brave. I'll give him that. He was yelling something, but it was so noisy that I couldn't make it out." Julian sat up and put his bare feet on the rug beside our bed. "Those bastards picked Chief Barry up like a sack of potatoes, carried him on their shoulders, and set him down on the rocks below me."

"No one helped him?"

"His son. And one fellow seemed to go to his aid, but it was too dark to make out who he was."

"Where were the rest of the police?"

Julian shrugged.

"That dear old man."

"Too little, too late." Julian stood up and started getting dressed.

"Where was Garland?" I lowered my voice. "After that? On Garrison? When they murdered Sandy?"

"I don't know, sweetheart. The last time I saw Garland was after the crowd had Sandy and was dragging him up the alley toward Garrison. I followed about ten paces behind the lot of them. Someone had knocked Garland down. Either as the crowd passed him, or he fell and they stepped around him to avoid falling themselves. I helped him to his feet. At first he didn't recognize me. He was very drunk. I shouted, 'Go home!' but he just stood there, wiping his forehead on his sleeve and blinking. I pointed toward Rogers Avenue. His eyes followed my finger, but he didn't move or say anything. It was obvious that something was happening on Garrison and it was my job to report it so I left him there."

"Why didn't you tell me this before, Julian?"

"Too many horrible things happened that night. I'll be remembering bits and pieces of it the rest of my life." He slipped on the clean shirt I'd laid out for him before going downstairs earlier.

I pushed back angry words and bitter tears. "I'm sorry, Julian. I know none of this is your fault."

He put his arms around me. "I'm upset too, baby." He kissed my forehead. "I'm mad and disappointed in people I've known my whole life. Or thought I knew. Upset with myself for being useless to help Sandy. Proud of the article I did Saturday night. And the work I'll do now and in the future. I'm not supposed to make the news, just report it. And I'm just one fellow—and not one prone to fisticuffs or arguments. Still, someone should have stopped that mob. I keep thinking that I should have rounded up like-minded citizens and blocked those idiots from getting into the jail. Me and people like me should have shamed Stowers and Smith and those boys. Or just stalled things until the cops got organized. I'll spend the rest of my life wondering how I could've kept that boy from dying on that pole."

10 a.m., Monday

Abigail had left by the time Julian and I came downstairs. Caroline was in the kitchen with Genevieve.

"You ready for your hot chocolate, Miz Mamie?"

"Put mine in the icebox, Genevieve. I'm not feeling up to it now. But, Julian needs something he can eat fast or take with him. He has to be back downtown in an hour."

"Have a seat, Mr. Julian. I'll fry you up some eggs. And we still got some of that good bread Miz Caroline baked last week. I can toast it for you."

Julian sat down at the kitchen table. "If you can add coffee to that, I'll be fine."

Caroline poured him a cup of coffee. "You look tired, son."

"I am, Mama. And sick at heart."

"Maybe you shouldn't go back to that mess today. You've done your part."

"Can't miss this week. Judge Hon called a special Grand Jury today." He consulted his pocket watch. "They'll be meeting soon. I want to be there when they get out."

"Is this how it works?" I sat down across from him. "Have you ever seen things happen so fast?"

He shook his head. "Not that I remember, but I haven't been at this all that long. People are riled. The businessmen are worried about how this makes Fort Smith look to outside investors and customers. The locals are defiant. They insist that Sandy shot Andy and as such he got what he deserved. The Negro community is on edge, expecting white vigilantes to show up at their doors. Everyday white folks are scared a horde of colored demons will slit their throats while they sleep."

"Lord Almighty," Genevieve muttered under her breath as she flipped Julian's eggs.

"There are good people in Fort Smith," Caroline said. "It might take a day or two, but they will calm down."

"The police failed everyone, Mama. They not only didn't stop it, but some people are telling me that they started it."

"How?" I demanded.

"I don't know exactly. We have a bunch of scattered pieces now. The Grand Jury will have to figure it out. That's probably why Judge Hon thinks this needs to be taken care of while it's fresh in everyone's minds. In the meantime, I need to talk to as many witnesses who'll let me. Colonel Parker wants me to put together a series of stories explaining what happened in a way the everyday reader can understand."

Genevieve put Julian's breakfast in front of him. "More coffee, sir?"

He nodded and held up his mug.

"I want to help."

Caroline and Genevieve looked at me in astonishment.

Julian drained his coffee cup. "How do you propose to do that?"

"People might talk to me who wouldn't you."

"What kind of people?"

"Coloreds."

Caroline, Julian and I turned to Genevieve in surprise.

"Miz Mamie is good to people like Miz Caroline here is. They like her and they'll tell her how they feel."

"Thank you for that, Genevieve," I said. "That means the world to me."

Julian turned to me. "Who else?"

"Nuns and prostitutes." I tried not to seem too glib. "I can do it."

"Not alone," Julian frowned. "It's a dangerous world out there. Especially right now."

"I can interview people and you can write it, Julian. I can do this."

"I can introduce Miz Mamie to folks in my neighborhood, Mr. Julian. I guarantee you no harm will come to this lady from Negroes."

"Wasn't Negroes that caused this tragedy, Genevieve."

"But we're suffering all the same."

"I don't know." He shook his head. "Let me think about it."

"Julian—"

"Not now, Mamie. We can talk about it tonight."

I bit my tongue. "Tonight."

The telephone rang. Caroline backed away from it. "I don't think I can take anymore bad news."

I picked up the receiver and held it to my ear. "This is the Mc-Grath home. Mamie speaking," I said into the mouth piece.

"Mamie, it's Anna Marie. I need your help again."

"Is something wrong?".

"It's about Garland Talbot. He and Orrin Fellows are here, hiding in our basement. Miss Bertha isn't as patient with that sort of thing as Miss Laura was. She wants them out of here."

"What do you want me to do? Call Abigail?"

"Garland is stubborn about that. He doesn't want her to know where he is."

"So what do you want me to do?"

"Come get them."

"Me?"

"They're afraid someone'll recognize them and call the law."

I tilted my head. "Why would anyone do that?"

"I think you know why." Anna Marie's voice trembled.

"My God!" Julian's chair turned over backwards when he stood up. Caroline clasped both hands over her bosom.

My voice was husky. "They didn't?"

"They're hiding in our basement. Talbot threw up most of the night they came here."

"What night was that?"

Silence.

"Tell me, Anna Marie."

"You know what night."

I leaned against the wall, trying to catch my breath.

Julian took my hand. "What is it?"

I pulled away from him and said into the mouthpiece. "Are they wanted by the police?"

"I have no idea," Anna Marie said. "But the police could make our lives miserable if they suspect these two were hiding here."

"I thought Mr. Fellows and Garland were on the outs about something."

"That was months ago. This is bigger than a fuss over money. They can't be linked to that lynching or stand trial or have their names or pictures in the paper. That kind of publicity could bring down bigger birds. Do you understand?"

"I need to think about this."

"Tick tock, tick tock, Mamie."

I covered the mouthpiece and tried to slow my breathing. I looked from Caroline to Julian and back. I had no idea what these two men had done the night Sandy died, but the thought of them being involved, however peripherally, sickened me.

I set the receiver on top of the telephone box and bent forward. How dare Garland do this to Abigail? To us? To me!

Visions of Andy lying in the hospital rose up in my mind. And of Sandy hanging on the Fort Smith Light and Traction Company trolley pole. And of Manny McKnight's dirty face.

"Mamie?"

Julian reached out to me, but this time I wasn't going to faint. This time I wasn't going to let anyone else protect me.

I pulled away from him and snatched the receiver from the top of the oak telephone box. "Anna Marie?"

"Yes?"

"No."

"What shall I tell them?"

"Just no. Not this time. Not ever again."

"Mami—"

* * *

The ball struck Andy Carr above the right eyebrow and fractured the skull, driving pieces of bone into his brain. The ball came out the right temple leaving a three inch track. Parts of the brain were shot out. Dr. Stevenson reports that there is little chance for recovery.

Southwest American

11 a.m.

Julian left before I came back downstairs. Caroline was in the kitchen with Genevieve, packing a large picnic basket.

"What's going on?"

"Putting together a few things for the Carr family," Genevieve said.

"I thought we might do beans for them."

"Maybe, tomorrow," Caroline said over her shoulder. "I have a feeling we need to go see them this morning. And there's no time to cook beans."

I froze. "You've heard something?"

"Yes. Well no. It's crazy I know, but I was looking in my notebook for Mr. Cravens telephone number for Abigail in case she needs a lawyer."

"Has she heard from Garland?"

"No, no. It was after she left. I got to thinking that a lot of people are going to need lawyers after Saturday night. I remembered Wilbur had his will done at Cravens and Cravens and I thought I'd written down the name of the young man in that office who did it. Wilbur liked him a lot. And I thought that maybe she might need someone if Garland has left her or something." She avoided my eyes.

"Do you think that's what happened?"

"They've been struggling for a while. Garland drinks too much, you know."

"And Abigail spends too much," I said.

"Yes." She still avoided my eyes. "Anyway, that old paper—the one where I was figuring out that coded message from Theo Lamb's Ouija board party a few years ago? It fell out of my notebook."

"What?"

"You know when the spirit of Maybelle Shirley got Abigail all riled up that night?"

"Sort of. What did it say again?"

"Tell John B to watch out for Andy."

I sat down at the table. "Oh, my." I didn't know what to say and didn't have any air to say it with if I did. "You don't believe that."

"Oh no, dear. I don't believe in fortune-telling ghosts, but it was quite a shock to see it."

"I can imagine." I was pretty shocked myself.

"And I decided that coincidence or not, I needed to go visit Della and those kids today. Perhaps God wants me to be there today. Not tomorrow. But today." She blushed. "I think."

I stood up. "I think so too. And I'm going with you."

* * *

"Pick us up in one hour," Caroline told the driver of the hack as she paid him.

"Yes, ma'am. You tell Miz Carr that we're pulling for Andy."

"I most certainly will, Leroy." Caroline hefted the basket of food on one arm and I carried three bottles of milk.

The Carrs lived on the corner of S 17th and E. As we approached the front door, we heard a rumble of voices, from sobbing children to angry shouts to murmured prayers. I knocked on the front door several times before Andy's daughter, Pansy, heard us and let us in.

"I'm sorry, Miz Caroline. We're a mite rattled right now." She escorted us to the kitchen where we put down the basket and bottles of milk. "Thank you for thinking of us. As you can see, we're filled to the brim with neighbors, family, and visitors. None of us have the time or heart to shop, cook and feed this mob. Mama's spent every moment at the hospital with Daddy. She's cleaning up and getting dressed to go back again right now."

"Never you mind, dear. Mamie and I will put out a spread."

"Bebe's gone home to change clothes and check on her family. She'll help when she gets back. I think we've worn her out so she'll be glad to see what you've brought."

Pansy was a pretty young woman about the same age Sandy had been. She was neatly dressed and had brushed and tied back her hair with a ribbon.

I smiled at her. "You look tired. Sit down and I'll get you something to eat."

"I don't think I can swallow anything right now."

"How about some tea?"

She nodded.

"How's your dad doing?" I put a kettle of water on the stove.

Pansy lifted her chin. "Daddy's dying."

"Oh no. Maybe not."

"Don't try to give me hope, Miz Mamie. If I hope and he dies, that'll hurt worse. If I hope and he lives but is not himself, not right, you know—" She tapped her own temple with her pointer finger. "—if he doesn't recognize us or isn't good old Andy anymore, I don't think I can bear it."

I squeezed my eyes shut trying to block another wave of tears. "What will happen will happen. We just came to help you deal with this." I gestured around me.

Pansy nodded and stared out the back window until I set a cup of tea in front of her.

On the long table, we laid out a platter of sliced ham, a large bowl of green beans, cornbread, butter, honey, and fruit cake.

"Gee thanks, Miz Mamie." A solemn-faced boy filled a plate and sat down beside Pansy. "My daddy's in the hospital," he said to me. "Again."

Pansy put her arm around his shoulders and laid her head on top of his. "James, do you remember Miz Caroline? She's Julian's mama. And this is Mamie. Julian's wife."

The boy nodded to each of us. "Daddy got shot, Miz Caroline. Right here." He pointed to his forehead over his right eyebrow.

"I'm so sorry, James." Caroline was warm and comforting as usual.

"He's going to die." James forked a piece of ham. "I'm not supposed to know that, but I do."

"Pardon me." Pansy went out onto the back porch, slamming the door behind her.

Caroline grabbed a shawl hanging on a hook by the door and hurried after her, leaving me alone with Della and Andy's youngest son.

Not knowing what else to do, I sat quietly beside him.

He watched me through lowered lashes. "They lie to me, you know."

"Who does?"

"Mama and the girls."

"Maybe they're trying to protect you," I said.

"They think I'm a baby." His lower lip trembled.

"How old are you, James?"

"Ten. Almost eleven."

"You're definitely not a baby."

"That's what Uncle Jim said."

"That's your mama's brother?"

James cut another piece of ham with the side of his fork. "Uh huh."

"So two Jameses live here." I smiled.

"Three. My cousin is James, too. After his mama died, they came to live with us."

"That will be good for your mother while your dad is in the hospital. And for you too."

James took a tiny bite. "How do you see that, ma'am?"

"Sometimes it's better for a boy your age to have a man to talk to in times of trouble."

"Ya think?"

I decided that was wrong. Then I thought maybe it was right after all. "Maybe."

"I got my big brother Meek too."

I'd forgotten about Meek. "You'll have each other."

"I hope Daddy comes home before he dies."

I blinked tears out of my eyes and tried again. "Andy's a pretty tough guy, James," I said. "He's always bounced back before."

"Mama's scared this time. So's Pansy and little Della." He took a bite of cornbread. "Margaret too. Meek says that the girls worry too much. He says that he and I have to be tough like Daddy and take care of Mama and our sisters."

"That's a good way to look at things." I had no idea if it was or not. I just wanted to sound like I did for James' sake.

"Uncle Jim says that things might be a lot different from now on. That he and Jimmy might need to move out."

"Maybe you shouldn't worry about that until it happens."

James frowned. "I don't want it to happen."

I was messing this up and I knew it. It was just as well that Julian and I would never be parents. "Me either." It was almost a whisper.

"Bebe'll be back soon." He took another bite of ham. "She said she was gonna cook fried chicken for us tonight."

The back door opened and Caroline came in without Pansy. I raised my eyebrows and she shrugged. "I'm going to talk with Della before she leaves for the hospital."

"Okay."

James watched her disappear into the crowded living room. "I was supposed to go see Daddy with Mama but now she says it's not the right time."

"Well, your mama would know best about that."

"Or she just doesn't want me to know what's going on." He drank the rest of his milk and stood up, leaving most of his food on the plate.

"She wants to protect you, James."

"What's to protect if every thing's just fine?"

* * *

I scraped James' plate and rinsed it. Through the window over the sink, I saw Pansy sitting on the back step, wrapped in the shawl Caroline had taken her. I watched for a minute before deciding to go outside and sit with her.

"It's noisy in there."

"I can't escape it." She pulled the shawl tighter around her.

"I know." We stared at a row of Jonquils blooming along the back fence.

"It's my fault."

"How could that be, Pansy?"

"I sneaked out to meet a boyfriend before Daddy came home that night."

"And?"

"Daddy was upset I wasn't home when he got here and he went back downtown to find me."

"And did he?"

A single tear trickled down her cheek and she nodded.

"What happened then?"

"I wasn't even with Jack when he found me. He got all upset all the same. Over nothing. He took me home on the trolley. I kept trying to talk to him. To explain. But he wouldn't look at me."

"What happened when you got home?"

"Daddy told me to go to my room and he'd talk to me later. Only there was no 'later.' That was the last time I saw him. What if the last time he talked to me, he was mad?"

I put my arm around her. There wasn't much I could say to comfort her. "Daddies are partial to their first born, especially daughters."

"Did he think I'd never grow up? That men would never find me attractive?"

"Probably," I said. "I expect he and Della are still learning how to let go of their baby."

"That whole time on the trolley he never said a word to me. Nothing."

"Maybe he didn't know what to say."

"And Mama says he can't talk now."

"He loves you, Pansy."

"I hope."

2:15 p.m.

When we got home from the Carr's, Caroline declared herself mentally and physically exhausted and retired to her room. I went upstairs and fetched my journal and pen. It was March and I hadn't written much since the fall of 1911. My last entry described the opening of the New Theater and the play, The Third Degree. How young I was then. No time for such foolishness now. I pulled the cap off the fountain pen and wrote. "I am a writer. A reporter and a writer." I dated and signed it. Then I turned to the next page.

I was three pages into a description of the worst Saturday night of my life when the telephone rang. I capped my pen and closed the journal on it.

I made it down the stairs by the fourth ring.

"Mamie?"

"Yes?"

"It's Garland Talbot. Please don't hang up."

"Abigail's worried sick about you."

"I know. I've made her life a living hell these past few years."

"So what are you going to do about it?"

"I'm going to lay low for a while. I can't call Abigail. She'll try to talk me out of it. Fact is, she'll be a lot happier when I'm gone."

"I doubt that."

"Believe me, she will. Besides, if I don't get out of here soon, they'll probably arrest me after what happened the other night. Doesn't seem right that hanging a nigger should cause such a ruckus after what he did to Andy. Maybe after everyone settles down, people will come to their senses. In the meantime, I need to get away from Orrin. He's not my friend. Tell Abigail that he isn't hers either. Tell her to watch out for Sister Clarence too. That whiskey is mine. Ours. I thought of it, I invested in it. Hell, I even came up with the hiding place."

I bit my lip. I wanted to call him a lowdown dirty murderer, but after I tamped down my disgust, I said, "So you're leaving town? Leaving Abigail in the lurch?"

"Until everything settles down. Until Fellows thinks I'm dead or the cops figure him out or that Chicago crowd figures out where he is."

"I thought the two of you were hiding out in Miss Bertha's basement?"

"He went to tend to business at St. Anne's and I slipped out."

"Where are you now?"

"Tell Abigail after I'm gone, maybe tomorrow, to check Mr. Guckenheimer's locker at the Frisco Station. She knows which key if she thinks about it."

"Garland, what're you talking about?"

"And tell her that I love her. I know that's not near enough. I can't even live up to my own expectations, let alone hers."

"Where are you going? What are you going to do?"

The line went dead.

"Aw, Garland." I slammed the receiver back on the hook. "You're a poor excuse for a—" I took a deep breath and tried to remember everything he'd said so I could put it in my journal. I was halfway up the stairs when the phone rang again. "Oh for Pete's sake, Garland," I cried and hurried back to the phone. "Don't hang up on me again!"

"I'd never hang up on you, sweetheart. What's going on?"

"Oh Julian. I just had the craziest call from Garland Talbot. I think he's leaving town."

"I would too, if I were him. They're considering him one of the leaders of that mob."

"Garland? He couldn't lead a bee to clover."

"Probably not. But, they'll arrest him if he sticks around town. He was a pretty visible part of the group drinking at Till Shaw's that came out and revved up the other drunks and those kids."

"Good riddance then."

"What did he want from you?"

"To give a message to Abigail."

"He hasn't got the guts to call his own wife and tell her he's leaving town?"

"I swear, Julian. You dare do something like that to me, you might as well not come home at all."

He chuckled. "Goodness you've gotten feisty lately."

"I've had to."

"I thought about what you said this morning. About interviewing people. I think you're right. Even if we both talked to the same fellow, we'd get different things. He'd tell me the basics. He'd tell you what he thinks and feels about it. Strikes me that could be useful in figuring out what happened on Garrison the other night."

"Does that mean you'll read the information I get for you?"

"If you think it'll help. I'll trust your judgment."

"I started already. This morning at the Carrs."

"Good. Think you can come down here for the City Council Meeting at four?"

"Will they let me in?"

"Maybe, maybe not. But people will be coming and going. Men especially won't be able to resist talking with you. When they do, just get them to tell you what they think and why. Write it all down right away. If you hear something important, tell me and we'll compare it with what I'll be hearing inside."

"Where do I need to go and when?"

3:45 p.m.

I stood under the street light in front of the Hotel Main, staring at the trolley pole where a mob had lynched Sandy a little over forty hours before.

An older man walked past me, paused, and then tipped his hat. "Good afternoon, Mamie. It's Sam McCloud. Do you remember me?"

"Mr. McCloud? Yes. You are the president of First National Bank. We met at the Goldman last fall. I was just—"

"I can't stop looking at it either."

I blinked back tears. "I knew him."

"The young Negro who was killed?"

I nodded. "Sanford—we called him Sandy—he kept our lawn. He wanted to learn how to drive so he could become a chauffeur, but our car broke down after one lesson and we hadn't gotten around to repairing it. He was aiming to get a better paying job so he could get married."

"I didn't know that about him, but I heard he was a polite young fellow."

"Yes sir, he was."

"I understand that he didn't have a gun so he couldn't have killed officer Carr."

"Even if he had a gun, he wouldn't have hurt Andy. He was scared and just trying to go home to his folks, I'm sure of it."

"I'm sure too."

We stood quietly for a moment, awkward in each other's presence, yet both inexorably drawn to this spot.

"Fort Smith is better than this, Mamie. I promise you, we'll figure out what happened and make sure the ones who did this are punished."

"Thank you, sir." I knew so many of the people on the street that night. How could I ever look at them again without seeing the ugliness in their eyes. Would I ever be able to sleep thinking that my neighbors had that in them? No matter how this situation was resolved legally, the community would be torn up for years to come. I would be too.

Mr. McCloud tipped his hat again and hurried off.

* * *

I sat in the green leather rockers in the Hotel Main lobby.

"The City Council finally met," Julian said when he arrived. "The aldermen expected Mayor Bourland to call an open meeting first thing this morning. By eleven when he still wasn't in his office, they were frustrated. So several of them sent him a letter setting the time and place and demanding, quote—action on the disgraceful violation of the law that took place on Garrison Avenue Saturday night—unquote. And six of them signed their names."

Mayor Bourland's lack of leadership on this topic was puzzling. If nothing else, he impressed me as an opportunist who'd be eager to seize the limelight. "Why do you suppose the mayor did that? Feeling guilty?"

Julian shrugged and handed me his notebook. "Maybe. Or maybe overwhelmed—not wanting to deal with the uproar. Or maybe trying to decide how to play this thing for political effect."

I thumbed through his notes. "The aldermen had already come up with a resolution by the time they met with the mayor?"

"Outraged people don't waste any time."

"Who wrote this?"

"TB Garrett. He's the most vocal but they're all mad as hornets." I read out loud,

Whereas the law has been outraged and the city of Fort Smith has been disgraced and humiliated by a mob, which took from the jail of this city and hanged Sanford Lewis on the night of March 23, 1912.

"Resolved that the city council of the city of Fort Smith condemn the action of the mob and each of its responsible members, as disgraceful and as meriting the prompt infliction of the severest punishment provided by the outraged law.

Resolved that it is the sense of the city council that no responsible participant in the mob is worthy of citizenship in this community, but deserves successful prosecution, extreme punishment, and no recognition as a resident of the city of Fort Smith.

"I can't believe this," I said. "I expected there would be no consequences suffered by any of these men for killing Sandy."

"I know. I was shocked too. And impressed," Julian said. "But read the rest."

I found my place. "There's going to be a police inquiry?"

"And they are going to fire people."

I looked up at Julian, my heart beating faster.

"Go on." He gestured with his head.

"And they are going to fund the investigation!" I closed the notebook and handed it back to Julian. "They're really going to do something about this?"

"It appears so." He tucked the notebook into his coat pocket.

"I can't believe it. A fair number of the men out on the street Saturday night were Fagan Bourland's friends or backers. I expected all this would be covered up."

"Exactly." Julian sat down beside me.

"I'm glad they're going to try. It's too late for Sandy and Webster and Loula. And for Pocahontas and for Andy and Della and their kids. What's been done has been done."

Julian nodded.

"But to do nothing would be worse."

"Yes," he said. "Much worse."

After a moment, I broke the silence between us. "So what else happened in the meeting?"

"They mostly huffed and puffed about the crime that 'embarrassed' our fair city. Guess they have to do that. The big news is that they suspended Chief Barry."

"Oh my," I said. "I thought Bryant Barry was one of Mayor Bourland's favorites."

"He is. But this is beyond politics as we have known them up to now. The real power in this town is money. And Fort Smith businessmen swing that hammer. They're trying to build this city up by opening stores and theaters and restaurants. They want to lure folks to Garrison Avenue with entertainment, food, shopping. And safety. Lynch mobs are bad for business. The aldermen knew this even if Bourland didn't."

"Who all was there?"

"It was a mixed lot. The only thing most of these folks had in common was their outrage that this should have happened. Everyone was upset about Andy. He's been a fixture in Fort Smith for so long that even if people didn't know him personally, they felt like they did."

"All those newspaper articles about him in Judge Freer's Court every week."

"Yes. And Andy's a hard worker. He has a big family to support, so he was willing to do whatever it takes to feed them all. Most of us crossed his path at one time or another."

"So besides their concern for Andy, what else took up so much time?"

"That this mob pretty much controlled the town Saturday night. The police seemed to egg them on rather than controlling them. It should have been a big money night but men who'd brought their families to town for dinner or theater were afraid for their safety."

"I kept wondering why no one was stopping it."

"Several others were suspended too—the Night Captain, Sam Smart and the Night Jailer, Stansberry."

"Good."

"They also suspended Pitcock."

"Wonderful. I don't like that man."

"You not liking him doesn't mean he's not a good cop, but there's to be a full police inquiry tomorrow to investigate how the department performed. We'll find out."

"Will you be called?"

"If they need me, I suppose. We'll see."

I took a deep breath. "Did they mention Sandy by name?"

* * *

I found the ladies room off the lobby of the Hotel Main. My face in the mirror was so pale that the scar on my cheek seemed almost blue. I splashed water on my eyes. The image of Sandy's face, beaten so badly that I didn't recognize him, flashed through my mind. Like so many others that night, I'd not done enough to stop Pitcock from hitting that boy. Would I have been more insistent that the beating stop if I'd recognized Sandy as Pitcock's victim? I was a foot shorter and a hundred pounds lighter than the Detective. Was that the reason I let Fort Smith policemen drag that poor boy back up Tenth Street and down Garrison Avenue, yelling at anyone who would listen that this "nigger" killed Andy Carr? I was disgusted with myself and the cops. Fighting new tears, I pinned up my hair and returned to the lobby.

"Miz Mamie! Imagine seeing you here." A middle-aged man called to me as I passed the bar.

I squinted in the direction of the voice. "Who is it, please?"

"It's Jim Brewer, ma'am. You know, from the Arkansas Garage on Tenth and B?" A lean figure emerged from the bar.

"Yes, Jim. It's nice to see you again." I turned and headed toward the lobby rockers.

"I'm a preacher too, you know." He hurried to catch up to me. "I don't usually drink. My religion frowns on it."

I shaded my eyes and looked up at him. "I don't judge people on their drinking habits."

"I'm not worried about that. I just finished testifying to the Grand Jury about Saturday night. My mechanic JW is in there now. I couldn't stand the waiting so I wandered over here, looking for a friendly face." He jerked a thumb toward the bar. "They made me buy something to sit in there."

"I'm sorry, Mr. Brewer. I didn't mean to be rude. Would you like to sit with me?" I sank into a rocker and gestured to the chair beside me.

"Thank you, Mamie. I must seem like a fool." He rubbed the palms of his hands together. "Truth is, my soul is troubled."

"Mine too, Mr. Brewer. Jim. I don't know if it will ever be at ease again."

"I should go on home. JW won't mind. It's just that there's been talk that I shouldn't tell the Grand Jury what really happened Saturday night. And now that I have, I don't know if I feel better or worse."

"What do you mean?"

"JW and me. Folks been saying it's wrong to testify about what went on when Andy was shot. They say that now that boy's dead, we should let it go."

"You know Sandy never shot Andy, don't you?"

He stared at his boots and nodded. "That boy didn't even have a gun, Miz Mamie. JW and I came out of the garage when we heard shooting and yelling. We no sooner stepped out the front door than that Lewis kid ran past our place of business, head thrown back, mouth open—eyes almost bulging out of his head. A bullet whizzed right past my nose. I ducked back, looking around and saw that Pitcock was about to shoot again. He was at least a block behind that kid, yelling for him to stop. I cussed him out for nearly killing me. He said that he had to shoot. That that nigger was too fast for him. I waved him away from my business afearin' he was gonna put holes in my cars—and told him to put that damned gun away. John B was following him at a distance. Guess he didn't want to get shot by mistake either."

"So how did John B get the gun? It was Saturday night. He told Julian that he didn't expect to be asked to support the police that night, so when he closed the Pony Express and left, he didn't take his gun."

"I don't know about that either way, ma'am. I just know old Pitcock ran out of steam at some point and handed his gun to John B who chased that boy down easily—and when the kid tried to get away again, he hit him on the head with the butt of Pitcock's pistol. Just knocked him silly with it—and then there was a flash and a loud bang. I thought John B had killed the kid at first. His legs buckled and he fell for the first time. But he got right back up and started to run again. It was then we saw that Andy was down not too far from where we were standing."

My heart beat faster. "You mean it was John B?"

"John B was just trying to arrest that boy. Pitcock's gun went off when he hit the kid with it. Andy went down straight away. Lifted him right up off his feet and put him on his back." He wiped his forehead with the back of his hand. "I never saw a man shot like that. In the head."

I flinched. "Poor Andy."

"Yes, ma'am. And John B was all lathered up and kept on hitting that kid until Jarnigan and Lacey got there to take over. It wasn't until then that he even realized Andy was hit."

"How awful."

"Yes ma'am, it was. As soon as the other cops took the Negro boy, John B looked around and saw Andy on the ground. He ran up to where we were standing over Andy and asked him if he was okay.

Andy muttered something. It sounded like, 'They've killed me!' or 'He's killed me.'"

"What happened then?"

"John B, he sorta screams. Raised the hair on my neck. Then he runs out onto Garrison and grabs a hack. Andy was talking gibberish by the time he got back. By then, JW'd done tore off a piece of cloth from his shirt and held it to Andy's wound, but it turned red right away and I knew that Andy was dying."

"I thought I heard he was getting better," I said.

Jim Brewer shook his head. "No ma'am. Andy ain't gonna survive this one, sorry to say. When John B came back with the hack driver, I knew from the look on his face that he thought Andy was dying too."

"What did he say?"

"Nothing. He was upset. Crying, you know. JW and I helped him get Andy into the carriage and they headed off for St. Edwards Infirmary."

"Is that what you told the Grand Jury?"

"Yes ma'am. The truth is the truth. There ain't no way to dress up this pig. John B shot his friend by accident. And many of the good citizens of Fort Smith got it in their heads that they knew what was best and they killed Sanford Lewis for it. An innocent boy. Was the worst night of my life."

I pulled out my handkerchief and handed it to Jim. "Mine too, Jim."

He wiped his eyes. "Guess I'm too soft for my own good. I've been tore up over this business since it all happened."

"Did you see them hang Sandy?"

He was quiet a long time. "Yes, ma'am. I did."

"It's like we were cursed." I pushed back with my feet and let the rocker go forward and back. This one had the slightest of squeaks.

A square-jawed man approached us. "I was hoping I'd find you here," he said to Jim. "I figured you'd gone on home and that I should too, but I guess I ain't ready yet."

"They done with you, JW?"

"For now." JW ignored my presence and focused on Jim. "I don't know what else I can tell 'em but they said they might call me again."

I held out my hand. "I'm Mamie McGrath, JW. Julian McGrath's wife?"

"Oh yeah." He looked at my scar rather than into my eyes. "I was jes telling Julian back at the courthouse what them folks on the Grand Jury wanted to know."

"I'm glad they called you." I smiled to put him at ease. "There was close to two thousand people on Garrison that night. Every one of them tells a different version of the story about the hanging. But as far as I can tell, you and Jim were the only witnesses to what happened to Andy."

JW looked over his shoulder, licked his lips and swallowed. "There was a big ole boy waiting outside the room where I was talking to Julian. Gave me the eye. Gave me the damned heebie jeebies. Pardon my language, ma'am, but that's the truth."

"Who was it, JW?"

"The one that told us that they hooked that kid to Sullivan's horse's saddle," he directed the answer of my question to Jim, "— and dragged him back up Court Street to Garrison."

I turned to look at Jim. He seemed spooked as JW. "You weren't testifying about the lynching, were you?"

Jim shook his head.

I turned back to JW. "You?"

He glanced over his shoulder again. "No, ma'am. Just how Andy Carr was killed."

"Then why would this man threaten you?"

JW blew his exasperation out through pursed lips. "Ma'am, pardon my saying this, but you don't know a damned thing about it."

"JW." It sounded like a warning or a threat.

JW choked back a reply, turned to me and tipped his hat. "Pardon me, ma'am. Everyone thinks they know what the right thing for me to do is. I don't need anyone else bullying me, not even a pretty little thing like yourself."

I stood up. "I'm not in the habit of telling people what to do, sir. I was asking you a question."

JW backed away, his eyes shifting from side to side. "Look, I didn't do anything wrong. None of this is my fault. I happened to be at the wrong place at the wrong time and saw something I shouldn't have. That doesn't make me a criminal."

"Calm down, buddy." Jim reached out to his mechanic. "No one's accusing you of anything."

"What's going on, JW?" I softened my voice and touched his arm with the tips of my fingers. "Was the Grand Jury that tough?"

A porter walked by and JW flinched.

"Here, sit down." I guided him to one of the rockers and gently pushed him into it. "We all need a break."

JW massaged the crease between his nose and forehead with calloused fingers. "It's too much, Miz Mamie. Seeing Andy shot down like that was bad enough, but that crowd. They was jes plain mean."

"I know."

"I liked Andy. He was the one what went to Muskogee and brought that young woman back to testify about the hack driver what killed Clarence Duff. I knew Clarence and it looked for a while like no one was gonna figure out who got him. But like always, Andy was the one. We counted on that old boy. Half the town knew him personally. The other half—" A tear escaped JW's left eye. "I'm sure gonna miss him."

I reached out to caress the top of his hand resting on the arm of the rocker, but froze, my fingers extended in mid air. "I know," I whispered and put my hand back in my lap. "None of us will get over this one."

"No ma'am, we won't."

7:30 p.m.

It was dark when Julian and I left the Hotel Main. We were both absorbed with our own thoughts as we waited for the trolley. When it arrived, he boosted me up onto the first step and I nodded to the motorman.

"Good evening, Miz Mamie." The man said.

"Good evening, Mr. Dyer."

I sat down in the last open seat which was right behind the motorman. Julian stood beside me, clinging to a ceiling strap.

"It's chilly tonight," I said.

"Yes ma'am. The weather's reflecting the mood of the town."

"That it is."

The car started up Garrison. We stopped at Texas Corner to let people off. I looked to my left, remembering the events a block away on Tenth and A only two nights ago.

I blinked and looked again.

A hulking figure crossed Garrison in front of the trolley.

I tugged at Julian's coat and pointed.

He ducked to look out the window. "What?"

"Garland," I mouthed.

He shrugged. "Maybe."

The car started up again and then braked, throwing everyone forward.

"Sorry, folks," Mr. Dyer said. "Can't get into heaven if I run down a nun."

I turned in my seat as we started again, watching a Sister of Mercy hurrying across the street.

"Is she following him?" I whispered to Julian.

He was staring out the window. "Looks like she might be."

"What's going on?"

He shook his head. "Nothing good."

* * *

We got off the trolley at Rogers and Greenwood and walked back to Lecta. Caroline had already retired for the night, but she'd left food on the sideboard for us.

"Your mother's a saint," I said as I filled my plate with a tiny sliver of ham and a spoonful of stewed apples.

"That she is," Julian made himself a thick ham and cheese with butter sandwich. "I didn't realize how hungry I was until now," he said.

"So what's happening tomorrow?"

"Apparently, the city council meeting wasn't enough. There are two events set for tomorrow. There will be an open meeting at the Grand Opera House at two. Colonel Parker and I will attend, but no women. But no worries there. I'll take notes. The police inquiry will start at ten. It's totally closed to the public but we can try to see if you can get the people being questioned to talk to you like you did today. One look at your sweet face and they can't help but talk to you."

Thrilled, I reached across the table and he squeezed my hand. "Really? I was helpful?"

"I wouldn't have any information about Jim Brewer or JW Walker without you."

"I'll put the details in my notebook for you."

"Wonderful. I'll have to get an article written tonight so it can make the morning paper, but I'll do it here so I can ask you questions."

"Did I tell you we visited the Carrs this morning?"

"It must be chaos."

"Those kids are scared and devastated, Julian. Pansy, the oldest, feels guilty because she had a row with her father about a boyfriend. The last words between them were harsh. And the youngest is smart as a whip. Sees right through their efforts to protect him."

"Before you go to sleep tonight, can you give me three or four lines about them. How they are doing?"

"You mean you would use it in your article?"

"If that's okay with you."

"I'm thrilled, darling. Beyond thrilled."

"Partner?"

"Partner."

"What else happened today? What was going on with Garland?"

"Now that's a story in progress. He called to say he was leaving and for me to tell Abigail that there's something in a locker at the Frisco station."

"What the heck is that about?"

I shrugged. "He was mysterious."

"And I thought Abigail was the overly-dramatic one." He laughed.

"He also said that Fellows wasn't a friend."

"That makes sense. A friend doesn't steal a man's car," Julian said with his mouth full. "Without Andy, he'll never get it back." He finished his sandwich and stood up. "Leave that for Genevieve. It's going to be a long day tomorrow and we have this article to get in tonight. We better get to work."

I put our used plates in the sink. "Go on up. I'll join you in a minute."

"Don't be long." He kissed me on the cheek and went upstairs.

* * *

As soon as I heard the bedroom door close, I cut another thick slice of bread and buttered it. I wrapped it in a cloth with hunks of cheese and ham and an extra big piece of Caroline's chocolate cake. After filling a mug with milk, I opened the door and listened. When neither Caroline nor Julian called down to me, I went out through the screen porch, down the single step and across the back lawn to the shed.

"Manny?"

"Are they comin' for me, Miz Mamie?"

"Not yet." The door squeaked as I pushed it open enough to squeeze through. "But it won't be long now."

He closed the door behind me and we were in darkness for a moment until he relit the lantern. "Does Miz Caroline or Mr. Julian know I'm here?"

"If they do, they haven't mentioned it to me." I handed him the mug and he drank down the milk while I set the cloth on the wooden floor and opened it.

Manny grabbed the ham and took a big bite.

"Slow down."

"Hungry," he grunted.

We were back where we'd started. All the progress Manny had made with Sandy teaching him how to paint and use a saw and fix fences was worthless now. They'd find him sooner or later. I choked back a tear. "You must turn yourself in."

"Why would I do that?"

"At least you wouldn't have to live in hiding like this."

"This shed's dry at least."

"Half the town saw you shimmy up that pole with the rope and half of them know you personally. They are about to arrest everyone involved—policemen even. Don't think that they won't be looking for you. Probably tomorrow or the next day."

"I done told you I didn't know it was Sandy. I wouldn't have done it if'n I'd have known." He bit into the cheese.

"Why did you get involved at all? Why would you do that to anyone?"

"I didn't kill him. Wasn't me. They jes needed that rope over the cross pole. Mr. Sullivan boosted me up there and told me to do that."

"Manny."

He swallowed. "I didn't know it was Sandy. Even when they hoisted him up there the first time. He looked up at me and I thought he was sayin' my name." Manny stared at the lantern. "But he didn't look like anyone I knew. Face was puffed up big as a balloon. And by then no one coulda understood him. Jes squeaks." He shuddered. "Made my skin crawl, though. I got down off that pole and ran."

"How old are you really, Manny?"

"What's it matter now?" He bit into the cake. "They gonna kill me over this."

"I hope not."

"If'n they're coming for me, I guess I better go, ma'am. They gonna find me sooner or later but I wanna at least see my next birthday."

"Stay another day. At least there's food here."

"Pardon my sayin' this ma'am, but I been thinkin' I'm hearin' Sandy in here in the dark—and he's sayin' he's gonna take me to hell with him." Manny shuddered.

"Shush, now. Sandy's not in hell."

"Even after killing Andy Carr?"

"They are saying it wasn't Sandy."

After a long silence, he said, "Guess I'm goin' alone then."

12

March 26, 1912
**Preliminary investigations into the Garrison Avenue riot on Saturday night
indicate that Sanford Lewis probably did not shoot Andy Carr.**

Julian McGrath, *Southwest American*

Tuesday, 7 a.m., March 26, 1912

"OH MY!" CAROLINE LOWERED THE newspaper, her eyes wide and her mouth pursed. "They're saying it wasn't Sanford Lewis who shot Andy after all."

Julian and I glanced at each other.

"You were asleep when we came home last night, dear. I didn't want to wake you," Julian said.

"That means they killed an innocent boy!" Her voice broke. "Totally innocent."

I looked into her eyes and nodded.

"Does Webster know?"

I shrugged and Julian shook his head.

"Genevieve?"

Genevieve stuck her head into the dining room. "Yes, ma'am?"

"Did you know Sanford was innocent?"

"Yes, ma'am. No coloreds in this town gonna believe that boy shot Andy Carr."

"Have you talked to Patsy?" Caroline folded her piece of the paper and laid it on the table cloth.

"She know too."

"And no one thought to tell me?"

"Patsy been too busy to come by, Miz Caroline. She been spending time with Webster and Loula. And the last few nights ain't been easy for them folks. They got younger kids they's scared for."

"I should have been to see them. I wanted to give them time. I thought it might be harder for them to talk to me since everyone assumed Sanford was a murderer."

Genevieve flinched. "That boy wasn't no murderer. He was a good-hearted, God-fearing Methodist."

Caroline's eyes filled with tears. "That poor child. I've been praying to God to forgive him that awful sin and take him into Heaven no matter what he did."

"We all knew he didn't have no gun and even if he did," Genevieve said. "—he didn't know how to use it."

"Then that child is in Heaven with Jesus." Caroline clasped her hands to her bosom. "Thank God."

"No question of that, Miz Caroline. Sanford be walkin' with the Lord right this minute."

Caroline turned pale and leaned back in her chair.

"What is it, dear?" I hurried to her side, afraid she was going to faint.

"What should I do? What should I do," she muttered.

"What do you mean, Mama?" Julian put his piece of the paper aside and leaned forward.

"They think John B did it?"

"By accident," I said. "I talked to two of the witnesses last night. He was trying to help Detective Pitcock arrest Sandy and the gun went off and hit Andy."

"Does Della know that yet?"

Julian leaned back in his chair and took off his glasses. "I haven't talked to Della. I don't know what she knows at this point. The Grand Jury only heard from eyewitnesses to the shooting last evening. Mamie talked with them right after that. And I put it in this morning's paper. I imagine folks are reading about it this morning."

"This is going to rock Fort Smith," Caroline said. "People will be coming to Jesus all over town."

Julian sighed. "Some'll be filling the churches begging for forgiveness. Others'll be right back at Till Shaw's bar pretending to be righteous."

I hadn't thought that part through. Sandy was still dead and Andy was still dying, whatever the details. "What about John B?" I covered my lips with the tips of my fingers. "And Jennie?"

"Yes," Caroline said. "Will they arrest him?"

"Depends on if the Grand Jury indicts him, Mama." Julian stood up and collected his jacket from the back of his chair.

"What will that do to the Carrs?" Caroline's shock at this development and all it's implications set my mind whirling all over again. I'd been so fixated on the simple fact of Sandy's death and Andy's mortal wound that I hadn't considered John B and his family. Somehow, knowing all this had been a tragic accident was soothing. Something manufactured by God for a purpose known only to Him. Murder was something else. Malevolent. Terrifying. An accidental shooting made sense and was a relief. Still tragic, but not the result of evil intent. But then, that made Sandy's lynching all the more horrific. Those men on Garrison the other night not only wanted Sandy dead, they wanted him to suffer. I shuddered, wondering if this would change how they felt about what they did.

"We have to take things one step at a time," Julian said as he put on his jacket. "Rather than jumping to conclusions, lets wait to hear what the Grand Jury and the Police Inquiry finds out."

"Yes," I said. "That mob was filled with men who jumped to—" I looked first at Julian and then at Caroline. "Why didn't they wait to find out what happened to Andy?"

"I'll tell you why," Genevieve said. "Even if'n they thought John B'd murdered Andy in cold blood, they'd wait for trial to make sure 'cause he be white. He be valuable. But Sanford's the grandson of slaves they wuz forced to give up. They don't think coloreds are worth spit now that we be free." She puffed out her cheeks.

I wanted to argue with her—reassure her that everyone is valuable. But I knew that wasn't a popular sentiment in Fort Smith. Troubled, I gathered my things and followed Julian out the door. It would prove to be a busy day.

* * *

After the mob dragged Sanford out of the cell, Chief Barry stood in the yard watching them pummel the boy. Mr. Lacey said to him, "If they got the right man, is it alright?" And Chief Barry gestured with his hand as if he didn't know. It was too late anyway.

Mamie McGrath Notes from interview with a witness who gave his name as "Anonymous Jones."

8:30 a.m.

Garrison Avenue bustled with business owners, city maintenance crews, shopkeepers, reporters, cooks, waiters, maids and office workers. It felt odd to me. I usually came to Fort Smith a few hours later when stores, restaurants, banks, and other companies were open for business. In front of the Hotel Main, Julian kissed my cheek and continued on to his office in the First National Bank building next door. I pondered another whole day waiting for people to wander by my station in the lobby and decided that I needed to stretch my legs a bit first. As soon as Julian was out of sight, I turned on my heel, walked back up Garrison onto North Tenth Street, past the New Theater on my left to the Pony Express on my right. A few yards away at the Horse and Mule Barn, a dozen animals stamped their feet and snorted.

I stood in front of John B's business for a few moments. This intersection was where Andy Carr was shot. I imagined his face with a bullet hole above his brow and an exit wound through his temple. Dear, funny, dedicated, kind Andy. Did he know the shot came from a policeman's gun wielded by his friend John B? Did he realize at that moment that the wound was mortal? Did he think of Della and his children? Does he now understand there's no hope?

Andy was such a Fort Smith hero. Whether at women's lodge meetings or when men gathered at bars to argue about who could spit a watermelon seed the furthest, Andy Carr stories dominated conversations. Even if you didn't know him personally, you felt like you did.

The door to the Pony Express opened unexpectedly and I jumped back.

"Mamie, what are you doing here?" John B's face brightened when he saw me. "Visiting the devil in his den this morning?" He was joking of course but his eyes were intent on mine, searching for something.

"I figured times are tough for you now and that you might not come to us. So I came to you."

His shoulders slumped. "Thank you for that. I'm about as down as a man can be and still walk. Jennie's at home with the kids. Mad at me. Scared. Sick at heart. And the folks who work for me, well, I gave them a day off while I think this thing through. Come on in and we'll have some coffee and mope together." He opened the door and I walked under his arm into the building.

He poured me a mug of coffee. It was a bit burned but it was hot and I took several sips while John B poured another and arranged himself behind his desk in the cluttered office. "I expect you want me to tell you what happened."

"If you want to, but I came to tell you how sorry I am about all of this."

He raised an eyebrow. "Really?"

I thought about my notebook in my purse. In the almost four years I'd known John B and Jennie, I'd never visited his place of business. In fact, I'd never had a private conversation with him unless a solitary waltz in a crowded ballroom could be considered private. Was this about friendship or a story? "Really," I finally said.

"Good. I'm beginning to feel like a cornered razorback."

"Why is that?"

"Let's not beat around the bush. You want something."

I blushed. "Sandy worked for us. I liked him. I like Andy and Della. I like you and Jennie. So yes, I want to know how this awful thing happened. I need to set my mind at rest."

He downed the rest of his coffee and set the mug firmly on his desk. "Fine. Here's the God's truth. Two private cyclones bumped into each other and there are casualties everywhere. The end." An unexpected tear trickled down his cheek and he looked out the window—as if that would hide the fact that he was crying from me.

I could feel my heart thumping in my chest. "Cyclones?"

He picked up a pencil and tapped the tip of it on a piece of paper lying on his desk.

I couldn't take my eyes off his hand—the knuckles were bruised and his pinkie was swollen. "I promise that I won't make it worse for you, if that's what you're thinking."

"I don't know what to think, Mamie." He saw me looking at his hand and he dropped the pencil.

"Meaning?"

"Why should I trust you? I look bad in this thing no matter what. I feel bad about it no matter what. If they decide to arrest me, I won't resist. If they don't, I'll spend the rest of my life wondering what I should have done instead of what I did. The truth is confusing enough for me. It'll likely be confusing to everyone else too. And I expect there'll be plenty folks out there who'll believe the worst." He flipped the pencil over and tapped the paper with the eraser.

"If you don't want to tell me, fine. I'll find out other ways."

The corner of his mouth quivered. "Okay."

"Okay, what?"

"I'll trust you."

"Why?"

"Because you're the one that knocked on my door this morning. I'm scared and mad and feeling guilty. And there's no one else here now."

"That's fair enough."

"Ha! Fair doesn't enter into any of this." He took a deep breath. "I don't know if I can say some of this out loud but here goes."

There was a long silence while John B struggled to put the right words together. I folded my hands in my lap and watched a variety of emotions flicker across his face—sorrow, irritation, anxiety, and confusion being only a few. "Andy was mad at me Saturday night," he said finally. "And he had every reason to be."

"The two of you have been friends for a long time."

"We have. I look up to Andy. He's good with people. He's willing to take folks as they come. Thats why he can bring in the lowest damn snake in the county. He does what he has to do. But in general, he's polite and respectful when he does it. Treats snakes and saints the same way most of the time."

"Everyone loves Andy," I said softly.

"The last few years, I've been working with the police department. On the side."

"I've heard."

"Learning from Andy how to do it better." He flipped the pencil lead down again.

"What's this got to do with Sanford Lewis?"

"That's my point. Not a damned thing. It was about Andy's daughter."

I straightened in my seat. "Pansy?"

"You talked to her?"

"She told me Andy was furious with her and she's afraid the last thing he ever said to her about anger and disappointment will be the last thing he'll ever say to her."

His nostrils flared. "Poor kid."

"Yes."

"You see, Mamie." He drew a square on a paper lying on the desk. "I'm a harmless flirt. I joke around and tell tall stories. Jennie knows this. Some of it I learned at my mother's knee. Pull out chairs and open doors for ladies. Tell them they look nice, even the plain ones. Think about how other folks feel and try to make them comfortable. Be entertaining."

That certainly described John B. He was unfailingly polite and charming. He offered to carry baskets and heavy bundles. He helped old folks across streets. He volunteered for all sorts of organizations. If anything, he tried too hard to please. "So Pansy came downtown to see a boyfriend and—you protected her?"

"More complicated than that. Pansy did have a boyfriend who worked somewhere on Garrison. Nice enough young man named Jack. They met and went for walks. Talked. It was at the early stages apparently."

"Andy and Della disapproved?"

"Of course."

"How did you find out about it?"

"Pansy and Jack came by here one evening." He turned the square into a the box by adding slanting lines to show the top and sides. "She was late and needed a ride home. So I gave her money for the trolley. And I didn't tell Andy and Della about it."

"My God. They thought she was seeing you?"

John B sighed. "Well." He drew a pyramid sitting on the box. "I'm not totally innocent here. I did help her sneak around. And then she started coming in to talk to me about this boy. She was afraid he was losing interest in her."

I didn't like where this was going. "John B, you didn't—"

"No, not that. She's a sweet kid, but I'm twenty years older than her. I like my life, love my family. My plans don't include a spare woman. I didn't mean to encourage her. I thought I was playing the part of a good uncle."

"Andy didn't think so, though."

"No. He came barreling in here Saturday night and sees her sitting there, chatting like you and I are now. Lamenting because Jack didn't show up at their meeting place. I swear, I never laid a hand on that girl. Never saw her anywhere but here. And this place is normally a beehive with folks coming and going. Come to think of it, someone probably told Andy that his daughter had been visiting me here. I was never alone with her. But—"

"But?"

"I confess, I knew she had a kind of crush on me and it was flattering. I like when people like me. I'm ashamed to say that now though, after all that's happened."

"So Andy confronts you and takes her home."

"I never saw Andy that mad before. He cussed me and herded her out the door. I'm sure all kinds of people saw or heard us fussing."

"Did you and Andy actually fight?"

"No. Andy was upset, but I didn't blame him. I was embarrassed and ashamed I'd let this thing develop." He lowered his eyes. "I'm a fool."

I didn't know what to think. John B was a handsome man in his mid-thirties. And generous to a fault. Being kind to an infatuated young girl was certainly in his character. But more than that? There were plenty available women in Fort Smith. For that matter, prostitution was legal and a lot more practical than wooing a friend's teenage daughter. If John B had seduced or tried to seduce Pansy, it would've been foolish to do it right here at his place of business with people coming and going. Fort Smith was full of gossips. Abigail Talbot would've been the first to exaggerate and spread something like this. If anyone thought John B was romancing Pansy, it was odd that no one had breathed a word of it in my presence. "So how did this end up with Andy getting shot?"

John B drew a bird inside the little house he'd sketched, sweat forming on his forehead. "I thought it was over. Andy hustled her off and slammed the door behind them. I sat here for awhile, worried about what he might say to Jennie. Sick that Andy thought I'd betrayed his trust. I figured the whole town would know by morning."

"Well, that certainly turned out to be true."

He looked up at me, his eyes filled with pain. He started to say more but then returned to his sketch, adding bars around the little jailbird. "I closed up shop for the night—and walked up to Kimmons Drugstore to buy a few things for Jennie. Our little Marjory isn't feeling well. I was just about to go in when Andy caught up with me. He'd cooled down some but he still wanted to give me another piece of his mind. What with all the electric signs and street lights on Garrison Avenue, it was bright as daytime and it being fairly nice weather, all kinds of people were out blowing off the stink. And with automobiles, hacks, horses, and trolleys coming and going, it was noisy. He bent my ear while we stood on the sidewalk in front of Kimmons. I told him he had a right to be mad but I was not interested in that girl. Besides, I told him, he should know his daughter better than that. That calmed him down a mite, so I apologized again. I told him I'd stay away from him and his family when it came to social events, but that we were still cops and there might be times we'd have to work together. He wasn't having it though and by that time, I'd had enough with the accusations and threats. Just as I turned to go into the drugstore, here comes Pitcock and Lacey and Jarnigan running past us toward Texas Corner."

"The argument was over at that point?"

"By that point, I'd been accused of being a pervert and threatened with violence. And nothing I said made any difference. I was boiling mad."

"At Andy?"

"At Andy. At myself. At the prospect of being a target of derision in this town. As I said before, I like to be liked. At that moment, I was mad at anyone or anything that threatened what folks thought of me—what I thought of myself. I had a head of steam on and no way to let it off. So, when those cops pounded by, I just took out after them."

"Did you have a gun?"

"Back here in the desk." He tapped the bottom drawer. "I wasn't exactly prepared for a fight. I'd thought I was going home for the night."

"Go on."

"You don't leave a fella anything, do you?"

"I don't mean to be cruel, John. But you aren't telling me everything."

"So now you think I'm a pervert too? That I take advantage of innocent young girls who have crushes on me?"

"I don't know yet. What happened next?"

"These two Negro kids were yelling at each other on Texas Corner. Pitcock and the two other cops grabbed hold of them. I skidded to a stop a few feet away, still het up. I figured the excitement was over, but then the girl tore loose and took off down the Avenue.

While everyone was gaping at her, the boy got away too—and he ran up Ninth with three of us chasing after him. I'd have caught him sooner except Pitcock was shooting at him and Pitcock wasn't the best shot on the force. So I hung back."

"Did he hit him?"

"Not that I could tell. Once Pitcock shot at him, that kid took off like a jack rabbit. Pitcock was slowing down by the time we hit B Street, so he handed me his gun. I was still revved up. I'd been accused of all kinds of things by a fella I held in high regard and I was hurt."

"And?"

"The kid ran past the Arkansas Garage on B and turned back this way when he got to Tenth. I ran that little bastard down in that intersection right there," he pointed out the front window. "—and cracked him in the head with Pitcock's gun. Then, the whole damn aggravating day finally got to me and I hit him until I dropped the pistol. And then, I hit him with my fists."

He clenched his right hand and jabbed at the air. "I hit him. And I kept on hitting him until Lacey took him away from me and even then I tried to kick him."

"Why?"

"Because I needed to hit someone. And he was there."

"Did you know Sandy?"

"Never laid eyes on him before."

"Where was Andy?"

John B raised his chin and his eyes met mine. "I'd lost sight of him back in front of Kimmons, but I never knew Andy to avoid a take down. I figured he was lagging back so he wouldn't get in front of Pitcock while he was shooting at that kid—just like I did."

"Where did he go?"

"At first, I didn't understand what I was seeing. People running toward something on the ground in front of the Pony Express. The clothes were familiar. I suddenly realized it was Andy lying on the ground. I handed the prisoner off to Lacey and ran over to him. He looked up at me, eyes wide and said 'He's killed me!' And I said, 'No, no, Andy. Don't say that. You'll be fine.' But I knew it wasn't so. That bullet went right through his head." John B's eyes reflected the horror of that moment.

"I'm so sorry." The words seemed hollow as I said them.

"This whole thing is sordid and confusing, Mamie. Andy was supposed to live a long time. He was meant to be sheriff or chief of police or mayor or congressman. And then to see him like that." John B covered his face and sobbed.

His hands were calloused. A working man's hands. My heart went out to him. I wanted to say 'there, there,' and pat his shoulder, but that seemed inappropriate. So I waited for him to collect himself.

"I was shocked," he said finally. "I couldn't fit the pieces together."

"Why?"

"Because I'm not sure when that gun went off. I don't remember that at all. I thought Andy was back on Garrison. Or behind me. I think now that he must have been trying to head that boy off. He must have come up Tenth instead of following us up Ninth. And somehow he stepped in front of one of Pitcock's bullets."

"Is that what you think happened?"

"I don't know." He shook his head. "I just can't figure it, Mamie."

Someone knocked on the door.

"It's open," John B called.

A well-dressed man who I didn't recognize came in. "John B Williams?"

John B sighed and stood up. "That's me."

"You've been called to testify before the Grand Jury this afternoon at two pm." The man handed John B a piece of paper. "I need you to sign here."

John B took a fountain pen out of the top drawer of his desk, uncapped it, and scrawled his name on the line the man indicated.

"Don't be late." The server pulled out the carbon and gave John B a copy. "We'll assume you're running."

"Of course. I understand. I'll be there."

The man left the door open a crack when he left. I stood up. "Is there anything I can do?"

"I can't think of anything." John B reached for his jacket. "I need to go home and prepare Jennie for what this might mean."

"And I need to get back to the Main."

John B straightened his shoulders. "I appreciate you coming here, Mamie."

"I appreciate you being honest with me, John B."

He put on his Stetson. "It was easier than being honest with myself."

We went outside. He locked the door to his office and we headed back toward Garrison.

Tuesday, March 26, 1912

Photographer Redner was charged with peddling lynching photos without a license. Because the adverse advertising might damage the reputation of Fort Smith, City Attorney Miles told a local photographer to refrain from producing any more pictures of the incident.

Mamie McGrath Notes

I sat in an upholstered rocker in the lobby of the Hotel Main waiting while Julian attended the police inquiry at the courthouse. People scurried about. Business as usual. Only it wasn't.

"Can I join you?" Burley Johnston stood in front of me, a newspaper rolled up and tucked under one arm.

"Please, do," I said. "I can't decide if I'm mad or sad right now. Whatever it is, a little company will help."

"How's Della?" He laid his jacket across the arm of a chair.

"As you can imagine. Heartbroken. Angry. Scared. And Jennie and John B are distraught too. Everyone is pretending Andy will recover but—"

Burley sat down in the rocker next to mine. "White folks are arming themselves for Armageddon. So are some of the blacks. All it'll take to start our very own war is for some damn fool to pick a fight with another damn fool."

"Surely people have more sense than that."

Burley sucked his front teeth. "If folks had any sense, that kid would be alive right now."

"Poor Sandy. He was going to be a chauffeur. Had it all worked out. We just never got around to doing it. Waiting for good weather mostly." I blinked back a tear. "Poor Webster. That's his father. Has anyone seen him?"

Burley shrugged. "Wouldn't know him if I did see him."

"He sharecrops in Moffett. Preaches on Sunday. A good man."

"Sounds like it."

The chairs squeaked ever so softly as we rocked back and forth. "Caroline?"

"Church."

"If it didn't make me feel like a hypocrite, that's where I'd be."

"Me too. Truth is, though, I'm mad at the Almighty right now." I gritted my teeth. "Furious."

"You'll burn in hell for that, Mamie McGrath."

"Probably."

A man walked into the lobby and headed for the bar. A second later, he came back into the lobby. "Pardon me." He grabbed the arm of a passing porter. "What time does the bar open?"

The small black man shrank from him. "In ten minutes, sir. Maybe fifteen. The bartender is late and the other one had to leave early."

"I need coffee."

"No coffee in the bar now anyway. Go to the restaurant."

"You're sure they have coffee?"

"Yes, sir."

The man released the porter's arm and the young Negro scurried off.

"Till?" Burley called.

The older man, already headed toward the restaurant, turned toward us. "Burley?"

"Is that you, Tillman Shaw?" Burley stood up and offered his hand.

"It's me all right." Till shook Burley's hand. "What're you doing here?"

"Waiting with Mamie while Julian attends to a little reporting business."

"Mamie?"

I stood up too. "It's me, Mr. Shaw. It's good to see you."

"Pardon my saying this ma'am, but you look a lot better than the first time I laid eyes on you, stretched out in the middle of Garrison Avenue."

I held out my hand. "I know Julian has talked to you, but I'm only recently back on my feet enough to get out and about on my own. I've been meaning to come visit you."

"Me, ma'am?"

"To thank you for rescuing me that day. Without you, I might have been lying out there on that street and someone else might have driven right over me."

"I'm glad to see you're better, Miz McGrath."

"Please, you saved my life. You can call me Mamie."

"I hardly did that, ma'am. Mamie. Where did you say Julian is?"

"He's at the courthouse, trying to get information about that police inquiry they're doing this morning."

"I just came from there."

"Oh." I tried not to gasp. "Can you tell me about it?"

"If we can go get some coffee while we talk. I been raked through the coals and my skin is singed."

"Oh?" I covered my mouth with my fingers. "That sounds awful. I think a cup of coffee would help me too. You, Burley?"

"My job is to watch over you. Guess a few cups of coffee won't get in the way of my body-guarding duties." Burley guided me toward the restaurant.

I bit back a tart reply. He was joking, but I was out of sorts and it felt like he and Julian were conspiring to hover over me everywhere I went. And after Julian had called me his partner just the night before too.

We were seated right away and ordered coffee and pastries.

Till sat across from me, tapping his fingers on the table, looking over his shoulder and sighing deeply.

Between Till Shaw's nervous tics, Burley's overly-solicitous manner, Sandy's horrible death, Andy being shot and in the hospital, and Manny hiding out in our back yard, I felt like screaming. "Why did they want to talk to you, Mr. Shaw?" My sudden question startled both of them.

"Well, um. I witnessed some things Saturday that they wanted to know about." Till looked around for our waiter.

"What things, Mr. Shaw?"

"Things that proper folks don't like to talk about in front of ladies." He turned sideways in his chair and avoided my eyes.

"I was there the other night. I am quite sure I'm able to handle whatever it is you told the men of this town."

"Mamie."

"I'm perfectly fine, Burley." I whirled on him, eyes blazing, "Andy is our friend. Sandy worked for us. Surely I have the right to inquire about this double tragedy."

Burley sat back in his chair as if my intensity was a burst of wind throwing him against a tree.

I glared at both of them. "I'm not a baby. Please don't treat me like one."

"Yes, ma'am." Burley held his hands up in the air. "Don't shoot! I'm a cranky old widower. I must've lost the getting-along-with-women knack."

I scowled at Burley and turned to Till Shaw.

"I give up too. You are tougher than Dr. Eberle when it comes to pinning a man down."

I let the corners of my mouth curl so that they couldn't be sure if I was smiling or snarling. "Then tell me what happened."

"How about I tell you what I know?"

The waiter poured steaming hot coffee into our mugs. Till grabbed his and threw it down like it was lukewarm. "More, please." He held up his cup which remained empty until the waiter had served Burley and me.

I blew on my coffee and leaned back in my chair, waiting for Till to gather himself.

"So they asked me about Saturday night. I told them about the craziness that went on. My saloon was packed. Lots of out-of-towners were here for business. The theaters were lit up. A steady stream of people coming and going filled the streets. The hotels were full of construction crews and cattlemen, all with full pockets looking for something to do."

"Or buy," Burley said under his breath.

"Exactly, son. After that young cop, Lacey, marched that kid past my bar, telling everyone that Andy'd been shot, everyone got quiet. Then Talbot started cussing and beating his hand on the bar. It was like a bolt of lightning. Stowers and Sullivan started in. And Fellows. Before I knowed it, drunks who hadn't even met Andy were screaming to lynch that—pardon the expression, ma'am—god-damned nigger. Even though Andy'd tucked half of my customers into a jail cell to sleep it off at one time or another, he was one of them when it came down to choosing sides. And they was bound and determined to make that kid pay for what they thought he did to Andy."

"But why Sandy, Mr. Shaw? He was a good boy. He wasn't a murderer. He was quiet-spoken and never in any trouble with the law before this."

"Pardon me, ma'am, but him being a good boy didn't enter into this. Those yahoos were liquored up and looking for trouble. Andy was an excuse and Lewis was a handy Negro."

I wiped away a tear with my knuckle, lady-like niceties like handkerchiefs forgotten. "It's so ugly."

"Yes, ma'am. It sure is."

"Was that all they wanted to know? What happened at your saloon?" Burley hadn't touched his coffee.

"No, they had lots of folks could testify to that, I reckon."

"What then," I probed.

"They wanted to know about when I was the jailer back in the day."

I sat my coffee down on the edge of the saucer and it sloshed onto the tablecloth. "What?"

Burley leaned forward. "You were the jailer?"

"For six years." Till waved for the waiter to bring him more coffee.

"What about it?" I pushed.

"Did I have any incidents like the one that took place last Saturday." Till watched the waiter pour coffee into his cup.

"Did you?"

Till threw down half of his coffee before turning to me. "I'll tell you just like I told the committee, Mamie. I had three incidents on my watch. One time the crowd petered out before they even got to that jail house. The other times, I had warning that folks were about to try something like that. So I got myself about thirty men with rifles and shotguns and ringed them around the building. And not one of them sons-a-bitches dared even come inside that fence. They knew that if they'd tried, I'd have blowed them away."

I stared at my hands. "So why didn't they protect Sandy the way you protected your prisoners?"

Till looked at me, all pretense of social niceties gone. "Exactly."

I glanced at Burley who was frowning.

"Anyway. I need to go open up my saloon. If anyone shows up. Yesterday, it was just my old regulars and they drank themselves into oblivion without much chitchat. Stowers and Talbot didn't show. I'm sure Fellows is hiding out somewhere until it all blows over."

"Will it?"

"Not for a while." He stood up. "It's good to see you up and around, ma'am. I promise to be in a better mood next time we meet."

"Me too."

"Will you be at the meeting at the Opera House this afternoon, Burley? I hear the future of Fort Smith lies in the balance."

"I'll try," Burley said. "But I don't think my opinion will sway many hearts, one way or another."

"Don't go that way, son. If this city is going to survive this setback, we need young minds like yours."

"Yes sir."

Till paid for our coffee and the untouched pastries and left.

Burley pushed the plate toward me. "Shouldn't let these go to waste."

I shook my head.

"Pardon my boorishness, but you're pale and shaking—and way too thin these days. Julian told me how upset you've been over this thing. We aren't trying to bully you. Really. We just care about you. Please eat something."

I sighed and chose a strawberry tart. "Thank you, Burley. I'm sorry I was mean to you. Just don't leave me of what's going on any more. Whatever it is, I might not like it, but I can stand it."

His nodded and brushed back an errant lock of dark hair.

I took a bite of the tart. "How are things with Marie?"

His smile broadened. "Now that is one interesting lady."

"I'm glad. Maybe Caroline will stop trying to be your matchmaker now."

He laughed. "You have to give her credit for trying."

"Not one of the lovely young women she invited to any of those dinners interested you. Why?"

He got serious again. "At first, it felt wrong to think of anyone but Flora. Then, I guess I was numb. And lately, I thought that if it was going to happen, fine—but I wasn't going to pursue it."

"And Marie?"

"She's everywhere I go. She's playing the piano when I walk into places. She's in the wings waiting for her turn to perform when Julian and I and the other guys are singing. And I just started noticing her. Don't put too much on it yet, Mamie, but maybe."

"Good for you. Take your time." I finished my tart and sipped my coffee.

Julian stuck his head into the restaurant. "There you are!"

"Come join us." I patted the seat of the chair Till had just vacated. "Did you get anything?"

Julian sat down and pulled out his notebook. That meeting at the Opera House this afternoon is turning into a circus. Everyone with something to say is coming."

"We heard," I said.

Julian took off his glasses and rubbed the bridge of his nose. "They are even letting the quote—better class of Negro men—unquote in—but they won't be allowed to speak."

"What about me?"

Julian glanced up at Burley and then at me. "No women or kids. I did ask."

"They don't think this impacts everyone?"

Julian signed. "I didn't say it was fair. Just who they say will be allowed in."

I tapped his notebook with my fingernail. "What else. Don't leave out anything. I mean it, Julian."

"I know you do—and I won't, I promise." He looked tired. "The police inquiry is on recess now. I'll have to go back soon. I can't go in and listen. They've declared it private. But I can see who's coming and going. And some of those folks will tell me whats happening in the meeting room. Some will even tell me what they were asked and how they answered."

"No secrets in this town," Burley muttered.

Julian grinned. "Nope. Eventually it all comes out. Here's who are serving on the panel." He put on his spectacles and thumbed through the pages of neat printing. "Fagan Bourland, Mayor. Vincent M. Miles, City Attorney. W. T. McAuley, Captain of Police, acting as bailiff."

"Bailiff? What are they expecting? Fistfights?"

"I think it's a formality, Mamie," Burley said.

"Yes." Julian peered at us over his glasses. "I believe it's customary even if a bailiff isn't likely to be needed."

"Oh." The people in this town were jumping out of their skins. Maybe it was a good idea after all, I decided.

"There will be two committees running the police inquiry. John Howell, Dr. Eberle and Sid Collier sit on the police committee. And C.E. Speer and C.W.L. Armour represent the citizens."

"An august group," Burley said.

"Aside from Mayor Bourland and Dr. Eberle, I don't know many of these names. Who are they?"

"Well, I know John Howell," Burley said. "He's a big cheese in the oil industry. Dabbles in politics. Lives and works here. Smart. Good man."

"And Sid works at the Feed Company. Don't know why he would be representing police interests. I'll have to find out that connection." Julian underlined Sid Collier's name. "Clarence Speer is a businessman. It makes sense he would represent those folks. Charley Armour is in real estate—and loans."

"I'm confused," I said. "What're all these groups supposed to be doing?"

"Everyone's got a different mission although in reality, they do overlap a little. Yesterday, as you know, the city council got together and huffed and puffed a bit before suspending the cops who were involved until more is known. They demanded the police inquiry and the public is so roused up, they decided it was better to direct all that anger toward something positive."

"So that's the one at the Grand Opera House this afternoon?" I uncapped my pen.

"Yes."

I scratched out a quick outline of who was meeting when and where in my notebook."

"The police inquiry," Julian continued, "—the one I've been in all morning—is charged with figuring out why the cops failed to protect Sandy."

I noted that too.

"The *Grand Jury* will determine who participated in the lynching. That'll be a separate thing. They already talked to three of the witnesses last night." Julian checked his pocket watch. "About time to head back and see what I can pick up. Think about going home, Mamie. You look exhausted."

"I'm fine. Think I'll sit here and see if anyone will talk to me about the other night."

"You got several camps," Burley said. "The 'we ain't gonna talk about it at all and maybe it will go away group,' the 'I didn't see or do anything group who probably did see or do a lot,' and the 'mad as hell group who wants justice'—whatever that can possibly be in a situation like this."

"And we have 'the broken-hearted crowd,'" I prompted.

"Well, if anyone will talk to you, don't wait too long before writing it down. It's easy to get people mixed up or mishear what they are telling you at times like this." Julian tucked his note book into his vest pocket and stood up. "Get as many quotes as you can. Be sure to tell them that you want to use them for a newspaper article. And ask them if you can use their names."

"I've never been much of a note taker," I said as I recapped my pen. "But I'll try. I do have a good memory though."

Julian kissed my forehead. "Do the best you can. That's all any of us can do." He nodded to Burley. "Thanks."

"No problem," Burley said.

"What was that for?" I turned to Burley as Julian walked away. "Babysitting me?"

Burley chuckled. "Mamie, you're the last person in the world who needs that. I'm as interested in this case as you are. I'm a concerned citizen and you and Julian are getting the goods. I'll leave if you want me to, but I'd like to know what happened in our city Saturday night—and you are my ticket for that."

Actually, Burley was sweet and earnest. Even though I was still mad at him for manhandling me the night of the lynching, maybe I was misjudging his motives for spending a morning with me. "I'm sorry I've been cross with you."

"I'm a singer and a businessman, not a newsman like Julian or a writer like you. But I want to be a part of this thing. There'll be some folks who won't talk to Julian because they don't want to end up in the clink for being a part of that mob. And there are some who'll tell you one thing—but they might tell me something else. And some, like old Till awhile ago, who'll talk to both of us just cause they need to lift a burden and neither of us are especially threatening. We can compare notes when you start writing it all down."

I thought about it. Even if Julian asked Burley to look out for me, having a second person around might be helpful. "Okay. But there might be people who will only talk to me alone."

"Maybe there will be some who'll only talk to me alone," he countered.

I hadn't thought about that. "We need a signal when we think that is happening."

"So I can participate in this little project you and Julian are conducting?"

"Deal?" I held up my almost-empty coffee cup.

"Deal." Burley clicked his cup against mine.

* * *

Noon

March 26, 1912–City Council suspends Police Officers.
Chief Barry, Captain Smart, Detective Pitcock and Jailer Stansberry were
dismissed until a committee can investigate the incident and report findings.

Julian McGrath, *Southwest American*

Burley left me to do some business, so I took that opportunity to slip over to the courthouse. I looked around for Julian, but not seeing him, I found a seat in the hall outside the room where people were being questioned.

"Imagine meeting you here," a uniformed police officer stood in front of me. "Not causing any trouble today, are you?"

"I like to think I never cause trouble, Mr. Pennewell."

"I was the one directing traffic last year when they were scooping you up off Garrison Avenue."

I smiled up at him. "Thank you for that."

"You look a lot healthier now."

"That took some time, but yes, I'm better."

"So why are you here?"

"Curious. How about you?

"Guess."

"You're waiting to testify."

"Smart girl."

I didn't have any reason to suspect Ed Pennewell of anything nefarious. But he saw me as being where I didn't belong and I found that annoying. I closed my notebook. "You were there Saturday night?"

"Me and a couple thousand other people." The bench squeaked as he sat down beside me. "Typical Saturday night on Garrison."

"People typically get lynched on Saturday nights in Fort Smith?"

"No need to bite my head off, missy."

"So what were you doing there?"

"That's a pretty general question if you're trying to pump me for information." He flicked an invisible speck of lint off his sleeve. "Planning on writing about what well-dressed ladies should wear to a riot these days, Miz McGrath?"

"Just curious, but it's no skin off my nose if you tell me or not." I turned away from him.

"You're mighty full of yourself, aren't you?"

"I could say the same about you, Mr. Pennewell." I reopened my notebook and sketched the hallway filled with anxious men waiting to be called into the inquiry room.

"That there's Bliss Pool," Pennewell pointed toward a young man sitting across from us. "He was there Saturday night."

"A member of the crowd?"

"Part of the group who attacked the jail, but whether he was a principled witness or there to do the Devil's business, who knows."

"So where were you Saturday when that crowd was forming?"

"Doing my job!"

"I see."

"Seriously, missy. I was on my beat where I was supposed to be." He reeked of hair oil, leather and indignation.

"What's a beat?"

"It's my territory. That stretch of Garrison Avenue I'm supposed to patrol."

"What stretch is that?"

"Why do you care? Pinning me down even before those bastards in there question me?" He gestured toward the door at the end of the hall.

"Okay, don't tell me." I finished my sketch and labeled it, Bliss Pool, witness."

"I wasn't going to." He folded his arms over his chest.

"Fine." I looked around for another subject.

He sighed. "Me and Lacey were assigned Garrison Avenue. From eighth to Texas Corner."

"Didn't you hear or see that mob?"

"I heard hollering over toward the jail once in awhile. Couldn't tell exactly what it was. There was a political rally going on that night too."

"And you didn't go help defend the jail?

He squirmed in his seat. "No ma'am. I was busy doing what I was supposed to be doing."

"And what was that, Mr. Pennewell?"

"We was rousting niggers for guns about that time."

"Why?"

"When Pitcock and Lacey arrested them niggers making a ruckus on Texas Corner, it drew a crowd of looky-loos out of the Negro bars. And then, one of the women, Pocahontas, got away and that Lewis kid ran up Ninth with Pitcock and Andy and John B hot on his heels."

"With Pitcock shooting?"

"How'd you know that, Miz McGrath?"

I frowned at him. "A bird told me."

He seemed taken aback by my tone—and maybe a little hurt.

I softened my voice. "Tell me the rest, Mr. Pennewell, please?"

"Pardon my asking, but why do you care about all of this so much?"

"Andy's a friend. And John B. And I was there, caught up in that chaos. It was the worst night of my life. And I for one want to know exactly what happened."

"Ah." His expression softened. "I'm sorry about that. It was the worst night for us too. Confusing and scary." He checked his watch and put it back in his pocket. "Looks like it's gonna be slow going in there. Might as well jaw some. Nothing else to do."

"I appreciate that."

"After Andy got shot and they took that boy to jail, those people on the Avenue got meaner. There was only a few of us, ma'am—and a lot of them."

"How many cops were with you?"

"Let's see. Eventually, there was Danner, Lacey, Booth, and Jarnigan—and me. Five. If you don't count Pitcock, Andy or John B.

"Any of them here this morning?"

"There's Sam Booth." He pointed. "Looks like he's gonna be grilled too."

"He's so young," I said as I reopened my sketch book.

"This job'll take the bloom off that pretty face soon enough, ma'am." Pennewell nodded to Booth who acknowledged our presence with a smile.

"So what did you do next?" I sketched Sam Booth's smooth, rounded jawline.

"After Andy Carr got shot, we started rousting niggers for weapons like I said before."

"Find any?"

He folded his arms across his chest. "We found guns, knives, sticks, chains. You name it. They're a dirty, dangerous lot. We probably prevented all kinds of crimes on the Avenue that night—from murder and robbery—" He leaned sideways toward me, his breath warm on my cheek. "—to rape."

Frowning, I pulled away from him. "And?"

He seemed disappointed that the mention of rape didn't distract me. "And we looked for Pocahontas. Eventually, we found her hiding in a house back off Campbell's Alley along with a bunch of other niggers. Arrested all of them too."

"This was the girl Sanford Lewis was arguing with?"

"That's the one. Pocahontas. She was a wild one, I tell you. Fighting and cussing. Never saw a woman black or white—save Pearl Starr—behave that way. She was drawing a crowd. Niggers coming out of those cribs on Campbell's Alley, out of Northum's Saloon on Tenth."

"So what then?"

"We amassed a following as we herded this howling-drunk young lady and her friends down Garrison."

"What time was this?"

"Getting nigh on to midnight."

"Who else did you see?"

He scowled. "Well, only other people I saw right about then was that fella that hangs out with that whore from Miz Bertha's. You know the one I mean? Always wears a top hat. Something's wrong with his face."

I leaned forward. "Is it shiny?"

"Yeah. That's the guy."

"Orrin Fellows."

"Yeah, well, didn't know his name. Looks like a wet weasel. He came running out of North Tenth and then slowed down when he hit Garrison. I'd have kept an eye on him, but that night, there was so many folks in downtown Fort Smith, you couldn't stir 'em with a stick. He blended right in and I had other fish to fry right then."

"What Orrin Fellows was doing down by the Pony Express?"

"What do you mean, Missy?"

"Just that I told Andy Carr something about Fellows that afternoon and Andy said he'd look into it."

"You think this guy shot Andy?"

"I don't know what to think, Mr. Pennewell."

He sighed. "I'll look into it once they're done with me, ma'am. If I still have a job after all this."

"So you were taking your prisoners to jail?" I prompted.

He rubbed his face with both hands. "When we got to the Fort Smith Western shop, we could hear that big crowd hollering over at the courthouse. I got scared that if we came barging in right then, they'd take our prisoners away and beat the dickens out of them. So we stopped and I tried to call the jail to see if we should bring this bunch in or wait—but no one answered. I figured they was a mite busy."

"And you didn't try to help your colleagues?"

"Ma'am, your tone is insulting."

"Perhaps that's your conscience you're hearing." I whirled on him, eyes blazing.

He seemed stunned by my anger. And then, offended.

"I'm sorry," I said. "That boy—Sanford Lewis—worked for us. He was a polite, hard-working young man. His parents are devastated by all of this—his brothers and sisters terrified. And why? Because he was arguing with someone?"

"He broke the law when he took off like that, ma'am. He should've done what he was told. Obeyed the officers' commands. If he'd have done that, Andy Carr wouldn't be at St. Edwards with a hole in his head."

"He was scared."

"Scared of what?"

"Of what happened to him. Of what you let happen to him!"

"Lower your voice, Miz McGrath," Pennewell said under his breath. "You don't know a thing about it and you're upsetting people."

I glanced around. Men waiting to testify were staring at me. Bliss Pool had stood up and was eyeing the stairs—as if he might run away. Sam Booth stood too, his hand on his holster. These people were involved in Sandy's death one way or another. "I'm upset. Why shouldn't they be?"

"This big bruhaha over a damned nigger," he sighed. "Okay, so it was ugly. All kinds of things in life are ugly. Folks got revved up. Andy is a popular fellow. They thought he was already dead and they wanted justice. If I'd been there when that nigger shot Andy, I'd have killed him myself."

* * *

Noon-thirty

I gathered my notebook and purse, hurried down the stairs and out onto the yard of the courthouse facing Parker Avenue.

At the foot of the steps, I stopped abruptly and dropped my purse. There, not twenty yards away from me, was the jail. A barred window had been ripped out of the wall and a railroad tie rested on the torn-up ground beneath it. A lone figure was taking photographs. Heart pounding, I sat down on the steps and watched.

"It's awful, isn't it?" Sam Booth handed me my purse and sat down beside me. "This is the third time I've come to look at it since it happened."

I wiped my nose with my handkerchief. "It's—" Actually, I couldn't think how to describe how it made me feel. "Won't they be looking for you in there?"

"They're taking a twenty-minute break."

"I didn't mean to accuse Officer Pennewell that way. I guess I just needed to blame someone and he sat down beside me.

"The good Lord knows there's plenty of blame to go around, ma'am." His voice was unbearably young. "Ed Pennewell's a good man though. He thought he was doing the right thing at the time. But now, he's like the rest of us who were out there on Garrison Avenue the other night, wondering what we could have done that would've changed anything."

I looked up at him, through tears. "But he seemed so defiant. So angry."

"Aren't we all?"

"I guess so. I keep thinking I should have done more—something more. But even now, I can't think what."

"Looking back, it's easier to see we should have put that boy in the county jail where we could've protected him better. But at the time, we were upset over Andy and Chief Barry barely gave us the time of day. The crowd was like a wave—tossing us around. We were struggling to keep our balance, just like you."

The photographer took a picture of the jail window.

"What's Mr. Redner doing?" I pointed.

"For the record, ma'am. They'll go in the final report of the Police Inquiry along with sketches and maps."

"Ah. Illustrations. Of course." Julian also took photographs to go along with his newspaper articles, but I still made sketches. The pain in my heart was still there, but thinking about how to preserve the story gave me something positive to do. I opened my book and began drawing the jail. "What was your beat?"

"Ma'am?"

"Your beat. Mr. Pennewell was telling me you all had an area of responsibility."

"Towson Avenue."

"So how did you end up with Mr. Pennewell and the others?"

Sam Booth seemed surprised by my question. "I was working Campbell's Alley and I heard shooting. So I came to check it out and ran into Mr. Pennewell in the intersection of Garrison and Towson. He told me about Andy."

"You know Andy?"

"Everyone knows him."

"He's quite the hero, isn't he?"

"Yes, ma'am. Reading about him in the paper's why I decided to become a cop. I want to be like him."

"Let's hope he recovers soon."

"Yes, ma'am."

"So what time did you meet Mr. Pennewell and the others?"

The young man narrowed his eyes. "Must've been around eleven. He said we should go round up Pocahontas in Campbell's Alley. He knew where she lived."

"He did?"

"That's what he said. So we got her and a couple of other women who were there—and five more next door to that."

"What did you arrest them for?"

"There'd been a complaint about Pocahontas. The others we charged with disorderly conduct and immoral purposes."

"Was Campbell's Alley your beat?"

"Part of it was."

"Could you hear what was going on here when you were bringing Pocahontas and the others this way?"

"Ma'am, Fort Smith was noisy last Saturday night. There was that political meeting and Judge Harp had those folks hooping and hollering. And the people who thought this black boy killed Andy were pretty het up. Teenaged boys blowing off steam. The blacks pouring out of the bars and saloons around Texas Corner were bellowing like bulls. Guns were going off left and right. And the people we arrested with Pocahontas were sounding off too. When you ask me about the jail specifically, well—" He shrugged.

"It was chaos?"

"Yes, ma'am."

I finished my sketch and showed it to him.

"That's a really good likeness of Redner over there." He pointed at the photographer. You ought to show it to the cops. Or the newspaper."

I smiled at him. "Not good enough for that, but helps me remember how things are." I titled and dated it.

"I gotta go back in now, ma'am. There'll be hell to pay if they call my name and I'm not there."

"One more thing. When you were taking all those people to jail, did you run into a crowd?"

"Oh yes, ma'am. There were thousands of people downtown Saturday night. Everyone going ever-which-away. So many, that Mr. Pennewell got scared someone would try to take our prisoners away from us. So we stopped and he went into the Western shop to telephone and ask if we should bring those people on up here."

"And the answer was yes?"

"Eventually, ma'am. We stopped several times along the way. And now, I do have to go back inside or they'll skin me alive."

"Thank you, Officer Booth. Be careful, you know—out there."

His smile was warm. "Yes, ma'am."

* * *

I hurried across Rogers and up Sixth Street to Garrison.

"Mamie!" Jennie Williams was a half-block away. "Can I talk to you a minute?"

I opened my arms. "I am sorry about all of this, Jennie."

She hugged me. "I tried to call Della, but she won't talk to me. We've known each other so long—and in her hour of need, she won't let me help."

I patted her back while she sobbed on my shoulder. "Everything's so awful. Confusing and awful."

"The Carrs think John B deliberately shot Andy."

"No, I can't believe that. I don't believe it."

"They think my John was trying to seduce their girl." Jennie flushed. "I don't know what to think about that. He swears it's not true. He says Pansy denied it to Andy when he confronted them about it."

"Then believe him until it's proven that you can't."

"I know him, Mamie. John's a good man. Fun. We have small children. I can't believe he'd do something like that with a child. Besides, he looks up to Andy. Even if John was seeing a woman, it wouldn't be Andy and Della's girl."

"I'm sure he wouldn't too. In fact, when I talked to him this morning, he swore to me he didn't as well."

Her lower lip quivered. "Did you believe him?"

"One hundred percent."

She grabbed my wrist. "Thank God."

"Two terrible things happened the same night at the same place. Not even the police have it all figured out yet. The Carrs can't heal— you and John B can't heal—until we know exactly what happened."

"What if they never do figure it out?"

I was taken aback. "Andy's hurt bad. That's all Della can think about now. Once things settle down, once we know if Andy will recover, maybe you can reach out to them. Until then, maybe it's best that you stay away while their feelings are hot."

"Mamie," Jennie lowered her eyes. "John says that Andy's as good as dead. He knew it the moment he saw him."

That took the wind out of my sails. "What did the doctors say?"

"John got Andy into a cab and rushed him to Saint Edwards right away. Doc Stevenson confirmed to him that the wound was mortal. John's first thought was to go get Della. At first, she wouldn't let him in. But he banged on the door until she opened it. When he told her about Andy, she called out to her brother to watch the kids, got her coat—and let John take her back to the hospital. But once there, she made it clear, that she wanted him to leave."

"Oh no, Jennie."

"He was devastated and furious. So instead of coming home like he should have, he went back downtown. A cop told him about the lynch mob, so he raced down to the jail to tell everyone that

Andy wasn't dead. But no one heard him—and if they did, they ignored him."

"I saw John B on the Avenue after it was all over."

"Where was he?"

"Leaning against the front of Till Shaw's Saloon. Crying, I think now. Or coughing. We spoke."

"I can only hope he comes home tonight."

I patted her shoulder. "I know."

* * *

Padgett's Café was unusually quiet. I nodded to Sophie as I sat down across from Reverend Matthews at a back table. "I hope I'm not too late," I said to him.

"You're fine. I need to be at the Grand Opera House at 3 pm. That's my only pressing appointment." A plate of half eaten beans sat in front of him.

Sophie brought me coffee and a menu. "What'll you have, Miz McGrath?"

"Buttered bread and a piece of cheese, I think."

"Okay."

I expected her to fetch my lunch, but she just stood there.

I looked up expectantly.

"I was there Saturday night, Miz McGrath. On the Avenue."

I waited.

"I saw you when they hung that nigger."

"Yes?"

"I knew you was friendly with Andy. You were here with him that afternoon."

"Yes, I was."

"They're saying now that the Negro didn't kill Andy after all."

I sighed. "It was a tragic misunderstanding. Two cyclones?" I stopped. John B's metaphor wasn't really an explanation. "Seems they lynched the wrong man."

Sophie's forehead wrinkled. "Is Andy gonna die?"

"They say he is." I avoided her eyes.

"So what'll happen to John B?"

"I imagine he'll be tried for murder. Manslaughter, maybe."

"They won't hang him?"

"See here, young woman." Reverend Mathews cheeks shook. "There's not going to be a repeat of the outrage perpetrated on this town by a gang of—"

"Drunken fools," I interjected.

"—out of control, murderous fools." Reverend Mathews' indignation matched mine.

"So what'll happen if they decide John B did it?"

"I imagine that'll depend on whether he meant to shoot Andy or not. The Grand Jury will decide that."

"So you knew that black boy was innocent Saturday night?" She cocked her head sideways and raised her eyebrows.

"I didn't realize he was someone I knew when they hanged him."

"You knew Andy and you didn't know whether that boy killed him or not?" The angry glint in her eyes was directed at me.

"What's your point?"

"Andy was your friend but you were upset they hung the nigger who murdered him? You didn't know any different then."

"I don't like your manners, Sophie," Reverend Mathews said. "Miz McGrath was reacting to a horror show. If the police had kept that boy safe until everything was clear, he'd be home with his kin right now—and half the kids and habitual drunks in Fort Smith wouldn't be murderers."

"I don't get it." Sophie's voice trembled. "Andy died by accident? And the folks trying to get justice for him are bad?"

"Sophie!" A man's voice bounced off the walls of the small café. "Quit tormenting the customers and get back to work!"

"Fine." She threw her pad of paper and pencil onto our table and untied her apron. "Take care of them yourself." She turned on her heel and marched out the front door.

Her boss appeared at our table before the door closed behind her. "Sorry," he said as he gathered up her belongings. "Sophie's friend was part of that mob Saturday night."

"Oh, what's his name?"

"Grover Bourland."

"I sat back in my seat. "The mayor's nephew."

"She'll get over it."

"I don't know about that," I said. "This is going to be a sore spot for years to come. I think."

"So," the manager wiped his hands on his apron. "What'll you have?"

I repeated my order and waited while the manager went to fetch it.

"Why did you want to speak to me, Miz McGrath?" The reverend turned to me.   \

"Two reasons, really."

"Okay." He checked his pocket watch.

"It's about Emanuel McKnight. Manny. Do you know him?"

"Ah yes, the dirty little urchin, my wife calls him."

"He works—worked with Sandy Lewis around our house." I stopped. "Caroline's house."

"Okay."

"He was one of the boys who climbed that pole the other night."

"And?"

"He's hiding in our shed as we speak."

"What does he say?"

"That the others put him up to it."

"Of course."

"And that he didn't know it was Sandy he was helping them kill."

"Is that possible?"

"I guess it is. I didn't recognize Sandy either. His face was destroyed by the time I saw him."

"What do you want me to do about Manny McKnight?"

"Take him in until the hearings are over. Feed him. Make sure he doesn't run away."

"I take it, he's prone to that."

I nodded. "He needs a firm hand."

"He needs to turn himself in." Reverend Mathews pushed beans around his plate.

"Yes, he does—but that won't happen. He's scared and surly—and alone."

"You could turn him in."

I sighed. "I can't."

He scowled. "Mmhm."

"Will you do it?"

"Miz McGrath, I'm busier than a bee in a tar bucket right now. I cain't be chasing a troubled kid all over town..."

"I see. I'd hoped—"

"—but if he'll come to my house tonight—on his own or screaming and kicking, I don't care which, Rachel and I'll take him in, feed him—and try to talk some sense into him."

"I don't know Florence Pahotski well, but she was his teacher and is inclined to stand up for him. She might help with a few dollars."

"Does that mean you're washing your hands of him?"

I sighed. "No, but that boy needs a whole bunch of things I can't provide right now. Like spiritual guidance. And a lawyer."

"I can do that."

The manager set a plate in front of me and refreshed our coffees. "Pardon me but I heard some of what you were saying to the Reverend here, Miz McGrath. You both should know there are people hiding out all over town, just waiting for the cops to come for 'em. Some have come to their senses and are sorry—and they are in need of the Reverend's services too. Others are defiant, like the

Bourland kid. And some are just plain old thieves and murderers. Con Sullivan's wanted for robbing a bank over in Van Buren, for instance. They scattered like rats when you turn the light on 'em."

"I reckon the Marshalls'll have to ferret out most of them," Reverend Mathews said. "But good people caught up in this—like John B Williams—will turn themselves in when the time comes."

"My point is, when you go to that meeting this afternoon, tell Paul Little that one's hiding out in Mena and another's in Heavener. Heard a customer talking about seeing them bragging on the midnight train at the Frisco. They was laughing and showing everyone that they had blood on their clothes."

I flashed on Will Manus' bloody hands that night and shuddered.

"I'll pass the word." Reverend Mathews checked his watch again. "You said you had two things to discuss with me, Miz McGrath?"

"I'll leave y'all to your conversation then," the manager took the cue.

I watched until he disappeared into the kitchen. I turned back to the Reverend, "At the meeting today, will you speak out for Sandy?"

"You know I will."

"You'll have to do it because even though they're letting black men attend, they won't be allowed to speak."

"What do you want me to say about him?"

"That he was kind and generous. Shy. Religious. He was in love. And he was eager to learn and just as inclined to teach others. His parents are the Reverend Webster and Loula Lewis from Paw Paw."

Reverend Mathews put his hand on mine. "And he deserved a lot more respect than Fort Smith gave him."

I bit my lip and nodded. "He did."

2:30 p.m.

I thought about returning to the courthouse where the police inquiry was still in session, as well as the Grand Jury. Both were supposed to be secret, but people couldn't help talking about what they'd seen or done or heard. Perhaps they needed to say things out loud to understand what we'd all lived through. Or maybe it wasn't real until someone else knew about it. After a few false starts, I finally decided to go back to the Hotel Main lobby and see who might come by.

"Miz Mamie." The colored doorman greeted me. "I have a message for you."

"Oh?"

"Yes ma'am. From Mr. Webster Lewis. He says he'd like to visit with you and Miz Caroline in the morning."

My heart beat faster. "Tell him we'll wait breakfast for him. Say eight am?"

"I'm sure that'll be fine, ma'am."

"Give him and Loula my love, Mr. Jefferson."

"I'll sure do that, ma'am."

I went into the lobby and sank down in my usual upholstered rocker. From there, I could see people entering and leaving through the front door, visiting the bar and the restaurant, going up the staircase or waiting for the elevator. I could even see guests coming and going from the pool room.

However, a great weariness overtook me and I dosed off.

"Go home, Miz Mamie. You're worn plumb out."

I opened my eyes. "Mr. Redner."

"Yes ma'am."

"What time is it?"

"I don't know. Pushing three, I guess. Everyone's heading over to the Grand Opera House to talk about what Fort Smith's gonna do about the lynching."

I sat up straiter. "What will they do?"

"Who knows?" The man sat down beside me. "Bunch of malarky if you ask me. Those business men never laid eyes on that kid that got hung. All they care about is making a buck. It doesn't look good when they're trying to make it sound like Fort Smith's a la-di-da modern city. Still stinks like cowboys and Indians to outsiders—especially nosy-stuck-up Northerners with fat bank accounts."

I rubbed my eyes. "Well, hanging people in the middle of town—no matter what else it is—is disruptive. There were so many people in town the other night that traffic couldn't get through."

"Don't matter much to me. I make a little money either way." He pulled an envelope out of his pocket. "These shots'll give me some income for awhile." He tossed it in my lap. "Maybe you'll write about that little incident for one of those fancy magazines. I'll let you use one of these for a percentage."

Curious, I opened the envelope and screamed. "Sandy!"

People in the lobby turned to look at us.

"My God, Miz Mamie. You about scared the peewaddling outta me."

"You took pictures?"

"A bunch. Sort through 'em. See, that one's the best lit. It was night after all. Hard to see the nigger's face, but you can see the pole and the rope pretty good." He tapped the top one with his fingernail. "And that one, you can see the people standing below him. Cain't

215

make out their faces so much but that's a pretty distinctive cap right there. And in this one, you can see the fella with the raincoat. He bought a copy of all of 'em."

"You're selling them?"

"Well, why not? People want keepsakes you know—and a man's got to make a living."

"On someone else's tragedy?"

He took the envelope away from me. "It's the nature of the beast, ma'am."

"What if his mother saw those? How do you think she'd feel?"

He scratched his head and grinned. "Never thought of the family. But who knows? Maybe I could package 'em as last photos of the beloved?"

"Get away from me."

"It was a joke."

"Not funny."

"You take things too seriously. I didn't mean nothing by it. This is news—no different from any other kind of illustrations. They're even copyrighted. The newspaper bought 'em. And I figure Mr. Little will use 'em to prosecute them hellions. Besides, I was there taking pictures that night when I coulda been home. Don't my family got a right to eat same as yours?"

"Maybe you should get a different job!"

"Miz Mamie, pardon my saying so, but you're no different from me. Both you and Julian are writing about this case. It's your golden opportunity to make good on the tragedies of others, as you put it."

"That's different. There's context and history and—context—"

He grinned.

Actually, he had me—but somehow, I knew it was different. I just couldn't explain it.

"I take it you don't want any?"

"Mr. Redner, I was there. I can't get those images out of my head. I won't ever forget them."

He stood up. "Fine. Be that way."

* * *

City indignant over lynching.

Julian McGrath, *Southwest American*

5:30 p.m.

I'd been downtown all day. I was tired and sick at heart. To push away the helplessness that had pursued me since Saturday night, I focused on my notes, trying to document everything I'd seen or heard.

"Ah, there you are." Julian sank into the chair beside me. "Have you been here all day?"

"I've been a lot of places. Talked to a lot of people."

He yawned. "Got anything good?"

"Yes and no. You?"

"Well, the citizen's meeting at the Grand Opera house was something. It'll be my lead tomorrow for sure. Get this. Fifty of the top business men in the city are putting up the money to make sure this is investigated and that the guilty are identified, indicted, arrested, and tried."

I sat up right. "Their own money? On top of the $1000 put up by City Council?"

"Yep. Sam McCloud led the way along with Angus McCloud and Fred Sicard. Also, Artie Berry, Ike Apple, Rudolph Ney, Chauncey Lick, Vincent Miles."

"The town lions," I murmured.

"I have the rest in my notes," Julian said.

"They're doing this for Sandy?"

"They are doing it for Fort Smith. They've invested a lot in this town and they want it to be a place where people can do business or enjoy a play or shop or eat dinner without a bunch of liquored up lunatics scaring everyone."

I remembered my short encounter with Sam McCloud below the trolley pole where Sandy had died. "It's more than that."

"Oh yes. Peace. Politics. Safety. Morality. All those things too. But business is number one."

"You're a cynic."

"I'm getting too old to be an idealist." He stood up and offered me his hand. "Mama and Genevieve will have dinner waiting for us."

"Where's Burley? I haven't seen him since this morning."

"He told me you gave him the slip so he tended to his own business this afternoon."

"I didn't give him the slip."

"Uh huh." Julian took my arm and we went out the front door to wait for the trolley.

"I didn't. He's going to talk to different folks and share the information with us."

"Okay."

"You're easier to find." He lifted me up onto the trolley and boarded after me.

"If I want to be found." I nodded to the motorman, "Good evening, Mr. Dyer."

"Good evening, Miz McGrath."

We sat down mid car.

"—shot him right out in the middle of the street." A woman behind us said to her seat mate. "I heard it from one of the Meeks."

"John B is such a friendly fellow. Civic minded. Generous." It was a man's voice.

I glanced at Julian. He shook his head.

"Doesn't mean he wouldn't shoot you dead if you cross him."

"You don't know that, Vera."

"They say he was messing around with Andy's daughter and when Andy called him on it, he shot him."

The man sighed deeply. "So why did they lynch that black kid?"

"The cops did that to cover it up."

"So all the cops and all the witnesses are in cahoots?"

"Everyone knows that."

"They do?"

"That's what they say."

"Oh Vera."

"Tone, darling. Tone."

"I'm glad ladies can't sit on juries. You and your girlfriends would hang a man for murder before hearing a word of testimony."

"Common sense."

I chanced another peek at Julian. He looked straight ahead, choking back a chuckle.

13

March 27, 1912 —Election Day
We want a good man in every sense of the word at the head of our city. If
the pay is not sufficient, let's increase the pay. Let's do it for every office in
our community.

Burley Clay Johnston, Letters from the People, *Southwest American*

9 a.m.

WEBSTER LEWIS KNOCKED ON OUR back door at eight am on the dot.

"It's Mr. Lewis," Genevieve called to us as she welcomed him into the kitchen. "And Miz Patsy too."

Caroline hurried to greet them. As I watched Caroline hug Webster and then Patsy, I realized how complicated her relationship with them must be. They had grown up together on the same or adjoining farms and felt the bonds of shared childhood memories. Yet, in Fort Smith in 1912, the social gap between them was vast. So vast that the regard they held for each other had to be hidden away in Caroline's kitchen.

"I'm sorry about what happened to Sanford, Mr. Lewis." It sounded flat and not nearly enough. I didn't tell them Sandy had pleaded with me to help him and that I did nothing. I was too ashamed.

"My heart is cracked open like an egg, Miz Mamie." Webster sat down on the kitchen chair Genevieve had pulled out for him. "All my insides is spilled out onto the ground."

"I know, I know," I murmured under my breath, but of course I didn't really.

"I keep thinkin' how careful he was with everyone else's feelings," he said. "And how those boys who kilt him didn't give a spit about that. And all those people watchin' him suffer didn't care how special he was. They jes knew he was black." Webster covered his face with both hands and his shoulders shook.

Caroline sat down beside him and put her hand on his shoulder. "Where's Loula and the kids?"

Webster was too overcome with grief, so Patsy answered for him. "They're too afraid to stay in PawPaw so they're at a friend's house for the moment."

"The crowd disbanded that same night." I tried to sound comforting. "Everyone knows Sandy didn't shoot Andy. I'm sure your family isn't in any danger now."

Webster didn't move but both Patsy and Genevieve looked up at me with fiery eyes.

"Things like that lead to other things like that," Genevieve said. "White folk get all roused up and it's like a stew on high flame. Eventually someone gonna burn."

"But—"

"These bad feelings go back a long ways, Mamie." Patsy sat down beside me. "What happened to Andy was a match thrown on kindling that was already bone dry. It's still dangerous out there. Black folks are upset and frustrated with how things've been going. And white folks know they haven't been treating us right, so they're scared and determined to keep us in our place. We—you and me and Caroline—have to keep everyone calm best we can or more boys—black and white—are going to start hurting each other again."

I remembered Pitcock beating Sandy. And the drunk who peed off the curb onto Garrison. And Officer Pennewell and the others manhandling Pocahontas. Suddenly, the fact that Negroes couldn't eat in white restaurants or wait in white waiting rooms or use white bathrooms seemed downright mean. Why did black people have to live in a separate community? And why did they have to come to the back door in white neighborhoods? I'd not thought much about those things before now, accepting my place and theirs without question. Was I blind? Dumb? Heartless? "Oh, Patsy, no."

She took my hand. "Suspicion goes both ways."

"What should we do? Hunker down?"

"We can't disappear. And we can't start a war, but maybe we can start fixing one thing at a time."

"Starting with?"

Patsy glanced up at Caroline and then back to me. "We get the vote."

"Who?"

"Women."

I caught my breath. Of course. That's exactly what we needed to do. "Is it even possible? Won't women just vote the way their husbands say?"

"Would you?"

I thought about it. "I might discuss it with him, but I doubt we'd always agree."

Patsy smiled. "See? We have our own ideas."

"Voting won't change how people think of each other," Caroline said.

"No, it's but a step."

Webster wiped his eyes and sat up straighter. "None of this talk'll bring back my boy."

I looked up at him. He was right. Words, however well meant, were just words. "What can we do, Reverend Lewis?"

"Nothin.' All I can do is reach out to the Lord and beg him to embrace my child."

Caroline crossed herself.

Like Sanford, Webster Lewis got right to the point.

* * *

We stood on our front porch and watched as Webster Lewis got into his wagon and urged his mules forward. Regardless of what the neighbors thought, Caroline insisted that Patsy and Genevieve stand with us, a kind of informal honor guard, as Mr. Lewis headed downtown to retrieve Sandy's body from the coroner.

"Where will he be buried?"

"We gonna be praying at the AME church tomorrow, Miz Mamie," Genevieve said. "But Reverend Webster, he say he don't want a church service cause who knows what white people might be thinking or planning on doing. He wanna get that boy in the ground soon as possible."

"But where, Genevieve?" I looked from her face to Patsy's.

"I don't mean to be rude, Miz Mamie. We all loves you like you was one of our own. But you ain't, ma'am. The world won't let you be."

Pain ripped through me. "But Genevieve—"

"Genevieve's right, Mamie," Patsy said. "Where Webster puts that boy isn't your business. Or yours, Caroline."

"Unhuh," Genevieve nodded. "That's the God's truth, ma'am."

* * *

March 27, 1912
Fort Smith Ministers Deplore Disgrace of City.
It was inevitable that when our officers showed their hostility to some, that all our laws should be brought into contempt. As so many other laws had been broken with impunity, it was easy for the mob to conclude that the law that safeguarded the accused was unpopular and to break it also. We hope that the adjudication of this matter will be the beginning of reform—an obedience to law.

Fort Smith Ministers Association

10 a.m.

Julian slipped out the door early because of all the hearings going on. After Patsy left to teach her classes at Lincoln High, Caroline went upstairs to say the Rosary, since she missed 8 o'clock mass. I waited until Genevieve was busy ironing before heading out to the shed with food for Manny.

"You look like you're about to cloud up an rain all over me, Miz Mamie."

I sighed and set the food on Wilbur McGrath's old flat-topped trunk. "It's not been a good few days."

Manny rubbed his hands together. "Eat first, then tell me." He took the bottle of milk and gulped down half. Then he leaned against the wall, panting for a moment before finishing it off. "Been a long time since I seen hide nor hair of you."

"I've been busy, Manny. There's a lot going on in this town right now."

"Pardon my saying this ma'am, but what do you care about any of it?"

I sat down on a barrel. "Trying to decide what to do about you."

He scowled and stuck out his lower lip. "You gonna turn me in?"

"No, but I think you should turn yourself in. The whole town saw you on that pole. I saw you. Everyone recognized you. If you go talk to Mr. Little now, maybe he can help you."

"That fella don't give a fart about me." He unwrapped the peanut butter and bacon sandwich I'd made him and tore into it. "He thinks the sun comes up jes to hear him crow. He'll lock me up soon as look at me," he said with his mouth full.

"Look around you, Manny. Isn't this shed about the same as a jail cell?"

"I can leave here anytime I want."

"And go where?"

"I can go see Mr. John B. He's been good to me in the past."

"He might end up in jail himself."

Manny's eyes widened. "The hell you say!"

"It wasn't Sandy who shot Andy. It was John B."

"Why would he do that? They's tight."

"It was an accident."

Manny chewed slowly. "So's we hanged that nigger for nothin?"

"Absolutely nothing."

He laid the rest of his sandwich back on the cloth I'd wrapped it in. "You sure it was ole Sandy? Looked to me like it coulda been any nigger on the street."

"Reverend Lewis is headed to town to get his body and take it home to his mother."

He thought it over for a minute. "At least that nigger had someone that cared about him. When I die, they'll leave me in the middle of Garrison for the dogs to eat."

"Oh, Manny." I shook my head. "You committed murder. Don't you understand? You're in real trouble this time."

"I'm a kid. A white one. They ain't gonna kill me."

"They could put you in prison for the rest of your life."

"Then I won't get rained on or have to sleep with the horses, ma'am."

"I think you need more help than I can give you."

He slumped. "You're throwing me out."

"No, but I want you to go talk to someone who can help."

"I ain't talking to no prosecuting lawyer Little."

"I'm thinking about a friend of mine. Reverend Mathews. He already said he'd try to help. You just have to go talk to him."

"Aw, that old guy smells like moth balls half the time."

"Do it, Manny."

"I can't jes saunter down the road in the middle of the day. Ole Pitcock'd put my butt in jail sure as shootin.'"

"Detective Pitcock has been suspended. Probably going to be indicted along with you and your friends."

"You're a ray of sunshine, ma'am, what with all your good news."

I tucked a piece of paper into his hand. "There's Reverend Mathews' address. Go see him tonight. Talk with him. Take his advice."

"You're just tired of feeding me. Maybe I'll go see Miss Pahotski. She never let me down like this."

I tucked a dollar bill into his hand. "You'll do what you will just like always. But for heavens' sake, listen to someone."

"Ain't no one cares about me anyways."

I was angry when I closed the shed door behind me but by the time I got to the screen porch, I was crying again."

* * *

At the Grand Opera House, Mayor Bourland suggested that since Judge Harp's political gathering at the courthouse broke up just before the lynching, many of the attendees participated in the mob. This is unlikely. Judge Harp and I came to the Southwest American office immediately after the rally. We had already copied two typewritten pages of Judge Harp's speech when we heard that Andy Carr was shot. This was long before they took Lewis to jail.

J. B. Parker to Mamie McGrath

14

March 28, 1912
They made a rush for the jail and I got there with them. I said, "Men, the nigger's not here, that's all there is to it. Look for yourselves." They looked around and seemed to accept that he wasn't there after all. But then someone climbed up at the north end of the jail and looked through the bars and saw the nigger and yelled, "He's here!"

Mamie McGrath's Interview with Sam Smart

March 28, 1912
At least a thousand white people got together at the Grand Opera House yesterday afternoon. They complained about Sanford Lewis being strung up on Garrison Avenue last Saturday. We know what happened because they let colored men sit in the gallery as long as they didn't say nothing. Webster Lewis and my great uncle Mosie Day went so we'd know what went on—specially the part where that tiny little mayor said he was called too late or he could have stopped that mob from hanging Sanford. Uncle Mosie said that man ain't got the sense God gave a goose.

Genevieve Day, *The Fort Smith Bell.*

March 29, 1912
Prosecuting attorney Paul Little arrests well-known city contractor John C. Stowers for the murder of Sanford Lewis on Garrison Avenue last Saturday night. His friends offered to put up a $20,000 bond but learned that the offense was not bailable due to concerns Mr. Stowers might leave town.

Julian McGrath, *Southwest American*

9:15 a.m.

It was a cool morning and I was bundled up. A shiny new Ford sped past where I stood at the trolley stop on Greenwood and Rogers. It skidded to a sudden stop just as the street car arrived.

"Good morning, Miz McGrath," the motorman said as I climbed aboard.

"Good morning, Mr. Dyer. How are you?"

"Sad times in Fort Smith, ma'am."

I sat down two rows behind him. "It is indeed."

"Everywhere I look I see a broken heart."

"Did you know Sanford Lewis?"

"Never set eyes on him that I know of."

"Andy?"

224

"Andy Carr's picture's in just about ever heart in Fort Smith, ma'am. I got a buddy who got his pocket picked twice in one month and old Andy, he found both them thieves. They made restitution, spent time in a cell—and moved on to a town where they ain't got no Andy Carr."

"I'm afraid Fort Smith won't have Andy Carr after this."

"Andy's toughed his way through worse than this." He started up the trolley. "And if he doesn't, don't you worry about Fort Smith, ma'am. We'll go on. We always do."

"Whoa!" Someone pounded on the side of the trolley. "Stop this thing!"

Mr. Dyer slammed on the brakes and opened the door. "Morning, Cotton. Joe."

Two unfamiliar men climbed aboard and sat down behind me.

"That damn darkie about broke my hand," a low voice growled behind me.

I leaned back in my seat and turned my head so as to hear better.

"I still think we should have just put a bullet in the little bastard's head," the second man muttered. "Quick and easy—and from a distance. No witnesses. No newspaper stories. No hoity toity women acting like we were the bad guys. Just a corpse floatin' in the river."

"Sophie over at Padgett's said Katherine Mivelaz told her Andy's still alive—sittin' up and eatin' scrambled eggs."

"How'd she know that?"

"Katherine's a Maledon and so's Jennie Williams and she and Della are still tight—at least for the time being."

"Even if Andy's eatin' high off the hog and dancing a jig afterwards, that nigger still shot him."

"I sure hope so, Cotton. Otherwise there's a couple thousand people saw us kill an innocent kid."

I opened my notebook and wrote, "Joe? Cotton?"

One of the men behind me lit up a cigar. "Ain't nobody gives a damn about that kid. Even if he didn't kill Andy, he's sure as shit done something just as bad—or would've sooner or later. I'm good with it either way."

Laying my notebook aside, I took a mirror out of my bag and held it in front of my face. Hand shaking, I positioned it so a partial reflection of the growly-voiced man behind me appeared. All I could see was a sweat-stained cowboy hat pulled low over a pair of thick black eyebrows.

"All I'm saying is maybe we jumped the gun."

I strained to hear Joe over the noise from the trolley.

"Pitcock pointed him out. That's good enough for me," Cotton said. "Then and now. I don't buy that bull about John B shooting Andy. They worked together all the time. John B's a good man. Just can't see him pointing a pistol at Andy and pulling the trigger. Nope. My money's on the black kid."

I patted my hair and put the mirror away.

"I think we walked into something a lot more complicated than it appeared."

"If'n you feel like that, then why'd you do it, Joe?"

There was a long pause. "My dander was up. I didn't trust the law to get justice for Andy."

"Hogwash! You trusted them ever other time there was a crime. If you didn't, we'd be lynching someone ever night of the week and twice on Sundays," Cotton grunted.

"That boy was like a snake that won't die when you whack it, wiggling back under your saddle blanket to sink his fangs in your behind the moment you drift off. I wanted to be sure he was well and surely dead afore more of them heathens got the idea they could just up and shoot a man in Fort Smith and get away with it. They's all laying in wait to take us down as it is."

My hands curled into fists, my nails digging ever deeper into my palms.

"Shit man. That nigger wasn't no demon. He was just a flesh and blood kid," Cotton said. "Just like me."

"You don't know that." Joe lowered his already deep voice to almost a whisper. "I was a mind to destroy wickedness—obliterate it once and for all, but now I'm scared maybe folks won't see it that way. Bad joke on me."

"Aw Joe, don't talk like that."

"A man can't help but wonder."

"Not me. I did the right thing. We did. No matter what them fancy arses putting their money down to persecute us think. You don't see them out protecting the town like Andy and John B."

"Main Hotel," Mr. Dyer called over his shoulder.

The car slowed and the seat behind me squeaked as the two men stood up.

"Appreciate you stopping for us, Dyer." The man with the bushy eye brows patted the motorman's back as he prepared to disembark.

"See you and the Missus in church this Sunday, Joe."

Cotton followed meekly behind Joe, his collar pulled up around his neck.

"What time is it, Mr. Dyer?"

"Pert near eleven, ma'am."

"Thanks." I stood up and scanned the Avenue to see where Joe and Cotton went. They were just disappearing into Till Shaw's Saloon when I caught sight of Abigail Talbot walking past them toward the Main.

"Pardon me, Miz McGrath. Going or staying?"

"Um—" As I craned to see where Abigail was headed, a black robed figure idling in front of the First National Bank caught my eye. She bent her head as if she were sitting in a pew at Immaculate Conception Church fingering her rosary beads,

"Well?" Mr. Dyer's voice rose.

As Abigail hurried past her, the nun turned and watched. When Abigail crossed Sixth, the good sister followed. Was this Andy's shiny-faced nun? If so, was she spying on Abigail? And if she was, why?

"Ma'am?" The motorman was getting impatient.

"I'm sorry, Mr. Dyer. I thought I saw someone I know. I'm getting off here."

I climbed down off the trolley and made a show of brushing dust off my clothes, until Mr. Dyer started up again. Temporarily forgetting Joe and Cotton, I turned to watch Abigail, curious about where she was going on foot and vaguely concerned about her. She was tall and cantankerous. Even yowling mad dogs scurried out of her way. Still, I was alarmed. I watched until they were both halfway down the 500 block of Garrison before falling in behind them.

Abigail's stride was long but the nun had no trouble pacing her. I, on the other hand, was almost running to keep them in sight. As they approached Third Street someone behind me called my name.

I turned. It was Theo Lamb dressed for her job at the Boston Store.

I quickly took her arm and walked her back the way we'd all come. "It's good to see you," I said. "I need help—and here you are."

"Life is so interesting." Theo's dark eyes sparkled. "I have a message for you."

I sighed. "Not from Maybelle Shirley, I hope."

"No, it's from Garland Talbot."

My mouth went dry. "He's not dead?"

"No, no," she chuckled. "Not from the beyond. He called me at the Boston Store through a new fangled instrument called the telephone? I was going to catch the trolley out to see you, but you got off when I was still a block away from the stop. I waved but you took off so fast, I thought you were going to run all the way to Oklahoma."

Arm in arm, we strolled a few steps further and stopped in front of Gilley's Saloon, where I stole a peek over my shoulder. Abigail was headed toward the Frisco Train Station and the nun was still a good fifty paces behind her. "Is he well?"

"Sounded well enough."

"Then what is he doing and where is he doing it? He has Abigail worried to death." My voice rose.

"And apparently you won't take his calls."

"It's a long story."

Theo patted my hand that was hooked through the crook of her arm. "Aren't they all lately?"

"So what did Garland want me to know? And why can't he just call or write Abigail himself?"

"He says that some guy named Orrin Fellows is dangerous—and that he has someone watching her all the time. Someone that knows if anyone calls her or writes her. Abigail should tell Fellows she doesn't know where Mr. Guckenheimer is buried. He said that's important. And maybe tell John B about all of this too since Andy's out of commission for now. Garland will be back when this thing with Fellows has been resolved."

"What is this thing with Orrin Fellows?"

"I don't know but it's surely illegal. And dangerous."

I glanced back again. Both women had disappeared. "Thank you, Theo. I don't know what all of this means but I'll tell Abigail."

Theo started back up Garrison, then stopped and snapped her fingers. "Oh, yes. One more thing." She faced me. "He said to watch out for a Sister Clarence too."

I took a breath before it hit me. "Oh my God!"

"What?" Theo's voice rose.

"I was just following a strange nun who no one seems to know—and she was following Abigail."

"Where?"

"Toward the Frisco train station." I was already running as I pointed. "Find a policeman. Or Julian. Or John B. Or someone to help me. Maybe Dino Esposito. His restaurant is nearby. Tell him to bring his gun."

Once again, my narrow skirt restricted my stride and I swore I'd never wear one like it ever again—fashionable or not. The cracks in the sidewalk and the spaces between the creosote bricks in the street were hazardous. I told myself that Abigail's life depended on me not falling. I was breathless before I could see the train station.

* * *

I am a Brakeman on the KCS and went out on the train the night of the lynching. I saw a noisy crowd get on the train. I did not recognize any of these people by name. I did not know the two men who were unusually noisy.

M McEachin, Grand Jury Testimony

People were coming and going as the noon train approached. Passengers waiting to board on the platform were lined up back under the colonnade that protected the front door. I couldn't see Abigail or the nun in the crowd. I increased my pace. What were the chances that Theo could find Julian or John B in time? The cops were caught up in the lynching inquiry over at the courthouse. Many of them anyway. And, despite the clamor for better policing and the search to find Sandy's murderers, I'd seen what happened on the streets of Fort Smith with my own eyes. I couldn't—I wouldn't wait for someone else to come rescue Abigail. I had to do this on my own.

The train had just pulled in as I reached the Frisco. I hurried through the colonnade into the white waiting room. People were picking up babies and bags and lining up in front of the double door out to the platform. No Abigail and no Sister Clarence. I peeked into an alcove on my right labeled "Women's Rest Room." A girl was pinning her long dark hair up into a bun. Startled, she turned to glare at me. I apologized for the intrusion and left. I peered over a long table between the back room and the more elegantly outfitted front waiting room labeled "white." A ticket taker turned to me. "Can I help you, ma'am?"

"I'd like to look for someone in there." I pointed through the door behind him.

"Oh, there's no one in there that would interest you," he said. "I'm sure your party is in here." He gestured with his head.

I stood on tiptoe. "I don't see them," I said. "A tall woman wearing a hat with great big peacock feathers on it? A nun with a shiny face?"

He frowned. "No one like that."

"Can't I just look in there?" I peered around him.

"That's not appropriate, ma'am. That's the colored waiting room. Was your party colored?"

"No."

"I guess they wouldn't be in there now, would they?"

"Oh for heaven's sake." Turning back to the front lobby, I looked left and right. Then I saw it. Baggage Claim. I tapped at the desk. "Did a lady in a big blue feathered hat and red hair claim anything?

"No, ma'am. Not today anyway," a young man said,

I stood there trying to figure out what to do next.

"Of course, the day's young."

I was probably overreacting. Abigail was a grown woman who'd been taking care of herself since long before I was born. Then what the baggage claim attendant said hit me. "Does she come here often?"

"Couple times a week maybe."

"Since when?"

"Oh, I dunno. Last fall?"

Suddenly, it all made sense. Whatever business Garland did with Orrin Fellows fell through on opening night of the New Theater. Whatever repercussions that caused, Garland deemed them too onerous and had Abigail run his errands for him. Now, after what happened Saturday night, he disappeared, leaving Abigail to deal with it entirely. And whatever it was, Sister Clarence wanted it.

I went out onto the platform and squeezed through the passengers who were boarding.

"Can I help you?" A conductor blocked my way.

"I'm looking for a red-haired woman wearing an outrageous blue feathered hat—and a nun."

"That-a-way, ma'am." He jerked a thumb over his shoulder.

I hurried down the platform to the far end of the station, turned left—and there they were. They turned to face me just as the engineer blew the train's whistle. My eyes focused on a tiny silver pistol with a pearl-faced handle, because Sister Clarence held it against Abigail's side. Abigail's face was suffused with defiance—the nun's with irritation. Their lips were moving, but it took a moment before the whistle's shrill assault on my eardrums faded and I could hear them again.

"I've been looking for you," I said to Abigail.

"Here I am." She had both arms in the air—one hand curled into a fist, the other holding her parasol.

"Back off, Miz McGrath." Sister Clarence's smooth baritone was familiar. Her watery blue eyes behind her round spectacles were hard—and the skin on her cheek above the wimple was red and shiny.

"Orrin Fellows!"

He blew air out of thin pursed lips. "Well, I guess Sister Mary Clarence has outlived her usefulness." Pointing the gun alternately at me and then Abigail, he pulled off the black veil, the starched white collar and the headpiece.

"Are you okay?" I said to Abigail as I raised my hands too.

She nodded. "He's trying to use me to find Garland."

As the train eased out of the station, Orrin Fellows ripped off the rest of the nun's habit. "That thing's uncomfortable and the god-damned skirt gets in the way."

Abigail and I glanced at each other and even in this bizarre situation, we both laughed.

"You have no idea, Mr. Fellows." I edged a step or two closer to them.

He glared at us, now holding the Derringer with both hands. "Stand still." The nun's habit had hidden the long-barreled pistols that he wore in holsters on each hip and across his chest. His bald head was crisscrossed with red welts and white scars that matched the less serious ones on his face and hands.

"Is your real name Marky?"

"The little whore tell you that?"

"I didn't know—not until now. It fits though. The fire in the room at the old McKibbon, no body in the embers, your burns. Anna Marie Cavanaugh asking me to deliver a basket from Sister Alberta. That's where you got the nun's habit, wasn't it?"

When he grinned a silver tooth flashed in the sunlight. "Gotta admit that was a stroke of genius. Not many people in this town smart enough to figure that one."

Abigail started to lower her arms.

"Back up! Arms up! Now!"

She slowly raised them—but not as high as before. "They're tired."

"What do you really want, Mr. Fellows?" I distracted him.

"My money." He turned toward me. "The money I invested in Garland Talbot's Guckenheimer scheme."

Abigail lowered her arms just a little more while he was looking at me.

"How much money was that?"

"A grand."

"A thousand dollars?" Abigail laughed. "I guarantee you Garland Talbot doesn't have that kind of money lying around." A tiny blue feather drifted off Abigail's hat, swirled around in the breeze, and stuck to Fellows' pants. "If he had anything like that, believe me, I'd know it."

"I got nothing to lose here, Miz Talbot." He moved the pistol from her side to her cheek. He couldn't quite reach her temple. "If you ain't got the money, I might as well kill you right here and now."

"In broad daylight?" I said. "With half of the city's business-men coming and going all day long? Not fifty feet away?"

He pointed the gun at me, decided better of it, and stuck it back in Abigail's face. "I couldn't get even a tenth of it from Garland's Buick—and he claims he doesn't have any cash. And Mr. Guckenheimer was long gone by the time that train got to Tulsa. Talbot claims not to know what happened to it, but my new partners in Detroit don't believe him—or me. I can't go back to my previous benefactors because they think I'm dead after that unfortunate fire."

I glanced nervously at Abigail, afraid she was going to do something stupid—like wrestle him for the gun. "How did that happen, Mr. Fellows?"

"My partners for that particular project were hard nosed. When the row burned up back in 1910, a lot of my investments went up in smoke too. I was into these—business men— for a lot of money. A lot. And they wanted it back. So I went into hiding over at the McKibbon. They looked for me almost a year until someone—probably that little whore working for Miz Laura, the one with mole under her eyebrow? Angelica? She looks young, but she's a smart cookie. Anyway, I think she led them to where I was hiding."

"How did she know?"

"Well, ma'am. A man can't hide out in a hotel room with nothing to do forever." The tone of his voice made me shudder. "I needed some company. You know."

Abigail sniffed. "You're old enough to be that girl's father, Fellows."

I found the idea pretty disgusting myself. "So you're saying that Anna Marie Cavanaugh told your partners where you were?"

"My previous partners, Miz McGrath. And no, that girl didn't betray me. They followed her when she visited me."

I caught Abigail's eye and we both choked back a giggle. Either Abigail was growing on me like a fungus or life or death situations made for strange partnerships.

"You really think that pretty young thing would turn down an extra dollar to save your hide?" Abigail blurted out. "No wonder you were stupid enough to go into business with Garland."

"She's right, Mr. Fellows. Anna Marie's looking for her Prince Charming. I seriously doubt you have enough money put aside to buy her a castle, glass shoes, and sixteen white horses. Besides, you're almost old enough to be her grandpa."

"No, no, no." He pointed the gun at me again. "They burst in after she left. And in their world, they like things to be—even."

"You mean balanced?"

"Exactly." His hand shook and the barrel of the pistol bobbed up and down. "I claimed their money burned up—so they burned me."

The horror of that experience flashed across his face—and for a moment, I felt sorry for him. "What happened next, Mr. Fellows?"

"I ran." He lowered the gun as he remembered. "I ran as fast as I could, down the stairs and out onto A Street."

"What did you do there?"

"Screamed. And ran. And screamed. I was near collapse when that little Angelica found me and knocked me down and threw water on me." His voice cracked. "There were horses rearing and stamping somewhere." He closed his eyes. "Finally they broke free and galloped off. I could feel their hoof beats in the ground where I lay with my clothes on fire—and my hair. I realize now that Angelica must have untied them so she could get to a water pump somewhere nearby. That water saved my life." He shuddered.

"Anna Marie Cavanaugh saved your life?"

"She did, Miz McGrath. Risked her life, her looks, her job for an old coot like me. Old enough to be her great grandpa really."

He stared off into space, reliving the horror.

Abigail slipped whatever she was holding in her fist into her bodice, then touched his shoulder. "What happened next, Orrin?"

"I didn't want those bastards to hear I'd survived and come after me again, so Angelica—Anna Marie, she got a cabby friend to carry me down to Miss Laura's. I was there in the basement healing for months. I almost died."

Abigail had lowered her hands to shoulder level. "I'm sorry that happened to you, Orrin."

He lifted the gun again. "Raise 'em! Now!"

"Me too," I said.

"Don't think I'm gonna let anything like that happen to me again."

"So that's why you became Sister Clarence."

"I should have stayed Sister Clarence. People respect nuns. They are polite to nuns. Orrin Fellows has had a tougher time of it."

He had me there. I didn't know a soul who wasn't nice to the Sisters of Mercy.

"Did you stay at the convent with them?" Abigail lowered her arms again.

"Oh no. I pretended to be on my way to visit my mother when someone greeted Sister Clarence on the street—and I never went near the convent for fear Anna Marie's big sister, Sister Alberta, might recognize the habit she'd lent us."

I laughed. "So Sister Alberta wasn't in on this?"

"Anna Marie made up some story about needing the habit for a play but didn't have the nerve to tell her sister face to face."

"Ah, so that's where I came in."

"Yes, she said you were nice about it."

"What?" Abigail cocked her head sideways and raised her eyebrow so that her monocle fell out of her eye orbit and dangled from its chain.

"I'll tell you about it later," I mouthed, hoping she would forget it before I was forced to reveal my ugly secret to the town gossip.

"Now, stop that!" Orrin Fellows exclaimed.

"Stop what?"

He pushed the barrel of the gun into my chest. "Being nice to me."

"Oh for heavens sake! Why?"

"Because I'm gonna kill you, Miz McGrath, and I don't want to like you."

I glanced at Abigail who'd caught her swinging monocle and replaced it on her face.

"You aren't going to kill us, Fellows." Abigail lowered her arms all the way, so that her elbows were at her waist, her palms—one empty, the other clutching her closed umbrella—shoulder high, facing him.

"I have to, now," he said to her. "If I let her go, she'll tell everyone that I'm Sister Clarence. And I have to be Sister Clarence for a while longer. My partners are going to kill Orrin Fellows unless Garland shows up either with the money or the Whiskey. And if I was him, I'd run like hell so I have to figure that's what he's doing. And you, whether you know it or not—you have it, Miz Talbot. You must."

"I don't know anything about Mr. Guckenheimer except that he was a friend of Garland's from Pennsylvania."

"Me either." I piped up just in case Fellows decided to ask me, which he didn't.

"You two must be the stupidest broads on the face of the earth." His scratched the side of his nose with the barrel of the Derringer.

Abigail and I looked at each other.

"Perhaps we are," I said. "So you're going to have to tell us what you want in plain English."

"Guckenheimer is the whiskey, Mrs. McGrath. They make it in Pennsylvania. Garland and my investors were looking ahead—to when that pipsqueak prosecutor, Paul Little, shuts down whiskey on Garrison or, even better, when all those snooty women get their pansy husbands to vote for that so-called prohibition amendment. The price'll go sky high. We'll make a fortune."

Abigail wrinkled her nose. "So where's the whiskey?"

"That's the question, Miz Talbot. Where is it? We already sold almost half the shipment and those customers either want their whiskey or their money back."

"So where's the money?"

He sighed dramatically. "You finally catching on, Miz McGrath? We ain't got no money. We got investors back east waiting for their loans plus interest and we got customers who want either whiskey or a refund. But we ain't got no money to pay off those loans with interest and we ain't got no whiskey to sell to make the money to pay off those loans with interest."

"Why not?"

"Help me, sweet Jesus," Orrin Fellows looked up to heaven and raised both his arms in frustration, the tiny pistol in one of them. "Because your "Mr. Guckenheimer" coffin didn't make it to Tulsa."

Quick as a cat, Abigail pushed on his back with both hands and he fell forward, hitting his head on the brick platform and knocking himself out.

"Quick, get the Derringer." She pointed to where it'd slid under a bench as she knelt awkwardly beside the unconscious Orrin Fellows to relieve him of his three holstered guns.

"You're amazing." I fished the Derringer out from under the bench and stuck it in my bag.

Abigail puffed as we rummaged through his pockets. "My corset is killing me!"

"Try running in these skirts," I laughed. "Fashion is what makes us the weaker sex."

Fellows stirred, moaning and holding his forehead.

"I've had just about enough of you, Fellows." Abigail bashed him on the head with her parasol. "Stay down, you polecat."

"I'll shoot you dead soon as look at you, Mrs. Talbot."

"Not without your guns." She hit him again and he covered his head with both arms to protect it.

"A man only has so much patience." He groaned.

The noise from the train faded in the distance.

"Now, Mamie?"

"Now."

"Help! Thief!" She screamed.

"Murder!" I screamed with her. "HELP!"

A door opened a few yards behind us and a man with a green eye shade came running. John B and Dino Esposito rushed around the corner of the train station, guns drawn. Theo Lamb and Martina Esposito followed them a few seconds later.

15

March 29, 1912
After indicting Sam Smith who spends his day gambling, Prosecuting Attorney Paul Little saw that varmint sauntering down the street, pretty as you please. Smith didn't even notice Mr. Little behind him. He walked right past Patrolman Frech too. Mr. Little had Mr. Frech run Sam Smith in for last Saturday's lynching. It's a little one, but it is a win for Sanford.

Genevieve Day, *The Fort Smith Bell*

March 31, 1912
I arrived at the jail at the early stages of the disturbance. There were two or three hundred men in the enclosure. They were without a leader or organization. At that time, they confined their energies to yelling and shouting that they would get the prisoner."

J. B. Parker, Testimony from Police Inquiry

April 1, 1912 - 10 a.m.

IT WAS A GLORIOUS SPRING morning. I eased the gleaming new Hudson 33 out of the Arkansas Garage onto A Street.

"Not too fast, ma'am," JW cautioned. "That's it. Nice and easy on them gears."

"It's so exciting that I forget myself."

"Yes, ma'am."

"She's a natural, don't you think, JW?" Julian called from the back seat. "She drives instinctively—like the car is a part of her body."

"Don't think she don't know how things work, Mr. McGrath. She can name ever part of this machine and tell how it's supposed to work."

"Oh for heaven's sake," I said over my shoulder. "What did you expect?"

Julian laughed and clapped JW on the back. "No compliments allowed, buddy. Of course, she's a good driver. She's good at just about everything. Took me twice as long to figure out that old Boehmer. First day I had it, I ran it up over the curb in front of the Saddle Shop and bounced off a water trough. About scared Ollie Fields' old mule to death. He broke loose and took off. Got almost to the river before Ollie got control again."

JW laughed. "That mule never set eyes on an automobile before then. Miz Fields neither. She refused to come to town to shop until that mule died in his sleep one night. And when Ollie finally convinced her to come to town, she pressed herself up against the buildings lest a wild Boehmer run her down in the middle of the sidewalk."

I braked at the corner of Tenth and A and turned right on Tenth, driving past the New Theater and slowing before turning right onto Garrison. Bert Stewart came to the door of his barber shop and waved.

I gripped the wheel tightly, afraid to let go lest I run over someone on the busy avenue.

"Just keep an eye out for people crossing mid block. They'll be thinking about something else and step right out in front of you," JW said as if reading my mind. "And slow down around the trolley stops too, for the same reason."

At the end of Garrison, I turned around and drove back up the Avenue. Just past the Goldman Hotel and Immaculate Conception Church, I veered right and headed out Rogers. At Lecta, I turned left and drove by our house, waving to Caroline and Abigail who were having their morning tea on the front porch.

"Show off." Julian chuckled.

"Quiet! I have people to impress."

"I don't think you need me anymore, Miz McGrath," JW said. "How about you take me on back to the garage before you start parading this fine machine around town."

"No problem." I loosened my grip on the steering wheel a bit. "You want me to take you to work, Julian?"

"You going to be okay on your own?"

I glanced over my shoulder, eyes narrowed in feigned irritation.

"Of course. You'll be fine." Julian was enjoying both the ride and teasing me.

"I'll drive around until I'm comfortable. Then I need to stop at Maggie's and get measured for a driving outfit."

"You can secure yourself from the elements a lot better now than when I bought the Boehmer."

"It's more than rain or wind. You'll see soon enough."

"She's a wild one, JW."

"Yes sir." JW grinned.

* * *

After the lynching, I saw John B Williams at the Main. I suggested he cut the body down. He said he would contact Putnam and left.

J. D. Parker to Mamie

I turned left onto Towson, and then right onto Rogers again. At Sixth I turned right and pulled up to the curb beside the bank. "I'll be back to pick you up at 4," I said as Julian got out of the car.

"Have fun, my darling." Julian kissed my cheek.

"I promise." I was already in love with the Hudson. I waited until he waved as he went into the bank building. Then I eased off the clutch and turned onto Garrison.

"Mamie!"

I nodded at Katherine Mivelaz who covered her mouth in mock astonishment as I passed the Boston store. Theo Lamb crossed the street in front of me. I beeped my horn at her and she jumped back playfully.

"You're teasing your friends, ma'am."

"I am at that, JW. After so many weeks of sadness, it's wonderful to have a sunny day for a change."

"Just let me off at the corner and you can head right on out Grand."

I pulled over to the curb beside John B's Horse and Mule Barn—and JW got out. "Enjoy your new toy, Miz McGrath. I could play with these automobiles all day."

"Now that I know how to drive it, will you teach me more about it? I'll pay for your time."

"Just call and make an appointment." He got out and crossed in front of me. I eased off the clutch and headed out Grand.

As I approached the Williams home, Jennie was in the front yard. Seeing me approach, she waved and came to the edge of the road.

I skidded to a stop. "You want to go for a ride?"

Her eyes sparkled. "Give me a minute to get the kids settled with John?"

"I'll sit right here."

"Mamie! Is that yours?" Medora Sparks called from her carriage.

"First day driving it on my own."

"Good for you! Was it hard to learn to drive?"

"A couple lessons at the Arkansas Garage."

"You are brave."

"Just tired of being cooped up—and rather than buy a horse and buggy, I thought I'd go modern."

"Have fun!" She clicked to the horse and continued on her way.

Jenny came running out of her house, wrapping herself in a shawl.

"Be careful now," John B came out on the porch after her.

"Don't worry." I called to him. "We won't be gone long."

"Just bring her back safe."

"Aw, that's sweet," I said to Jennie. "He's worried about you."

She tied a scarf around her hair. "No, he's worried who'll take care of the kids if I get killed and he has to go to jail."

I was stunned until I realized she was joking. "We're off then." I turned around and headed back toward Garrison to show off my shiny red car one more time.

"Can you talk and drive at the same time?"

"Got a lot to say, do you, Jennie?" I looked at her and we both giggled.

I swerved to miss a mud puddle and bounced off of a rock.

Jennie held on to her seat. "Whoa!"

"It's a car, Jennie. Not a horse."

That set off another round of giggles. I had to pull over to the side of the road and compose myself.

Jennie's laughter turned to tears. "Don't mind me," she rubbed both eyes. "It takes all my energy to be calm and supportive. I'm the one who usually falls apart when something goes wrong."

I squeezed the steering wheel. "Oh, don't worry. I fell apart regularly this past summer. Must be the year for it."

"I'm glad you came by, Mamie. I don't know whether our friends are staying away because they think John B murdered Andy in cold blood or if they just don't know what to say to us."

I ducked my chin. "Maybe a little bit of both. Do you think he would kill Andy?"

She shook her head slowly. "Not in a million years, Mamie. Not my John."

"No one that knows John believes it."

"There's so much to figure out here. John heard they're going to arrest that McKnight hellion and his buddies."

I took a deep breath. "Have they found them yet?"

"Not yet." She rewrapped her shawl. "They're children in men's clothes. The whole idea of those babies in a jail cell makes my skin crawl. You can't put boys in with hardened criminals. They'd beat them at the very least. Rape them. Maybe even kill 'em." She shuddered.

I leaned my head onto the steering wheel. "I—I never thought of that."

"That nice young cop, Sam Booth, told us that the other day. John must have known it, but it was news to me. Couldn't help but think of our little Ray. What would such a thing do to a kid? Turn him into a heathen? An outlaw? A pervert?"

"Nothing like that will happen to Ray. John B would kill anyone that tried to hurt your kids."

"Yeah." She nodded with tears rolling down her cheeks. "I know he would. He'd protect us with his life—but what if they put him away, Mamie? What if they hang John for killing Andy?"

"He didn't mean to shoot Andy. They can't hang him for an accident. Besides John B was one of the good guys—a sheriff's son. He was too—too—, " I searched for the right word. "—nice."

Jennie looked up at me like I was crazy. "Do you know who I am, Mamie?"

I squirmed in my seat, searching for a lucid response. "I—I—"

Her laugh was mirthless. "Have you ever heard of George Maledon? Or Annie Maledon?"

Mortified by my apparent ignorance, I shook my head.

"George Maledon was Judge Parker's hangman." She stared out the Hudson's windshield. "He was a bantam rooster of a guy. Scrawny but tough. A German immigrant. He hung about sixty men during the course of his career. Shot several others who tried to escape. That's how he earned his living, fed his family."

"You knew him?"

She turned to watch my eyes. "He was my uncle, Mamie."

"I've heard of him."

"He died last year."

"Oh, Jennie. I'm sorry."

Her eyes watered but she refused to let a tear escape. "He was eighty and lived in Tennessee the last few years of his life so I didn't see him much."

I didn't understand where we were going with this conversation.

"His oldest daughter, Annie, was murdered. Shot in the stomach by her lover—and she didn't die right away. She suffered."

"Oh no, Jennie. When was this?"

"Back before the turn of the century. It about killed George and Mary."

"I imagine so."

"Before she died, she told them who shot her. Why. And where the bastard was."

"So they got him?"

"Yes, and tried him. And the jury found him guilty."

"Thank heavens for that, at least."

"Yes, justice. Right?"

"I guess." I visualized another hanging body. Was that justice? I wasn't sure—but what else do you do with someone like that?

"We thought so. An eye for an eye, you know."

"So did your uncle hang the man who murdered his daughter?"

"He would've, except the son of a spitting snake had a good lawyer and he got his sentence commuted to life in prison."

"Oh, I see." Was that justice?

"My uncle gave up at that point. He quit his job. Perhaps he was tired of the uncertainty. He told me one time that he took pride in executing those outlaws—rapists and murderers mostly. He put them away quickly with the least amount of suffering possible. He wasn't there to judge them—just to carry out their sentences. Maybe all of that wasn't so clear cut when the victim was your own daughter."

"Maybe not," I murmured, remembering Sandy's suffering as that crowd tortured him.

"I'm scared, Mamie. Anything can happen. It's bad enough that Della's a widow." The tear Jennie had been fighting spilled down her cheek. "I don't want anything bad to happen to my husband."

I put my arms around her and cried with her.

When no more tears would come for either of us, I put the Hudson in gear and we continued on our ride. The hum of the automobile's engine soothed us and the fresh air dried our tears. Soon we began to feel better. More hopeful at least.

"Do you know that detective that was involved that night," Jennie asked.

"Sort of." I wrinkled my nose. "I'm sure he does what he's supposed to do. He has a family to feed just like your Uncle George."

Jennie pretended to stare at the road but she was really watching me out of the corner of her eyes. "And?"

"He's aggressive. That night wasn't the first night I saw him mistreat someone. Of course, he thinks I'm a nosey know-it-all who judges him harshly."

"Are you?"

"Oh yeah," I chuckled. "That's exactly who I am. For all I know he may be a great provider, tender lover, and proud papa. But whenever I see him, I think of that night."

"The reason I ask, last month John B came home with a crazy story. You know how little Ray loves spending time with John. It had been awhile since they'd had an adventure so John promised to take him to see the Nelson-Togo fight."

"Oh I remember Julian and Burley talking about that. Was at the Grand Opera House, right?"

"Yes. And the two of them were excited. Ray ran around telling everyone who would listen that his Daddy was taking him to see Battling Nelson the Durable Dane."

"What does that mean?" I slowed as we headed back down Garrison for the fourth time.

Jennie laughed. "Who knows? It's something John taught Ray. I presume it's a nickname for one of the boxers."

"Okay. So what does this boxing match and the Durable Dane have to do with Pitcock?"

"Well, John B and Ray got down here a little early. The ring wasn't even open yet but they didn't want to go do something else until time, so they stood in line. I shudder to think about it even now, but suddenly they were in the middle of a shootout."

"On Garrison?"

"Apparently, I'm the only one who sees this as a problem. Ray and John B had a merry old time. John B told me it was over in the blink of an eye but that if it had lasted much longer, he would have hustled Ray out of there one, two, three,"

"I take it you didn't believe that one."

"Not even the story that had the line parting and giving them a chance to move up."

"So what did happen?" I pulled up in front of the First National Bank where Julian was standing on the street corner chatting with Burley Johnston. They shook hands and Julian crawled into the back seat. Burley tapped on the hood and gave me a thumbs up signal.

I turned around. "Give us a minute to finish?"

"You want me to get out?"

"No, no, stay put, sweetheart. This won't take but a minute."

"Fine." Julian took out his notebook and pen.

I turned back to Jennie. "So John B and Ray were standing in line waiting to get into the boxing match. What happened next?"

"Well—" Jennie turned toward me. "As they were waiting, a big Negro man runs in front of them. Then they hear loud bangs and bullets whizzing by."

"Say what?" Julian laid aside his journal. "What happened?"

"It was Pitcock, chasing after this guy who was shooting back at him."

Julian leaned forward so as to hear better. "In the middle of a crowd?"

"In front of the Grand Opera House," Jennie repeated. "On Garrison. Where a bunch of people were waiting to get into the boxing match."

"I wonder how many other times he did that," Julian said as he leaned back in his seat. "A dangerous habit."

"Not to defend him, but why would he do such a thing?"

"What do you mean?"

"Just this, Jennie. Don't policemen try to arrest people alive?"

"That's the idea."

"And this was unusual enough that Ray and John B mentioned it to you."

"What are you getting at, Mamie," Julian said from the backseat.

"Well, seems like someone told me—maybe John B himself— that the night Andy was hit, he lagged behind Pitcock because he was shooting at Sandy as he ran. Andy either did that too—or went the other way—to try avoid Pitcock's bullets and head off Sandy."

"You think it was Pitcock who shot Andy!" Jennie covered her mouth with her fingers.

"Well, it was Pitcock's gun because John B wasn't wearing one. And John told me he didn't even realize Andy was down at first. He thought he was behind him coming off of B onto Tenth, not in front of him at the Pony Express. Granted John B beat that kid half to death with Pitcock's gun, but I'm beginning to think maybe Andy was shot before Pitcock gave his gun to John B."

"But John B believes he shot Andy," Jennie cried. "And it's eating him alive."

"So what are you thinking," Julian asked. "Pitcock knows he accidentally shot Andy and that's why he let that crowd think Sandy did it?"

"He did whisper the cell number in your ear."

"What?" Jennie spun around to look at Julian in the back seat.

"At the jail, after they got the boy situated, Pitcock came out and whispered the cell number to several people—including me."

"He wanted them to hang that boy?"

"It seems so," Julian said.

"It all comes back to Pitcock." I put the Hudson in gear. "John B was too upset to know anything for sure. The witnesses may or may not have been in position to see who was holding that gun when it went off. I'll ask them. But regardless of how it happened, Sandy was killed because Pitcock was afraid he'd be blamed. I'm sure of it."

"Oh my poor John," Jennie said as we headed back up Garrison.

* * *

Julian and I lay together in the darkness of our bedroom. "Tired?"

"Exhausted."

"Can you stay awake long enough to tell me what's going on with the police inquiry?"

He yawned. "Sure. Some of them tell me more than others. A few of the older men follow the rules and don't say anything to anyone."

"Just about every family I've spoken to knows someone involved in someway," I said. "It's awful."

" Did I tell you what Jack Roberts told me?"

"Pretty sure you didn't. Don't think I know Jack Roberts."

"Young man from a well-known Fort Smith family still sowing his oats."

"Sounds like most of them." I yawned.

"He cornered me in the hall outside the men's room in the courthouse. He thinks the Grand Jury will call him. It'll be a while before they get to all that so he wanted me to write everything down now before he forgets it."

"There's probably more to it than he's willing to tell."

"He said he and his buddy Chris were drinking at an unnamed bar when they heard the commotion and went over to the jail that night. He emphasized several times that they never got any nearer than the fence."

"Too emphatic. Implies he thinks you might not believe him," Julian chuckled. "In that case, he thinks right."

"Up to something?"

"Probably. He said they watched the crowd pull Sandy out of the jail. He didn't hear John B or anyone else yell that Andy wasn't dead, though. He was insistent about that."

"Interesting that he seems to think that there's a difference between lynching a man for murdering a man that's not dead yet."

"It is, isn't it?" Julian yawned. "He says he didn't see his friends —including this Chris, Harold Christmas, Nick Fararri, Ben Black, Grover Bourland, Grady Templeton or Tom Lyle— standing inside the fence at the jail. He did see them standing in front of the Main after the lynching. He doesn't know where they were during the hanging though."

"That doesn't make sense, Julian."

"Never said it did. I asked him if he was drunk and he said no. When I reworded the question to 'had he been drinking,' he said, 'well, they'd been playing a game.' Turns out, he himself drank about a dozen shots at one place, maybe two or three at another."

"How is it that he's alive to tell you this?"

He patted my leg. "You're becoming quite a skeptic, my dear."

"You get held up by a nun, it sours you on trust."

His laugh was more of a sleepy cough. "Anyway, he said every time he took a whiskey, Harold Christmas did too. So I said, after all of that you must have been schnockered. And he said, no, not especially."

I choked back a belly laugh before remembering the results of that binge. "So is he more worried about his folks finding out he was poisoning himself with drink or that he participated in a public murder?"

"Maybe both, Mamie. Maybe both."

We lay there, each thinking our own thoughts until his breathing became regular. I touched him. "Julian?" He snorted and turned away from me.

I lay on my back, hands over the blanket—twisting my wedding ring. I struggled to understand the events of the day. Patsy and Genevieve had been annoyed with me that morning when I tried to reassure them that white hostilities had settled down. I didn't understand why that upset them and my feelings were hurt. Then, I thought about Manny McKnight. I'd peeked into the shed after dinner only to find he'd left. I hoped he went to Reverend Mathews' house or was visiting Miss Pahotsky—but I doubted he'd done either. That boy was the most vexing person I'd ever run across. Fort Smith had failed him. John B, for all his good will toward the boy, had failed him. And I had failed him most of all.

I closed my eyes and tried to sleep. John B's worried but determined face when he rescued Abigail and me at the Frisco floated in my imagination. Then Pitcock searching through the rubble at the intersection of Tenth and B supplanted it. Was he looking for the thirty-eight John B thought he saw that night? Bullets? A meaningless whirl of images flipped through my mind distracting me from the most bothersome thing about the day—Joe and Cotton. I yawned and rolled away from Julian. They looked like ordinary guys. The kind of men who stepped aside to let me pass on the sidewalks of Garrison Avenue. They probably had jobs or owned businesses—had wives and children, mothers and fathers, brothers and sisters. They were normal, everyday people trying to live good lives. Yet they were more worried about what people thought of them than the fact they'd murdered someone. Someone important. At least to his family and his community. Joe and Cotton thought they knew best— better than the police or the legal system. They knew so much better that they couldn't trust the government to get to the bottom of who shot Andy. Dear, dear Andy.

Bad as that was, as mad as I was at Joe and Cotton and Manny and even John B, something else was keeping me awake. I'd done the same thing. I didn't even like Abigail Talbot. She was snooty and nosey and a blabbermouth—and yet, when I saw Sister Clarence following her, I couldn't wait for the cops either. I rushed right into something bigger than myself—uninformed, fueled by arrogance and attachment and fury, ready to dispense my own brand of know-it-all justice. We were all lucky that Mr. Marky/Fellows/Sister Clarence was such a push over. I'd done a foolish thing intruding into Abigail and Garland Talbot's messy life and I was never, ever going to do it again. Ever.

16

Free Bridge Celebration.
Airship Flights Daily, Big Floral and Industrial Parade,
Balloon Ascensions, Baseball
SPEECHES BY GREAT MEN
Fort Smith and Van Buren

Monday and Tuesday, April 1-2, 1912

April 1, 1912–Race War Postponed. Prospect of Outbreak in Arkansas Fol-
lowing Lynching Disappears.

Asbury Park Press, Asbury Park, New Jersey

April 2, 1912–"Where the hell is Asbury Park?"

Elias "Sarge" Eacret to anyone who would listen

April 2, 1912–Andy Carr, died yesterday morning. It wasn't fair what hap-
pened to Reverend Lewis' boy Sanford, but that don't mean colored folks
don't hurt for Detective Carr's family. He was fair and polite and we felt safe
when Andy was on duty.

Genevieve Day, *The Fort Smith Bell*

April 2, 1912 10:30 a.m.

A BLACK FORD WITH THREE grim-looking men inside stopped and the driver blew it's horn. Caroline and I jumped at the raucous noise. A horse shied and the line of people waiting at the Greenwood Avenue gate to Oak Cemetery swayed in alarm.

An angry policeman ran out into the street and tapped the window with his baton. "Move on!"

The men inside the Model T argued back but drove away.

As we entered the cemetery, we saw Andy's family and friends gathering under a small tree on a slope to our right. The hearse bearing Andy Carr to his grave hadn't arrived yet—and there was already a small crowd.

"Yoohoo!" Abigail's falsetto raised the fine hairs on the back of my neck. She waved her handkerchief like we couldn't see her towering over the other women waiting for the service to begin.

246

Heads turned and eyebrows shot up. I cringed but resolved to be as kind to Abigail as I could. We'd taken down a criminal together after all and my being polite to Abigail pleased Caroline.

We went into the graveyard and joined the group waiting for the coffin to arrive.

"Good morning, Miz Caroline." Burley took Caroline's hand to steady her on the uneven ground. "Mamie."

"It's a sad day, Burley Clay," Caroline said.

"Tragic ma'am," he responded. "For the Carrs and for Fort Smith. Andy was special."

"It's good to see you, Burley."

"You too," he whispered into my ear. "I have something to tell you later."

"Why don't you come by the house after this?"

"Sounds like a plan."

"There you are." Julian found us as we reached the edge of the plot that would be Andy's last resting place. "I was wondering if you two would make it in time."

"It wasn't that far of a walk and the weather was comfortable enough." I kissed his cheek. "Do you have time to come home for lunch? Burley has something to share with us and I don't think this service will take long."

His eyes focused on something over my head. "Okay."

I turned to look. John B and Jennie stood outside the fence as if trying to decide what to do. "Oh the poor dears," I murmured. "Should I go talk to them?"

"Why don't you, sweetheart. They look like they could use a friend."

The horse-drawn hearse was pulling into the cemetery a few yards away as I reached the fence.

"Aren't you two going to join us?"

"We don't want to cause trouble but we wanted the family to know we care," Jennie said. "I want Della to know that at least."

John B's shoulders were slumped, his arms crossed over his chest with his hat dangling from one hand.

"You're looking pretty down in the mouth, John B."

"He was my friend—dead by my hand. That's pretty hard to bear."

"It must be awful."

"It's the worst thing I've ever had to face." His eyes were damp. "I hope wherever he is, Andy knows how sorry I am."

Jennie took his arm. "John's not been sleeping since this happened. Worried about what will happen to us and his businesses if he has to spend a considerable time behind bars. Worried about Della and the kids too."

"The Meeks' will look out for her, I'm sure. And Della's a spark. She'll keep that family going."

The hearse stopped in front of the grave and the pallbearers stepped forward.

"I should have at least done that for him—carried his coffin, but his family didn't want me." A tear trickled down John B's cheek into his handlebar mustache. "I don't blame them. I should have protected him."

Jennie caressed his face while I stood mute, the rod iron fence not separating us so much as the tense gloom.

A group of policemen led a small procession to the grave site. Then Della and the children walked up the hill and stood grim-faced as the coffin was set over the grave. Della's brother and nephew joined them along with other members of both the Carr and the Meek families. Locals who'd followed the hearse filed after them, hats off and hands folded. Reverend Mathews was there—and Father Horan. And Mayor Bourland and other city officials.

From where I stood with the Williamses, we couldn't see or hear much that was being said at the grave site. Della and the children were surrounded by mourners.

"Come on, John. Let's go on home. Della knows we were here. Let's not intrude now."

John B draped his arm around Jennie. "Y'all come over for dinner one of these days," he said to me. "Jennie makes a great pot roast."

"Just give us a date and we'll be there." I blew them kisses. As I turned to climb the hill and join Andy's friends, relatives and colleagues gathered to say goodbye, I saw the black Ford drive past the gate once more—all three of the toughs inside craning their necks. To see what was going on? Maybe to make out who was there?

Noon

"Both Andy and Sandy are in their graves now," Caroline said as she poured us each a glass of cold milk straight from the icebox. "It's time to put this whole thing in perspective and move on."

Shocked at my mother-in-law's words, my mind whirled. Did "moving on" mean letting everyone who did this horrible thing get off scott-free? Did it mean forgetting about Andy and Sandy? Like they never lived at all? Like what happened to them didn't matter?

"I know that's the way Fort Smith deals with unpleasant things, Mama—but given that the Grand Jury hasn't announced its findings, it may be premature to move on just yet," Julian said as he and Burley put extra sections into the kitchen table to make room for all of us.

Caroline lowered her eyes. "After this, I don't want to know what goes on in my neighbors' hearts. It scares me."

"Me too," I said softly.

"You and Julian are so brave, poking dragons like you do. I'm afraid that, sooner or later, you'll get burned."

I gave her a hug. "Maybe those dragons will just disappear in a puff of smoke rather than be exposed."

"I hope."

Julian tried to give her a light hug, but she clung to him.

"Mama?"

She stepped back, squared her shoulders and called to our guests in the front parlor. "This is going to be informal. Come on back and grab a seat."

Abigail and Burley made their way down the hall and sat down around the kitchen table, searching for—and not finding—a light conversational topic. Miss Peach followed, pushing Sarge in his wheel chair. Caroline and I set a platter stacked high with chicken salad sandwiches, a tureen of Caroline's fresh tomato soup, and a bowl of potato salad in the center of the table.

"Go ahead, eat up." Caroline wiped her hands on her apron and waited for everyone to dig in. "There's apple cobbler for dessert."

I'm all for that." Julian picked up the platter of sandwiches, took one and passed it on to Burley.

I had no appetite but I sat down across from Julian and smiled wearily at him.

"The cops are pointin' fingers at each other and anyone else they can. White folks are scared Negroes are goin' to slit their throats. Black people are hunkered down expectin' another lynch mob at any moment." Sarge started in as Miss Peach pushed him up to the table. "And I don't blame any of 'em. Them damned-fool sons of rebels all decked out in sheets are a nasty lot. They're the kinda men that only got guts when the odds are fifty to one in their favor."

"Why the Klan's nothing but a political party around here," Abigail admonished as she sat down across from him. "Most of the members are either old men beating a dead horse, or young whip-persnappers showing off for each other. Either way, I didn't see any white robes the other night. Just drunks and kids."

Miss Peach glared sideways through her eyelashes at Abigail. I gave her a tray of food. We paused, eyes locked, both of us still holding it. Then, the moment passed. She backed away and walked toward the back parlor to eat alone. I couldn't imagine that's what she wanted, but she was scrupulous about following Fort Smith's rules. Once after my blunder at the Goldman Hotel, I asked her about it. She'd shrugged. "I got to take care of my family, Miz Mamie. If'n I follow the rules, it's more likely there won't be any misunderstandings. That's better for Mr. Elias and it's better for you too." At the time, I'd nodded as if I understood—but in reality, I was contemptuous of the rigid arrangements between white folks and black.

Julian took the seat beside Sarge. "I heard that fool, Will Manus, has been showing people the pictures that Redner fellow took of the lynching. He even points himself out, saying his clothes are still stained with Sandy's blood."

"That photographer thought he was gonna make some money," Burley said, "...but someone reported him and he got called before the police court for peddling souvenirs without a license."

"What kind of fool does that," Abigail said. "Things aren't tense enough in this town already?"

"He claimed he tried to get a license but the city clerk refused to issue him one because he didn't like the content. And then, the City Attorney, Vince Miles saw them and was appalled. He gave Redner a lecture. You know, propriety and city image and the like. Convinced him to destroy the negatives and everything he'd already printed up—to spare Fort Smith's good name."

"Ha!" Sarge barked. "You can bet your bottom dollar he put a few back."

"I understand why Miles did that, but Redner's already sold a bunch of them. They're all over town," Julian said. "All limiting supply will do is drive up the price in the secondary market."

"You'd think Will Manus'd be scared they might arrest him—especially if he's in Redner's photographs."

"He's stuck, Mamie." Burley pulled his chair close to the table.

"What do you mean stuck?"

"He didn't do that alone. There were at least fifty or sixty of 'em involved. He's letting the others know that he's still with them. That he's not sorry."

"Oh Burley, how can that be?"

"He's scared. Not just of the law—but of his cohorts. And like any other fool, the last thing he wants is to be thought of as a fool."

"It's better to be known as evil?"

Burley's eyes danced. "Oh yes, ma'am. Evil is powerful, at least."

"A disturbing thought."

"That Manus boy's only got one oar in the water," Abigail said. "Why act exactly like what you don't want people to think you are?"

No one except Abigail seemed hungry but we ate enough to satisfy Caroline's attentive eye. As we began dessert, the conversation picked up again.

"This thing is bad for business," Julian said. "I like to think those fifty business men put their money down to ensure this crime is investigated properly did it for moral reasons. But they also did it to protect their investments. Who wants to eat at the fine restaurants or patronize those beautiful theaters if you're afraid you'll be confronted with a violent mob on the Avenue?"

"Not me," Abigail put a dollop of whipped cream on Sarge's cobbler and then one on her own before passing it to Burley.

Burley sat it down without serving himself. "I was going to wait until it was just me and Mamie and Julian, but I reckon y'all will hear about this soon as you set foot on Garrison."

"Ya might as well spill the beans now, boy." Sarge sneaked his small flask out of his waist coat pocket, took a sip, and then eased it back in again. "There's not much happens about town that red-haired vixen over there don't spread around like offal afore the flies can light on it." He nudged Abigail who pretended not to ignore him.

"Well," Burley said, "I heard this morning that the night Andy was shot, he was already onto that Orrin Fellows, who we now know—thanks to these two ladies engaging in fisticuffs with him," he nodded to Abigail and me, "—had been disguising himself as a sainted Sister of Mercy. Fellows said he was hiding from some Detroit businessmen, but once you know someone's a liar, it's hard to figure if anything he says is true or not. Anyway, Andy was investigating how Garland's Buick came to be stolen and sold for way more than it was worth."

"How'd you know that?"

"I was doing what you told me, Julian. Hanging out over in the court house. Cathey Pitcock was showing off for his men. He said Andy had told him to be on the lookout for a big shipment of Guckenheimer whiskey that disappeared somewhere around here. Pitcock claimed he already knew about it and was planning to liberate it from the bad guys and get a cash reward for it."

The final piece slipped into place. "Mr. Guckenheimer!" I slapped my hands against my thighs. "He's not a dead person. He's a coffin full of whiskey."

Abigail perked up. "Garland stole whiskey from people who were stealing whiskey from someone who was stockpiling it?"

"Exactly." Burley grinned. "And last night, I realized that means that someone is sitting on a lot of money—even more once

Prohibition comes. And both Fellows and Garland intended on being that person."

Sarge leaned forward. "I been drinkin' mostly Jake since I came back to Arkansas—unless I'm visitin' my darlin' niece here. And that son of a gun Garland was sittin' on good stuff? I've a mind to dig out my old horsewhip and give him a good whackin.'" His raucous laughter turned into a prolonged coughing spell—which caused Miss Peach to run into the dining room and slap him on the back several times. "Dammit, woman. I'm fine. Stop beatin' me to death. I've got somethin' to live for now."

"Sarge is fine now," Abigail said. "Do go on, Burley."

Miss Peach put her hands on her hips and shook her head. "You got too much merriment going on here for white folks. This man's not well and he don't need no encouragement when it comes to carrying on."

"I'm sorry, Miss Peach," Burley said. "It's my fault."

"Humph." Miss Peach obviously didn't approve of whatever she thought it was that we were doing. After a warning glare at Sarge, Abigail and Burley, she returned to her lunch in the back parlor.

When her door closed, we dissolved into muffled giggles.

"Guess we needed that." I wiped my eyes with my knuckles.

Julian turned back to Burley. "Start where you want. But we're on to you like a pack of wolves after a lamb."

Burley's eyes twinkled. "Now that I'm visualizing a pack of wolves nipping at my heels, I'm much calmer. Thank you for that image, Julian."

After another round of snickers, he tried again. "So Fellows was flat broke after his last project and he convinced Garland to pony up his savings to purchase the Guckenheimer, not realizing that Garland wasn't as big a fool as he appeared." Julian turned to Abigail. "Pardon me, ma'am."

"Don't tell me that Garland wasn't always as drunk as he seemed?" Caroline sank into her chair like a balloon that'd run out of air. "So that's why that Mr. Fellows attacked Abigail. He thought she was in on it."

"But I'm not," Abigail protested. "I'm the secretary of the Fort Smith Women's Christian Temperance Society. I wouldn't. I couldn't."

"I know, dear," Caroline soothed her. "Remember how worried you were about Garland when this all started?"

"It's taken years to build up our standing in Fort Smith." For once Abigail's mask slipped and she seemed frightened. "You can't convince me Garland had anything to do with killing that boy."

Caroline put her arms around Abigail. "There, there, dear. It'll work out. Wait and see."

"He has a horror of such things," Abigail dabbed at her eyes with her kerchief.

"I know he does," Caroline crooned.

Burley shrugged. "Could be Fellows thought Abigail knows more than she does. Or maybe he thought Garland was somewhere sleeping it off and he'd use his absence to steal his share from her."

"Whew, I'm confused. Where's Garland now?"

"That's what I'd like to know, Mamie." Abigail leaned over and tapped the table with her fingernail. "This is embarrassing. I'm the treasurer of the Women's Christian Temperance Union, you know."

"I know, dear." I tried to keep the amusement out of my voice. "Where would Garland have hidden all that booze?"

"I don't know, Julian. Garland knows that my position in the WCTU would require me to destroy contraband like that. I'm sure that's why he hid this enterprise from me."

"Destroy it?" Sarge was incredulous.

"If I knew where it was, which I don't."

I folded my arms across my chest. *So if Garland wasn't always as drunk as he appeared, was Abigail who she presented herself to be?* A carload of coffins filled with Guckenheimer whiskey would make it possible for Garland to keep Abigail in all the fine things she coveted. Especially if the talk about banning the stuff came about. I flashed on the confrontation with Orrin Fellows at the Frisco. *What did Abigail have in her fist? Why was it so important that she hid whatever it was in her bosom?* I suddenly realized that conversation around the table had quieted and all eyes were on me.

"What?"

"How did Andy know about Fellows?" Burley repeated himself. "Who told him?"

"I had coffee with him at Padgett's the day he died. Remember, Julian, I told you that?"

Julian straightened his spectacles with his knuckle. "I do."

"What did you talk about?"

I lowered my eyes. "Garland, Mr. Fellows, and Sister Clarence."

Burley's eyes widened. "What did he say?"

"Nothing. He just got up and left."

Caroline's eyes grew wider. "Someone shot him over whiskey?"

"But they said John B did it." Abigail stood up and pushed her chair in. "What's a person to believe if the story keeps changing?"

"Maybe that black boy did shoot Andy with Pitcock's gun. Ever think of that?" Sarge said with his mouth full of cobbler. "It's possible."

"John B swears Sandy never had a gun. Maybe a pocket knife. But Andy was shot not stabbed." I shuddered at the prospect of that reality. "On the other hand, Sandy was beaten, shot, stabbed, dragged by a horse, and strung up."

"It's worse than that," Burley sighed. "I got it from Katherine Mivelaz that someone told the Carrs that Pitcock made it look like Sandy did it to cover up John B shooting Andy after a quarrel—and he went so far as to tell those raging drunks in front of the jail which cell that boy was in."

Sarge pounded the table with his fist, "Hold it. Is John B tight with Pitcock?"

"I don't know," Julian said. "I never saw them in one place together except when we all had dinner at the Goldman before the grand opening of the New Theater. I don't believe they even spoke."

"Then why would Pitcock cover for John B?"

"Dunno, Sarge. Cops looking out for cops?" Burley shrugged.

"Probably just rumor," Julian said.

"I saw Orrin Fellows down around Texas Corner that night."

Everyone grew quiet.

"You what?" Julian looked angry.

I took his hand. "I just remembered. During my encounter with Pitcock on Garrison, I saw Fellows turn the corner of Tenth and Garrison and head back toward the Main."

"Was he armed?" Burley's voice cracked.

I closed my eyes, trying to remember. "He was tucking something inside his coat pocket. Something small."

"Like the little Derringer?" Abigail pretended her hand was a pistol. "The one he was holding on me the other day?"

"For heaven's sake," Caroline frowned. "Who *did* shoot Andy?"

* * *

I didn't see the police arrest anyone but black folks that night.

Sister Alberta Cavanaugh to Mamie McGrath

I paced in front of the window in the front parlor. "I just don't understand why those people couldn't wait for a trial. Isn't that what we were taught in school?" We'd left the dishes for Genevieve to clear later so that Julian and Burley and I could collect ourselves before court was due to start again.

"It's all about how you see the world," Sarge said as Miss Peach rolled him into the room. "Say I stole a dill pickle off Burley's plate—just forked it and popped it in my mouth."

Miss Peach rolled her eyes and headed back down the hall.

Burley seemed startled. "Go for it, Sarge. I prefer raw cucumbers anyway."

"See, Mamie, folks are different when it comes to family," Sarge said. "That boy don't mind me stealin' his pickle for lots of reasons. First off, he likes being part of our crazy family and losing a fine dill to a fellow tribe member—especially a revered elder like myself, well, it just ain't worth a fight. Of course, he don't care for pickles anyhow. So he can get himself a plain ole cuke and be happy. Would have been different if'n an outsider took it off his plate though."

Julian jerked his thumb at Burley. "Old Burley there's got a sweet tooth, Sarge. He'd cut your heart out if you went after Mama's chocolate pie."

"Let's say a stranger came after Burley's pie...," Sarge's voice rose. "...you'd see more of a fight. But if it's someone he knows and don't like..."

"Like a Negro?"

Sarge nodded. "Someone you can see right away ain't family—and thus is undeservin' of family pie."

"Someone who used to belong to you," Abigail said softly. "Whose sole value was in how much cotton they could pick. Then some arrogant Yankee insists they were never your property at all and had an equal right to chocolate pie same as you."

I folded my arms over my bosom. "So this is *still* about the Civil War?"

"It's about losing a way of life that seemed right and moral, Mamie. At least for those of us who benefited from it." Abigail sat stiff-backed in her chair, her jaw tightening as she gritted her teeth. "Folks like you, my dear, see the world as a garden of plenty. You don't care if a black person gets pie because you can always make more when this one's gone. But other folks think there are only so many pies in the world and if some black man eats one, that's one less for you and yours."

The more people explained how they felt about Negroes, the more confusing it got. "But why didn't they wait to see who really killed Andy? And why did they murder Sandy and not John B?"

"Because he ain't black." Genevieve stood in the doorway with a basket of vegetables.

We turned to her. Abigail scowled. Sarge studied his fingernails. Julian's cheeks were cherry red. We'd been so intent on our conversation we'd forgotten to be careful with our words.

Burley and Caroline both arose. Caroline took the basket out of Genevieve's hands and began storing its contents in the pantry.

Burley pulled a chair out from under the table and nodded for Genevieve to sit down.

"Mr. Burley, that's mighty kind of you, but I'm still wantin' to be mad."

"So be mad sitting down, for goodness sake. You've been running around taking care of everyone but yourself."

She looked at each face sitting around the table. "I might rest my feet a bit."

"We're all pretty upset about Andy right now." Burley's voice was kind. "Seems like we all thought he'd live forever, you know? We thought he was a giant so long, that him being vulnerable just like one of us—well, we're scared, Genevieve."

She unfolded her arms. "Now see, that's what I'm sayin.' Y'all need to get back to normal."

"What are you and yours going to do?"

"Our normal's not as comfortable as yours, Mr. Burley—but we'll put our grievances in our pockets for the time bein.'"

"I don't know how this all started," Burley said, "...or when it'll be over. But I am sorry, Genevieve."

She covered her face with her hands. "Don't make me hope, Mr. Burley. I can't bear it when it don't happen."

"I'm sorry too." It was almost a whisper even though I felt like I was shouting it.

Abigail fished a clean folded hanky out of her sleeve. "Here, here. Keep it. I have ten more just like it back in my dresser drawer."

"Thank you all. But there ain't nothin' you can do to bring Reverend Lewis' boy back. Jes let it be. We'll find a way on our own."

"I don't have to apologize for anythin,'" Sarge growled. "I done lost a leg—my favorite one, too—to change this shit."

Genevieve sniffed and lowered her hands. "I appreciate that Mr. Elias. You're such a pissant now, I hate to think what you'd have been if'n you had two legs."

3:30 p.m.

After everyone left, I went out on the screen porch with a cup of hot tea and my note book. Although Julian had warned that on a regular beat, a reporter didn't dare miss a day, I was exhausted. Facts blended with personal interviews and gossip. I needed to clear my head and think about things in order, one at a time. I opened my notebook and wrote, " Sanford Lewis." And underlined his name twice.

How well did I know him? He was shy around me. Respectful. Hardworking. I remembered how leery Sandy had been of Manny at first. And then how kind. I remembered him bringing Caroline vegetables from his father's garden in PawPaw—and Caroline sending him home with hand-knitted socks in an assortment of sizes for the children of Reverend Lewis' ministry. He liked to read and Julian shared our collection of Hopalong Cassidy books with him—one at a time. If he'd lived, he would've been grooming our flower gardens and trimming the bushes about now. And we'd be driving my new Hudson together.

I thumbed through the sketches I'd made at the courthouse. Bliss Poole. Sam Booth. John Jarnigan. Cathey Pitcock. I turned to a new page and picked up my pencil. Twenty minutes went by quickly. I stared at what I'd done until my eyes drooped and I dozed off.

"It's a good likeness."

I opened my eyes. "It's good to see you, Patsy."

She sat down beside me. "I hear you're on a mission."

"Who told you that? Caroline?"

"She's one of several." Patsy leaned back in the wooden porch lounge. "They tell me you aren't eating like you should—and you aren't sleeping either. Want to tell me what's eating you that's on top of what's eating the rest of us?"

I closed my book and held it against my chest, hiding my sketch of Sandy. "I don't understand myself."

Patsy stared at the buds forming on our Magnolia tree. "Oh?"

"That night, I ran toward the noise and saw Lacey and Pitcock herding a young Negro man down Garrison. He was handcuffed and his hands were bleeding and broken. His eyes were swollen almost closed. His nose was mashed up toward his forehead and toward the side of his face. He had a horrific cut across the top of his head and I saw his skull through it. Every time he fell down, they'd kick him or drag him. I had no idea who he was. I swear."

"Do you really think you could have stopped it? A tiny woman against the mountain of hate displayed on Garrison Avenue that night?"

"He spoke to me, Patsy. He begged me to help him."

"And..."

"I didn't even recognize his voice. The most important thing I could have done was recognize him. Comfort him in his moment of need. Speak up for him, not some stranger accused of shooting Andy—but our employee and friend." I stole a peek at Patsy, figuring it would be the last one before she hated me. "I'd have known without question that Sandy would never hurt anyone. That they were punishing the wrong man. And I would have fought with every last ounce of my being if I knew it was him."

"As far as I know, no black person fought for him either, Mamie."

"No, that's not it. I *should* have realized it was Sandy. Look at the sketch. He was wearing the same shirt he always wore when he came to work here. Clean and nicely-pressed. He'd take it off and hang it inside the shed and put on the old soft cotton one his Mama made him. He wore that one when he was doing our lawn. When he was through working, he'd get water from the well and wash up in the bucket we have back there. And then, he'd put that good shirt back on. He wanted to look nice while he was in town."

"So, you're beating yourself up because you didn't recognize him and because you didn't recognize him, you didn't fight hard enough?"

"Worse than that. If I'd known it was Sandy, I would have fought to my last breath—and might have won too. I already had run ins with Pitcock and he'd have been scared that I'd report all of his misdeeds if he didn't stop this awful thing. He would've backed down. I know it."

Patsy seemed confused.

"If I'm strong enough to fight for a friend, I'm strong enough. So why didn't I fight for whoever it was?"

Patsy shivered and pulled her shawl tighter around her shoulders. "It was a huge crowd. Over a thousand people who could've intervened and didn't."

I sighed. "I can't speak for a thousand people, Patsy. What keeps me awake is why I just watched. Like Garland Talbot watched them murder Henry Smith in Parris, Texas."

"Oh Mamie."

17

April 11, 1912
Local contractor, John Stowers, who was jailed for leading the mob that lynched Sanford Lewis last month was released on a $5,000 bail by Judge Hon. Stowers is erecting a large building here and is under bond to finish it within a required time. Concerned that Stowers' incarceration would prevent the completion of the project, bondsmen took the initiative to secure his release.

Julian McGrath, *Southwest American*

April 15, 1912
Disaster at Sea! Titanic sinks on Maiden Voyage.

Julian McGrath, *Southwest American*

April 19, 1912
After the lynching of a innocent young Negro on Garrison Avenue last month, the good people of Fort Smith realize the weakness of our present political system of municipal government. Now is the time to unite to insure the adoption of the commission form of government for Fort Smith.

Julian McGrath, Southwest American

April 23, 1912 10:30 a.m.

I STOOD IN FRONT OF Immaculate Conception Church.

"Good morning, Miz McGrath." A small man came down the steps. "Is something wrong?"

"Just waiting for my mother-in-law, Mayor Bourland. She's still in line at the confessional." It was the first time I'd seen him without his entourage.

He took off his hat and pressed it to his chest. "I can't imagine that dear woman has sins enough to justify more than a 'how do ya do' in the confessional."

I smiled uncertainly. "If unburdening her soul to Father Horan makes her feel better, who am I to challenge it?"

"So you're Catholic too, are you?"

"Converted."

"Ah yes, so you and Mr. McGrath could marry."

I tried not to frown. Julian and I'd been married four years now. In all of that time, Fagan Bourland had never said more than ten words in a row to me—and then only in formal situations when it was required. After all, I couldn't vote for him. He struck me as the kind of man who never wasted time on people who couldn't—or wouldn't—do anything for him.

"Did you hear about that big ship that went down in the Atlantic?"

"Yes." I looked around for an escape. "The Titanic."

"The newspapers are full of it. Seems there was a St. Louis reporter on the Carpathia, the ship that plucked those poor souls out of the freezing water. He has spent the last days since the incident interviewing survivors. Lucky, eh? He'll make a lot of money off someone else's tragedy." He leaned forward. "Like you and Julian."

"There are more reasons than money to record what's going on around you, Mayor."

He hissed, fine drops of his spittle hitting my face. "Name one!"

"History."

He must have liked my answer because his hostility melted into awkward friendliness. "I grant you that my contributions to Fort Smith are historic. I helped create business opportunities around here—lots of them starting back before the turn of the century. I worried about this place. Put my heart and soul into it. Took as much pleasure in watching it evolve as I did watching my children grow."

I cocked my head sideways. "Okay?"

"How does what I said and did on Garrison Avenue after a lynching translate to history more than my other contributions?"

"What you do and say matters because you have power, sir."

"Ha!"

"You don't think so?"

"They chew me up and spit me out, you know. They challenge my motives. Act like I'm a cheat and a crook."

"Who does?"

"My political enemies. And the newspapers."

"Do you give interviews?"

"I want them to write me as I see myself—not as some showboat reporter sees me. The press hasn't treated me fairly since the unfortunate problem with my wife years ago. She was found innocent in a court of law, but the newspapers found me guilty of any number of sins—and I didn't even have a damn trial."

"You didn't shoot Mrs. Allen."

"No."

"You were carrying on with her though."

Whether from pride or embarrassment, he flushed. "I was a good deal younger then, Miz McGrath. And a man is helpless when caught up in passion like that."

I forced myself not to laugh. "Why are you telling me these things?"

He studied his shoes for a moment, then glanced up at me with a deliberately charming smile. "I write things myself from time to time, you know. But I have to pay them to run them—and when I do that, folks think it's self-serving. What I need is someone who'll listen to me and be fair."

"You should talk to Julian then."

He smiled wider. "I'd rather talk to you. Then you can tell Julian or whoever you want."

"Why?"

"You're a lot prettier than Julian."

I bit back a sharp retort. "Julian is the reporter. They pay me for stories. Not the news but my opinion of the news."

"That's what I need. A friendly opinion."

His charm was moldy—like he was so used to telling people what to do, he'd forgotten how to make them want to do his bidding.

"Now isn't a good time, sir. My mother-in-law will be out of church any minute. How about we meet later at Julian's office?"

"Good God no. That's like telling my story to Abigail Talbot in the middle of Garrison Avenue."

"How about Padgett's?"

"How about something quieter and more elegant?"

"I'm a married woman, Mr. Bourland. I don't need rumors any more than you do. How about Espositos?"

His shoulders slumped in mock defeat. "Italian food is spicy?"

"Tasty. And the Espositos are friends of mine."

"Noon?" He put on his hat and arranged it just so on his head.

"How about twelve forty-five?"

"My God, you drive a hard bargain."

That was the point.

* * *

Noon

"You mean he's coming here?" Martina wiped the flour off her hands.

"I want him to tell me about his behavior the night of the lynching, so I need a place that's relatively quiet but not too private."

"He isn't what you call a gigolo—no—a philanderer, is he?"

"He's more of a bully."

She led me to a corner table in the smaller sining room. "Why does he want to talk to you?"

I sat down and took off my gloves. "He thinks the newspapers aren't telling his side of it and wants me to write something nice about him."

"People are angry about the lynching?"

"For some people it's a matter of conscience or religion. For others, it plain old bad for business. And for still others, a political opportunity."

"This mayor is in trouble." Martina poured me a cup of tea.

"Why do you think that?"

"Right after the riot, they had a big meeting at the Grand Opera House and Dino went. He said that the mayor said things that made the audience laugh at him, and in not a nice way."

"I heard that too. He was trying to say he could've stopped them from hanging that boy if he'd been called to the scene sooner. But what he did say was that if the folks at the meeting would give his police force another chance, they would do better."

"Yes, yes. That was it. If you try to hang that poor boy again, I promise you that the police will stop it this time." I forced the idiocy of that comment out of my mind lest I burst out laughing—or crying.

"How about some bread and butter while you wait?" Martina tried to change the subject and rescue my mood.

"Not yet," I murmured. "I'm not really hungry."

"You never eat much." Martina frowned. "You need something to keep you going."

"Just stay close while I'm talking to him. He knows he's in trouble and that his rivals smell blood."

"I'll stay near," Martina said. "Just in case."

* * *

12:45 a.m.

When the mayor arrived, it took him a few minutes to get from the front door to where I sat in the small dining room. He went from table to table, shaking hands and asking after kin and the businesses of Martina's diners. By the time she led him to me, he was glowing with personal satisfaction.

"Just visiting with a few of my supporters," he said as he pulled out his chair. "They don't doubt me."

"No, sir, doesn't look like they do."

"So this little lady is Missus Esposito?" He gestured toward Martina who stood beside our table with a basket of Italian bread.

"Martina, this is Mayor Fagan Bourland. Mayor Bourland, this is Martina Esposito. She and her husband Dino own this place."

"Well, nice to meet you, ma'am. I hear good things about this restaurant. Good things indeed." The mayor's eyes glowed with political fervor.

Martina and I exchanged amused glances. "Would you like some wine?"

"You aren't trying to trick me, are you?"

Martina looked confused.

He pointed at me. "I'm sitting here with a newspaper reporter who'll write it up that I got drunk before my official work day was over."

Martina pulled a pencil from behind her ear. "So water or coffee instead?"

"Oh, red wine please." The mayor lowered his voice. You Italians are much more used to wine this time of day, I hear."

"None for me, Martina."

After Martina went to fetch the wine, the mayor leaned across the table and said behind his hand. "That one's like a ripe tomato— round and juicy."

I flinched.

"You don't like that kind of talk?"

"It's beneath you, sir."

He looked into my eyes and slowly grinned. "Can't imagine anything more welcome after a long, hard day."

"Is that what you want me to write about you?"

"Why not?"

"I thought you wanted me to talk about the good things you've done and are doing."

"I'm teasing, Miz McGrath. Men are like that. Ask your husband."

"Men may like it. Even some women might. But I don't."

He sighed. "I didn't mean to offend you."

Martina brought him a glass of wine. "The special today is lasagna."

"What exactly is that, Miz Esposito?"

"Noodles, meat, cheese, tomatoes."

"You're on." Mayor Bourland boomed. "Miz McGrath?"

"Soup?"

"That's it?"

"That's it."

"I'm buying."

"And tea, Martina."

"Save room for dessert. I made lemon cake."

Mayor Bourland clapped his hands together. "Wonderful. Save us a couple slices then."

Martina went back into the kitchen.

"Now, Mayor. Tell me what happened to Chief Barry. I understand he was the bravest man out there that night. Julian tells me he literally threw himself between that mob and the jail. Why did you fire him?"

His smile melted. "I thought maybe I'd tell you about all the new construction. The First National Bank. The New Theater. Union Station."

"Bryant Barry," I said firmly.

"My God, you're stubborn."

"Yes."

"I like Bryant. We've been associates for years. He's always done a good job for me. Every step in my political career, I've reached out to him. Trusted him. In fact, he did a good job the night of the lynching. Could have done an even better job if they'd have called him earlier."

"So the fact that his men didn't come to help him was because—"

"Look, this whole thing was a flat out miscalculation. It'd been raining and cool. Other than the theater crowds and Judge Harp's political rally, it was just another Saturday might in Fort Smith."

"Not enough police on the street?"

"We had enough for a normal night."

"March 23 wasn't normal?"

He peered down his nose at me. "You were there. Did it seem normal to you?"

"What made that Saturday different?"

"Why, Andy Carr, ma'am. None of this would've happened if Andy had gone home, had dinner with his family and fallen asleep curled up with that pretty wife of his."

"So if John B and Andy hadn't chased after Sandy when he ran from Pitcock, none of what happened would've happened?"

He leaned back in his chair. "I've thought about that. All the small decisions we make every day. What if Andy hadn't came back to town that night? What if John B's little girl hadn't been sick and he hadn't gone over to Kimmons to buy her medicine?"

"What if Pitcock hadn't missed his trolley?"

He took a sip of his wine. "Yes, ma'am. What if?"

"I know what they think happened, Mayor. But I have always wondered. What if it was something else entirely?"

"Like what?"

"Maybe someone didn't want Andy poking into their business. Their illegal business?"

He sipped his wine. "What if that nigger did shoot Andy because—well, because he was a nigger—and then hid the gun?"

I stared at him for a moment. "What do you want me to write about you, sir?"

Satisfaction made his grin smug. "That I am productive, dedicated to this city and do not—now quote me carefully on this—I do not support the idea of changing Fort Smith's style of governance. My political enemies are trying to use this incident to weaken the power of the mayor." He slapped the table with the palm of his hand, rattling the china and silverware. "My power."

"How would you have handled this incident had you been downtown before Sanford Lewis was lynched?"

"I know those men who were out there misbehaving on Garrison, ma'am. I would have told them to back down and they would have."

"Simple as that?"

"Simple as that."

"Why weren't you there then?"

"I first heard of the trouble about eleven forty-five."

"I heard they called several times and no one answered."

"I don't know about that. I answered the phone when it rang."

"Go on," I said.

"Let's see. I got dressed and went downtown. As I was walking past the Goldman, I met a group of men on their way home who told me the Negro was dead."

"So you did nothing?"

"Miz McGrath, you get a most unpleasant wrinkle between your eyes when you are—what? Indignant?"

I relaxed back into my seat. "More like intense, sir."

"When I got to the Main, I found the hellions were still there, trying to set that dead boy's clothes on fire. I told them to disperse and they did."

"Just like that?"

"Well," He took a deeper swallow of the Cabernet. "They did return while I went to the jail and called Putnam's."

"Someone told me John B called them."

"Mr. Williams may have called as well. All I know, the undertaker was there when I got back. The lynchers had returned too and they were trying to burn the corpse again. I climbed into the undertaker's wagon and told them to disperse." He paused.

I resisted the urge to respond, sitting quietly while his eyes went from defiant to troubled to defensive.

"Any good citizen could have persuaded them to stop, Miz McGrath."

"Did you think that perhaps it was that easy for you because Sanford Lewis was already dead by the time you got there? And the only people left on Garrison were the ghouls?"

He was—at long last—at a loss for words. Stripped of his mask, Mayor Bourland's real feelings flashed across his face. I read them as embarrassment and sadness.

Martina set a plate of lasagna down in front of him and his mask returned.

"My, my!" He rubbed his palms together. "Smells wonderful, Miz Esposito."

Her acknowledging nod seemed cool. She set my bowl in front of me, raised a knowing eyebrow—and left.

Picking up his fork, he poked at the unfamiliar food in front of him. "You don't suppose this is spicy, do you?"

"It's flavorful. One of my favorites." I tasted my soup.

"Italians get carried away with seasonings sometimes." He cut a small piece off the lasagna with the side of his fork. Lifting it to his nose, he made a face. "Garlic?"

I laid down my spoon and looked up at him. "I take it the Irish like their food plain."

He took a bite. "Meat and potatoes, mostly. A little cabbage now and again."

"What do you think?"

He took another bite. "Hearty. A man wouldn't go hungry in Italy, I think."

"So you like the garlic?"

"Will have to explain to my sweet Julia." He laid his fork down.

"Done already?"

"Are you, Miz McGrath?"

I looked into his eyes. "We'll see, sir."

He laid a bill on the table and got up. "Give Miz Esposito my thanks for a lovely meal."

"You didn't answer my question."

He finished off his wine. "What question?"

"Why did you fire Chief Barry?"

He sighed. "Political expediency."

* * *

"Political expediency, my foot." Julian laughed that night as we lay in bed together. "Fagan didn't have a choice."

"How so?"

"The public outcry. Important people. Powerful people. They wanted someone to blame for the 'uncivilized ugliness' as Mama put it. And Bryant Barry was the sacrificial lamb. It's hypocritical

because no one behaved well that night. Everyone in that crowd—
even the spectators—are culpable on some level. Even me.
Especially me. You tried to stop it at least. I just recorded what
I saw."

"So you feel bad about it now?"

Julian took my hand. "As a human being, I was as bad as everyone out there. Some watched out of curiosity or in support of those
thugs who beat the tar out of Sandy and then murdered him."

"Some prayed."

He was visibly surprised. "You?"

"Not formally. Not out loud. Father Horan did. And Reverend
Mathews. And others in the crowd. Dino. And Burley."

"That makes me feel some better. I woke up just now because
my conscience wouldn't let me rest. In my dream, I was on the Hotel Main portico above the crowd again. I was pleased with myself.
I already knew it was Sandy they were torturing, but I was happy
I'd found a place with a good view all the same."

I put my arms around him and he laid his head on my shoulder.
"I kept saying that it wasn't my job to make things happen, but
to report on things that did happen. Now I'm not so sure that's an
honorable ethic."

"Oh Julian," I crooned as he wept. "You are the most honorable
man I know. You couldn't have stopped that crowd. No one person
could have. Not even Fagan Bourland no matter how he tries to put
the blame elsewhere. He wasn't even there until after Sandy was
dead, for goodness sakes."

"That everyone else behaved badly is no excuse either." Julian
rolled onto his back. "Mama taught me that since I was a kid."

"Perhaps there's a difference between doing something evil and
watching it."

"There is," he said. "But not much."

"At the jail, Chief Barry tried—and he had three or four supporters with him. I heard people were so determined to get into that
jail that they literally picked that dear old man up and put him back
on the rocks where he couldn't interfere. Finally, he gave up and
went to find a telephone. He called the fire department to use their
hoses to disperse that crowd, but one of Chief Trowbridge's men
refused. He was afraid that those folks were so revved up that they
would cut the hoses after one blast. Without those hoses, his ability
to fight real fires would have been limited."

We lay there, staring at the ceiling.

Finally, he said. "Do you think that was really the reason Trowbridge's man said no?"

I didn't know much about how the fire department works or how many hoses they have or how many they need. "No," I said. "But I think it was a reasonable fear."

"Jailer Stansberry and his guards were armed, but they didn't shoot into the crowd—and those bastards knew they wouldn't."

"How could they be so sure?"

Julian shrugged. "That crowd was like a swarm of angry bees. If you charged into them at one point, the middle would fall back, luring you into following them while the flanks closed in behind you. There weren't enough jailers or guards to fight their way out if they did get surrounded. So they didn't try."

"Till Shaw seemed to think he could've protected Sandy. He said he would've ringed the jail with sharpshooters."

"Till says that now. All the bigwigs say that now. But when it counted, no one did." Julian sat up and dangled his feet over the edge of the bed. "As I watched the lynching from above, I noticed a woman in the window of a building across the street. A Negro woman. When she realized I'd seen her, she backed away into the darkness behind her. I wondered who she was and thought that she was wise to hide like that."

"She must have been angry," I murmured.

Julian rubbed the back of his own neck. "I looked back after Sandy was dead, but I couldn't see her anymore. I keep dreaming about her though. She was probably someone's daughter or wife or mother. It must have been excruciating for her."

I crawled up behind him and massaged his neck and back.

"Ah," he said. "That feels good."

"I wonder if the guys who did this feel as guilty as we do?"

"I doubt it."

"They come from good families. Neighbors, the sons of prominent people, business men."

He flinched when I touched a sore spot. "Except for the fact that they killed the wrong guy, I think they're proud of themselves, Mamie. Some of them will say it was their responsibility. Mistrusting officials to provide justice goes way back around here. And the fact is, there'll be no lasting consequences for their behavior."

"Nothing?"

"Oh, they'll be indicted and arrested. Too many of the big investors in this town want that to happen. And that's truly an extraordinary thing. But no white jury will convict them—and of course white juries are the only kind of juries there are. Before the year is up, we'll be back to normal. The men who did this will continue doing business in town. Till Shaw's already planning to spring John Stowers if they arrest him. He needs him to finish refurbishing his bar. And mark my words, no one will touch John B. Williams either—whether he's found to have been careless or not. By fall, he'll be sprinkling water on Garrison to keep down the dust—and tipping his hat to every lady walking past the Pony Express, same as always."

"Doesn't seem fair."

He stretched and stood up. "That night, the Avenue was filled with people and carriages and horses and cars. There were well-dressed men and women in town for a play or dinner or drinks—some of them never heard of Andy Carr. They were simply caught up in the excitement. A free peek at someone else's tragedy, then home to top off the evening with a hot toddy. Folks waiting for the midnight train watched because it was an interesting way to pass the time—like an exciting moving picture show. Then there were the usual drunks and opportunists. Some caught the fever and cheered while Sandy was being murdered—others grumped about the traffic it caused on Garrison."

"It was almost like a carnival for awhile," I said. "I saw a couple moving through the crowd. She'd bump up against a well-dressed man while her partner picked his pockets. I'm guessing they had a profitable night."

"I always thought it was fun to go down town," Julian put on his robe. "I looked forward to rodeo or Christmas or military parades. The energy on the Avenue was exciting. I'd either hold Mama's hand or sit on Daddy's shoulders. I wonder if it'll feel different now."

"Do you miss your father?"

"I do, but he's like those fading photographs hanging in the front parlor. A nice memory, but faint and growing more distant by the day."

"That's how I feel about my parents too. It's not that I didn't love and respect them. It's just that their time with me is over, and I've done and seen things on my own that are just as impactful as the lessons they taught me. And some of the lessons I've learned replaced their ideas about right and wrong."

"What do you mean?"

"Lots of things, really. They wanted the Union to be strong and the rebels to be punished. They hated the idea of slavery, but neither ever knew a slave. Or a freedman either as far as I know. Or an Indian. I can't imagine them being caught up in a crowd like the one that killed Sandy, but I also can't imagine them spending time with good people like Patsy or Webster or Genevieve—or Sandy. It was a moral concept to them—not real people."

18

I wasn't in the jail yard. Just looking over the fence, you know. They were pulling the window out when I came up. I didn't recognize anyone.

Interview of Chris Wegman by Mamie McGrath

Someone told me that Grover Bourland was beating on the jail. In fact, Grover himself told me that he and Ben Black were at the jail break. Roy Templeton told me that Grover Bourland was breaking the jail.

Chris Wegman's Grand Jury Testimony

Friday, April 26, 1912, 10 a.m.

EVERYONE WANTED TO SEE TEDDY Roosevelt speak. Garrison Avenue was packed with automobiles, carriages, trolleys and foot traffic. Caroline, Abigail and I planned on listening to his speech from the windows of Martina and Dino's private residence above Esposito's. There was no way to drive down that far, so I parked the Hudson on Thirteenth Street and we walked. By the time, we got to the First National Bank, the wall of humanity was impenetrable. At least, Caroline and I thought so.

"Out of the way! We have important business." Roadblocks didn't faze Abigail.

Startled by Abigail's imposing attitude, people stepped aside. Caroline and I followed as she pushed through the throng. While I avoided angry eyes, Caroline murmured embarrassed apologies as we stormed past friends and neighbors.

"Coming through!" Abigail poked a gentleman in a black derby. When he didn't move right away, she hit him on the shoulder with her parasol. He jumped aside in alarm as Abigail, head down, rushed past holding Caroline's hand.

"Mamie!"

"Mr. Sicard." I was mortified.

"It's Fred," he reminded me.

"Fred. Has Mr. Roosevelt started yet?"

"He's making his way to the bandstand now. I'm not sure we can hear him from here. I'm thinking I'll have a better view from my office." He gestured at people hanging out windows and crouched on second and third floor balconies and porticoes. "Where are you going?"

"Esposito's."

"Be tough or they'll stomp you to death."

"Mamie!" Abigail's voice was like a foghorn, rising over the multitude surrounding us.

"Sounds like someone's looking for you."

"Abigail Talbot and my mother-in-law."

His expression changed. "Tell Mrs. Talbot that I had a message from her husband this morning. And business to do with her as a result. Have her either come by the bank or telephone me."

"Of course, sir. Nice to see you again. Give my regards to Mrs. Sicard."

"Ella."

"Yes, to Ella."

He turned and fought his way back to the bank.

"MAMIE!"

I could see Abigail's hat and parasol a half block in front of me. I pushed past a woman holding a small child on her shoulders, squeezed under the smelly armpit of a man who was waving a flag—and eased past a bored horse and his equally-bored owner sitting in the carriage behind him. Then I stood on tiptoe and looked around. I was still a block from Esposito's. Abigail and Caroline were no where to be seen. I gathered my skirt around me and worked my way to the curb on the North side of Garrison.

Just as I was stepping up onto the sidewalk in front of Padgett's, a heavyset man bumped up against me and I bounced off a woman who ran her hands down my body. I thought of the couple picking pockets the night Sandy died and realized what was happening. The man had already disappeared into the crowd, but the woman was determined to wrench my bag out of my hands. Planting my feet, I held on to it for dear life.

"Let go, you scarred-up bitch, before I gut you." She was tall and fleshy with thin orangey hair. While I didn't doubt she could hurt me, I didn't think she would.

"Go find an easier target." I jerked my purse out of her hands and backed off the sidewalk, falling on my behind.

The woman pounced and we engaged in a prolonged tug of war. The crowd around us either ignored the fight in their eagerness to see Mr. Roosevelt or cheered us on.

"My money's on Lucindy," a familiar voice said. "She's twice that lady's size."

"Kinda like a mama bear taking on a boar hog. Could go either way." That was Grover Bourland, for sure.

"I'll put down fifty cents." That twang was Will Manus.

"You're on," Grover said.

Lucindy straddled me and tried to yank the purse out of my hand, but I'd tangled the soft-corded strap around my wrist in the fall. When she couldn't get it loose, she grasped the bag in both hands and fell back off me. At that moment, I flailed at her with both arms and both legs. One of my wild kicks landed in her stomach. A rush of air spewed out of her nose and mouth. She dropped my purse and fell on me. I bucked and kicked. Her sour breath made my eyes water. My bag was now squeezed between us—pressing into both of our bodies. I pushed and squealed for help to get her off me. It seemed like we lay there forever, fighting for air. Her lips were turning blue when a pair of brown hands slipped under her arms and flipped her off of me.

"Hey now, Lucindy. Ain't you got anymore sense than to try and smother a fine lady like this in the middle of Garrison Avenue?"

Still unable to speak, Lucindy lay in the curb, holding her stomach.

"Here, Miz Mamie." A young girl held out her hand. "Let me help you up. Lucindy ain't gonna go after you no more. She's done for the day."

Clutching my bag to my chest, I let her help me to my feet. "Thank you."

"No, ma'am. I owe you some thanks."

I dusted off my clothes. The lace around the cuff of my left sleeve was ripped loose. "Do I know you?"

"No, ma'am, but I know you. You were mighty kind to someone that meant the world to me. I been meaning to come visit you. Miz Patsy and Miz Genevieve been telling me I owe you that much. I just ain't had the heart to get out until today." My rescuer had wrapped a brightly-colored scarf around her head but the rest of her clothes were simple and dark.

"Pocahontas?"

"Yes, ma'am."

"I'm so sorry about everything."

"Me too, ma'am."

"Would you like to get a cup of coffee or something?"

"I would, but you know that kind of thing ain't allowed." I remembered Patsy describing her as bold and a little wild. I wondered if she'd lost that spirit now—after Sandy.

"We can meet in the family quarters at Esposito's. There's a back entrance. I'll have someone lead you upstairs."

"Everybody's nervous as a long-tailed cat in a room full of rockin' chairs. Not you, though, Miz Mamie. Not you."

"No," I said. "Not anymore."

"I used to be brave too. Now I can't sleep nights afearin' they're comin' for me like they did Sanford."

I shook the dirt out of my skirt. "Back door. I'll have someone let you in."

* * *

It was too noisy for a speech so Mr. Roosevelt simply waved his hat and grinned at the folks filling the west end of Garrison. He'd already left for Van Buren by the time I got to Esposito's. Abigail and Caroline forgot all about the aborted campaign speech once I arrived and they saw my disheveled state.

"Should we call Dr. Stevenson?"

"No," I told Abigail. "Just a few bruises and a lot of dirt."

"A decent woman can't walk down Garrison Avenue in the middle of the day and not be accosted by heathens. We might as well move to the country where it's safe." Abigail paced in front of me while Martina dabbed my scratches with Merthiolate, leaving red stains on my skin. "Next thing you know, they'll be raping pretty young things in front of the Grand Opera House."

I winced as Martina doctored one of the larger scratches inflicted by the woman's long nails. "Wasn't men."

"I don't care if they were ten years old. Boys get ideas early these days."

I tried not to laugh. "It was a woman."

"What?" Caroline sat up straight in her chair.

"A man and a woman tried to steal my purse. The guy got scared and took off, but the woman was more aggressive."

"Oh, my!" Caroline fanned herself with her hands. "And in broad daylight too."

"So what did you do?" Martina put the stopper back in the bottle of Merthiolate and folded the cloth she was using to doctor my wounds.

"I—um—fought back."

"What?" Caroline was ready to cry.

"I had that little gun we took off Orrin Fellows at the train station in my bag. They were looking for money but I was afraid they might shoot me with the Derringer if they found it."

Abigail raised her eyebrows. "Why didn't you shoot her with it?"

"It was in my bag and I didn't know if it was loaded. And if it wasn't loaded, I didn't have any bullets to put in it."

"You've been carrying it around all this time?" Abigail picked up my purse and peered into it.

"To be honest, I forgot I had it until she was on top of me grinding that bag into my thigh. That's when I felt it."

Abigail opened the Derringer. "One bullet." She closed it and put it back in my bag. "Better not miss if you take it out. No do overs."

"I don't need it. Just forgot I had it."

"Seems to me that if you're going to roll around in the gutter with a common criminal, britches might be more appropriate attire." Abigail was in her most elegant day dress with elbow length gloves and a starched-high collar.

I looked down at my purple velvet skirt. One of the side seams had split and my petticoat was showing. My shoes were scuffed and the strap on the right one had broken during the fight. Both of my gloves were intact and on my hands. But, the netting I routinely draped over my turban was ripped. "Oh no," I put both palms over my forehead. "I've lost Julian's grandmother's broach."

"It's okay, my dear. Julian will only care that you are okay," Caroline said. "It was an ugly old thing anyway."

Her comment hung in the air for a moment and then she covered her mouth with both hands, trying to stifle her giggles. And then we were all laughing at the ridiculousness of my broach and my inelegant state of undress.

"All this for a tiny gun you don't even know how to shoot," Martina snorted. "Next time just carry my butcher knife."

"At least you don't need to load it," Caroline said merrily.

There was a small knock at the door.

Martina started toward it but Dino opened it from the hallway first. "Here you go, young lady." He gently guided Pocahontas into the parlor. "This here is Pocahontas Ross. She was Sanford Lewis' intended."

Our snickers stopped.

Pocahontas stood in the center of the braided oval rug. "Th-thank you for bringing me here."

"Have a seat." Martina pointed to an easy chair.

Pocahontas seemed shy and uncomfortable but she nodded and sat down, crossing her legs demurely at the ankles.

"Pocahontas rescued me this afternoon." I smiled at her. "That woman—"

"Lucindy."

"Pardon me?"

"That woman was Lucindy. Everybody knows that."

Unlike everybody else in Fort Smith, we were unfamiliar with Lucindy—but since she tried to rob me, I harbored ill feelings toward her.

"A horse kicked her in the head." Pocahontas tapped her own temple. "So she ain't been right since."

"The poor thing." Caroline clasped her hands in front of her. "I'll pray for her."

"Don't worry about her, ma'am. That was Rufus she was with. He's her baby brother. She took care of him when he was little, and he watches over her now."

"Doesn't look like he's doing her any favors getting her to rob people," Abigail sniffed.

"They's hill folks. Only get to town when they need seed or flour. They do it for fun. Sometimes they get enough for a pair of shoes or something. Mostly they eat hardy over at Padgett's and head on home with maybe a dime or two left over. Lucindy never hurt anyone—maybe cussed out store clerks who won't give her a cookie or something like that. And Rufus, he always runs away if'n it looks like they's gonna get caught. After court, Mr. Carr or Mr. Pitcock always saw that Lucindy got home okay. Don't know how she'll get home this time what with all the cops being gone and all."

"Mr. Pitcock?" I'd built up such malice toward Cathey Pitcock that I had a hard time imagining him do good deeds like escorting Lucindy home.

"Rufus has a still up there and Mr. Pitcock brings back a jug or two. A nice ride in the country and he gets paid for it same as if he worked a beat."

"Stand up straight, Pocahontas," Abigail commanded.

She frowned. "I reckon I'm about as straight as I'm ever gonna get, ma'am."

"How old are you?"

"Fifteen going on sixteen."

"You could get a good job doing laundry or cleaning or taking care of someone's house."

"Thank you, kindly, Miz Talbot, but I got other plans. I'm a singer, you know." She clasped her hands across her chest. "I'm gonna travel around Arkansas and Missouri and Oklahoma—maybe even get down to Nawlins one of these days."

"How will you eat? Where will you stay?"

"I gots people, Miz McGrath. "They let me stay with them if'n I sing at they's churches and family reunions and all."

"Patsy didn't tell me you could sing," I said.

"Oh yes ma'am. With only the wind to beat time or with an old banjo Sanford bought me last summer. I can play a piano alone or with bands and orchestras and all. You name it. Mr. Wiley taught me."

"That's good," Martina piped up. "Might make enough money to settle down."

Pocahontas folded her arms across her chest. "Without Sanford, they's no point to settling."

"It'll hurt a long time," Caroline said. "I still ache for my precious Wilbur. But you are young. There will be other suitors."

"Naw, I don't need me no man. At least no share croppin' farmer. They smell like chewin' tobacco and mule sweat."

"Where's your family?"

"Spread out all over the place, Miz Mamie. "—but I kinda out growed 'em for now, if'n ya know what I mean."

"Won't you miss Sandy?"

That stopped her. "I loved that sweet boy, the Lord knows I did." Tears filled her eyes. "Ain't never gonna be anyone like Sanford again. But he wanted to get married and have babies. We argued about that all the time. That night he was telling me all about the life he was gonna build for us."

"What were you doing on Texas Corner?" Abigail came off sterner than she intended—and she aimed for sternness. "Trying to find a man with some money?"

Pocahontas was clearly offended by Abigail's implications. "No ma'am. I was going to my job."

"Doing what?"

"Singin,' of course." Pocahontas fidgeted. "I was singin' for the Methodists first. Was gonna try for some change down around Texas Corner, but got arrested afore I could do it."

I glanced at Caroline before lowering my voice. "Where were you going after you made some money?"

The girl lowered her eyes. "After singin' Ragtime at whichever saloon would have me, I was gonna get the midnight train to Muskogee so's I could sing for the Baptists over there in the mornin.'"

"No one showed up?"

"Lots of em showed, Miz Mamie. That's what me and Sanford was arguing about. He didn't like so many handsome black farmers knockin' back a little beer afore hearin' the show. He was afraid one of them was gonna hurt me."

Abigail blew up. "Weren't you afraid to be up on that part of Garrison with no one to protect you?"

"No ma'am. I knowed them men since I was a toddler. Most of 'em are fifteen or twenty years older than me. They wasn't gonna hurt me. But you couldn't tell Sanford nothin.' Last time I take up with a preacher's boy."

Pocahontas could talk a mean streak, I'd give her that.

"Them cops were rougher than they needed to be. We wasn't doing nothin' wrong. We's just fussin.' That's all. They came runnin' up and was acallin' me all kinds a mean names. Sanford, he tried to take up for me, but these was grown men with a belly full of booze, wantin' to lay hands on me. And Sanford wasn't havin' it."

"So what'd you do?" Abigail made it sound like an accusation.

"I ran, Miz Talbot. You'd a done the same."

"Well, I never—" Abigail's outrage trailed off into irritable silence.

"Where'd you go?" I tried to keep my tone friendly and respectful, unlike Abigail.

"I was a stayin' with an auntie who lives in a house behind Campbell's Alley."

"Was that who was with you that night?"

"Naw, that was some old girl who played the accordion when I sang."

"What happened to her?"

"Don't know exactly. Maybe she didn't run when Sanford and I did. She was with the policemen when they found me though. Why you askin' me all these questions? I ain't done nothin' wrong."

I bowed my head. "I'm sorry, Pocahontas. I don't doubt you. I'm just curious."

"She's more than curious," Abigail butted in. "But she doesn't mean you any harm, young lady. None of us do."

"I was fond of Sandy—Sanford. He was a nice young man and I still feel bad that I couldn't stop that mob," I said.

"Yes, ma'am. I know that feeling."

"How about some tea or coffee?" Martina changed the subject and lightened the mood. "And some iced sugar cookies?"

Caroline clapped her hands. "I thought you'd never offer. Lemon or chocolate icing?"

Martina stood up. "Some of each."

"I'll have tea and a couple of the lemon," Abigail said. "Have to watch my figure, you know."

"Come on then." Martina led us into her smallish dining room. The table was already set.

Pocahontas stood in the doorway, eyeing the platters of pastry and candy.

"Come sit by me, dear." Caroline took her arm and guided her to the chair. "Abigail will steal your cookies if you don't watch her."

We all laughed. And after a moment, Pocahontas joined in.

"I have brownies too, ladies. Just out of the oven." Martina set them in front of Pocahontas. The smell was heavenly.

"What do you like, Pocahontas? Tea or coffee?"

"Coffee, ma'am, if'n you got cream to go with it."

Martina poured everyone coffee or tea as they wished and then sat down. "No rules here, ladies. Pass the goodies around." She handed Abigail the lemon cookies.

"Grab yourself a brownie, dear." Caroline urged Pocahontas. "—and pass them on to Mamie. She loves those things."

After a few minutes, Pocahontas began to feel more at home and her talkativeness returned. "They got the best food in Nawlins. Fish right out of the sea instead of rivers or lakes. Red beans and rice. I got me a friend down there who says I'd have work ever night asingin' in the Quarter. Lotsa folks like me down there. I'm jes tryin to get enough put back to pay my way. Was almost there but it took almost all I had so's I could get out of jail."

"Why did they arrest you?" Abigail reached for another brownie and two more chocolate cookies."

"Disturbin' the peace. Everyone on Garrison that night was a whoopin' and hollerin' and havin' fun. Me and Sanford was arguin' but they was jes words. We wasn't fightin' or nothin.' We's workin' things out." She finished her coffee. "Mr. Pitcock and Mr. Lacey busted in on our conversation. Yellin' at us and cussin.' Callin' me bad names. Beatin' up on Sanford. At first they said he had a gun, which is why they was bein' so mean to us. But Sanford didn't have no gun. Then they claim he had a knife—like it was some big ole dagger or something. Was jes a lil old foldin' thing like you'd use to trim your nails. About that long." She held her fore finger and thumb about two inches apart.

"So why'd they say he had it?" Martina said

"Ma'am, pardon my sayin' so, but you ain't never been a Negro in Fort Smith or you wouldn't ask that."

"You were scared?"

"Yes, ma'am, Miz Mamie. I's so scared that what happened was gonna happen that I caused it to happen." Her voice broke. "I been praying on it with the congregation at church but it all comes back to me. Jes me being there made it happen. Sanford was trying to look out for me and they kilt him for it."

"What happened when you ran, Pocahontas?" Caroline's eyes were soft and her voice soothing.

"Mr. Lacey and Mr. Jarnigan chased after me. Sanford ran cause I did. But he ran the other way so they'd chase him and not me." Tears welled up her eyes. "Mr. Pitcock, he started shootin' at Sanford right off the bat. Everyone was duckin' and a runnin' tryin' to stay outta the way of them bullets."

"Did you see Detective Carr? Or John B?"

"No ma'am. Just flashes from Pitcock's gun and all kinds of folks runnin' and yellin.'"

"So you got away."

"Almost, Miz Mamie. But warn't long afore they came lookin' for me. Girls come and go out of my auntie's house all the time. That night there was five or six of us home when Mr. Pennewell knocked on the door and rousted everyone out into the street. I was hidin' in an old chiffarobe, folded up like a clean sheet. They found me when I got a cramp in my toe and they heard me whimper. The cops walked me and the other colored ladies what was with me up Rogers to the Court house. Folks was makin' a racket there—shoutin' and a cryin' and bein' mean. I don't know why but they put me in a cell all by my lonesome. The women's jail."

"I'm sorry too, dear," Martina said. "We were sitting downstairs having coffee and waiting for things to blow over. If we'd only known, maybe we could have helped."

Something flickered through Pocahontas' eyes. Resentment? Exasperation?

"Don't know how anything y'all coulda done woulda made any difference, Miz Martina. They musta already had Sanford in that jail when they brought me into the other one. It chilled my bones to hear 'em. They was drunk and mean. They didn't know what a kind sweet boy he was." Tears spilled down her cheeks. "I didn't want to marry Sanford because of Sanford, you know. It was because of me. I loved him with all my heart and if'n I'd a been any other kind a girl, we'd be married now and Sanford—he'd be alive."

I handed her my handkerchief.

"I keep thinkin' that I broke his heart the same night people who didn't know him kilt him for no reason. He musta felt so down. So alone. So hurt." She wiped her eyes.

Caroline squeezed Pocahontas' hand. "Maybe he's happy now."

"Maybe."

I didn't buy that. What if hurt feelings went with you into the hereafter and poked at your heart long after it stopped beating?

* * *

It was mid afternoon when we left Martina and Dino's apartment. Pocahontas went first, taking the backstairs out onto the alley behind Esposito's. We waited a few minutes before exiting through the crowded dining room.

We weren't in any hurry. As we walked up the Avenue, we stopped to look in store windows. Abigail and Caroline chatted about the latest clothing styles while I thought about Manny and John B and Andy and Pocahontas and Joe Tucker. As we approached the First National Bank, I remembered seeing Mr. Sicard earlier in the day.

"Abigail, I forgot to mention it, but when we got separated in the crowd this morning, I ran into Mr. Sicard. He wants you to either call him or stop by as soon as you can."

"Did he say what it's about?"

"I imagine it's something private."

She glanced up at the big white building. "Garland takes care of our business dealings. Do you suppose there's a problem?"

I shrugged. "Whatever it is, Mr. Sicard wouldn't share your private information with me."

"I'm sure it's nothing serious, dear." Caroline patted Abigail's arm. "Maybe it's some legal documents coming due or something like that."

"What kind of legal documents?"

"Hard to say. When Wilbur was killed, there were legal papers I needed to sign. I had no idea what it was all about. Finally, I talked to Mr. Cravens and he assigned some nice young man to get me through it all without too much trouble."

"I suppose I should go in and see what Mr. Sicard wants." Abigail checked her reflection in a store window. Her impossibly-red curls were in place. Her lips were impossibly red too.

"You look fine," Caroline said. "Would you like me to go with you? I'm sure they have a place where I can sit when you go into see Mr. Sicard."

"Would you? After that business with Orrin Fellows, I'm nervous about what Garland might have gotten us into—and left the getting out of to me."

"I'll be glad to sit right outside the office when you go in," Caroline said.

"I have an errand to run and then I can get the Hudson and come back for you."

"Far be it from me to inconvenience you, Mamie McGrath." Abigail's voice rose.

"It's no inconvenience. I'm a mess after my encounter with Lucindy and her brother." I pointed to the torn seam. "Martina just pinned my skirt together. I'll drop in at Maggie Mitchel's before heading back to the Arkansas Garage. A few stitches and I'll be more confident. I wouldn't want to embarrass you when you meet with your banker."

Abigail eyed my tousled attire. "Okay."

"I'll be back here with the car in a half hour."

"What if it takes longer than that?"

"I'll wait an hour and then go home. You can call when you're finished and I'll come get you."

"I'm sure thirty minutes will be adequate." Abigail folded her parasol at the door of the bank. She let Caroline enter first while giving me a glance filled with pure terror. Then she lifted her head and swept into the bank like she was the newly-famous Molly Brown who'd survived the recent Titanic disaster.

At the dressmaker's, Maggie decided there was nothing she could do about my ripped skirt that afternoon. After a short discussion, I tried on the new driving outfit I'd ordered the week before I bought the Hudson. She'd been making my clothes long enough now that she only had to adjust a single seam and press it. I checked the clock. It'd been twenty minutes. Rather than running back to the garage, I put on my new driving ensemble and called the Arkansas Garage to pick me up in front of the bank.

I fidgeted in front watching people pass. Every time I came downtown, things had changed. Passenger service at the Frisco had just been transferred to the big new Union Station on South Seventh and Rogers. It'd only been a few weeks, but it definitely changed the volume of foot traffic on Garrison.

"Miz Mamie!" JW pulled up to the corner of Sixth and Garrison.

I hurried to greet him. "The others aren't out yet. I'll take you back to the Garage."

"Aren't you fancy these days, Miz Mamie?" He put the brake on and climbed into the passenger seat.

"That's the idea." I put the car in gear and within five minutes we were in front of the Arkansas Garage.

"Jim and I are planning a driving demonstration. From here to Waldron and back—to show off these wonderful automobiles."

"Maybe I can ride with one of you? Write an article about it?"

"We were hoping you'd do something like that. Help us sell more cars for women and families. Not just enthusiasts."

"Let me know when the day is set and I'll be here,"

"Thanks, ma'am." JW crawled down out of the car.

"No, thank you for bringing the car to me. Was everything okay? Do I owe you any money?"

"It's fine. A few maintenance charges on your bill, but the ride was free."

"I'll come by tomorrow and pay up."

When I got back to the bank, there was still no sign of Abigail and Caroline so I parked and waited.

Someone knocked on my window and I jumped.

"Well, Miz High and Mighty, looks like your evil eye worked."

I almost didn't recognize Cathey Pitcock without his uniform. "Evil eye?"

He leaned against my front fender. "Always acting like God made you special and everyone else plain."

"I didn't get you fired, Mr. Pitcock. You did that on your own."

"I got a family to support. My dough goes toward food and clothes for my wee ones—not bright shiny automobiles. And even if they find me innocent, who'll hire me now? He leaned against my door window and the smell of whiskey overwhelmed me.

"I'm sure I don't know."

"I didn't think you'd have any wise words for the likes of me and my family, Miz McGrath."

I thought about his children. Of all the victims of Fort Smith's most shameful night, certainly the families of the police officers involved were the most innocent. "When is the trial?"

"When Judge Hon says it is."

"Don't you like Judge Hon?"

"About as much as I like a swarm of wasps."

"What will your family do if you're convicted?"

"Damned if I know." He pulled a small bottle out of his coat pocket and polished it off with a flourish. "All I can hope for is that the good Lord will intercede and send a good Samaritan to take care of them."

"Given your behavior that night I wouldn't expect much help from the Almighty, Mr. Pitcock. However, I'm sure your family will find fortune and good will in this town."

His eyes glittered. "You best watch your smart tongue, Miz Mc-Grath. I may not be a policeman anymore, but I'm still a man and I won't tolerate your sass."

He was taller and heavier than me—and most likely armed. That he'd been drinking made him even more dangerous. "Mr. Pitcock, I have nothing to do with the trouble you're facing. I doubt they'll ask me about what I saw you do that night. However, I'm willing to tell them if they do. And I'm sure they'll be interested in how you threatened me just now."

He stepped back and rested a hand on the Hudson's front fender, leaving oily finger prints on it. "We'll see how it all works out, won't we?"

"Guess we will."

* * *

"That man is rude and unsightly," Abigail complained as she crawled into the backseat of the Hudson. "Telling me I owe him money!"

"Who? Mr. Sicard?" I was scandalized.

"No, of course not, Mamie." Caroline squeezed into the backseat beside Abigail. "Fred Sicard was the model of courtesy and helpfulness."

"Who's rude then?"

"That, that Peacock man!" Abigail's shudder shook the car.

"You mean Pitcock?"

"He says that since the Guckenheimer deal with Garland fell through, he wants his money back."

"Since being fired, he needs money. He was loitering around here a few minutes ago worrying about what will happen to his kids if he goes to jail."

Abigail nostrils flared. "His children are not my concern."

"How much did he say he invested?"

"Two hundred dollars."

"What?" Caroline and I said together, each of us turning to look at Abigail in sympathetic outrage.

"Do you have two hundred dollars?" Caroline put her hand on Abigail's shoulder.

"Not that I know of. Not in cash anyway."

"What did Mr. Sicard want?"

"It seems that Garland put our house and a piece of land near Cavanaugh in my name."

"Why would he do that?"

"I have no idea, Mamie. None at all."

Abigail was a bad liar but it wasn't my business anyway. I started the car and headed toward her home. As we approached the turnoff to her house, instead of slowing, I accelerated past it.

"Mamie, what're you doing?" Abigail complained from the back seat.

"Don't look behind us, but we're being followed." I turned right on Dodson and sped to the next corner, turning right into an open carriage house.

"All day?"

"Would have been pretty hard following us through that crowd this morning," I said. "I'm guessing just from the bank."

"Why would someone be following me?" It was her innocent little girl voice and I wasn't buying it anymore.

"You've heard from Garland more than you've let on, haven't you?"

"How could you think that?"

"In fact, you know exactly where he is."

Abigail sank into sullen silence.

"Abigail!" Caroline suddenly figured it out as well.

"It's because I'm protecting Garland. I don't think they'll come after you too."

The Model T following us was neither as fast nor as maneuverable as the brand-new Hudson. It either missed our sudden turn onto Dodson or the driver didn't realize which side street housed our current hiding place.

"Let's pick up Julian and go home now. Abigail, you need to come with us. I don't think it's safe for you to be alone."

"Garland," she whimpered. "He's hiding in a secret room in our house."

"Is he safe in there?"

"I hope so," she said softly.

* * *

Back in town, I parked in front of the First National Bank again. "I'll hurry," I told Caroline and Abigail. "But just in case," I handed Caroline my bag. "There's that one bullet in the Derringer."

"Don't worry." Caroline took the purse. "We can manage. Just hurry."

I ran into the building and up the stairs to the third floor. "Julian," I said from the door to his suite of offices. "We need you."

Startled, he looked up from his typewriter. "What's happening?"

"We need you at home now."

He stood up. "Okay."

"Is something wrong, Julian?" A middle-aged man in an office across the hall called.

"Some family problems, Mr. Parker."

"Put what you're doing away and I'll take care of it later."

"Yes, sir."

I paced while Julian fussed with his desk.

"Might want to call—"

He stopped and cocked his head up at me. "Call who?"

I froze. Andy was gone. John B shouldn't get into this for his own sake. Chief Barry and Pennewell were gone. Lacey. Phillips. I didn't know Chief Moss, but he was in charge. I had to trust him. "Call the cops to send a detective to our house."

"Are we in danger?"

Were we? "Not immediately. But we need to report a problem now."

Colonel Parker came to the door of his office. "I'll take care of things, Julian. You go deal with what's wrong."

Julian frowned. "I'm almost done here."

It had been a long day and my impatience simmered. "We're waiting in the car."

He picked up the telephone receiver.

Concerned about Caroline and Abigail, I hurried back to where I'd left them. A dark-haired man and his horse stood by the automobile, chatting with them.

"No—" I dashed around the Hudson, ready to knock him down.

"Mamie?" The man turned to me. "Are you okay?"

"You're a welcome sight, Burley."

"So I'm hearing. What can I do for you?"

"Julian is calling the police now, but it would be nice if you could come to our house. These people think Abigail has something of theirs—and, especially since Orrin Fellows is in jail, they want it back. I want to be sure these ladies are protected before we try to rescue Garland."

"I'll head out there now." He mounted his horse.

"We'll be right behind you as soon as Julian comes down." I called after him.

He raised his hand in acknowledgment.

I got in the car and turned around in my seat. "How long have you known Garland was hiding in your house?"

She lifted her chin. "Since the day we fought off Orrin Fellows at the Frisco Station. That morning, I went out into the old carriage house where we used to keep the Buick. I wanted to store some winter clothes, so I left the door open. The sun shown through—and I saw an outline under the straw. I got a broom and swept it clean. That's when I knew there was a room under the main area."

"You never noticed the trap door before?"

"Either our carriage in the old days or our automobile the last few years was always parked over it. Deliberately so, I realize now."

"How did Garland know about it?"

"It was Garland's great grandmother's house. He visited there when he was a boy."

"I forgot old Miz Talbot lived there," Caroline said. "You'd have liked her Mamie. She was quite the storyteller. Lived to be one hundred and one years old."

I turned to Abigail. "So what did you do? Try to flush him out?"

"I didn't dawn on me who was down there. I was thinking maybe an animal or a bum. I got a shovel off the wall and tapped on the door. That liked to have scared Garland to death because he thought his enemies had found him. He yelled to stay back or he'd shoot. That's when I knew it was him—and I told him in no uncertain terms to put down that gun. Of course, he recognized my voice and I climbed down to see him. I gave him a big old kiss and a hug. Then I remembered how mad I was."

"Uh oh," I chuckled. "Poor Garland."

"The place is like a cozy palace. Rugs on the floors, curtains on another door leading to a tunnel where Genevieve comes and goes, bringing him food and anything else he might need—including newspapers."

"Why was he hiding from you?"

"He says that he didn't want me to be in danger."

I bit my lip to keep from laughing. He didn't think Abigail could keep a secret.

Julian opened the car door and got in. "What's going on?"

"The people who lent Garland and Fellows the money for the Guckenheimer project are following Abigail."

With that, I headed home. The black Ford passed us going the other direction as we turned onto Rogers.

* * *

"What are we going to do?" Caroline sank into her chair in the front parlor.

"We're going to sit tight," I said. "I'm sure these people will realize Abigail's with us eventually."

"I would be perfectly safe at home." Abigail ran her hand across the mantel. "They're threatening Garland, not me." A faint coating of dust darkened the fingers of her white glove. She wrinkled her nose and pretended to sneeze.

A knock at the front door startled us. Abigail and Caroline grew quiet.

"I'll get it," Caroline said after a moment.

I put my hand on her sleeve. "No, I will. Stay in here with Abigail just in case."

I hurried into the hallway and peeked out the front window. Burley stood on the porch.

"Did anyone follow you?"

"I don't think so, but there's a Ford with three unfamiliar faces in it, parked across the street."

I glanced that way as I opened the door and let him in. "Julian's in the kitchen, talking to Genevieve."

We went down the hall to the kitchen, leaving Caroline to console Abigail.

Genevieve sat on a kitchen stool, playing with the hem of her apron. "Mr. Talbot said that I shouldn't tell anyone where he was. Specially Miz Talbot. Not even Miz Mamie or Patsy."

Julian acknowledged Burley and me as we came in and sat down at the table.

"You're sure there was no one else?"

"I'm positive, Mr. Julian. No one but me. I have three jobs. And I got to fetch and tend to my own family too. No time for tellin' tales about Mr. Talbot."

"Of course, we know you're busy," I patted her hand.

"Ya'll got me worried what with folks hustlin' in here like a bunch a hogs tryin' to git in outta the rain. What's goin' on?"

"Seems that Mr. Talbot's enemies think they're going to follow Miz Talbot until she leads them to him. I don't think they plan on letting up until they find him."

Genevieve shook her head. "I about had enough excitement for a lifetime, Miz Mamie. What're we gonna do?"

"Have you ever seen anyone following you when you took him food?"

"I usually go at night. Mr. Talbot wants that I come in through the tunnel that opens out on the back street rather than from the house or through the garage."

Julian and I exchanged glances.

"There's a way to get into that bunker through the house?"

"Yes, ma'am. There sure is. Mr. Talbot's great granddaddy, Mr. Tom Howard, added all kinds of ins and outs to that place back afore the war."

"How do you know that," Julian asked.

"The Howards owned my grandma when she was a girl. She talked about how skeered that ole man was when the war started. Course, that wasn't nothin' new. He was peculiar. Always skeered. Of bein' hungry. Of someone breakin' in and hurtin' him or the ole lady. Of ghosts. Of varmints. He got rid of all his other slaves back in 1860 cause with all the war talk, he got to thinkin' they's gonna kill him sooner or later. Only one he kept was my grandma—and she say he eyed her like she was gonna turn on him any minute. Course she was only ten or eleven at the time and even if she wanted to bash his head in and run away, where was she gonna go back then?"

"So he built ways to get away?"

"Ya gotta remember, Mr. Julian. That place was a farm back then. They sold land to keep them alive in later years. Now it's town. I don't got any idea where all he put doors. My grandma told me about one that was hidden inside a chiffarobe. I think it led to a barn but there ain't no barn in that neighborhood now. And there's supposed to be somethin' under that big ole front porch."

"Do a lot of people know about this?"

"Jes really ole folks."

"Thanks, Genevieve."

"Ya'll need somethin' to eat? I got ham in the oven and the fixins' are jes' about ready.

* * *

Burley peeked out the front window. "Looks like they gave up for the night."

"Then I want to go home," Abigail said. "I want my own things around me."

"It's safer here." Burley turned to her. "They might be waiting outside your house."

"I doubt that. They have to eat and sleep sometime."

"I have an idea," Burley said. "Those guys just want the whiskey, right?" He sat down beside Abigail.

"But I don't have any whiskey, Burley!"

"But they think you do."

"What are you cooking up?" Julian said to Burley.

"Just this. I don't believe these are the same men who burned Orrin Fellows. They think they killed him, so while I imagine these people are just as bad as the first bunch, they probably just want the whiskey or the money—and once they have it, they'll leave Garland alone."

"So how do we do that?"

"Send them on a wild goose chase."

"I repeat," Julian said. "How do we do that?"

"First thing we have to do is talk with Garland."

Julian glanced at me.

I stood up. "Let's do it."

Abigail's posture was imploring.

"No."

"What's a poor little woman like me to do?" She whimpered.

I'd seen Abigail take down Orrin Fellows with her parasol. Her vulnerable southern belle act was as thin as chicken broth. I started to tell her so, but Caroline interrupted me. "For now, stay right here. We can sit out on the front porch so if someone is looking for you, they can see you. It'll keep them busy until Julian and Burley and Mamie get back."

"But I want to see Garland too."

"It'll work out, dear. In the meantime, you and I can play dominoes and get caught up on our gossip. Or maybe we can ask Theo to come tell our fortunes."

Abigail perked up. "Yes, do give her a call. Maybe Maybelle Shirley has some answers."

"Yes, dear. Maybe she does."

I fetched the jacket and gloves of my driving outfit and readjusted my turban. Then Julian, Burley and I slipped out the back door and through the screened in porch. At the back gate, I paused. "Can either of you see anything?"

They each peered over a different stretch of fencing.

"Nothing unusual," Burley said.

"Not this side either," Julian agreed.

We slipped out the gate and into the car. It was getting dark, but I waited until we were on Rogers before turning on my lights.

"There's no one following us," Burley declared as I turned onto Greenwood and then turned again a block before Abigail and Garland's street.

"Think we can find the entrance to the back tunnel?"

"Where can I park this thing so that it's not obvious?"

"There." Burley pointed. "I know the Murphys and they're in Hot Springs this week."

I pulled up in front of an older home. We got out and walked toward the Talbot property about a hundred yards up the road. Without Genevieve's directions, we would have never found the small split in the tall bushes in the dark. One by one, we slipped through and followed a narrow path. About fifty feet from the backyard gazebo where we often had tea when we visited, we came upon two dense hedgerows about ten feet apart—and taller than Julian and Burley. We stopped at the large pine with a lover's heart carved into the trunk that Genevieve had described. I felt around the trunk until I found a skeleton key hanging from a nail about four feet from the ground. We squeezed past it into a long strip of land, hidden on both sides by the hedges. From there, it wasn't hard to spot a sloping door that resembled the entrance to a potato cellar.

"This must be it," Julian whispered. "Let's try not to scare him."

"Don't know how to avoid that." I inserted the skeleton key into the lock.

"Who's there?"

"It's me, Garland. Mamie McGrath."

"What the hell are you doing here? Are you alone?" His voice was soft, like he was far away.

"Burley and I are with her, Garland," Julian said.

Silence.

"Garland?"

"That little traitor."

"Don't blame Genevieve," I said. "I made her tell me how to find this bunker."

We stood at the door, waiting.

"Is Abigail okay?"

"She's fine, but we need to talk to you," I said. "Help you."

"I don't need your help."

"I'm afraid you do."

Another minute of silence.

"It's not a trick?"

"No trick. I promise."

"I have a shotgun here."

"Okay."

"Come on in. If it's not as you say, I'll shoot you dead."

"Aw, Garland. You aren't going to shoot me. You'd have Sarge on your back for the rest of your life."

"That one-legged pipsqueak." Garland snorted.

I lifted the old door. Black material—to keep sunlight from creeping into his living space, I presume—hung across an opening at the foot of a steep rock stairway. As we climbed down, the heavy wooden door slammed shut behind us—leaving us to feel our way down the rest of the way.

At the foot of the steps, Julian pushed the heavy black curtain aside. Garland didn't have a shotgun, but he was holding a wooden chair over one shoulder ready to bash the brains out of an unwelcome intruder.

"Oh for heavens sake, Garland. Put that thing down."

"You're a sight for sore eyes, Mamie." He set the chair down and motioned for me to take it.

"Thanks. It's been a long exhausting day." I sat down and folded my hands on my lap.

"Burley. Julian." He gestured toward another chair and an upholstered settee.

As they sat down, Garland stood for a minute, wringing his hands. He'd lost weight since I'd last seen him, the night that Sandy died. He might have been nervous, but he definitely wasn't drunk. "Would you like some water? It's about all I got. Wasn't expecting company."

"No, thanks," Burley said. "We're good."

Garland sat down on the edge of the settee beside Julian. I realized that he'd shaved his cheeks and chin—and that his bushy mustache was streaked with gray.

"So you found me."

"You can't hide here forever."

"I didn't have no part in hanging that kid."

"But you were drinking with a lot of the men who did. You should come forward. Tell your story. The Special Grand Jury is still hearing testimony," Julian said. "Hiding out makes you look guilty."

"You saw me there, Julian. You know I was in no condition to participate in a mob."

"I saw you leave, Garland." I said softly. "I know you didn't touch Sandy—but I know you didn't stop them either."

Garland leaned forward, his forearms on his knees and I realized he was crying.

I put my hand on his shoulder.

"It was so awful," he sobbed. "I knew those men. A lot of them were just kids. But some were longtime friends."

"It's sad," I said. "People you see every day can't meet each other's eyes."

"I don't know how to explain it, Mamie. I've never been one for fisticuffs. Never had the stomach for it. I just, you know—put on a show."

"How do you mean?".

"I'm big. Meaty. Long of bone." He held up his fist. It was twice as big as mine. "But I never hit anyone in my life."

"That's admirable, Garland." I looked at first Julian and then Burley—and both avoided my eyes. "It is," I said firmly. "It is."

"You're about the only woman in this state who'd say a thing like that, Mamie. Women choose men who are strong. Decisive. Protectors. I not only can't face my friends, I can't face Abigail." His voice quivered. "When my friends needed me to stand with them, I let them down. I let Andy down and John B too."

"Wait. What about Sandy? Shouldn't someone have stood up for him?" My voice rose.

"You've got to understand how it was," Garland continued. "We thought—everyone said—that boy shot Andy dead. Murdered him in cold blood. Folks were stirred up. If the blacks would kill a lawman in the middle of the street, what's to stop them from killing decent white folks all over town? We had to stop them. Put the fear of God in them. Protect our families. Our homes. A man's honor bound to do that."

I backed away from him. "So you're hiding away down here because you *didn't* commit murder?"

"It was a righteous killing, Mamie. My friends came together to combat evil. And I took one look and ran away. When it meant something to be a white man—a solid member of this community, I was puking down by the tracks near the Frisco station. And when that murderer was swinging, I was boarding a train. Didn't even care where it was going. Just needed to get away from that horror— and my shame."

"The decent people of Fort Smith are outraged by what your friends did." I spit out the bitter words. "I'm outraged and disgusted by their behavior."

Garland stood up. "You'd rather be attacked in the street than be protected by strong men? Be locked inside afraid for your life? Your honor?"

I stood up to face him. "I'd rather have the police do their jobs and then let the judge and jury sort it out. That's what Andy believed in too. Law and order. That crowd of so-called strong men debased Andy's memory by torturing and killing an innocent boy."

"Mamie," Julian reached out to me. "Calm down."

Garland began pacing and gesturing with his hands. "The law takes too long. Hordes of niggers were already gathering on Garrison and Tenth that night. Decent people were on the sidewalks after theater and dinner. Voters were attending Judge Harp's political rally. If those blacks got riled up enough, there would've been a massacre. And now—" He pointed to a pile of newspapers beside one of the chairs. "Now the world's gone crazy. Locking up good citizens—ruining their lives. For what? A nigger boy who even if he didn't shoot Andy as they are claiming now, had probably done his share of robbing and going after our fine white women?"

I stamped my foot. "Nothing like that happened that night!"

"Because Stowers and Sullivan and Tucker and the boys took care of it. Taught those niggers a lesson."

"My God, are you blind? Obtuse?"

He stopped and leaned down so his face was near mine. "You're a Yankee, like that damned fool uncle of yours. Your ideas are irresponsible and dangerous. They're going to get you killed one of these days."

"It's better than being a murderer," I shouted.

He lowered his eye brows and showed his teeth.

"Whoa. Garland. You're making yourself sick here." Burley grabbed his arm just as he was about to hit me.

"Mamie, darling, shush." Julian pulled me away. "You aren't going to win this fight. It's been going on around here for generations—and probably will for a good many more."

"So much for never hitting anyone," I taunted Garland.

Julian put his arms around me and pressed his lips against my ear. "We came here to help the Talbots—not argue politics. This isn't helping them."

"He's more worried about what his murderous friends will think about him than what's good for this town," I whispered back.

"I know. It's disgusting, but it's how he feels. He was sharing his shame about letting his buddies down. It's hard for him to tell you things like that. Personal things."

"But Julian, what about Sandy?"

"He can't hear you if you don't hear him, my love. Bite your tongue and listen."

Across the room, Burley had coaxed Garland back onto the settee and they were talking quietly.

"He's scared." It was a sudden realization.

Julian nodded.

"Why?"

"That's what we need to find out."

"I still want to box his ears."

Julian held me tighter. "Take a breath, Tiger."

"Do I have to apologize?"

"Recommended."

I slumped like a beaten dog. "Okay."

* * *

"I really need a drink," Garland said as we sat together on the settee.

"Coffee maybe."

"You're relentless—like Abigail."

"Oh please. This is a fragile truce. Don't go there."

He laughed. "I'm sorry, Mamie."

"Shall we start again?"

"What other choice is there? My wife and your mother-in-law are best friends. We can't destroy their get-togethers with arguments like this."

"You could just assume I'm right."

"That I'm obtuse? What is that? A perfumed dandy?" His pretend scowl wasn't as intense as his real one.

"It's an angle, I think."

"See, they're playing nicely now," Burley said to Julian.

"About time." Julian sighed dramatically.

"We'll be good." Garland took my hand and held it up. "I'll miss it, but there's still Sergeant Elias Eacret to fight with. He really will shoot me if I get carried away. Great fun."

"The reason we came looking for you is your problem with Mr. Guckenheimer. Orrin Fellows may be in jail and Anna Marie Cavanaugh is back with her brothers in Oklahoma for the present, but your investors and your customers are getting antsy," Julian said.

"I've been hiding out and sobering up so I could deal with them."

"Abigail's worried about you."

"That old girl knows this'll blow over."

"She may believe it, but you're compromising her social life, Garland. She's the secretary of the WCTU now. And you're planning on dealing whiskey," Burley said. "What're you going do about that?"

"Hang on to it a while. I figure this is going to be a waiting game. Won't do to dig Mr. Guckenheimer up until most places are dry. I got merchandise put back for a few of my special friends like Till. He pays me a little bit every now and then to keep me afloat. He sees it as insurance for when things get dry."

"So all your potential clients are okay with you?"

"Most of them."

"So who're those men following Abigail?"

"Ugly mutts in a brand new Model T? Those would be my investors—or their associates at least."

"So since you're trying NOT to sell whiskey right now—how are you planning to pay them back?"

"Still trying to figure that out."

"Do they want whiskey or cash?"

"Cash but I'm sure they'll take product, Burley. What are you getting at?"

Here's my idea. I swear, I'm not going to hijack you, Garland—but where do you have the majority of the Guckenheimer stashed?"

"Here, there—everywhere."

Burley caught my eye.

Garland sighed. "I have it stored all over town."

"In lockers?"

"Funeral homes, warehouses, cellars, graves, barns—you name it."

"Perfect. So tell me where the smallest stash is. Doesn't even have to be all whiskey. Some bottles can be colored water if you want. Just make sure the top layer is the real thing."

"And?" Garland put his hands on his hips.

"Make sure it's separate from any of your other product."

"And?"

"Have Mamie here deliver a note to your investors telling them where they can find that stash."

Julian frowned. "I don't like it. What if they hurt her?"

"She'll have them sign a receipt for a stated amount of booze equal to the amount of money owed."

Garland rubbed his palms together. "Burley, my boy. I'm beginning to see what you are getting at. Great idea."

Julian was still troubled. "What if they come back on Mamie when they realize that most of the whiskey bottles aren't whiskey at all?"

"First off, who would doubt that sweet little face? And secondly, if we time this right, they'll never know they've been had."

"I'll do it," I said.

Julian nudged me with his elbow.

"I will—and I'll be fine."

Garland scowled. "What if it doesn't work? Why would they believe Mamie? She's not even family."

"Send Abigail with her, then. That way when we pull the trigger on this thing, they won't be able to come back on her. And we might ought to get John B to help out while we can."

I folded my arms over my chest and blew out my cheeks.

"Trust me," Burley said. "One more caper and you and Abigail can retire from crime."

"Are you going to tell her—or do you want me to explain all this to the Secretary of the Women's Christian Temperance Union?

19

ABIGAIL OPENED HER FRONT DOOR a sliver. "Is everything set?"

"So they say."

"Where is everyone?"

"If I point, someone might see and that would blow up the deal."

She opened the door wider. "Who's with you?"

"Just me," I lied. "Might as well get used to it. It's just you and me doing this."

"Give me a minute." She closed the door in my face.

Without an invitation to go inside, I paced the long front porch. John B and Julian watched from a wooded lot across Lexington. Pretending not to see them, I turned and walked to the other end of the porch. Burley was hiding somewhere in the neighborhood with his horse. I felt safe enough.

Abigail came out straightening her hat. She handed me a large basket while she pulled on her gloves. Muttering under her breath, she fussed with the door lock until it slid into place with a dull clunk. "Ready?"

"Everything is set up."

"Did you find those men?"

"Burley did. They're staying at the Goldman. He said they'd be delighted to meet us for brunch."

"Why did he have me pack up those bottles of Guckenheimer?"

"Samples." I panted as I lugged the basket down the steps to where I'd parked the Hudson in front of the carriage house.

"We can't hand them over in the Goldman in front of God and everyone who matters."

"We won't."

"I must see to my reputation. I'm the secretar—"

"We're just meeting these fellows for a talk. Burley's got it all worked out."

"What will people think?"

I hefted the basket into the backseat of the Hudson. "Don't worry. Your friends will think you're quite the heroine after this."

We crawled in and arranged ourselves. I started the car before I remembered. "Do you have the keys?"

"Yes." She patted her purse. "Although I don't see why we need them. We haven't been out to that old barn in years. It's probably filled with rats and rattlesnakes."

I shuddered. "They didn't tell me about rattlesnakes."

"You know men. They don't tell you about things like that unless you ask."

I still had Orrin Fellows' Derringer—and its one bullet—in my purse, but it seemed like an ineffective weapon against snakes. "Should we take a hoe or something, just in case?"

"I'm not going into that creepy old place—with or without a hoe."

I turned the engine off and folded my arms across my chest.

We sat quietly, staring out the front windshield of the car. After a few seconds, Abigail blew air out of her pursed lips. "Oh for heaven's sake." She got out and marched over to the carriage house. "I'm not exactly dressed for a barn."

"You never are," I said under my breath.

A few minutes later, she emerged with a large sickle and a hoe. "Just how big are these snakes?"

"However big they are, we're prepared to do battle with them." She put the tools in the back seat.

I turned on the engine.

"Wait, wait."

"What?"

"I'm dewy and my hat is crooked." She fished her hanky out of her bosom and patted her upper lip. Then she adjusted the big Merry Widow. "How's this?"

"A little more."

"Better?"

"Perfect."

* * *

At the Goldman, I was relieved to see the black Ford parked out front. A valet helped Abigail out of the Hudson while another one gave me a receipt to retrieve it after our brunch.

"Who is this we're meeting?" Abigail said out of the corner of her mouth.

"A man named Oleg Pavlov and his two sons."

"Are they from here?"

"I don't know. Hot Springs, maybe?"

"Where does Garland come up with these people? First that Orrin Fellows. Now Oleg something or other. Doesn't he do business with anyone whose name starts with a C or an S, for goodness sake?"

I tried not to giggle. "Wonder if the sons' names start with O too."

An enormous pear-shaped man with a thin black mustache crossed the lobby to meet us. "Mrs. McGrath, I presume."

I stretched out my hand. "Yes. And you must be Mr. Pavlov."

"At your service, ma'am." He bent to kiss the back of my glove.

"And this is Mrs. Talbot."

"Ah, Mrs. Talbot—wife of the missing Mr. Talbot. I'm glad to meet both of you. My sons are waiting for us in the restaurant." He guided us through the door.

The sons stood as we approached our table.

"Mrs. McGrath. Mrs. Talbot. This is my eldest, Oral."

I swallowed a chuckle as I extended a hand to Oral, who looked a lot like his father. "Nice to meet you," I mumbled.

"Oral." Abigail emphasized the O and smirked at me.

"And this is Konrad." Oleg pointed to his other son, who was younger, taller, thinner, and blonder. "With a K. His mother is from Germany."

"Oh," I said.

"People here usually spell it with a C, you know." Konrad pulled out a chair for me.

"Yes, I know."

"I imagine that causes a lot of confusion." Abigail avoided my eyes as we sat down.

Oleg rubbed his hands together. "Can I order for the table?"

"Of course," I said, hoping he wouldn't order fish.

Oleg lifted the menu and conferred with the waiter while Abigail and I chatted with Oral and Konrad.

"Where are you from," Abigail asked.

"Detroit." Konrad was the more talkative of the brothers. "Born and raised."

"Oh, I thought you were from Russia."

"Our grandparents came over when they were teenagers."

"Yes, well. That's taken care of." Oleg took over the conversation as our waiter scurried away. "While I'd much like to chat about the old country, we have business to take care of this morning."

Out of the corner of my eye, I saw Julian and Burley being seated across the room from us. Although I hadn't realized I was nervous, I relaxed. "Of course, Mr. Pavlov. We understand that you financed a business transaction with a Mr. Fellows and Mr. Talbot."

"Yes. This was some months ago and although our loan isn't due for a few months, we've heard there were problems here in Fort Smith."

Abigail sat up straighter. "Yes?"

I pinched her and she jumped.

"Pardon me. I'll speak for my aunt."

Abigail's eyes narrowed, but she didn't say anything more.

"Two unexpected situations—totally out of Mrs. Talbot's control—have changed the outlook of your business here in Fort Smith. First, Mr. Fellows was arrested for assault and theft. Apparently, he didn't have bail money so he was a guest in our jail here for some days. Then, as we've heard it—a young woman came to his rescue. She paid his bail—and he was released. He was supposed to be available for trial when his case came up. However, they left town and no one has seen them since."

Oleg leaned back in his seat as the waiter served us wine, a plate of cheeses, crackers, fruit, crumbled up boiled eggs mixed with chives and a dish filled with something black. "Ah, special treat for these special ladies."

"What is that?" Abigail pointed.

"Beluga Caviar. You must try it. It's exquisite." Using a wooden spoon, Konrad dipped some onto toast along with hard-boiled egg and some thick cream.

"What is caviar though?" Abigail picked up the toast and sniffed it.

"Fish roe," Konrad said. "Eggs."

She cocked her head so that she could examine it more closely through her monocle. "I don't know..."

"Please, Mrs. Talbot," Oleg said. "It's very special. Considered quite a treat on the continent."

"Oh?" She perked up.

"Only the wealthy get to enjoy it here." Oleg practically purred.

"Well, maybe." She touched the tip of her tongue to the Caviar sitting on the toast.

At first, I thought she didn't like it, but the expression I took as revulsion turned into rapture. She took a bite. "It's wonderful."

"How about you, Mrs. McGrath?"

"Thank you, but no. Fish makes me sick."

"Oh such a shame." Oleg snapped his fingers for the waiter. "We'll find something you will love too."

"No. I'm happy with just toast and jam. And coffee. No wine for me."

"Oh Mamie, I'll eat yours." Abigail finished her toast.

"We have one convert," Oleg laughed before ordering for me.

"Go ahead," I said to the others. Eat."

Oral dipped himself a large portion and spread it on his toast.

"My brother doesn't say much," Konrad said as he prepared a second piece for Abigail and one for himself.

"Not much to say." Oral focused on his caviar.

"So, Mrs. McGrath," Oleg said as we ate. "One of our partners is on the lam. What about Mr. Talbot?"

"I don't suppose you heard about the trouble we had here the end of March?"

"We don't keep up with the Fort Smith news, I'm afraid." Oleg dabbed at his lips with a napkin.

"A young black man was lynched in front of the Hotel Main a few blocks from here. An innocent man, I might add."

"What's that got to do with my money, Mrs. McGrath?"

"Please." I smiled at him. "Call me Mamie."

"Okay, Mamie. What's the unfortunate death of this Negro got to do with my business?"

"They're indicting the people who lynched him."

"And?"

"No one's seen hide nor hair of Garland Talbot since that night."

"Has he been arrested?"

"Not that we know of."

"Mmmm," Abigail moaned as she took another bite of the caviar. We all laughed.

She opened her eyes. "What?"

"Nothing, dear. We were enjoying you enjoy your food."

"Actually, I was inquiring about the whereabouts of your husband, Mrs. Talbot."

"No idea," she said with her mouth full.

"None?"

"The police don't have him. He's not at home. It's been six weeks now. He could be dead for all we know," I said.

Konrad poured himself another glass of wine, "What about the whiskey?"

"Mr. Talbot never shared any information about his business with Mrs. Talbot."

"Why would I believe that?" Oleg growled.

"Mrs. Talbot didn't even know there was a project—and she certainly never saw any whiskey."

"So who's going to pay me?"

"Mrs. Talbot doesn't have cash. Until her husband is found—or returns on his own, there's no money for the kind of debt you hold for Mr. Talbot and Mr. Fellows. And in fact, the contract is between you and them. Not Mrs. Talbot."

"You mean I poured $500 dollars into a project that'll have zero return?" Oleg's voice rose and people at other tables turned to look at us.

"Not completely," I said.

Last year, Mr. Talbot and Mr. Fellows lost a friend. They brought him to Fort Smith, already in his coffin. His visitation was at my house."

"And?"

"Mr. Talbot wouldn't let us open the coffin."

"Okay, where is this going?" Konrad wanted to know.

"There was no ceremony at the church."

"Let me guess. No one ever actually saw a body, right?"

"Not a soul."

"And what was the name of the dearly departed?"

"A Mr. Guckenheimer."

"Damn!" Oleg slammed his hand on the table.

"Do you know, Mr. Guckenheimer?" Abigail asked with her mouth full.

"A personal friend, ma'am." Konrad turned to me. "So where's old Guck buried?"

"I have no idea. There was no graveside ceremony."

"What's going on, Pop?" Oral woke up. "She's saying there's whiskey buried somewhere in Fort Smith?"

"Well," I cleared my throat, "There's one other thing."

"What?" Oral was suddenly very interested indeed.

"We've searched everywhere since Garland Talbot disappeared, as you can imagine. From bank vaults to each place of business Garland ever owned, worked at, longed for—or walked by. Nothing. However, Abigail found a key the other day. We're not sure, but we think it's to an old barn out on Jenny Lind Road. We're planning on going out there to look for it this afternoon."

Oleg waved the waiter over. "More coffee for Mamie here."

"Abigail is not sure of her status now. Is she a wife or a widow? Other than her home, she doesn't have much money. Her husband was a good man, but he had two fatal flaws. He was a drunk and a gambler. Everything Abigail thought she owned belongs to someone else now."

"Not a penny in the coffers," Abigail said piteously. "Garland lost our automobile to Mr. Fellows last fall. And my mother's wedding ring the spring before that. I've even hocked our furniture for food."

I scowled at her, but the Pavlovs seemed to be buying her plea of poverty. "So you've lost—and Mrs. Talbot has lost—to the same scoundrel, Orrin Fellows."

"I invested a lot of money in this venture, Mamie."

"I understand that, sir—but I have a suggestion. I can't do anything about your lost opportunity. But if Mr. Guckenheimer's casket is full of whiskey—and if it's out there in that barn on Jenny Lind, will you be satisfied with that?"

"What if I'm not?"

"Well, sir. See that man over there? The good looking one with the dimple in his chin?"

"Yes?"

"That's prosecuting attorney Paul Little. He was the son of the governor of Arkansas at one time. He's the man who wants to make Fort Smith dry. There's word he might succeed too. Of course, if he finds that whiskey, imagine what he'll do with it. On the other hand, he's a big man in this town. Looking to be a judge one of these days. He knows the law that well. Imagine what he'll do if he thinks you are misusing a widow like Abigail."

Abigail's poor-little-me eyelash flutter was practiced, but effective.

"So what happens if I take the deal?"

"I had a lawyer write up the terms and I have a friend over there..." I pointed at Burley who was having coffee with Julian. "—who will notarize our agreement."

"Then what?" Konrad seemed almost amused.

"We all get in our cars and go see what's in that barn."

Oleg pushed back his chair. "What if there's nothing there?"

"Then there's nothing to be had, is there?"

"Okay, you got us," Konrad said. "But if there is whiskey out in your barn, why do you want to get rid of it, Mrs. Talbot? It could support you for a long time. Especially if whiskey is banned."

She lifted her chin. "I'm the Secretary of the Women's Christian Temperance Union."

* * *

I braked as we hit a bumpy stretch on Jenny Lind Road. The bottles clanked around in the basket in the backseat.

"Are they still behind us?"

I glanced in the mirror. "Staying close."

"What's to keep them from reneging on this deal?"

"Nothing but the paperwork I had them sign—and whether or not they believed me."

"We'll be out here away from town." Abigail glanced over her shoulder. "They could shoot us—or you know—"

"Other than that being an ugly thought, I doubt either Oleg or Oral have the inclination or the ability to catch either of us."

"And Konrad?"

"The three of them are more interested in money than women—besides, we have backup."

"You're sure?"

"Positive."

I swerved to avoid a hole and bounced off a large rock. Abigail hung on for dear life. "Reminds me of our trip from Hope to Fort Smith with Mama and the sick kids in the back of the wagon. Bad roads and Indians."

"When was this?"

"I was thirteen. The Indians thought I was beautiful and tried to kidnap me for immoral purposes. Mama chased them away with a shotgun."

"Really?" That was a story I'd never heard before.

"They like pretty little white girls, you know."

"Is that a fact?"

"That and whiskey."

"I think we're pretty safe." I pointed at John B sitting on his horse beside the barn as we pulled up in front of the door.

The Pavlovs parked behind us.

And Julian and Burley followed at a distance.

I got out of the car and walked back to talk with Oleg. "We have a couple bottles left over from Mr. Guckenheimer's visitation. Would you like to sample them?"

Oleg rolled out of the backseat of the Model T and stretched. "A nip would be welcome. The ride about shook my guts out."

"I'll have a swallow too." Oral emerged from the front passenger seat wearing a long duster and goggles. "I don't know which is worse—the dust or the ruts."

"It's not as bad as some, not as good as others," I said.

Konrad set the brake and turned off the engine. "Lots of good land out here. The Talbots aren't farming it anymore?"

"Don't think farming ever interested Garland—and he's the last of his line."

Konrad took off his goggles and wiped his face with the back of his sleeve. "He ought to sell it."

I shrugged. "Abigail has the key, but she's not been out here in ages. Says there might be snakes around, so watch your step."

John B got off his horse and I introduced him to the Pavlovs.

"Nice to meet you, Mr. Williams." Oleg shook his hand.

"John B is both a businessman and a lawman," I said.

"Oh?" Oleg glanced at me nervously.

"Just a sideline." John B grinned. "I'll probably be taking some time off later in the year."

I opened the back door of the Hudson and took out the basket. "I got hurt last year and still have trouble opening bottles." I handed the Guckenheimer to John B along with some small glasses. "I'll have water myself."

John B handed Oleg the first shot. "Tell me what you think?"

Oleg held up the glass so that the afternoon sun shown through it. Then he sniffed it and wrinkled his substantial nose. "It's Rye?"

"Yes, is that a problem?"

The Pavlovs laughed.

I glanced at John B, unsure if that was a good or bad sign. He shrugged.

I held my breath.

"Most assuredly not a problem, Mamie." Oleg turned the glass to view the amber liquid from all angles.

Konrad and Oral flanked their father as if this was a well-practiced ritual.

Julian and Burley arrived and tied their horses to what remained of a corral beside the barn.

Oleg remained transfixed by the whiskey.

"What's taking so long, for heaven's sake?" Abigail frowned.

"About to taste it."

She threw open the door of the Hudson and tramped through the grass, holding her skirts up—and inspecting the ground lest she step into a viper's nest.

"Is something wrong with it," she said to Oleg.

"Shush," Konrad and Oral said in unison.

"Well, I never."

Oleg closed his eyes, brought the glass to his lips and took a sip. We waited.

Then he threw back the entire shot in one gulp. "Ah."

Abigail stamped her foot. "Is it any good or not?"

A slow grin spread across his face. "I can make money with this, Mrs. Talbot."

"Good."

"Are we sure there's a coffin full of the stuff in there?" Oral flipped his thumb toward the barn.

"I have no idea. It's the only place Garland's stash could be though." Abigail produced the key from her bosom. "Shall we look?"

As we headed toward the barn, I reached into the backseat and grabbed the hoe.

"Surely, it's not guarded by serpents, Mrs. McGrath."

"You never know, Oleg. It pays to be prepared."

"The boys will protect us."

"I'm sure they will—and John B and Julian and Burley. But I'm prepared—just in case."

Abigail inserted the key into the lock and pushed open on the old wooden doors. She stepped back, allowing Burley, Oleg and John B to go inside first.

* * *

The inside of the barn was dark. Julian found the side door and opened it, allowing more light to pour through.

"Is there anything in there?" Oral peered into the darkness, his hands in the pockets of the long duster.

"Packed to the rafters," John B called. "Everything from old iron bathtubs to broken chairs. Might as well sit in the car, this is going to take a while."

"Fine." Abigail turned on her heel and hurried back to the Hudson.

"Watch out for snakes," I said as Konrad elbowed around Oral and went inside the barn.

"Don't you worry about that." John B stood just inside the door, his palm resting on the butt of his holstered gun. "I'm keeping watch while the others look for that coffin."

I followed Abigail back to the car.

"Think it's going to work?"

"Shush." I jerked my eyes toward Oral who was leaning against the Ford. His role was apparently to keep track of us—either that or to eavesdrop on our conversation. Of course, maybe he just didn't like closed-in dusty places either.

Abigail nodded and changed the subject. "I've only been here a time or two. Once, about twenty years ago, Garland came out looking for his mother's ring. Don't remember why he thought it might be here."

"Did he find it?"

"No, but he did find her portrait. She was a tight-fisted woman with a mole right between her eyes. Insisted on being in charge of everything and everyone. After the war, she was afraid of being poor again so she spent the rest of her life buying expensive things and hiding them."

"What kind of things?"

"Jewelry. Guns. Saddles. Paintings. Quilts. Had to be nonperishable and easily converted to cash. Garland told me once that there's a wine cellar hidden somewhere on the property. I looked for it when he first disappeared but never found it."

The Talbots had an odd extended family. I imagined Abigail sitting alone in that big old mausoleum of a house trying to figure out where all the supposed riches were hidden.

Burley appeared at the door of the barn. "We found it!"

I stuck my head out the window. "Mr. Guckenheimer's coffin?"

"We're about to open it now."

I threw open the door. "Are you coming?"

Abigail pursed her lips.

"Well?"

"Yes, yes. Let's get this over with." She got out of the car and we walked back up the path to the barn with Oral following us.

As we all crowded around the barn door, John B kept a watchful eye on us. "It's awful dark in there," he said. "Why don't y'all just bring that coffin out into the sunshine. There's no body around to see and I'll make sure no one intrudes."

Abigail coughed. "Yes, just bring it outside. We can always put it back if it doesn't hold what you think it should."

Abigail, Oral, and I retraced our steps coughing and dabbing at our tearing eyes. Oleg followed but stopped to peer back over his shoulder.

"You're a suspicious man, Oleg." I smiled.

"Trying to distract me, Mrs. McGrath?"

"I suspect it takes more than a smile to distract a man like you."

A small crash startled us and we squinted into the dusky barn.

Burley and Julian pushed the coffin out on the small cart on which it had rested through the months it'd been stored. Once in the sunshine, I realized that though it was ornate, it wasn't nearly as fancy as I'd remembered.

Julian felt around for the clasp that held the lid closed.

Oleg and his sons leaned forward.

The lid opened slowly and the sun reflected off the contents, blinding me for a moment.

"Count them, Konrad," Oleg said.

Konrad bent over the casket filled with crates of whiskey. "Will an estimate do?"

"How many?"

"The coffin is 80 inches long, 14 inches high and 25 inches wide." He measured with his hands. "Looks like."

"The cases?"

"They're 16 by 12 by 13 ½. Standard. Twelve bottles per crate. Five crates length wise and two across. That's 120 quarts."

"What's the going price?"

"$2.70 per bottle," Oral said.

"By the shot, numbskull."

"About eight cents an ounce."

The Pavlovs looked at each other.

"That makes back your investment and then some," Konrad said. "Sell as shots would make even more. Wait until whiskey is scarce and we'll do even better."

Oleg turned to me, his eyebrows making a V on his forehead. "You're sure there's not any other coffins around?"

"You know as much as we do. The only one who could say yes or no on that is Garland Talbot and he's been missing for months."

"Yes, well I'd hoped for more. I bought in expecting more."

I silenced Abigail with a glare. "It is what it is, Oleg. Take it or leave it."

"I'll take it for now. But, I won't drop this. I'll be on the look out for Mr. Talbot in the days and months and years to come."

"Let us know if you find him." I turned to Julian. Abigail and I are going home now. Your mother has invited Theo to read our fortunes this afternoon. Jennie will be joining us. And Katherine Mivalez."

"In that case, Burley and John B and I will pick up some cigars and retire to the screened in porch when we get back."

"I'm sure Genevieve will have snicker doodles for you."

"Won't be the same without Andy and Della." Julian closed the barn doors and set the lock.

"Della and I will have lunch next week if she's up to it. Or the next after that." I turned to the Pavlovs. "How will you get that thing back to the Frisco?"

"Mr. Williams here has a Horse and Mule Barn—and he says he can rent me a wagon and driver to get it to town. Oral here will watch over it until we get back."

"Dad." It was almost a whine. "Why can't Konrad stay here?"

Oleg spun on his older son. "Because I have other things for Konrad to do."

I picked up the hoe that I'd left leaning against the Hudson. "In case you see any snakes."

Oral shuddered but he took the hoe.

"Thanks for the lovely lunch."

"You drive a hard bargain, Mrs. McGrath—but don't think we won't be back to check on things from time to time."

Julian opened the door of the Hudson and I crawled in. "He leaned down to kiss my cheek. "Good job, my love."

He walked around and helped Abigail into the passenger seat. "Glad it's over?"

She straightened her hat. "Is it really over?"

"Your part anyway."

***

The remains of a Mr. Oleil Pavlov disappeared while being transported to Saint Louis. Cathey Pitcock, Train Detective, isn't dismissing theft but it seems unlikely anyone would steal a body. He suspects the coffin was simply misplaced and the company is conducting searches of all of their facilities. The Pavlovs are extremely upset.

Julian McGrath, *Southwest American*

20

May 3, 1912
I didn't see a man climb the pole at any time. Whipple and I are on good
terms. I didn't see Will Manus. I do not know Grover Bourland. I saw the
two boys when they slid down, but I didn't see a man climb the pole.

Will Henry interview by Mamie McGrath

Eighteen persons including six former police officers were indicted for
offenses committed during the lynching of Sanford Lewis.

Julian McGrath, *Southwest American*

ABIGAIL HAD A NEW HAT. It was about time, if you asked me.

"It's quite becoming, dear," Caroline was telling her as Julian and I came in the door.

"I had Mr. Ney order it for me. It's called 'The Shirley.' What do you think, Mamie?"

It was less formal than the Merry Widow she'd been wearing for years. Instead of the gigantic dyed feather arrangement on the crown, she had chosen a fat blue and white striped satin bow pinned to a fashionably-small-brimmed velvet hat. Knowing how important style was to her, I said, "It's elegant, Abigail."

"Never play poker, Mamie. What's wrong?"

"Yes," Caroline looked at Julian and then back at me. "What's happened?"

"The Grand Jury delivered the indictments today," I said.

Abigail froze, her hand at the base of her throat. "Not Garland?"

"No."

"Thank God." Caroline kissed the crucifix she wore around her neck.

Abigail relaxed her hand. "At least they won't be hanging the old fool for murder."

"Garland's safe at least for now," I said. "But they're charging John B with Aggravated Assault and Manslaughter."

"John B's as big a fool as Garland." She ignored my anger. "Going to spend a fortune getting out of this one."

"I hope he has a good lawyer." Caroline stepped in to keep the conversation civil.

"I'm sure he does, Mama. There are others though." Julian handed her the list of names.

She examined it through her lorgnette. "Oh dear."

We all watched her.

"Oh no, the poor dear." She turned page over. "Tsk, tsk, tsk."

"Oh for heavens sake, Caroline," Abigail said. "Who are the hellions that caused this disaster?"

"Emanuel McKnight and Grover Bourland are being charged with first degree murder."

"Babies!" Abigail's hat brim hid her eyes from me, but I could tell from her voice that she was upset. "Do you suppose they'll hang them?"

"Hard to say. Depends on how much evidence they have on them, the make up of the jury—and how good their lawyers are."

"Humph! That just means that Bourland kid will get off and the McKnight one will die."

"Oh no, Abigail. How can you be so sure?"

She turned to me. "Because his supporters are mostly women. Flo Pahotsky. You. Every housewife who ever gave him shoes or a clean shirt or a ham sandwich. His jurors, however, will be men."

"John B was always good to him."

"Not much John B can do for him now, is there?"

The reality of Manny's situation hit me.

"Abigail's right," Julian said. "John B and Joe and probably even John Stowers will get bail. And the Bourlands will get Grover out, but who will stand up for Manny? Certainly not the men who got him into this in the first place."

"I want it all to go away." Caroline sat quietly, hands on her lap, face white. "I've seen bad things happen in this town before, but this touches everyone. What good does it do to tear families apart? What good?"

"It's not about good—or justice. We claim to be Christians but deep down inside we're as hard-nosed as any Israelite warrior seeking vengeance." Abigail clenched her jaw. "An eye for an eye."

"No, ma'am," a deep voice said from the kitchen down the hall.

We all startled.

"Webster, come in here," Caroline called.

After a few unintelligible whispers, Webster Lewis appeared at the pocket door between the front parlor and the hall. Patsy was a step behind him and Genevieve flanked him.

"What did you say?"

He avoided Caroline and spoke to Abigail. "We want justice for Sanford, Miz Talbot. Vengeance belongs to the Lord."

Abigail didn't back down, but her voice softened. "You're a better Christian than me, Mr. Lewis."

I touched his arm. "What are you going to do?"

"I don't know yet, Miz Mamie. I gotta take care of my other kids right now. And Sanford's poor broken-hearted mother. But we ain't droppin' nothing. We'll decide what to do in the Lord's good time."

"We didn't hear you come in," Abigail said. "Pardon my saying so, but why are you here?"

"That was me, Miz Talbot," Genevieve said. "I heard the indictments come out tomorrow and I figured Mr. Julian would have that list already. So's I sent my boy Calvin to tell Reverend Lewis."

"It'll be in the morning paper," Julian said.

"I reckon that's a mite too long for me, Mr. McGrath."

"You aren't going to knock some heads together, are you?"

"No, Miz Talbot. I want to end up in heaven with my son, not in eternal flames with his murderers. But I still need to know who they think did this to my boy."

For a moment, none of us knew what to do or say. Then Julian handed him the paper. "The police are arresting them now. They'll all be in jail tonight and in court by morning. The ones they find, that is."

"I appreciate your trust, Mr. Julian."

Fear rose up in my heart. Was this the right decision? Right or not, I was proud of Julian—even while praying for peace.

Webster looked at the paper, squinted and looked again. His hand began to shake. Finally, he handed it to Patsy who so far had simply stood beside him. "I must be more upset than I thought. I can't make out them scribbles."

Caroline stood up. "Sit here." She guided him to her own chair.

"But Miz McGrath—"

"Shush. There's nobody here but us. We're family right now."

Patsy nodded to Caroline who sat down on the settee.

"Officers Cathey Pitcock, R.O. Lacey, John Jarnigan, Ed Pennewell, and Phillip Ross are charged with malfeasance in office." She looked up. "Does that mean they're permanently fired too?"

Julian nodded. "I think so."

She continued, "Morris Campbell, Ben Black, Con Sullivan, John Stowers, Harold Gaches, Cotton Kingwood, J. S. Tucker, John McEachin, D.L. Owlensky, F.G. Powell, Frank Hornsworth, John Mood, Manuel McKnight. Grover Bourland." Her eyes sought mine. "First degree murder. Cathey Pitcock. Assault with Intent to Murder. John B. Williams. Involuntary Manslaughter."

"That's not all, is it?"

"No." Julian lowered his head. "Someone on the Grand Jury told me there were others who they didn't feel they knew for sure were involved. They rolled those cases over to the next Grand Jury to investigate."

Patsy handed the paper back to Julian who put it in his pocket. "Are you okay, Reverend?"

Genevieve touched Webster's shoulder. "No, ma'am. I don't think I'll ever be okay again." He was trembling. "But I'll survive."

Seconds passed as we all focused on our own thoughts.

Webster's eyes were red rimmed when he finally looked up. "So what happens next, Mr. Julian?"

"After everyone is arrested and arraigned, they'll set a date for the trials. Might take three or four months to prepare."

"Will I be able to watch those trials?"

Julian glanced at me. "I don't know, Reverend Lewis, but I'll ask around and see what the lawyers say."

"I appreciate it. I surely do."

"How's Loula?"

Webster turned to me. "No better than the last time you asked, ma'am."

I swallowed hard.

"Thank y'all kindly," he said. "Don't think I could have closed an eye tonight without knowing their names."

"Don't forget, Webster," Caroline said. "Don't go visit those fellows tonight. They'll be in jail and their families are innocent."

He nodded her way. "Yes, ma'am."

21

Sad to say not one penitentiary sentence has come from the lynching of Reverend Lewis's boy Sanford. In spite of more than thirty indictments, only a few have been caught. Their trials will be in Waldron this summer. We're waiting for justice, Judge Hon.

Genevieve Day, *Fort Smith Bell*

June, 1912

"THIS PLACE IS FALLIN' DOWN," Sarge said as Miss Peach and I helped him up the stairs to the courthouse. "No wonder Judge Harp wanted to rebuild it."

"He staked his career on getting it done." Julian carried Sarge's wheel chair up the stairs behind us. "Although, it seems to me that with all the new building in Fort Smith this past couple of years and with all the damage caused by that tornado, a new courthouse should be in the works."

"Seems to me a better city jail would be in order after what happened to Sandy." I was puffing by the time we got up the stairs. "Now what?"

"In there." Sarge pointed.

As Miss Peach helped him into his chair, I noticed how frail he was becoming. The old man was my only living blood relative. The realization that he wouldn't be with me forever left a lump in my throat.

"I still don't understand why they called you," I said. "You were inside Esposito's when Sandy died."

Sarge patted my hand. "Not sure myself."

"Sarge?"

He shrugged. "I'll tell you when I know."

"Call me when he's finished and I'll run back over to help with the chair," Julian said.

Miss Peach dabbed at Sarge's face with a damp cloth. "There won't be no need, Mr. Julian. I can manage that thing going down them stairs."

"We'll be fine." I blew Julian a kiss as he left and turned back to Sarge. "The Grand Jury, Sarge? Really?"

"Mamie, I don't have one damn clue."

"Fine." I folded my arms across my chest. "Did they call you, Miss Peach?"

"No, ma'am. Them white men didn't ask me any questions to begin with and they ain't asked me to testify either."

I tapped my toe. "What could it be, what could it be?"

"Mamie."

"What?"

"Relax."

"It's just that I thought I had this all figured out. And now it's clear I don't."

"Go ask one of them what they're doin' here and get off my back." Sarge pointed at a couple of men sitting across the room. They were avoiding my eyes too.

I pulled out my notebook and sketched them. I'd never seen one of them before, but the other seemed familiar.

The door to the Grand Jury room opened. "Mr. Eacret?"

"I'm here," Sarge said.

Miss Peach stood up. "Do you need me to push him in?"

"No need," the man said. "I'll do it."

As soon as the door closed, I turned to Miss Peach. "You were pushing Sarge home when everything started happening that night."

"Couldn't hardly get up the street there were so many folks out, Miz Mamie."

"Did you see them bringing Sanford to the jail?"

"No, ma'am. We were back inside Esposito's afore then."

"What could you have possibly seen that they want to ask Sarge about?"

"Well, we heard the shooting, you know."

"You heard shooting?"

"Mr. Pitcock was shooting at Sanford. And Mr. John B and Mr. Andy were behind him so's not to get shot themselves. And of course, that other guy with the top hat mighta been shooting too. A lot was happening and it was hard to tell."

"The top hat?"

"I don't know his name, but his face is all messed up."

"Orrin Fellows?"

She shrugged. "Folks was screaming and running and pushing each other, that night. I spun Mr. Eacret around and we came back down Garrison as fast as I could. We banged on the door at Miz Martina's restaurant and hid out there until things settled down."

"Orrin Fellows was shooting?"

"Maybe. He came around the corner on Eighth and nearly ran into us. He was putting a big gun away and taking a little one out of his pocket."

"Did you see Andy get shot?"

"No, ma'am. We never saw Mr. Andy at all that night."

I paced back and forth. I'd told both Andy and John B about Orrin Fellows and Sister Clarence. Both had promised to look into my suspicions about him. What if this had nothing to do with Andy being mad about Pansy? I stopped, opened my book and scribbled a whole different scenario. At the end, I added three question marks.

"Ma'am?"

I looked at Miss Peach.

"Nothing ever comes out even." Her eyes were kind. "We won't know until we know. Maybe we won't never know it all."

"I can't stand it, Miss Peach. Looking at people I know and like, wondering which one is lying to me—or which one is just wrong. Or who really did what that night. I used to think things were clear. Folks either did or didn't shoot each other. But, John B was so busy being mad that he didn't realize the gun he hit Sanford with, Pitcock's six shooter, went off and hit Andy. He's taking responsibility for killing Andy because the folks at the Arkansas Garage say that's what happened—but he's gone over it in his head so many times now, he's not sure what did happen exactly. Everyone else is just going by what they've heard, but what they've heard varies based on who's talking. It's driving me crazy." I stopped. Everyone in the waiting area was looking at me and I realized once again that I'd raised my voice.

"Sit down, Miz Mamie." Miss Peach patted the seat beside her. "Maybe some things just aren't knowable for certain. Comes a time, we have to look ever thing over and decide what we think is true."

I stared at my hands. "That's belief, not fact."

"Yes, ma'am. And if it's making you crazy, think what Mr. John B's going through."

* * *

We got Sarge down the stairs and into his wheel chair again. I hurried back to call Julian and let him know to meet us at the Main Hotel restaurant for lunch. Then I rushed to keep up as Miss Peach pushed Sarge back toward Rogers.

"So what did they ask you about?"

He shook his head. "Give me time to digest it, Mamie. We can talk over lunch."

I glanced at Miss Peach, concerned at this new somber Sarge. By the time we got to the Hotel, Miss Peach and I were both sweating. I tried to encourage her to join us in the restaurant, but as usual, she preferred solitude. Julian wasn't there yet, but the greeter escorted me and Sarge to a table and a waiter brought our drinks.

"Are you alright?"

Sarge sighed. "Just tired and sick of this whole business."

"They wanted to know if you saw John B shoot Andy?"

"In part."

"Did you?"

"As far as I know with my own two eyes, that kind man never shot anyone."

"So what was the other part?"

"They wanted to know if I knew who did, either by seein' it or hearin' about it."

"Well."

"I didn't see Andy Carr get shot. Period."

"But you've heard something?"

"Nothing new. Nothing I could testify to, but it got me thinkin.' Andy was a hero to a lot of folks in Fort Smith, but the same stuff that makes you a hero to some folks might make you a bad guy to others."

"Is that what you think happened? Someone shot him for revenge?"

"No, I think Jim and JW saw what they saw. An accidental shooting,"

"For sure?"

"No. Not for sure."

* * *

Bert Stewart, a well-off and respected Negro barber, bought a house at 901 North 11th Street. On August 9, a neighborhood committee confronted Mr. Stewart as he prepared to move into his new home. They told him that "while it was nothing personal," they would not allow "the color line" to be broken and threatened violence if their demands were not obeyed.

Patsy Lincoln, *The Fort Smith Bell*

August 12, 1912

I stared out our bedroom window. A warm rain drenched our flower beds. Recovering from a cold, I was bored and cranky. "Why did Judge Hon move the trial?"

Everyone was preparing for the trip to Waldron—press, witnesses, defendants, lawyers, law clerks, transcriptionists, police—everyone but me.

"There are between twenty and thirty thousand people living in Fort Smith," Julian said as he packed a small valise. "Two thousand of them were witnesses or participants. At least ten thousand are related to the defendants in someway, either by blood or marriage or as neighbors or they do business with them or go to church or lodge with them."

"So that means they would be disqualified by the judge?" We'd finally decided that I would stay home while he went to Waldron, but I wasn't happy about it.

"Yes, and we have a sizable population of black people."

"And black folks can't serve on a jury?"

"Not in any world we live in. Women either."

"Why not?"

"Folks around here don't take to change easily."

"Absurd," I muttered under my breath.

Julian closed his suitcase and sat down beside me on the bed. "What's wrong, sweetheart?"

"I don't like not knowing what's going on and I don't like being excluded."

"I know."

I blew my nose and pouted.

"Are you mad because I'm taking the Hudson?"

"Of course."

"And that it's filled to the brim with other people?"

"Especially that."

"You can still get around on the trolley when you feel up to it."

"That's not the point, Julian."

He put his arm around me. "So the next time there's a lynching and the judge changes the venue for the trial to Waldron, I promise not to borrow your car and fill it up strangers when you're feeling poorly."

Only half-playfully, I growled like an angry tiger.

He laughed and after a moment I did too.

"So, why Waldron? Aren't jurors from there more likely to be biased in favor of white defendants?"

Julian shrugged. "That's what people have been saying, but seems to me that we'd run into the same problems with bias here— or anywhere actually."

"But why Waldron? Why not Greenwood, say?"

"I don't know for sure, but maybe it's because Judge Hon is from Waldron. He knows people."

I rolled my eyes. "Seems like a lot of money and inconvenience to me."

Julian kissed my forehead. "Still warm. Get some tea, sweet-heart, and go back to bed."

"Telephone me long distance—" I followed him downstairs. "—and let me know what's happening."

"If I can, but you can always call the paper and see how things are going."

"How long do you think this'll take?"

"At least a couple of days."

Caroline and Abigail were sitting in the kitchen, having tea with Patsy.

"I made you lunch, Mr. Julian." Genevieve handed him a small basket.

"Thank you, Genevieve."

"I don't know what to hope for," she said. "I like Mr. John B. But if he shot his friend in cold blood—"

"We're all hoping it's like he said. An accident."

"But him beatin' up a black boy jus cause he got scared and ran away—"

"I know," he said.

Patsy handed Julian an envelope. "A down payment on inside information for an article in the *Bell*."

"I'll remember."

"Are you all going to keep this young man here all morning? He can't do a thing for anyone if he's still here taking orders from the lot of you," Abigail said. "Be on your way, Julian. Shoo."

"I'm off." He hugged Caroline and went out the back door. A minute later, we heard the Hudson roar to life.

* * *

By ten o'clock, Genevieve had cleaned up the kitchen and head-ed home to take care of her own household. Leaving through the front door, Abigail and Caroline were on their way to a charity lun-cheon at Adelaide Hall. Patsy went out the back door and headed to the same trolley stop. I watched the three of them converge as they reached Rodgers, their umbrellas bobbing in the rain.

It was the first time I'd been alone in the house with no press-ing tasks in a long time. I closed the front and back doors, but it was too hot to close the windows. I did pull the curtains together to darken the room. Then, yawning, I slipped off my shoes and curled up on Caroline's settee in the front parlor. It wasn't long before I dosed off.

A distant thump. I opened my eyes. Sweat dotted my face. I shivered and realized that my fever must have broken. I stretched and rolled over, pulling one of Caroline's crocheted throws around me. My dreams were nonsensical flickers. I was opening doors. Cellar doors. Closet doors. Trap doors. I cringed in the dark. Squeaking floorboards. Footsteps coming closer. Warm breath in my face. Sharp pressure under my chin. "What?" I startled awake.

"No use screaming, Mamie."

I pulled away from the prick. "I'm not alone."

"Do you think I didn't check the house before I woke you?" Orrin Fellows' eyes blazed into mine.

"What do you want?"

"The same thing I've always wanted, dear child."

"I don't have your money."

"Ah, but you know where it is, I'll wager." The light streaming through the window over the settee illuminated his scars.

"Where's Anna Marie?"

"Anna Marie decided she had better things to do than travel from shadow to shadow with an old man hard on his luck. Besides, she was getting pretty long in the tooth for my taste."

Something in his voice scared me. "Is she okay?"

"Depends on your definition of 'okay,' I guess."

I hid my fear behind a show of anger. "How did you find me?"

He snorted. "Did you forget I was here for Guckenheimer's visitation? But, the reason for this little visit?" He leaned forward until his face was inches from my nose and thundered. "Where's the Guckenheimer?"

"The Pavlovs took it."

He pushed the blade tip deeper into my chin and pulled me forward with it. "All that beautiful Rye Whiskey? All of it?"

"All of it." Following the pressure of his knife, I sat up and put my bare feet on the floor. "Looks like you got everything out of Garland Talbot you ever will. The man's penniless unless you like dusty old picture frames and cracked mirrors."

Fellows flicked the dagger. A trickle of blood stained my bodice bright red. "Maybe *you* are the valuable property, my dear. Some people would pay to get you back—that handsome husband of yours, the crazy old man in the wheel chair. Maybe even one of the publications you work for would pay a ransom. What a story, eh?"

The sight of my own blood should have terrified me, but it didn't. I'd gone through two miscarriages and been run over by a wagon in the space of two years. I'd seen a young man tortured and murdered in front if my eyes. Instead of squealing in horror, I thought of Sarge and Caroline. I even thought of Abigail and Garland. This time, there was no hope that one of my many saviors—Julian or Burley or Dino or John B or Andy—or even Till Shaw—would be there to rescue me. Then I thought of the Derringer loaded with one bullet in my purse, hanging in the hallway. "Depends on what it is you will take to spare my life," I said under my breath.

"I didn't say anything about sparing your life, Mamie. You're a talker. You'd tell your story—and mine—to every newspaper in town and every woman's magazine. You'll write about how I beat you and raped you and cut you."

Rape? "No, I won't. I promise."

He laughed again. "That's disappointing. Nothing I love more than scaring pretty young women." He grabbed my arm and pulled me to my feet. "Where's that shiny new car?"

"Julian has it."

"A horse and buggy?"

"Sold off a few years ago."

"So we'll take the trolley down to the bank. I'm sure Fred Sicard will authorize a sizable withdrawal in exchange for your pretty head."

I jerked my arm out of his hand. "I'm not worth anything to anyone. Sure, my father left me some money but I won't see any of that until I'm thirty-five–ten years from now."

"Don't give m—"

I pushed him with both hands.

Cursing, he fell backwards over Caroline's sewing basket. Even on his back with his knees in the air, he sliced at me with the dagger.

I sidestepped around him and ran to the hallway. My dress was wet. I looked down. The cut under my chin was bleeding more than I expected. I glanced back into the parlor. Fellows had rolled over and was pulling himself up on one knee. I pulled my bag down off its hook.

Fellows snickered. "Are we really going to do this?"

"Are you going to leave now?"

Our eyes met. As each of us tried to appreciate the other's determination, I stuck my hand into my purse and gripped the butt of the Derringer.

"I think not," he said. "Without you, finding the Talbots' stash might take longer than I want."

"My family will be back soon."

"Ha!" He brandished the big knife at me.

"You don't scare me."

"That, my dear, is a grave miscalculation on your part." He lunged forward.

I raised my hand and pulled the trigger. The bullet creased his bicep and plowed into the wall behind him.

Fellows seemed as surprised that I'd shot him as I was that the little gun had fired. He looked at his arm and grinned. "So, Mamie," he taunted as he edged closer to me. "We've both drawn blood."

I retreated a step at a time, my eyes on the blade in his hand. When my back was against the hall wall, he slashed my left forearm. However, he was not quite as close as he thought and the knife left a deep scratch instead of the massive wound he'd obviously intended. Still another stream of blood added to the gore on the floor, his and mine.

I looked to my right. The front door was at least ten feet away. As close as he was, he'd catch me before I could get to it. He had effectively blocked my way to the kitchen too. My only escape was up the stairs behind me to the bedroom I shared with Julian.

Sidestepping until I felt the opening, I bolted up the stairs, missing a step and banging my shin on the second riser, slipping in my own blood. Fellows roared and followed. Halfway up, he grabbed my bare ankle. I screamed and tugged to get my foot free. Slowly, it slid out of his bloody hand and I scampered the rest of the way up to the landing.

Fellows leapt after me, swinging the knife into the nothingness behind me. I ran into the bedroom, slamming the door behind me so hard that it bounced back open. I reached my dresser just as he appeared on the landing. Roaring, he raced across the bloody parquet, holding the dagger over his head posed to plunge it into my neck. As he started his downward thrust, I stabbed him in the stomach with Martina Esposito's butcher knife she'd given me the night Andy was shot and Sandy was hung.

Fellows' scream turned into a breathless grunt. Trying to get it loose, I jerked the blade down and to the side. He dropped his knife and I kicked it away.

"Don't think you're going to get away." He rolled onto his back, grimacing.

I knelt over him. "Was it you?"

"Wha—" It was a gurgle.

"Did you shoot Andy?"

His eyes turned inward as he bled to death on the floor at the foot of my bed.

I tried to stand up but nearly fell again. I held onto the furniture and made my way out into the short hallway. The single flight of dimly-lit, bloody stairs was terrifying. Aside from the wounds Fellows had inflicted on my chin and arm, I'd cut myself with Martina's butcher knife in several places—and bruised my bare foot kicking the handle of the heavy dagger away from him. I realized I couldn't make it down them on foot without falling. So I sat on the top riser and scooted until I dropped to the next. It seemed like forever, before I reached the phone.

* * *

I was standing on the front porch when the police arrived. They seemed horrified at my bloody clothes and ugly wounds, but they listened to my story before running inside and following my bloody footprints up the stairs. Shortly after that, Caroline and Abigail arrived in a taxi.

"Mamie!" Caroline threw her arms around me.

"I'm sorry," I sobbed. "I got blood all over your settee."

* * *

August 13, 1912
Stowers and Williams Trials in Waldron Attract Hundreds

Southwest American

August 14, 1912
Stowers acquitted.

Southwest American

August 15, 1912
Williams acquitted after jury deliberates nineteen hours.

Southwest American

22

GENEVIEVE HAD SCRUBBED THE HOUSE from top to bottom and her son Calvin sanded and painted over the stubborn stains on the walls and woodwork. She burned my bloody clothes in a barrel behind the shed. While I was stiff and sore, I was definitely on the mend and eager to see friends and family so Caroline and Abigail with the help of Katherine Mivelaz decided to hold an open house. Sarge was less than enthused but he showed up early to complain and argue with Garland. To keep them busy, Genevieve served them my mother's lemonade in quantities sufficient to keep them calm, so calm that both were snoring out on the screened in porch by eleven-thirty. This allowed Miss Peach to spend the rest of her day alone in the back parlor reading a book Patsy lent her.

Reverend Mathews, his wife Rachel and little Frankie brought news that Emanuel McKnight was being held in the Greenwood jail. They were hopeful that he wouldn't be tried since John Stowers and Con Sullivan had been acquitted. Miss Pahotsky was working with the authorities to bail him out.

"The boy sent you a note." Reverend Mathews took a folded piece of paper out of his vest pocket and handed it to me as they were leaving.

Miz Mamie, it said in a large childish script.

Sorry I did what I done. I just wanted them boys to think I was tough as they thought they were. I see now that Grover is as windy as a sack of farts. And Harold is a pissant kid like me. Miss Pahotsky is trying to help me. She's as big a fool as you are, ma'am. When I see him on judgment day, I'll tell baby Jesus how good you kind ladies been to me,

Emanuel McKnight

I dabbed at my eyes with a fresh kerchief. "I don't know how to feel about this, Reverend. It seems like no one will pay much of a price for murdering Sandy. Still, Manny is so young, much younger than he looks."

Reverend Mathews nodded. "To be honest, I don't know what's right here either. Should one so unsophisticated and vulnerable to the suggestions of older friends like Harold Gaches and Grover Bourland—and adults like Stowers and Sullivan—be punished for a crime when the instigators weren't? It's a quandary and I've been praying on it." He patted my good shoulder. "Take care of yourself, Mamie. You've had too many run ins with fate for a person your age."

* * *

Ed Pennewell and Sam Booth surprised me a half hour later.

"I'm sorry I was rude to you that day, Mr. Pennewell," I said as he sat beside me in the parlor. "I jumped to conclusions, just like everyone else did."

He sipped the tea Genevieve brought him and bit into one of Caroline's warm snicker doodles. "We were all upset, ma'am. And you were asking questions that we were trying not to think about ourselves. Like what did we do that we shouldn't have—and even worse, what didn't we do that we should have? Not sure I know even now."

"I wake up some mornings," Sam said, " and think, should I go talk to Reverend Lewis about his boy and apologize for not being able to stop it? But then I think that man is entitled to his anger. It's pure and reasonable and justified. My feeling bad doesn't undo it, and so I let another day go by without talking to him. I'm ashamed."

"I feel the same way," I said. "Like I failed everyone and there's no fixing my mistakes this time."

"Miz Mamie, you did more than most that night."

I felt my lower lip quiver. "Not nearly enough."

"I wish we'd have been here when that Fellows guy attacked you," Pennewell said as they were leaving. "Seems like all I've been doing is going to court for one thing or another. All I want to do is be a cop. Learn from this, of course, but get my job back and go to work again."

I waved as they went out the door. "Good luck," I said under my breath. My knife fight with Orrin Fellows had changed how I felt about the police. I now understood what violence felt like personally. How could I criticize their mistakes when my reaction to the whirlwind wasn't anymore rational than theirs?

* * *

I was chatting with Della Carr when Theo Lamb stuck her head in the door. "Can I join y'all?"

"Come on in," I said. "Do you know Pansy and Jimmy?"

"No, but I want to." Theo stretched out her hand to Pansy. "I have a message for you, Pansy."

"From who?" Pansy looked surprised. "Everyone I know can talk to me face to face."

Della frowned and shook her head slightly.

Theo smiled at her and said, "Don't worry, Mama Bear. I'm here to help your cub."

"Wait. Are you that fortune teller?"

Theo sat down beside Pansy. "Something like that."

"So what's the message?"

"Who it's from is more important.

Pansy cocked her head sideways. "Okay. Who's it from?"

"Your daddy."

"Come on now." Della stood up. "Haven't we suffered enough? Hasn't Pansy been through enough?"

"Shush, Mama," Pansy said without breaking her gaze into Theo's eyes. "What does he say?"

"Six words."

"Go on." Pansy's voice was husky.

"I forgive you. I love you."

Pansy covered her face with both hands. "Daddy says that?"

Theo nodded.

With tears running down her face, Pansy held out her arms to Della. "Mama."

While Della embraced her oldest child, I turned to Jimmy. "You taking good care of your Mama and sister?"

"Yes, ma'am." He nodded politely, but he kept his eyes on Della and Pansy.

* * *

"Did you come to see me or the Carrs?" I said to Theo after Della hustled her children out the door.

"Both, actually."

"That was kind of you. Whether it was true or not."

Theo laughed. "Why would you think it wasn't true?"

"Is that my darling Theo?" Abigail swooped into the room.

"And my second message of the day is for you, Abigail."

"From Maybelle Shirley again?"

"No, this is from me." Theo's dimples deepened.

"Do we need the Ouija board?"

"Only if you won't take advice from a living friend."

325

Abigail frowned. "Do I need advice?"

Theo patted Abigail's gloved hands. "You have a choice to make. But don't forget, you can also choose not to choose."

"What kind of a fortune is that?"

"A difficult one, I should imagine." Theo turned to me. "But one that will change the world. One way or another. Support her if you can."

I was surprised but I nodded. "I'll try."

"Mamie McGrath, you better do better than just try." Abigail took out her monocle and shook it at me for emphasis. "And I know those cuts hurt, but stand up straight and lift your chin, for goodness sake. Do you want folks to think you don't have any gumption?"

I sucked in air reflexively.

Theo patted my newly-straightened back and left.

I turned to Abigail. "Do you think it would be okay with your friends if I came to your next meeting?"

"The Women's Christian Temperance Union?"

"I thought I would write about what you are doing."

Delight drifted through her eyes followed by doubt. "What would you say about us?"

"Something positive, I imagine."

"This is important."

"I know."

"You won't say anything, you know—too political?"

The stitches in my face made it hard for me to smile. "I promise."

* * *

John B arrived before Jennie. As Genevieve led him into the front parlor, I could tell he was still troubled. I turned to Abigail and said under my breath, "I need to talk to John B alone."

She cocked her head. "Really?"

"I have some questions for him."

"About the trial?"

"Among other things,"

"I'd thought I'd work with you, Mamie. You know, help with the writing."

"Then as a reporter, you will understand how important confidentiality is."

She looked confused. "From whom?"

"I won't know until I talk to him," I said.

As she flounced out of the room, I nodded to John B. "How are you doing?"

He took off his wide-brimmed Stetson. "Better now that I can plan for my family and businesses."

I gestured toward the chair and he sat down.

"I wanted to talk to you about the time you came to visit me at the Pony Express," he said. "About the things I told you."

"I've kept your secrets, John."

"I know and I appreciate that."

"You're still troubled?"

"On the surface, a man has to carry on. But inside, I'm different."

"How?"

"I drink more. Think more. Work more."

"We've all been changed by this, John. Think how this impacted Webster and Loula. And the Carrs. And Fort Smith in general. It's changed how we think about each other—and what kind of city we want to live in. Looks like they will have the votes to change the form of city government finally. And I think Bourland will be out next election."

"I'm going to move my business," he offered. "Expand it. Change it some."

"That's good."

We sat quietly.

"I have to wonder if they acquitted me because they believed me or because I'm white." The words came out in a rush.

"Does it make any difference?"

"Probably not to my friends and family, or even my customers."

"But it does to you?"

He avoided my eyes. "I would have been upset if they'd convicted me, of course—and maybe even resented it because I'm white and deep down I must think that makes me a better citizen, a better businessman, a better person. But I'll tell you now, I'm guilty of beating that boy. It's like he wasn't worthy of my concern that night, because I was upset and being a part-time cop gave me the authority. When I close my eyes and remember it, I'm enjoying hitting him—but when I open my eyes, I hate myself for it."

I remembered my passion that night. I was out of control too. Acting on how I felt, not what I knew. "It's a lot easier to see these things now that it's all over, isn't it? No time for reflection while it's happening."

His Adam's apple bobbed. "No. No time."

"And Andy?"

His face collapsed. "I'll never get over that either. When I try to sleep, I see him lying there. The horrible wound. The look of surprise on his face. And resignation. I don't think he was mad at me anymore. Just shocked that he'd been hit. But I don't—can't—feel the same kind of guilt about Andy that I do with Sanford. I didn't see Andy on Tenth and A that night. I thought he was behind me.

And both of us were definitely behind Pitcock until he just stopped and said he couldn't run anymore. Hell, I only know that gun went off because Jim and JW saw it. I can't remember it at all."

"Maybe it's time to believe your instincts, John. How hard can that be? Right?"

His acknowledgment was so slow and sad, that I almost didn't recognize it. "Right." He stood up. "The whole danged Williams clan will be here soon. Best not to mention these things to Jennie. She's relieved by the outcome of the trial, of course."

"Of course," I whispered.

"But now, I got some mending to do. With Jennie. And others."

"Stay away from Pansy, John. She's healing slowly, but she's healing."

"Don't worry. It's not likely our paths will ever cross again. Andy was our only link."

"And don't expect the Meeks to take too kindly to you anytime soon."

He sighed. "Can't expect them to."

"Rumors."

He blushed. "Yeah."

* * *

Patsy brought me an armful of books and we chatted about literature and art and what was happening at the latest Grand Order of Olanthe meeting. She regaled me with stories about some of the events at Mame Josenberger's Hall. Weddings. Dances. Even visitations. Then we talked about what it might feel like when we could vote. I worried I wouldn't be informed enough to choose the best candidate. She assured me that when suffrage came, we'd study the people and issues carefully. It seemed so unlikely but Patsy was determined and she made me feel determined too.

"I haven't seen Webster since the verdicts came down in Waldron. Is he mad at me?"

"Why would you think that, Mamie?"

I twisted my wedding band. "Maybe because I couldn't stop it?"

"If you take things too much to heart, you'll break. He knows it wasn't your fault."

I startled. "It's not just Sanford is it?"

"History has made us careful with our feelings, because we always lose in our dealings with white folks."

Tears filled my eyes. "I'm not trustworthy?"

"It's not that so much as that you just can't stand in our shoes."

I wiped my eye with a knuckle. "I know."

She gave me a hug. "At least you try."

"So Webster's not coming back to see us?"

"Give him some time."

It was easier not to talk after that. So we just relaxed together, each lost in our own thoughts. Patsy had a knack for making me feel comfortable in her presence. I wished I had the same knack for her.

* * *

When Patsy left, I joined everyone waiting for me on the screened in porch.

"General Robert E. Lee robbed Pennsylvania blind," Sarge was saying as I stepped out into the fresh evening air. "Tried to steal ever freedman he saw and send him back into slavery."

"He was a strategist and a tactician." It was good to see Garland out of hiding after so many months. He was pale from lack of sunshine, but otherwise he seemed to be up to their traditional General Lee fight. "And the kindest man on the face of the earth."

"Only if you were white and you obeyed without question."

"Now, now, gentlemen," Burley interrupted merrily. "It's time to agree to disagree on a few of these issues. The General in question has been dead half a century now." He smiled at Marie DuVal who was sitting beside him. "We gotta start coming back together on this stuff."

Marie nodded. "Time to concentrate on today's problems."

It struck me that today's problems were the grandchildren of the arguments that led to the Civil War, but I didn't say that out loud.

"How are you feeling?" Julian reached out to me.

"I had nice little cry with Martina Esposito when I gave her a new butcher knife to replace the one that—well, you know. I told her that she saved my life when she gave it to me. And we both marveled at all the little things that had to happen for that knife to still be on my dresser months after she gave it to me."

"Some things are just meant to be, Mamie." Theo sat on the porch swing, drifting slowly back and forth. "The magic of the universe."

"That's what Martina thinks too," I said. "She's going to light a candle in front of the Blessed Virgin at Immaculate Conception Church every day this week."

"I already started." Caroline smiled up at me. "It doesn't hurt to meditate on these things during rosary. You've beaten the odds several times now, dear."

"Garland and I are going to buy a new car," Abigail said loud enough to alert our neighbors down the street. "A newer one. And I'm going to drive it too. You won't have anything on me, little girl." She tried to wink at me but it went all wrong and we got tickled.

"Julian tells us that Colonel Parker is going out on his own with a new version of *The Fort Smith Weekly Herald* and that the two of you are going to be writing for him," Garland said.

"Maybe," I said. "It won't be like the *Southwest American's* focus on news with departments on all kinds of things that support the business."

Abigail sniffed. "What in the world are you talking about, Mamie?"

"Instead of articles about mine explosions or murder or accidents or—bad news, Mr. Parker wants to focus on parties and clothes and church socials."

"Sounds delightful," Caroline said. "This town needs to let bygones be bygones. Just not talk about stuff and eventually it'll go away."

"That could make for a pretty dull job, Mama," Julian told her.

"You mean you'd rather be covering trials and city government fights and lynchings?"

"I think we would," I said. "Maybe work with Mr. Parker on weddings and clothes and coming out parties part time. Maybe work for the *Southwest American*—or even some of the other local papers—one story at a time."

"They'll let you do that?"

"Looks like they will, Mama."

"Well what is this world coming to?"

Lightning bugs flickered as the dusk gathered. I sat down in one of the porch chairs beside Julian, listening to Abigail berate the "little" fellow in power now.

"I liked Mayor Johnston," she said. "None of this would've happened if he was still mayor of Fort Smith."

"Now, sugar," Garland sighed. "That's not what you said back when he was mayor."

"Don't be silly." She spun on him. "I always liked Mayor Johnston. Never did trust Mr. Bourland."

As they yammered on about the passenger service at the new Union Station and whether or not Julian and I should join one of the lodges, I relaxed. They were funny, annoying, and very dear to me. And then I wondered why I'd procrastinated returning that butcher knife to Martina after the lynching—and then, I wondered who Fellows really was.

23

And then —

September 20, 1912
Oleg Pavlov and his two sons, Oral and Konrad were arrested in Fayetteville
for selling liquor without a license. After being indicted by commissioner
Perry in the United States Grand Jury, U.S. Marshall J.O. Johnson put them
in the Federal Jail on default of bond.

Julian McGrath, *Southwest American*

Emanual McKnight was released into the custody of his teacher, Miss Flor-
ence Pahotsky this afternoon. He'd been indicted in the lynching of Sanford
Lewis in March of this year. Given his tender years and the fact that most
of the other accused participants had received bail while waiting for trial
months ago, Judge Hon accepted Miss Pahotsky's pledge that she would
personally guarantee McKnight's presence in court when called.

Julian McGrath, Southwest American

January 8,1913
Joe Tucker was tried in Greenwood and acquitted in the death of Sanford
Lewis who was lynched in Fort Smith, March 23, 1912. The sheriff could not
find state's most important witnesses—they include a local auto dealer and
Deputy Constables Meyers and Creekmore. After the court refused a contin-
uance until these witnesses could be found, the state requested a dismissal.

Julian McGrath, Southwest American

January 12, 1913
Famous New Orleans entertainer, Miss Pocahontas Ross, performed at
Josenberger Hall last night. Was good to see her back in Fort Smith. And,
Lord can that child sing. Mr. Wiley was proud as could be of his old student.
She'll join us at the AME Church before she heads north to Harlem. She say
that's where black folks are making music and movies and writing poetry
and she wants to be part of that.

Genevieve Day, *Fort Smith Bell*

January 23, 1913
Till Shaw's Saloon at 623 Garrison Avenue has reopened after being com-
pletely remodeled by Fort Smith contractor John C. Stowers. With a new
glass front, a steel ceiling and mahogany fixtures, Till says that the facility
demonstrates the fine quality of Stowers' work.

Southwest American

March 16, 1913

*Prosecutor Paul Little dismissed the last of the Special Grand Jury in-
dictments in the shooting death of Deputy Constable Andy Carr and the
lynching of Sanford Lewis a year ago. They were against three young
boys—Emanuel McKnight, Harold Gaches and Grover Bourland. McKnight
was the boy who placed the rope through the cross arms of the Trolley pole.
Witnesses said that he was hoisted up onto the shoulders of grown men to
carry out that task.*

Julian McGrath, *Southwest American*

July 17, 1913
*Mr. and Mrs. Howard H. Redner and Mr. and Mrs. Reese, J. B. Morris and
others will attend the National Photographers convention
Kansas City next week.*

The *Fort Smith Herald and Elevator*

March 3, 1914
*The body of Emanuel McKnight, a young boy well-known in Fort Smith,
was found in the ruins of a train accident in California this week. A paper
with Miss Florence Pahotsky's telephone number was in his pocket. A slight
lad of tender years, he was arrested in 1912 for participating in the lynching
of Sanford Lewis. He was released through the efforts of benefactors who
felt he was unduly influenced by older men. The boy tried to find peace with
relatives in California only to meet an untimely death.*

Mamie McGrath, *Southwest American*

April 3, 1914
*Sister claims body of young boy killed in train accident in California is not
that of her brother, Emanuel McKnight, of this city. The grieving sister had
the body exhumed and maintains that although the clothes looked like her
brother's and letters in the pockets were addressed to him, she could not
identify the corpse. As of this date, no one has heard from Emanuel McK-
night since the accident.*

Julian McGrath, *Southwest American*

February 18, 1915
*The regular meeting of the Sunshine Club was held at the home of Mrs.
John B Williams at 1611 Grand Avenue on February 10. The event was both
enjoyable and profitable,*

Mamie McGrath, *Southwest American*

May, 1915, Van Buren
*Cathey Pitcock, former Fort Smith Chief of Detectives, was injured twice in
two days while working for the Iron Mountain Railroad. First, he stumbled
over a box improperly placed at the foot of a stairway in the Argenta Station.
He fell hard and banged up his knee. The next day while sitting in the company depot in Fort Smith, a large piece of electrical equipment fell on that
same knee, further damaging it and causing him to curse loudly.*

Julian McGrath, *Southwest American*

July, 1915

Fort Smith history is being featured in a movie titled "High Road to Fortune," directed by WP Wilson. Although some roles were played by professional actors, familiar faces filled important parts as well including Harry P Lyman as the hero and George Rye as the villain. John B Williams played Zachery Taylor, Helen Louis Pyle was Betty, and Allen Kennedy played Jefferson Davis.

Julian McGrath, *Southwest American*

July 20, 1915
Cathey Pitcock is suing the Iron Mountain Railroad $3000 for his first injury and $5000 for the second. It don't seem right that the man, who beat up on the coloreds all those years, can collect such a fortune just because he can't walk straight and don't know when to duck.

Genevieve Day, *Fort Smith Bell*

July 27, 1915
J. B. Parker and Sons, who three years ago established the Fort Smith Weekly Herald and made a splendid success of it, have launched **The Daily Herald** *as an afternoon paper.*

Colonel Anderson, *Van Buren Argus*

October 13, 1915
Last night, a circuit court jury ruled against Reverend W. C. Lewis of Moffett. Thinking it only fair that the man that started the riot that killed his boy, Sanford, in 1912, should pay for what he did, the Reverend sued John B. Williams. He said that while $25,000 won't bring Sanford back to his grieving mother, Reverend Lewis had planned to use the money to help other coloreds with law troubles.

Genevieve Day, *Fort Smith Bell.*

December 12, 1917
Well-known Fort Smith Union Civil War Veteran, Elias Eacret, affectionately known by family and friends as Sarge, passed away in his sleep Sunday night. He will be remembered for his courage, irascible nature, and his kind heart. His niece, author Mamie McGrath, her husband newspaper reporter Julian McGrath, and his mother Mrs. Caroline McGrath will host a viewing at their home on Lecta Avenue this Thursday evening.

Southwest American

Garrison Avenue is a gift to Joyce Faulkner from her hometown, Fort Smith, Arkansas. Many of the locations referenced in the novel are chapters of her own story—St. Anne's Academy, Immaculate Conception Church, the Goldman Hotel, the First National Bank, the Malco Theater (formerly known as the New Theater)—and Garrison Avenue itself. After graduating from St. Anne's in 1966, Faulkner studied writing at the University of Arkansas in Fayetteville. She also holds degrees in Chemical Engineering from the University of Pittsburgh and Business Administration from Cleveland State.

This drama began when Faulkner came home for her fiftieth high school reunion in 2016. The historians at Miss Laura's, the Fort Smith Historical Museum, the National Historic Site and the Fort Smith Historical Society wanted to know why there was so little about the area in Faulkner's many books. The answer was that she had spent the last fifty years in Pittsburgh,PA and Cleveland,OH with short stints in places like Rochester, NY, Monterey, CA, Tsuruga, Japan, Austin, TX, and Orlando,FL. She and her husband had traveled to Canada, Germany, Poland, Korea and Africa. Every job assignment and every vacation gave her new plots, legends, characters, points of view—and books to write. It was time, her classmates and old and new friends insisted, that she focus on Arkansas. She agreed.

Months later, emerging from a superficial survey of area history, she and her husband planned a four-month research trip. What she found was a city steeped in adventure, intrigue and great characters—enough to feed a writer's soul for years to come. They moved back permanently in the spring of 2018. *Garrison Avenue* is the first in a new series of Joyce Faulkner books set in Fort Smith.

Dr. Micki Voelkel is an Arkansas native. She is the Associate Dean in the Center for Business and Professional Development at the University of Arkansas-Fort Smith. She publishes research in the field of adult education and gender justice. She holds a B.S in Performance Studies from Northwestern University, an M.Ed in Adult Education and an Ed.D in Workforce Development Education from University of Arkansas in Fayetteville.

She has a varied background in writing and performing arts. She has more than 30 years experience in community and professional theatre as an actress and director. She lives in Van Buren, AR with her husband Bob, and a toy poodle named Tokyo. *Garrison Avenue* is her first novel.

Many thanks to these researchers, archivists, librarians, genealogists, historians and editors. Also, thanks to the descendants of the folks who people these pages. Your help was critical to the creation of this novel.

Fort Smith Historical Society
Sherry Toliver

University of Arkansas at Fort Smith
Shelley Blanton, Archivist, The Pebley at UAFS
Professor Billy Higgins, Historian at UAFS
Professor Michael Crane, Historian at UAFS

Fort Smith Museum of History
Leisa Gramlich, Director
Caroline Speir

Fort Smith Historic Site
Cody Faber
John Hagan

Sebastian County Records Retention
Willard Wentz
Reginald Moore

Fort Smith Public Library, Genealogy Section

Fort Smith Visitors Center
Carolyn Joyce
Russ Jester

Fort Smith Historian
Charles Raney
Joe Wasson
Mary Jeanne Black
Judge Jim Spears
Ben Boulden
Stan Kujawa

Descendants of characters in this novel
Burley Clay Johnston, III, George Allen Johnston
George Simmons
Maeva Mayes
Mike Hackett, Jim Sellen
Sarah Vick Sullivan
Della Jayne Douglas
Lucy Sicard Buergler
Sherry Tolliver

www.ingramcontent.com/pod-product-compliance
Lightning Source LLC
Chambersburg PA
CBHW050921030726
47503CB00007BB/2398